Girl's Guide to Witchcraft

Girl's Guide to Witchcraft

MINDY KLASKY

RED
DRESS
I N K
TM

GIRL'S GUIDE TO WITCHCRAFT

A Red Dress Ink novel

ISBN-13: 978-0-373-89607-3
ISBN-10:   0-373-89607-7

© 2006 by Mindy L. Klasky.

www.RedDressInk.com

Printed in U.S.A.

ACKNOWLEDGMENTS

I count myself beyond lucky to have had so many guides in the creation of this one.

Many thanks to the "book world" people: my agent, Richard Curtis (who fielded countless phone calls and talked me through endless possibilities with his trademark patience, humor and understanding), my editor, Mary-Theresa Hussey (who was brave enough to take a chance on Jane Madison and me), Adam Wilson and all the other creative, energetic folks at Red Dress Ink who turned this book into a reality.

Jane's voice is a blend of dozens of girlfriends through the years, some of whom speak louder than others. Many of my friends loaned bits and pieces of themselves to this book—I explicitly owe (in rough order of my meeting them) Pam Rude Robinson, Kimi Morse Reist, Heather Hutton Kuyk, Jane Johnson Ricker, Joan Craft Laoulidi, Tracy Palmer Berns, Kimberly Burke Sweetman and Melissa Jurgens. If anyone else finds herself in this book, thank you (or, I apologize!).

A book like this does not get created without the flexibility of "real world" people—all my thanks to Pauline Apling and Nkechi Feaster for covering in the CSS Library, and to Sylvia Miller for her boundless support and enthusiasm (but especially for treating me to tea at the Four Seasons, with far less drama than poor Jane experienced).

My family remains an endless source of support—I thank Mom and Dad, Ben and Lisa, and all the Maddrey/Andress/Fallon clan. A special thanks goes out to the North Carolina Maddreys for introducing me to Stupid Fish. This book would never have been completed without Mark's problem-solving, grocery-shopping, laundry-completing and—quite simply—love. The less said about feline assistance, the better.

Finally, I am grateful to my parents and all the teachers who turned me into the librarian and voracious reader that I am today. In an attempt to repay the smallest part of that debt, I am donating ten percent of my profits from this book to First Book, a national nonprofit organization with the single mission to give children from low-income families the opportunity to read and own their first new books. For more information about First Book, please visit their Web site at www.firstbook.org.

To correspond with me and keep track of my writing life, please visit my Web site at www.mindyklasky.com.

For Mark, because.

1

They don't teach witchcraft in library school.

Vermin—check. Mold and mildew—check. Difficult patrons—check. But there was no course in witchcraft, no syllabus for sorcery. If only I'd been properly prepared for my first real job.

I was probably responsible for what happened. After all, I was the one who recited the Scottish play as I pulled a gigantissimo nonfat half-caf half-decaf light-hazelnut heavy-vanilla wet cappuccino with whole-milk foam and a dusting of cinnamon. "Double, double, toil and trouble," I said as I plunged the steel nozzle into the carafe of milk.

"What's that from, Jane?" asked my customer, a middle-aged woman who frequented the library on Monday afternoons. Her name was Marguerite, and she was researching something about colonial gardens. She'd had me track down endless pamphlets about propagating flowering trees.

"*Macbeth*," I said.

See. It *was* my fault. Everyone knows that it's bad luck to say the name of Shakespeare's Scottish play. At least for actors it is. Still, I should never have risked the curse. I probably deserved everything else that happened that day and in the weeks that followed. Every last thing. Even the—

Well. No need to get ahead of myself.

I rang up Marguerite's coffee and crossed back to my desk. Strictly speaking, it wasn't necessary to walk by the online catalog. I didn't *need* to straighten the pens. I didn't *have* to set out more scratch paper. I wasn't *required* to organize the newspapers.

But all that busywork gave me an opportunity to walk by Jason Templeton's table.

Jason was my Imaginary Boyfriend. Oh, he was real enough. He just didn't know that he was my boyfriend. Yet.

Jason was an assistant professor at Mid-Atlantic University. He looked exactly like that movie star in last summer's blockbuster—you know, the one who suavely seduced two different women while he double-crossed the Mafia and stole the Hope Diamond? Except his hair was caramel-colored. And curly. And he was on the skinny side. And I've never seen him in a tuxedo—he's more of a J.Crew sort of guy.

Okay, maybe he didn't look exactly like a movie star, but when someone is your Imaginary Boyfriend, you give your fantasy a little breathing room….

In fact, since fantasy was my only romantic outlet these

days, I gave my dreams a *lot* of breathing room. After all, they were the magical cure. My dreaming about Jason was helping me to move on, to get over the near-legendary Jilting of Jane Madison.

I knew I should be over Scott Randall by now. Any man who would choose climbing the law firm ladder at his firm's London office over being my beloved husband, to have and to hold, from this day forward, for better or for worse....

Well, he wasn't worth having. Especially when he'd hooked up with some British slut his first week on the new job. And when he had the nerve to write to me—*write* to me!—and ask for my engagement ring to give to her....

But Scott Randall was the only man I'd ever loved.

Really.

And how sad was that? I was twenty-nine years old, and I'd only loved one man. He'd been my high school sweetheart. I'd never even dated seriously in college; Scott and I had made our long-distance thing work. College, then grad school for me (twice—first for a worthless English master's focusing on Shakespeare, then practical library science!) and law school for him. We'd lived together in D.C. before he took off for London.

He'd dumped me almost nine months ago, and it still felt like a part of me was dying every time I looked at my bare left hand.

So, Jason Templeton was actually a great development for me. Even if I wasn't ready to confess my attraction to him. Even if I hadn't quite brought myself to take a risk, to move him from the Imaginary category to Real Flesh and Blood.

At least I had convinced myself that—however un-consciously—Jason came to the Peabridge Free Library to see me. Well, to see me, and to study the relationships between husbands and wives in Georgetown during the two decades immediately following the signing of the Declaration of Independence. My best friend, Melissa, said that boded well—he had a romantic soul and a scholar's mind.

I was certain that one day he would look up from the letters of George Chesterton. He'd reach for the sharpened pencil that I'd have standing ready (no ink permitted around the original letters), and I'd say something witty and sly, and he'd smile his gorgeous, distracted smile, and then we'd go out for lunch, and our scholarly discussion would turn to personal histories, and we'd take a long weekend drive to North Carolina to visit George Chesterton's ancestral home, and we'd stay in a bed-and-breakfast with a king-size sleigh bed and lace curtains and homemade scones, and…

I hurried over to my desk and opened the top drawer. There, nestled safely among Post-it notes and Hi-Liters was my personal copy of *Gentlemen Farmers.* Jason's first book. University Press of Virginia had brought it out the year before and it received great critical acclaim. Okay, it got one column inch in the alumni magazine, but they really seemed to like it.

At Melissa's urging, I had ordered a copy of my own; it had finally arrived in yesterday's mail. She was the one who made me realize that a scholar needed recognition. He needed support. He needed a loving helpmate.

Before I could carry the book over to get Jason's autograph, the phone rang. I glanced at the caller ID and saw that it was Gran. I could let the call go, but then my grandmother would leave her one message: "Jane Madison's grandmother." Answering machines had been around for decades, but Gran refused to believe that they could be trusted with substantive messages. She was eighty-one years old; who was I to try to change her?

"Library, this is Jane," I said, trying to sound crisp and professional.

"Make me a promise, dear."

Oh no. We were back in "promise" mode. Gran went through these phases. She would read articles or watch television or listen to the radio, and she'd dwell on all the ways that people could die. As she was fond of saying, I was the only family that she had, and she wasn't going to lose me without putting up a fight. (Not until I blessed her hearth with a great-grandchild, in any case.)

In the past month alone, I had sworn that I would not go hang gliding, rappel down the outside of the Empire State Building or practice free diving in the Caribbean. Those promises were a small price to pay, I suppose, for Gran having raised me.

Every once in a while, though, I wondered if my actual parents would have been so insanely concerned about my safety. I mean, what were the chances that I'd ever engage in such risky behavior, promise to Gran or not? But I suspected that the car crash that took my parents' lives started Gran on her quest for "promises."

"Jane," Gran said. "Are you listening to me?" I'd waited too long to reply.

"Of course. I was just helping a patron at the circulation desk." I glanced across the room at Jason, smile at the ready, but he didn't look up from his notes.

"Make me a promise."

"Anything, Gran."

"This is serious!"

"Of course it is. You have my best interest at heart. You always have my best interest at heart. I'm the only grand-daughter you're ever going to have."

"Don't get smart with me, Little Miss Librarian."

I glanced at the clock in the lower right corner of my computer screen. "Gran, I've got a meeting with Evelyn in five minutes. I'm going to have to run."

"Promise me you won't lick any toads."

"What!" I was so surprised that I shouted. Jason did glance up then, and I managed a harried smile, pointing at the phone and shrugging elaborately. Great. Now he'd think I was a crazed mime.

"Promise me you won't lick any toads. I read an article about South American toads—they have poison on their skin, and it makes people hallucinate, and those poor people get into car crashes, and they don't even remember to try to get out of the wreck, and they die terrible, fiery deaths."

"Why would I lick a toad, Gran?" I tried to stop the chain reaction at the first link.

"I remember that poster you had on your bedroom wall. 'You have to kiss a lot of toads to find a prince.'"

"That was in fifth grade, Gran. And it was frogs. You know, from fairy tales."

"We form our basic personalities very early," she insisted,

and I could picture her shaking her head. "People don't change. You'll always be that fifth grader."

Great. Ten years old forever. I was doomed to spend the rest of my life with braces, stick-on tattoos and bangs. And I'd always be chosen last for the softball team.

I sighed. Maybe Gran wasn't so far from the truth. I *did* still have freckles, sprayed across my nose. And my hair still had too much red in the curls that hung halfway down my back. And my glasses continued to slip down my nose when I least expected them to, making me blink my hazel eyes like a dazed chipmunk. "Gran," I said. "I don't even remember the last time I *saw* a toad."

"All the more reason for me to worry."

What did *that* mean? "Fine, Gran. I promise. No toad licking for me."

"Thank you, dear." I could hear the relief in her voice. "You'll see. You'll be grateful when the decision is staring you in the face, and you'll know what to do because you've already made up your mind."

"I'm sure I will, Gran." My acquiescence drifted into silence as I watched Jason stack up his notes. I knew his routine better than I knew my own; he was preparing to leave so that he could deliver his noon lecture. He was shutting down his laptop, stowing away his books, capping his pen, clasping his satchel… And then he was gone. No autograph for *Gentleman Farmers* today. No blazing Templeton smile. No anything. "Oh, Gran…" I sighed.

"What's wrong, dear?"

She might have been an eighty-one-year-old woman. She might have believed that my fate depended on my ability to withstand the siren call of toads. She might have worried about the most absurd disasters ever to preoccupy a human mind.

But she loved me. She loved me despite my unsightly freckles and unruly curls and smudged eyeglasses. And it seemed like I was never going to find another person who would—never find a *man* who would.

I shook my head. "Nothing, Gran. I just wish..." I closed my eyes. "I wish I had a magic wand. I wish that I could change things."

"Things?"

I came to my senses just in time. The last detail I needed to share with Gran was the existence of my Imaginary Boyfriend. She was still waiting for me to get over Scott, a man she'd never truly liked. If she heard about Jason, she'd immediately start planning our wedding, my baby shower, our child's first birthday party, all before I could complete my confession. I forced myself to laugh. "Oh, Gran, you know. Just *things*. Make the day sunny. Find the perfect shoes to go with my new skirt. Finish shelving our new books."

"Jane, you know there aren't any shortcuts. No magic wands in the real world."

"Of course not," I sighed, glancing at my clock: 10:30 a.m. sharp. "Sorry, Gran. I really *do* have to run to that meeting."

As I hung up the phone, I wondered what other promises I'd make before the month was over. I shook my head and crossed the floor to Evelyn's office. She sat behind her desk; it was half-buried beneath the piles of important papers that had cascaded across its faux-leather surface. I glanced at the prints on the walls—the regimented gardens at Mount Vernon and the colonnaded porch of Monticello—and I wondered once again how my disorganized boss could have chosen to work in a library collection based on order, harmony and the rational strength of the human mind.

"Jane," Evelyn said as I stopped in her doorway. "Good news and bad news." She waved me toward a chair.

I always felt vaguely guilty when I sat across from her desk, as if I were reporting to the principal of my elementary school. It didn't help that Evelyn looked exactly like the mother superior in *The Sound of Music.* You know, the one who looks like John Wayne in a nun's habit? Poor thing.

I smiled as I sat down. "The board decided that we should hire three new reference librarians, and I'll be in charge of the department?"

She shook her head ruefully. "I'm afraid not."

Unease curled through my gut. This looked serious. "I'll take the good news first, then."

She blinked at me, and I realized that she was a bad-news-first person. She'd be the one to eat her pickled beets before anything else on her plate, holding her nose if she had to. I never understood that—what would happen if you filled up on pickled beets? Or got sick on them? Or had to leave before dessert? What if you didn't have any room left for chocolate cheesecake parfait?

"The good news, then," she said. "The board has authorized a special fund for a new project."

I smiled in anticipation, but Evelyn looked away. All

righty, then. The good news wasn't actually all that good. I braced myself mentally and asked, "What sort of project?"

"You know that we've been trying to increase walk-in traffic. We want to be more a part of the neighborhood."

I nodded, but I bit my tongue. It wasn't like we had a treasure trove of novels and picture books. The Peabridge and its grounds might occupy a city block in Georgetown, in Washington, D.C.'s most historic neighborhood. It might be nestled amid Federalist townhouses and cobbled streets, still looking like the colonial mansion it once had been. It might have grounds that were the envy of city gardeners up and down the East Coast.

But the Peabridge contained the world's leading collection of books, manuscripts, incunabulae and ephemera about life in eighteenth-century America. Not precisely afterschool fare, and hardly a draw for a Mommy and Me book club.

Evelyn went on. "The board decided that we should expand our base by taking a page from Disney's book. You know how they set up Epcot—each European country in its own special 'land.'" I nodded warily. I couldn't see any good place that this idea was heading. "Well, we'll do the same thing here. We'll turn the Peabridge into colonial America."

"Turn it into…" I trailed off, bracing myself for the hit.

"Yes!" Evelyn exclaimed with the enthusiasm of a parent explaining the joys of drilling and filling cavities. "We'll wear *costumes!*"

"You have got to be kidding," I said before I could stop myself. I felt guilty, though, when Evelyn's face dropped. "Costumes?" I glanced toward Jason's now-empty table.

What sort of Imaginary Boyfriend would be attracted to a woman in hoops, a bodice and a mobcap?

"The coffee bar just isn't enough, Jane. We still don't have the foot traffic that the board wants. Dr. Bishop has already made arrangements with the Colonial Williamsburg Foundation. They have some extra stock just sitting in a warehouse. The costumes will arrive by next Monday. You'll see. This will be so much fun!"

Fun. Evelyn might look forward to new clothes. She could set aside that boxy pink-and-brown suit that was designed for a woman two decades younger. Me, though? I'd feel like I was dressing up for Halloween every day of my working life. Where was that magic wand when I needed it?

I settled on a logical argument: "Evelyn, we're supposed to support serious scholarship!"

"And we do. We will. But there's nothing that says we have to be sticks in the mud while we're doing it. After all, we don't want anyone to think of us as Marian the Librarian, do we? We don't want to be boring and fussy and…" She trailed off, searching for a suitably terrible word.

I swallowed hard and realized that the worst bit of news remained untold. After all, the costumes had been the *good* news. I braved her gaze. "And the bad news?"

Evelyn answered in the grave tone of a physician diagnosing a fatal disease. "The board discussed salaries."

No one became a librarian because they wanted to be rich. And absolutely no one took a job at a small private library—a library that had to dress its librarians in eighteenth-century embroidered silk just to get patrons through the door!—because they thought they'd retire early. I'd originally come to the Peabridge on an internship while I was studying to get my master's degree, and I'd stayed because I liked the people—Evelyn, the rest of the staff. The patrons. I wasn't expecting to become a millionaire.

Still, I wasn't prepared for Evelyn's next words. "We're going to have to cut your pay by twenty-five percent." She rushed on. "I argued against it. I really did. But you know that there are still board members who don't think that we need a reference librarian at all, that we only need an archivist."

I couldn't say anything.

I'd already reduced my vacation budget to a one-week car trip to the beach. I brought my lunch every day (or snuck a gigantissimo latte from the bar). Breakfast was a Pop-Tart when I bothered at all.

Well, at least I wouldn't need to waste money on a professional work wardrobe anymore. But twenty-five percent? Not possible. Not even in my worst nightmares.

"Rent," I croaked. "If you take a quarter of my pay, I can't pay my rent. I'll be out on the street, Evelyn. I'll be living beneath Key Bridge, pushing a shopping cart to the library's front door every morning."

"Now, Jane," Evelyn said, moderating her tone as if she were talking a jumper down from the top of the Washington Monument. "I told the board that twenty-five percent was too much, that we couldn't do that to the staff. We especially couldn't do that to you—I know that you're already relatively underpaid, even in our field."

Well, it was nice to hear her say that, at least. In fact, she actually looked pleased as she prepared to make her grand announcement. "Jane, I came up with something better. I'm offering you a *home*. Free of charge, for as long as you work at the Peabridge."

"A home?" I blinked and wondered if I'd slipped into some alternate universe. I resisted the urge to glance around for hidden cameras, for some signal that this was a wacky new reality show.

"It's perfect!" Evelyn raised her chins from her chocolate-colored blouse and gave me a broad smile. "You'll continue to work for us, we'll make the salary cut, but you'll live in the guesthouse, in the garden out back!"

The guesthouse. What guesthouse? The Peabridge gardens were extensive, but there was no guesthouse. There was a gazebo, and a pagoda, and an obelisk and... Then it hit me like an ice pick to my belly.

"Do you mean the old caretaker's shed?"

"Shed?" Evelyn's laugh was a bit forced. "You've obviously never been in there. It's practically a mansion!"

Sure. In someone's sick nightmare. Every time I walked by the ramshackle building, it gave me the creeps. The hair on the back of my neck literally stood on end, and the walls seemed to create their own clammy drafts. "Evelyn, I can't live in a dusty toolshed."

"It's not a toolshed! It used to be home for a gardening professional, for a trained specialist in colonial horticulture! It has a kitchen. And a separate bedroom."

"And a toilet? Is there even running water out there? Electricity?"

"Of course! Do you think that we're barbarians?"

I stared down at my black slacks and my favorite silk blouse that was cut to show off my, alas, minimal décolletage. The outfit was my "Monday best," chosen to lure Jason's attention right at the start of the week. This would be the last time I'd wear it to work. Starting next week, I'd be dressed like Martha Washington.

Barbarians? No, but I thought the Peabridge board was entirely out of line with reality.

What else was I going to do, though? Move back in with Gran? Park myself on the floor of Melissa's one-room apartment? How was I ever going to move Jason from the Imaginary Boyfriend category to the Real, if I lived in a cardboard box under Key Bridge? If I was arrested for defaulting on my student loans?

"Rent free?" I asked.

"Rent free."

"Utilities included?"

"Utilities included."

I *was* tired of fighting with my landlord to fix the leaky ceiling in my current apartment. Thieves had broken in twice in the past year (not that I had anything worth stealing). My commute by public transportation was nearly an hour, each morning and each afternoon.

A one-minute commute.

I could sleep until 8:00 a.m. and still make it to work on time. I could dash home during the day and whip up a quick lunch. I could offer to help Jason with a research project, stay up late working beside him at my kitchen table then offer him a nightcap.

I could have it all—a *real* boyfriend, a successful library job, a home of my own, Scott Randall and missing magic wand be damned. I held out my hand, smothering my flash of embarrassment when I saw my chewed fingernails. Hmm… Another goal, breaking that lifetime habit. "Done," I said.

Evelyn's fingers were cool on mine, and her smile was encouraging. "Done." She smiled.

There. My job was secure. I had a new home. I was going to be spared wear and tear on my admittedly limited wardrobe.

Then why did it seem as if I was about to tumble headlong over a precipice?

"This might be the craziest thing you've ever done," Melissa said on Sunday as we clambered out of Gran's black Lincoln Town Car.

She would know. We'd been inseparable since the second week of third grade, when we went stomping through puddles during one waterlogged recess. We were wearing identical peacock-blue knee socks that day, and our feet and legs were stained for weeks. It's amazing how closely bonded two girls can become when they're laughed at by every child in their P.E. class. The experience wouldn't have been so scarring if Mrs. Robinson hadn't chosen that week to introduce our science class to the fauna of the Galápagos Islands. Especially the blue-footed booby.

"Thanks for the vote of confidence." I was already wrapping a bandanna around my hair, trying to lasso my curls. As I often did, I wished that I'd been blessed with Melissa's perfect hair. She wore it shoulder-length, so that the honey waves framed her gamine face. Everything about her was petite; she was only five foot two. But she packed more energy into her overalls than I'd ever imagined having.

Case in point: she was already emptying the trunk, fishing out dozens of bags filled with the finest cleaning supplies that Target had to offer. If a chemical shone, sparkled or wiped, we had purchased it, relying on a grandmaternal grant for funding. I collected my share of the loot.

Even in the full light of a spring Sunday morning, I felt the chill of the cottage's strange power as we approached the front door. A cool finger walked down my spine, making me unable to resist the urge to look behind me to be certain that nothing was looming over my shoulder. "There!" I said. "Don't you feel it?"

"You still think the place is haunted?"

"Not haunted," I said, feeling slightly foolish. "It's just that there's a power here. A…presence."

Melissa whistled the theme from *Twilight Zone* before lowering her voice to a Rod Serling rumble. "Jane Madison thought that she was moving into an ordinary cottage in an ordinary Georgetown garden."

I couldn't help but laugh. Of course it was cold, even clammy, next to the building. I was standing in the shade. How silly could I be?

I dug the keys out of my pocket and selected the new one that Evelyn had given me. She had been as good as her word; a locksmith had come out during the week and installed a solid dead bolt on the door. I hadn't had the nerve to try it alone. Now the brass key glinted, bright as gold, as I slipped it home and turned.

I took a deep breath before pushing the door open. "Ready?" I asked Melissa.

"Ready as I'll ever be." She stepped forward, Gran's mop and broom looking like pikes in her hands.

The door opened without squeaking. The locksmith must have seen to the hinges. The rest of the cottage, though, looked as if it hadn't been touched by human hands in more than a century.

Billowing white sheets clumped over furniture in the parlor, disguising shapes that might have been couches or chairs or massively mutated ottomans. Dust was thick on the floor, and the front windows were so flyspecked that they looked like some rotten form of stained glass. A braided rug was rolled up against the far wall, and the hardwood floor looked dull and diseased. By craning my neck, I could just make out the appliances in the kitchen, and I thought they might once have been white.

"I don't even know where to start," Melissa said, even *her* spirit daunted.

"Might as well tackle the worst bits first," I said grimly. "Do you want the kitchen or the bathroom?"

"I spend enough time in a kitchen at work. I'll take the bathroom. Besides, it's smaller." She grinned.

We split up the cleaning supplies and activated our divide-and-conquer strategy. I asked myself, how bad one kitchen could be when it hadn't even been used for decades?

The answer: bad.

I started by sweeping, figuring that it made sense to get rid of the dry dirt before I tackled the wet. I disturbed enough spiders to repopulate every farm this side of Charlotte's web. I discovered that my new home had mice—or at least it had hosted them in the past, when there was some semblance of food around. I learned that contact paper detached from shelves when the glue was old enough. And it left behind a gold-colored dust that made me sneeze if I peered at it too closely.

Even as I swept, though—and scrubbed and scoured and mopped—I couldn't help but be pleased. This was *my* home that we were cleaning. This was my pied-à-terre; my escape from the hustle and bustle of the workaday world. With every squeeze of a spray bottle, I was beating back the cottage's chilly atmosphere. I was subduing that *Twilight Zone* specter, pushing away my whispering fears.

Some time well after noon, I glanced out the kitchen window (newly glinting from a liberal application of Windex). I couldn't help but laugh out loud. The cottage lined up at the end of a garden path. While the yellow cowslips and deep pink candytuft had died back at the peak of the summer's heat, I could still make out the bright white stars of foamflower stalks.

Endless volumes of colonial horticulture had not been wasted on *this* librarian.

And Gran's housekeeping lessons weren't wasted, either. When Melissa and I folded back the dustcovers on the furniture in the living room, we were pleasantly surprised to find a pair of deep, overstuffed couches covered with hunter-green fabric that looked untouched by time. In the bedroom, we discovered a four-poster with an actual feather mattress. My own clean sheets fit it perfectly.

We rolled out the rug in the living room and admired its tightly braided pattern. Gran's vacuum cleaner worked like a charm, sucking up the last stray evidence of the cottage's abandonment. After I coiled up the vacuum's power cord, we collapsed on the couches and surveyed our handiwork. "I don't believe it," I said.

"Still feel your Ghost of Christmas Past haunting the place?"

"Any ghost who was living here has been asphyxiated by ammonia." I brandished the nearest spray bottle. "Fairies, begone, and be all ways away."

"Titania. *A Midsummer Night's Dream.*"

It was an old game that we played. Smiling to acknowledge Melissa's Shakespeare skills, I glanced over her shoulder. "What's *that* door?" I asked, gesturing toward the hallway.

Melissa followed my gaze and shrugged. "The basement? I tried it and it's locked."

Just as well, I thought. There was no telling what creepy crawlies lurked down there. I sighed and pulled myself to my feet. "So, are we going to reward ourselves with burgers?"

"And fries. Your treat."

Neither of us could bring ourselves to shower in the sparkling new bathroom; we wanted the fruit of our labors to remain unblemished for just a while longer. I did take a moment to splash some water on my face at the kitchen sink, and I removed my grimy bandanna, allowing my hair to spring out around my ears. Taken together, Melissa and I looked like refugees from a stowaway's convention, but that was going to have to do.

Besides, Five Guys Burgers and Fries did not exactly require the height of fashion to set foot inside its doors. The counter was already three-deep when we got there, and we took a moment to stare up at the menu, red letters stamped on a broad white board. Simple: hamburgers, fries, toppings (extra charge for cheese and bacon). Cold soda. Peanuts to munch on while we waited. The smell of hot grease made me salivate like one of Pavlov's dogs.

It was a sign of how long I'd known Melissa that I could order for her without confirming what she wanted. I stepped up to the counter and asked for one good burger (cheese, bacon, grilled onions and mushrooms, lettuce, tomato) and one pitifully flawed burger (mustard, ketchup, nothing else at all in the world, poor bare thing), along with a large order of fries for us to split. Before I could finish giving Melissa grief over her denuded choice of lunch, we found ourselves at a Formica-covered table.

The first bite was heaven. Hot beef and melted cheese and crispy bacon, with juice running down my fingers and a tiny rivulet snaking beside my lips. I closed my eyes and resisted the urge to moan out loud.

"Hey," Melissa said. "Isn't that your Jason?"

I whirled around without thinking.

So much for cool. So much for suave. So much for calm and self-possessed and witty and urbane. If my whiplash motion had not drawn his eyes to me, my explosion of coughing would have. Five Guys Burgers made a perfect meal, but they were lousy down the windpipe.

When I was finally able to breathe again, I saw the true extent of the disaster. My Imaginary Boyfriend was not merely sitting in the same dive-y restaurant that I shared with Melissa. He hadn't just seen me choke on a bite of hamburger the size of a pack of cards. He wasn't only privy to my dirt-streaked arms and my stained T-shirt.

He was eating with another woman.

A woman who, even seated, clearly had the body of a classically trained ballerina. She was tall and thin—*willowy* is the phrase that you read in books. She had soft brown hair with chunks of buttery-blond that I could tell weren't highlights—it was her own naturally perfect coloring. Her eyes were pale blue, framed by the longest, darkest lashes that Lady Maybelline had ever touched.

Who was I kidding? Maybelline? That woman didn't buy her cosmetics at a drugstore. Even Sephora would be too downscale for her. She probably had colors mixed by hand at some boutique in New York. But the most astonishing thing about her mascara? It was totally, completely water-proof.

The woman was crying.

And that made me even more jealous of her. Not only was she sitting across the table from my Imaginary Boyfriend. Not only did she have a body to die for and a face to match. Not only did she have more elegance in her elongated pinky than I had in my entire body. But she could cry without her nose turning red and her face going blotchy. I hated her.

"Don't look!" I hissed to Melissa. Well, as much as anyone could hiss a command that had no *s*'s in it. I made a big show of eating a French fry. One little French fry. One that wouldn't put too many inches on my hips. "What are they doing?"

"How can I know, if you won't let me look?"

"Melissa," I warned, swallowing some Diet Coke as I tried to wash away the scratchy feeling left over from choking.

She gave in with a grin. "He's offering her his napkin. She's wiping her nose. No. She's *dabbing* at her nose. My God, she looks like a princess."

"I don't need to hear that!" I stuffed three emergency fries into my mouth, and the salty, steamy potato almost drowned out the report.

"Hurry up," Melissa said with a sudden urgency. "Finish that bite. They're coming this way."

I gulped and swallowed and even found a second to take a sip of soda. By the time Jason stopped by our table, I'd pasted a smile on my lips, but it felt fake to me. An Imaginary Smile for an Imaginary Boyfriend.

"Jane," he said, and my heart leaped somewhere up to the vicinity of my larynx.

"Jason," I managed before prompting, "Um, I think you've met my friend Melissa. Melissa White." I needed to find out the name of the woman who was with him.

He nodded. Almost as an afterthought, he turned toward the spectral creature who drifted behind him. "Jane, Melissa, this is Ekaterina Ivanova."

Ekaterina Ivanova? Just like some Russian princess. Like

Anastasia's long-lost granddaughter. I waited for her to extend her hand, but she didn't. It was just as well. My own chewed nails and greasy fingertips would have defiled her forever. She inclined her head toward us, and I felt as if the very Queen of the Wilis had deigned to acknowledge our existence. She said, "Jason, I need to leave," and her voice was scarcely more than a whisper.

He shrugged and smiled at me, and I told myself that there were volumes behind that grin. He would rather sit with Melissa and me. He would prefer to help himself to some of our fries. He wanted to joke and relax with real women, rather than his ice statue of a companion.

Melissa came unstuck first. "It was nice meeting you," she said to Ekaterina. "Good to see you again, Jason."

I muttered something, and then they were gone. "Who do you think she is?" I asked, before the door had closed behind them.

"I don't know, but she definitely wasn't happy."

"She must be Russian. Did you hear that accent? Didn't she sound Russian to you?"

"I could barely hear her speak."

"She's Russian, though." I heard the words tumbling out of my mouth, faster and faster, as if I needed to reassure myself. "She must be one of his grad students. A lot of Russians study American history. You know, there's a whole tradition of foreign students specializing in the colonies. Alexis de Toqueville wasn't the first, and he certainly won't be the last."

"De Tocqueville was French." Melissa took advantage of my distraction to snatch the last of the fries from the greasy paper sack.

"You know what I mean."

"We're in Georgetown, Jane. The man is a professor at Mid-Atlantic. Probably half the people he knows are academics."

"Did you see her mascara?"

"Yep." Melissa downed the last bite of her burger before she nodded. "It probably cost more than a month of your pay at the Peabridge."

"Who bothers with mascara on the weekends, anyway?"

"On the weekends?" Melissa batted her eyelashes at me. I could not think of a time when I'd seen her wearing mascara. Or lipstick. Or blush, foundation, or eyeliner. She always said they just melted down her face while she worked at the bakery.

I sighed and set aside the vision of the Ice Queen. She probably specialized in early women's suffrage movements. She looked the type.

"Are you through?" I asked Melissa, already collecting our spent napkins and plastic cups of ketchup.

She nodded and tossed her pristine napkin onto the tray. I tried not to compare it to my stained one. Well, how was a girl supposed to stay neat while eating a burger? Didn't it show a healthy appetite to let the juices run down your wrists?

We walked back to the cottage, and I was pleased to see that our hard labor had withstood the test of time. If anything, the surfaces glinted more in the afternoon light. "Okay," I said after taking a deep breath. "Time to do the actual moving in."

"It should only take two trips."

Melissa was much better at spatial relationships than I. That must have been a skill that she developed during all those years of choosing the right mixing bowl, of finding the correct Tupperware for leftovers. Back at my old apartment, she made us slide the Lincoln's front seats up as far as they would go before she wedged in all of my possessions—first onto the car's huge backseat, then into the trunk. There wasn't all that much, actually. After all, I'd been a starving grad student for years, and my library job hadn't paid a fortune, even before my salary was gutted by the board. Before the London Disaster, I'd spent most of my time hanging out at Scott's apartment, watching his TV, eating off his plates, using his household appliances.

Mostly, I had clothes. Black clothes. Clothes that I could mix and match in an instant, with a generous apportionment of handmade jewelry to accessorize. My collection ran to necklaces and earrings, although I'd invested heavily in brooches when they were popular a couple of years back. Most of my holdings were cheap, scavenged at yard sales and art fairs, but a few were true treasures, garnered in museum shops and tiny galleries around town. What could I say? A girl has her weaknesses.

In the end, though, we had to run a third trip back to my old place. Neither Melissa nor I trusted Stupid Fish on a car seat with any other belongings.

Stupid Fish was the world's oldest neon tetra. He'd been a college graduation gift from Scott. He'd lasted through English grad school, library school, even through London. When I found out about Scott and the British slut, I almost flushed Stupid Fish. But it was hardly the tetra's fault that he'd been purchased by a jerk.

And so he lived on. Stupid Fish the Superannuated Tetra. Stupid Fish, who had a ten-gallon tank all to himself, because I wasn't about to compound my mistakes by getting him any little fishy companions. Not at this late date.

We moved the tank by emptying out half the water. Melissa carried it to the car (she'd always been stronger than I). She'd even thought to bring a cookie sheet to cover the tank and keep the water from sloshing out as we drove across town for the last time. After she carried it into the house and set it on the counter in the kitchen, I added some spring water and watched Stupid Fish swim around. As ready as I was to be out of the fish business, I was pleased to see that he made the move without obvious trauma.

Before long, Melissa decided to head home. She lived above Cake Walk, the bakery that she owned, down by the canal that ran through Georgetown. Mornings started at an ungodly hour for her. I thanked her a million times for helping me with the move, and she shrugged it off, like best friends do.

She walked down the garden path, and I was alone in my new home.

I strolled from room to room, a little amazed by the amount of space that was mine. It was the height of luxury to have separate rooms—I had lived in studio apartments for all the years since I'd flown Gran's nest. I made a cup of tea and sipped it while curled up on my hunter-green sofa.

I realized that I was exhausted. After all, I'd been up since dawn, packing up my old place, readying this one. It was time to go to bed, so that I could make it to work on time the next morning. Monday was a prime Jason day and I wanted to be rested.

I changed into my preferred sleepwear, a pair of men's flannel pajamas cut off at the knees, so faded that I could barely make out their Black Watch plaid. Making one more tour of my home, I turned off all the lights before climbing into the featherbed and putting my glasses on the night-stand. I lay back on my pillow and closed my eyes, but before I could drift off to sleep, I remembered the chilly feeling that I'd encountered walking around the cottage in the past.

That was not the right thing to think of.

I told myself to relax. I told myself to give in to the bone-deep exhaustion in my arms and legs. I told myself to go through the multiplication table, to bore my brain to sleep.

Around six times seven is forty-two, I gave up. I put on my glasses and found the fuzzy bunny slippers that Gran had given me for my last birthday. I smiled at their floppy ears the way I always did. I walked into the bathroom, grateful that Melissa had latched the decorative shutters over the single window, keeping nighttime spooks from peering in at me. I filled my toothbrush cup with water and made myself swallow slowly, all the time looking in the mirror and telling myself how foolish I was being.

When I set the cup back on the counter, I saw that one of the tiles was cobalt-blue, darker than all the others, as if it had been replaced some time in the past. I touched it, and to my surprise, it pivoted easily to reveal a cubbyhole. As I peered closer, I saw that there was a brass cup hook planted in the top of the space. And dangling from the hook was a key.

It wasn't a large key, no longer than the one that worked

my new deadbolt. But it was the strangest key I'd ever seen. It was forged out of black iron. Instead of little jagged zigzags of teeth, it had a sturdy black rectangle with an intricate shape cut out of the middle. I slipped it from the hook, and it was heavier in my palm than it should have been.

I could hear my blood pounding in my ears. Stop it, I said. There is nothing spooky or mysterious about this key. It must fit some door around the house. A lot of homes had hiding places, built before people trusted banks, before they poured their life savings into stocks and bonds.

Nevertheless, I turned on every light as I walked out to the living room. The cottage must have blazed in the middle of the Peabridge gardens like a centenarian's birthday cake. I didn't waste my time in the kitchen. Surely, I would have found a secret door when I cleaned that morning. The bedroom walls were bare, too, and there was nothing suspicious in my tiny closet. The bathroom, the hallway, the living room—all straightforward lath-and-plaster walls.

And then I saw it.

The basement door. The basement, which I was going to let live in peace, with its spiders and its mice and whatever else had scurried down there for shelter.

But there was the door, right off the living room. It had an iron lock. An iron lock that matched the key in my now-trembling hand. The clammy feeling washed over me again, nearly knocking me over with its force.

I found my purse on the coffee table and dug out my cell phone. I punched in a nine and a one. The phone whined in my hand, as if I'd brought it too close to a computer screen. The noise grated on my nerves, making me even more aware of the potential danger that lurked below. My left thumb hovered over the one again as I set the key in the lock. Filling my lungs and biting down on my lip, I turned the key and opened the door.

3

I fumbled for the light switch in the place I expected it to be, at the top of the stairs, but there wasn't one. Gripping my cell phone closer and feeling more than a little foolish, I swept my fingers in front of my face, swiping blindly into the darkness, hoping to find a cord or chain for an overhead light. Nothing.

The phone glowed green, shedding just enough light from its picture panel that I could make out the stairs beneath my feet. When I moved to the next step, though, weird shadows ganged up on me, and I had to stifle a shout.

Light. I needed more light.

Swearing under my breath, I retreated to the kitchen. After I set the phone down on the counter, it only took a moment to pull my box of thunderstorm supplies from beneath the sink. During the spring and summer, Washington saw its share of major thunderstorms, and my old apartment had lost power at least once a month. I'd become an expert at arranging candles to maximize the reflection of light off a book (candles lasted longer than flashlight batteries), and I had invested in pure beeswax to reduce unsightly drips and splatters. I dug out a fat taper from beneath the cans of tuna (emergency dinner) and the water spray bottle (emergency air conditioner.) I found the Zippo lighter at the bottom of the box and returned to the basement stairs.

I was so nervous that it took me three tries to get the Zippo to catch. When I finally had the candle burning, I tossed the extinguished lighter over to the braided rug. Raising the flame in front of my face, I sheltered it from drafts with my 9-1-1-poised cell. I could hear the phone's angry static, resonating down the basement stairs.

In for a penny, in for a pound, I thought to myself. That, unfortunately, made me think of the *Merchant of Venice*'s pound of flesh, which of course turned my mind to blood, to my *own* blood pouring down the stairs. *Then,* all I could imagine was the fairy tale Bluebeard: the domineering pirate who gives his ladylove free rein throughout his castle, but demands only that she avoid the tower room, the one filled with blood.

I shook my head and raised the candle higher. Even though my voice quavered, I counted out loud as I moved down the steps. "One. Two. Three."

I wouldn't have started counting, if I'd known there were thirteen steps. Like I needed any more harbingers of bad luck.

The air in the basement was cold, and I thought about

running back to my bedroom for a sweater. I was honest enough, though, to admit that I'd never make it back downstairs if I gave myself that chance to escape. Instead, I held the candle out toward the walls and looked around.

And then I laughed aloud.

I was staring at books. Rows and rows of books. They filled their mahogany shelves. They leaned against each other like plastic drink stirrers in a trendy martini bar. They were tossed onto the floor as if some temperamental undergrad had grown tired of studying for finals. I finally dared to take a deep breath, and I was comforted by the rich, familiar scent of leather.

Pleased at the treasure trove despite my now-laughable fears, I took another step into the basement room. My slippered feet settled onto something soft and yielding, and I looked down at the most luxurious rug I'd ever seen in my life. I don't know anything about carpets, but this one glinted in the candlelight with a soft sheen that whispered silk. The pattern was a riot of crimson and indigo; intricate twists and turns were woven into the design to tease my eyes into thinking that I could make out meaningful shapes.

A wooden reading stand occupied the center of the room. It was made out of the same dark wood as the bookshelves, finished with the same soft gleam. The surface was slanted toward me, and I was reminded of those high-end architects' desks that, although seeming to be the ultimate in elegance and sophistication, I'd always feared would lead to a strained neck, a backache and a checkbook full of buyer's remorse.

A single book rested on the stand. Its leather cover was stained and weathered; its pages rippled between the covers, sheets heavier than ordinary paper. Parchment, then. I looked for a title on the spine, but there was none.

My search took me to the side of the stand, and I discovered a statue crouching beside the high table. It looked like one of those Egyptian cats with its tail curled around its front paws, a guardian from a mummy's tomb, but it was huge. The thing came up to my waist, and as I took a step back, the cat's eyes seemed to stare out at me, somber and unblinking. They were made of glass or plastic or something, and they glittered as they reflected my candle. I resisted the urge to put my hand on its head.

I was afraid that it might be warm to the touch.

Instead, I looked around the rest of the room. In addition to a couple thousand haphazardly strewn books, there was a large humpbacked chest in the far corner. It looked like a steamer trunk, with peeling leather and a broken padlock that made me think of the *Titanic*.

And there, against the far wall, was an armoire. One door stood open, revealing a tangle of clothes—velvet and satin and a twisting length of feather boa. Both the trunk and the armoire were made of the same mahogany wood as the shelves and book stand. They were all bare of any decoration, any initials, any design that might hint at who had owned them or left them there.

Next to the armoire was a huge couch—ancient black leather as cracked and battered as if the furniture had come through a storm. A half dozen pamphlets were strewn across its cushions, and I wondered who had last read them. Who had—apparently—expected to return in short order.

My cell phone chose that moment to beep its displeasure at having been kept on alert for so long. I bit off a shriek at the mechanical sound, combining the beginning of a scream with the middle of a gasp, and I ended up sounding like a hiccuping cow. Angry with myself, and more than a little embarrassed, I snapped the phone closed. As an eerie, static-free silence filled the room, I couldn't help but glance over my shoulder to make sure there was still a clear path to the top of the stairs.

Skirting the statue of the cat, I moved around to the front of the tall, tilted book stand. My hand reached out toward the book. No, *I* didn't reach for it. I'm not stupid enough to reach out for an unknown book in an unknown library with a creepy, glass-eyed cat statue staring at me like I might be the Invading Mouse Queen from Hell.

But my hand just didn't recognize the danger it was in. We were in. We, my hand and I.

It reached out, and it turned back the cover, and it flipped past the first creamy, empty page. It brushed against the words spelled out on the title page, words that were dark and strong and printed in that pointy, ornate, gothic font that people use for tattoos that say *Death* or *Fear* or some other life-nonaffirming thing: *Compendium Magicarum*.

I had to squint to make out the second word. *Magicarum? Magic?*

The clammy sensation that I'd always associated with the cottage chose that moment to trace my spine again, making my skin dance along my vertebrae. If anyone ever asks you,

you should know that your hair really *can* stand on end. At least the short hairs at the base of your neck. And there's no amount of rapid breathing that will make them lie down again. Not while you're afraid. Not while you think that something might jump out at you from the shadows.

I made myself laugh, even if the sound came out pretty shaky. Pretending to be defiant, I turned the page, expecting to see more information—the name of the author, or a statement of who had printed the book, something about its provenance.

The next page, though, was filled with script. Carefully scribed Ye Olde English letters marched along, row after row. They made me think of monks sitting at long tables, holding quill pens and shivering as they reproduced countless Bibles.

No monk, however, would have written the words that were etched across the top of the page: *On Awakyning and Bynding a Familiarus.*

A familiarus. A familiar, surely.

I had read about the Salem witch trials. I knew about those poor old women who were accused of speaking to the devil through black cats. (Yes. Black cats. Like the statue beside the book stand. That chill rippled down my spine again.)

I told myself that I couldn't run upstairs now. It wouldn't do any good. Not now. Not since I knew about these things in my basement.

I put the cell phone down beside the book. As I brushed my hair back from my face, my fingers felt clammy on my forehead. I cleared my throat and touched my voice box, as if the chill would slow my beating heart. I spread my hand across my chest, willing myself to calm down.

When that mental command did no good, I resorted to one of the things I did best—laughing at myself. Purposely making my voice creak like an old soothsayer's, I ran my fingers beneath the words and read aloud:

"Awaken now, hunter, dark as the night.
Bring me your power, your strong second sight.
Hear that I call you and, willing, assist.
Lend me your magic and all that you wist."

There was a flash of darkness.

Okay, I knew that didn't make any sense. I knew that a "flash" was supposed to be light, that I was supposed to use the word to describe stars and glinting and color.

But this was an explosion of darkness.

My candle flame disappeared. The light from the stairs disappeared. The sight of my fingertips, pressed against the jet-black word *wist* on the parchment page, the book itself, the table, the room—all of it just disappeared.

And then, it jumped back into existence, except that everything was *more* than it had been before. Everything was sharper, clearer. I felt like someone in the projection booth of my life had just responded to an audience member's drunken roar: "Focus!"

This time, I didn't try to swallow my scream, but I still didn't manage a full *Friday the 13th / Texas Chainsaw Massacre* shriek. More a startled exclamation: "What the hell?"

And those three words changed everything. One moment, I was alone in my basement, surrounded by an impossible collection of books, holding a wavering beeswax candle and trembling in my bunny slippers. The next, I had company.

The statue beside me awakened.

At first, it moved like any other waist-high cat you might choose to imagine. It uncurled its tail from around its paws and stood up from its seated position. It shook its head back and forth. It stretched its front paws forward, digging its claws into the crimson-and-indigo Turkish carpet and extracting them one by one. It opened its mouth in a gaping yawn, showing me the ridged roof of its palate and its hand-long fangs, sharper than the knives I'd thrown into the kitchen drawers upstairs.

Before I could speak or move or even think of retrieving my cell phone, the cat tucked its head toward its chest and bunched all four feet together. It arched its back like a Halloween symbol, a rigid curve of spiky fur.

But when it came out of the arch, it was no longer a cat.

I found myself looking into a man's eyes. In the candlelight, I couldn't decipher their color—they might have been green or amber or hazel. They were slightly almond-shaped, complementing strong, angular cheekbones that I would have given my own eyeteeth to possess. His hair was jet-black and very short, standing on end as if it had been gelled. He wore the most close-fitting black T-shirt I'd ever seen and a pair of black jeans that were stretched so tight across his crotch that I glanced away immediately. His shoes were sleek leather, vaguely European.

He surveyed me from head to toe, taking a long moment

to linger over my bunny slippers. He took his time licking his lips before he settled his right hand on his hip and shook his head. When he spoke, he could have been making a guest appearance on *Queer Eye for the Straight Guy*. Girl. Whatever.

"Girlfriend," he said. "We have *got* to get you some better shoes."

A half dozen responses crashed through my mind. "What do you know about shoes?" I started to ask. That got pushed aside by "What just happened?" And "Did I really see what I think I saw?" And "What are you doing in my basement?" And "How did you get in here?" And "Are you really a familiar?" Spluttering, I settled for "Who the hell are you?"

"I'm Neko, darling."

"Neko? Just Neko? How about a last name?" Or *was* that his last name? I realized I was gaping, and it wasn't any more attractive here in my basement than it was when Melissa and I went out to Le Bar, and I couldn't think of a reply when the guy making martinis flirted with me. Like *that* happened on a regular basis.

"Just Neko," he said. He looked around the room and clicked his tongue in patent disapproval. "Oh, my! You *have* let things slip, haven't you?"

My cheeks flushed, even though I didn't have any reason to be ashamed of the basement. Once a librarian, always a librarian, I guess. The cascading books did make me feel vaguely uneasy. Like I'd been caught red-handed ducking out of work early, leaving part of my job undone.

Wait.

A statue of a cat had just transformed into a living, breathing man before my very eyes, and I was worried about shelving books according to the Dewey Decimal system? I shook my head. "Just a second," I said. "Before you start to criticize me, let's get a couple of things straight. First, I take it you're a familiar?"

"And I take it you're a witch."

"No, I'm a librarian."

"Who just happens to work spells. No need to be coy with me, girlfriend."

"I didn't work a spell! I just read some words in that book!"

Neko stalked around the book stand, viewing the volume from all angles. He wrinkled his nose, as if he could smell something unpleasant steaming up from the pages. He cocked his head when he'd completed his circuit. "And you just happened to have a beeswax taper in your hand when you read it? And sheer coincidence made you offer up the powers of your mind, your voice and your heart? Then trace the letters with your finger? You don't read *everything* out loud, do you? Not very good librarian behavior, that."

I looked at the candle, almost surprised to find that I still held it. "This is all some joke, right? Did Melissa put you up to this?"

"Who is Melissa?"

He truly sounded puzzled. So puzzled that I didn't even bother asking about Evelyn. Or Gran. No one else would have had the time to pull together this prank. Even if they'd known I was moving into the cottage. Even if they'd known how to transform a cat into a man.

But if it wasn't a prank...

I suddenly felt weak in my knees. Was he a madman? Was he dangerous? He didn't *seem* likely to harm me, but what could I truly know? I didn't think that I was actually going to faint—I'd *never* fainted—but sitting down suddenly seemed like a really good idea. And a shot of vodka was an even better one. My voice shook as I asked, "Can you come upstairs?"

"Can a drag queen sing?"

Well, could a drag queen sing? I have to admit I wasn't an expert on the subject. I mean, I'd seen *To Wong Foo, Thanks for Everything, Julie Newmar*—it was a campy staple at grad school. I was a big fan of Bugs Bunny, and it seemed like he spent half his time in a dress and lipstick.

But Neko was asking a rhetorical question. I didn't need to give an actual reply. Instead, I turned around and walked upstairs, clutching the railing and trying not to feel too paranoid about the flamboyantly gay, black-clad, feline familiar stalking behind me.

In the kitchen, I finally blew out my candle and dropped it onto the tile counter. I opened up the freezer and fished out the bottle of Stoli that I'd stashed there after the last run from my old apartment. "Drink?" I asked, as I tried to remember where I'd put the glasses.

Neko made a small moue of distaste. Apparently Stoli

wasn't his alcohol of preference. Tough luck for him. I found the tumblers on my third try—second cabinet to the left of the sink.

"Do you have anything to eat?" he asked. "It's been a while since my last meal."

The clear bottle rattled against the glass as I poured. "Not much. I haven't been to the grocery store yet."

The grocery store. Here I was, standing in my kitchen in the middle of the night, discussing my larder with an apparition that I'd summoned to life through the power of an ancient spell book.

Yeah. Right.

I downed a large swallow of vodka and poured another. The Russian heat burned down my throat, and I resisted the urge to shake my head and gasp.

Anxious for something to keep my hands busy, anything, I picked up the candle. I tested the wick to make sure that it was cool, and I tossed it back into the emergency supplies box. It landed against one of the cans of tuna. Hmm…tuna? "I've got this."

"That will have to do," Neko said, but he smiled as he craned his neck, examining the cartoon fish on the squat can's label.

I dug out my can opener, secretly pleased that I remembered which drawer held the tool. As I cranked the handle, Neko leaned closer. He wove his head back and forth as I worked the opener, and I thought that I heard a gurgle deep in his throat. Or was that a purr?

I pressed the detached lid back into the can and started to drain the packing water into the sink. "No!" Neko cried, and I jumped back. "What are you doing?"

"Um, draining the tuna?"

"That's the best part!"

I looked at him as if he were truly crazy, but he was dancing back and forth beside me. I wondered how long it had been since he'd eaten, how long he'd been frozen as a statue in my basement. Could it be decades? Centuries? How much did he know about canned tuna, anyway? And packing water? What exactly was going on here?

I put the can down on the counter and reached for a fork. Before I could hand him the utensil, Neko pounced on the food. I looked away, disgusted by his slurping directly from the can. Before I could say anything, there was a pounding knock at the door.

Neko glanced up. "You'd better get that."

"Who could it be?" I shot a look at my watch. "It's three-twenty in the morning."

"It'll be the warder."

"The warder?" I couldn't tell if my voice broke because of the strange word, or because Neko had already emptied the contents of the can. "Be careful!" I said, as he started to lick the lid. "You'll cut yourself!"

"Warder," Neko repeated, reluctantly setting the container on the counter. It was clean enough that I could set it out for recycling. The knocking resumed. "They don't like to be kept waiting. If you're lucky, you'll get one of the luscious ones."

I glanced down at my flannel pj's and my bunny-shod feet. No time to dress for this meeting, "luscious warder" or not. I settled for kicking off my slippers and grabbing my Polarfleece blanket from the back of the couch. I draped the throw around my shoulders and pulled it close at my neck.

I was sure that some glamorous movie star could have pulled off the look, but I felt like a barefoot little girl playing dress-up.

The pounding resumed, and I hollered, "I'm coming!"

I crossed to the door and waited for Neko to come stand beside me. After all, he seemed to have some idea who was out there. The amazing cat-man, though, only hovered in the kitchen doorway. He scratched at his jaw and said, "He'll only get angrier if you make him wait."

Clutching my blanket close, I threw the deadbolt and opened the door.

The man who swept in looked like he had escaped from a movie set. He was tall—he had a good foot on me. His dark hair swooped to silver on his temples, and he wore it a little long. He was clean-shaven, not even wearing the sideburns that Ashton Kutcher had made all the rage. His eyes were probably brown, but it was hard to tell because his pupils were enlarged from the nighttime dark. He wore a well-tailored suit of charcoal-gray, cut to accentuate his height, and his white dress shirt was open at the neck. The tendons on either side of his throat strained like metal cables.

He filled his lungs, and Neko took a mincing step back into the kitchen. The newcomer whirled toward me. If he'd been wearing a cape, it would have swirled out behind him. "What the devil do you think you're doing? Awakening a familiar on the night of a full moon?"

"What the devil?" I actually laughed out loud. It wasn't that the words were actually so funny. It was just that I'd never heard anyone use them before. Not in real life, in real anger. They sounded too high-flown, too Mr. Rochester or Heathcliff or someone like that.

My amusement probably wasn't the response he expected. I think that I was supposed to fall to my knees, cowering in terror. This guy was accustomed to people—to witches?—being afraid of him. "What the devil?" I repeated, and I closed the door behind him.

"What is your name?" he demanded.

"You're the one pushing your way into my house," I said, trying to ignore the fact that my feet were getting cold on the hardwood floor. "Don't you think you should tell me yours first?"

He glanced at Neko, who gave a slight shrug. Even if my, um, familiar wanted to provide this stranger with information, he couldn't. The warder eyed me evenly and said, "I am David Montrose."

"Jane Madison," I said, extending my hand. As soon as I said it, I wished that I hadn't given him my last name. If we'd been in a bar, I would have just said, "Jane." He shook my hand, but he seemed a bit surprised. Seizing the moment, I pushed my glasses back up on the bridge of my nose. "What are you doing here at three-thirty in the morning?"

"I'm one of Hecate's warders." The words meant nothing to me. "I was summoned by your unlicensed working tonight."

"My unlicensed working… You mean reading from that book downstairs?"

"The spell book?" he said, and even if he meant it to be a statement, it actually came out like a question. "The *Compendium?*" He must have heard his tentative tone, because he cleared his throat and said, "You worked a spell without first registering with the Coven." There. Now he sounded like the big bad wolf, and I had no doubt that he could huff, and puff, and blow my house down, or whatever else warders did when bad witches forgot to register and awakened familiars on the night of a full moon.

"Look," I said. "I don't know what this is all about." I looked over at Neko, who obligingly nodded his head in agreement.

"She really doesn't," he said to Montrose. "The poor thing doesn't know much of anything at all. Just look at those glasses—can you believe how wrong they are for her face?"

"Thanks." I scowled at him, but he only turned his palms toward me—a universal gesture for "what else do you want from me?"

"You expect me to believe that?" Montrose's words remained aggressive, but his tone wavered again. I thought he was beginning to realize that I wasn't some dark, mysterious pirate sailing the witchcraft seas. I was a totally lost amateur, hoping that my Sunfish sailboat didn't drift too far past the pier.

"I don't expect you to believe anything!" I said. "Look. I'll tell you what happened, but I'm not going to get down on my knees and beg your forgiveness. I didn't do anything wrong." Montrose opened his mouth, clearly planning to quote section and verse from some volume on witchcraft infractions, but I went on before he could interrupt. "Go on. Go sit in the kitchen. I'm putting on some real clothes, and I'll meet you in there."

Montrose stared at me in obvious surprise. I don't think that anyone had ever told him where he should go and when he should do it. I confirmed my suspicion when I caught Neko staring at me, a look of theatrical horror widening his eyes.

"Neko?" I asked. "Do you know how to put on the teakettle?" He nodded, apparently unable to find his voice. "Good. The tea is in the pantry. Top right shelf." I turned toward my room, pleased at having taken control of the situation. Then, I remembered. "No. Not right. Left." Back to my room. "Wait! Second shelf from the top."

"I'll find the tea," Neko said, as if he were more afraid to deal with a crazed homeowner who had lost her tea bags than he was to confront Hecate's warder. Whatever the hell that meant.

Back in my bedroom, I shut my door carefully, making sure that the latch snicked all the way closed. When I was reasonably certain that the cavalry wasn't going to come barging in, I tore off my flannel pajamas. My shorts and T-shirt from earlier in the day were crumpled on the floor, but there was no way I was going to confront Montrose—or anyone else—in those stinky things. I flung open my closet door and reached for the first hanger.

A black silk blouse. French cuffs. No way that I was going to find cufflinks at this late hour.

Next up was a knit dress, more or less unwrinkled after its transport on the backseat of Gran's car. I slipped it off its hanger and shook it out, cringing at the loud noise when it snapped in midair. I fumbled for a bra, swore when the straps twisted into a knot, and bit the inside of my cheek when the hooks tangled on the wrong eyelets.

This was ridiculous. I'd been dressing myself for how many years? I just needed to slow down. Take my time. Forget that I'd turned a giant cat statue into a man and summoned some sort of cosmic cop to my doorstep. Easy.

I tugged the dress over my head and decided that I wasn't going to fight panty hose and shoes, cold toes or not. With any luck, Montrose would be out of the house before he noticed the oversight.

Fat chance. When I walked into the kitchen, Neko immediately stared at my feet. "Would you like me to get your slippers?" he asked, glancing at the bunny ears that were just visible behind the couch.

"No. Thank you." I made my reply frosty. At least, he had managed to find the tea bags. And the sugar.

"You don't have any cream," he said, and he made it sound like a mortal sin.

"I drink mine black." I hoped to convey the fact that I wasn't running an all-night diner. Neko looked wounded. Montrose was not amused.

The water was just coming to a boil, so I used the routine of making tea to cover my apprehension. I rescued three mugs from the shelf above the sink and found a teaspoon and saucer to hold our used tea bags. I poured boiling water into the mugs. I gestured to the tin table in the kitchen and waved the men to their seats.

Only when oolong steam was rising to moisten my cheeks did I meet Montrose's eyes. His fingers closed tightly over the handle of his mug, and I could hear the tension as he forced his voice to be civil. "Thank you, Miss Madison," he said.

"My pleasure." His "Miss Madison" made *me* more formal than usual. Off my game again, I sipped from my mug and burned my tongue. I put the tea on the table and took a deep breath. "All right, then. You're a warder. What is that? Some sort of cop?"

He started to protest, but he settled for a tight-jawed nod. "I enforce the Covenants."

"The Covenants?" I wished that Melissa were with me; she could whistle her *Twilight Zone* theme. "Let me guess. The witches form a Coven? And their laws are the Covenants?" Another nod. "You do realize that I'm not a witch, right?"

"You worked a spell." He kept his voice perfectly steady, and even I couldn't argue with his logic. "You have the power. You found the key, and you opened the book. You read from the page."

"Anyone could have done that."

"If you didn't have the power, the key would have stayed hidden."

Oh.

I tried again. "Even if I *do* have some power, I'm not a witch." I counted off my explanations on my fingers. "One—I don't wear a pointy hat. Two—I use a broom only for sweeping. Three—I've never even owned a cauldron." Ha ha ha.

Montrose was not amused. "You lit the pure beeswax taper, didn't you?"

"Yes, but I didn't—"

"And you touched your brow, your throat and your heart?"

"Yes, but I—"

"And you traced the words in the spell book with your finger?"

"Yes, but—"

"And you read the spell aloud?"

"Yes—"

"And yet you still say you didn't work a spell. You awakened a familiar." He shook his head and pointed to Neko. "*That* familiar. On the night of the full moon."

Neko froze, halfway through testing his tea with the tip of his tongue. He cast a fearful look at Montrose. I was already beginning to feel protective of the black-clad guy. After all, he hadn't asked to be awakened by me.

I said, "So what's the deal with the full moon? I mean, how does it change things?"

Montrose sighed. "Any familiar awakened on the night of a full moon has freedom to roam." I stared at him. He said, "Neko can go anywhere. He doesn't have to stay in the same room as your *Compendium*. He isn't bound to you the way that a normal familiar is bound."

So much for feeling protective. I turned on Neko. "Were you going to say anything to me about this?"

"Probably not." He shrugged and pursed his lips into an air kiss. "Don't ask, don't tell."

I turned back to Montrose, feeling more than a little betrayed. "Look," I said. "Why don't we cut to the chase? Just for the sake of argument, I'll say that I worked a spell. You're the police, and I broke the rules. Do I pay a fine? Have to show up at witch court?"

"You have to stop using your powers. Until you've

trained with someone who knows the consequences of working magic."

"Well, that's easy enough." My relief actually felt something like a laugh. "I can promise you that I'm not going to work any more magic. Ever. This is all too weird. It's not like I *planned* any of this, you know."

"No spells, then."

I nodded, relieved at how easy this was going to be. "No spells." As soon as it was daylight, I would toss out every one of my beeswax tapers. I'd risk being without power in a dozen thunderstorms before I'd relive a night as strange as this one. And I'd figure out how to get rid of my... familiar in the full light of day.

"I'll be monitoring you," Montrose warned.

"You go ahead and do whatever you have to do." I tried to keep my words defiant.

Actually, I had about a million questions. How could he monitor me? How had he found me in the first place? How had he known that I'd transformed Neko? And how could he honestly expect me to believe that witchcraft existed in the middle of Washington, D.C., in the twenty-first century?

Before I could even decide whether to ask my questions, my jaws tensed with a gigantic yawn that I barely managed to catch against the back of my throat. I cheated a glance at my wrist and saw that it was almost four o'clock. That thought made me even more exhausted, and the next yawn escaped. I remembered to cover my mouth, though. Gran would have been proud.

Montrose must have thought that I was sending him a

message. He set his mug down on the table with a decisive gesture and rose to his feet. "Of course, you're responsible for whatever your familiar does—for *all* actions that he takes."

"Of course," I said, trying to sound as if I negotiated magical responsibilities every day of my life. "I won't be working any magic, so he'll have nothing to do." I glared at Neko, who managed a perfectly arched "who, me?" eyebrow.

"And one more thing, Miss Madison," Montrose said. I cocked my head to one side, still surprised by how odd my name sounded with his formal diction. "That." He pointed to the counter.

"The aquarium?"

"The fish."

"What about Stupid Fish?"

"Keep an eye on it." Montrose looked at Neko, who became completely obsessed with picking a bit of lint from his spotless sleeve. "You never know what bad things might happen when you're not paying attention."

Bad things. I glanced at the basement door and thought of the dozens of books down there, the countless spells that might result in any number of disasters. I shuddered and shook my head. "I'll pay attention," I vowed, silently promising never to set foot in the basement again.

"Just make sure that you do," Montrose said, and then he disappeared into the night.

5

"Oh my God!" Melissa said. "What did you do?" She held up a finger before I could answer, turning to the counter behind her and picking up the pot of Toffee Kiss coffee. She filled a large paper cup and slipped on a finger-preserving corrugated sleeve before handing it to a ginger-haired man who looked like he was only just waking up, despite the fact that it was after six in the evening. He paid her with exact change and took the cup. No words were exchanged. Ah, the joys of being a regular. And Cake Walk had more coffee regulars than the Peabridge Library could ever hope to attract.

When I had Melissa's undivided attention again, I shrugged. "Montrose left. I locked the door after him and went back to sleep."

"I don't believe that you're being so blasé about all this! I would have totally freaked! I mean, you worked a spell from an ancient magic book!"

"What am I supposed to do? Run out into the street screaming, 'I'm a witch! I'm a witch!' It's not like I can call the cops and report myself. They'd lock me up for observation. I'd wonder if I hadn't imagined everything, if not for Neko."

"He's still there, then?"

"Asleep on the couch. At least he was this morning— curled up in a sunbeam. He barely stirred when I left for work."

"I can't believe you just left him there!"

"What else was I going to do? Sit and stare at him all day? I needed to get to work. The last thing I'd need now is to be fired. I'd lose my paycheck *and* my house."

"But Montrose said that with the full moon—"

"I know!" I'd been worried about my familiar's dire potential all day. Melissa looked startled by my sharp tone, and I forced myself to repeat a bit less forcefully, "I know. But I couldn't figure out anything else to do with him. And, I have to say, he just doesn't *seem* dangerous."

Melissa snorted. "And what about Stupid Fish?"

"What else could I do? I hauled the aquarium into my room. It's sitting on the floor."

"Poor thing!"

"He's a fish," I said dryly. "I'll get some sort of table for him tonight. I guess I should consider myself lucky that the bedroom door locks. Otherwise, there's no telling what Neko might do for a snack."

"Why didn't you just whip up another spell? Conjure up a table to put the aquarium on."

"It's not like I'm a sudden expert on this stuff! And I'm

not getting anywhere near that book again." I remembered that strange flash of darkness, the sudden power that had risen from nowhere. "I mean, I have no idea how I did what I did, but I'm not going to play around with it. Even if I hadn't promised Montrose—"

My words were interrupted by a pair of women who walked through the door. "What's left?" one of them asked, already reaching into her purse.

"One Lemon Grenade." Melissa pointed toward the pastry, sitting lonely beneath a glass dome. "Two Ginger-Butterscotch Dreams." The giant cookies leaned against each other on a hand-thrown pottery plate. "One Fusion Swirl." Raspberry jam glistened in a Caramel Blondie. "And half a dozen Bunny Bites."

The miniature carrot cakes were my favorite. They were a lot of work, especially when Melissa took the time to pipe miniature orange carrots on top of the cream cheese frosting. I had the women pegged as Dream girls, though, and I wasn't disappointed. They paid up, promised to be back the next day and headed out the door.

Melissa passed me one of the Bites. The frosting melted over my tongue, and I closed my eyes in near ecstasy.

So what if I was a witch? So what if I had managed to work a spell? So what if the books in my basement might contain secrets to the entire universe, if I only took the time to investigate them, to explore them and put them in order?

I chewed and swallowed, reminding myself that I didn't need to do anything with the witchcraft collection. I wasn't going to let it interfere with my life ever again. It was a one-time mistake, like the Brazilian wax that Scott had coaxed me into trying, or having my eyebrows threaded. I wasn't going to go there. Not ever again. Anything else would be just too strange. And there was no time like the present to get life back to normal (whatever *that* meant, with a familiar napping on my couch).

I took a deep breath and forced a bright smile as I very purposefully changed the topic of conversation. "So?" I said. "Enough about the Wicked Ways of Witchcraft. Tell me about your date!"

Melissa was determined to find *the* Man by the time she turned thirty. Although she hadn't met him yet, she knew that the Man was educated. He was sensitive and caring and not intimidated by her running her own business. He was independent enough to give her breathing room, but reliable enough that he'd show up when he said he would. He had to be physically stronger than she was, and taller, and he had to have all his own teeth and hair. Too preppy was out, too grungy, too punk. Basically, she was looking for an impossible fiction, created by magazines and beach reading and endless, repetitious conversations with girl-friends.

But Melissa structured her search. She auditioned one new candidate every two weeks, rotating her stock from various resources: Dedicated Metropolitan Singles (an or-ganization devoted to conducting volunteer activities with teams comprised of equal numbers of men and women); *Washington Today* personal ads (the magazine was read by lawyers, lobbyists, and other upwardly trending intellectuals); FranticDate.com (not really the name of the Web site, but I could never remember what it was actually called); and Independents (recommendations from friends, relatives and anyone else who thought they should have a say in her love life).

"This one was a Dedicated, wasn't he?"

"Oh, yeah," she said, popping a Bunny Bite into her own mouth. The guy must have been a disaster. Melissa never ate her own wares. "Dedicated to his mother."

"We're talking a Norman Bates–type thing?"

"Just about. He phoned mumsy when he picked me up, ostensibly to make sure that she'd gotten home from her card game all right. And then he called her during dinner. And she phoned *him* while he was walking me home."

"But what was he like? I mean, couldn't you work with him on the phone thing?"

"Oh, the calls were only the beginning." She checked her watch to make sure that it was six-thirty before she walked around the counter. When she reached the door, she flipped the hand-lettered Walk On In sign to Walk On By and turned off the outside light. She flipped another switch, and the four two-tops at the front of the shop disappeared in shadows.

I picked up a towel, well-accustomed to the routine. I didn't pay for my Bunny Bites, but I washed plates, coffee carafes and whatever else was left around at the end of the day. As Melissa filled the sink with hot, soapy water, she shook her head. "I tried to compliment him on his tie, and he told me that his mother had brought it back from Singapore. I asked him what had made him sign up with Dedicated Metro, and he said that his mother's garden club was a sponsor."

"Sounds like a real winner." I shook my head and started drying the Dreams plate.

"I'm telling you, I was through all Five Conversational Topics, and we hadn't even finished our appetizers."

Despite all her practice, Melissa got nervous about dates. She was always afraid that she would say the wrong thing, or—worse—say nothing. So before each and every encounter, she drew up a list of Five Conversational Topics. She wrote them down on a piece of paper and committed them to memory. She tried to use them sparingly, exploiting the complete depths of each subject before going on to the next. Typically, they were masterpieces of open-ended questioning, and I'd never known her to go through all five. Two, usually. Three, if she was with a guy who was really hard to draw out. Four, if he was the shyest man in the world—most of her Four nights had been FranticDate guys.

But Five? And with the appetizer plates still on the table?

"What did you do?"

"I yielded to the inevitable."

"And that was?"

She shrugged and pulled the plug in the sink. We watched the water swirl away, and the slurping sound at the end seemed a comment on our love lives. "I asked him what his mother thought made an ideal woman."

"You didn't!"

"Oh yes, I did." Her jaw was grim as she dried her hands on a towel.

"But what if he'd realized you were being sarcastic?"

"What was the worst that would happen? He'd refuse to see me again?"

"And what did he say? What was his mother's ideal?"

Melissa shook her head. "A woman who could cook and

clean and manage a household's finances, all the while popping out babies as if the pill had never been invented." She put coffee into the brewing baskets, getting ready for the next morning's rush. "That last bit was my editorial. He didn't actually mention the pill."

"What did you talk about after that?"

"Nothing."

"Nothing?" I was fascinated by this tale of dating disaster. It was like a giant bruise, and I couldn't keep from poking it.

"I decided not to waste any more topics. Five's my limit." She shrugged. "Even dessert was the pits—molten chocolate cakes. I make better stuff in my sleep."

I started to challenge that harsh judgment. After all, molten chocolate cakes were molten chocolate cakes. They couldn't be all bad, even if the date had been a complete disaster. Loyalty made me shake my head, though, and I clicked my tongue in disapproval. "Another wasted night."

Melissa turned to the calendar that hung over the phone. She burrowed around in the mug of pens on the counter until she found her red felt-tip pen. Red for date nights. It was supposed to be a sign of romance, but it had become more like blood. She drew a giant *X* across the previous day and then switched to a black ballpoint to cross off the current square.

I sympathized with her. I really did. But a little voice nagged at the back of my mind: Twenty-six first dates in a year? That could drive anyone crazy. And what would happen if she actually *did* like one of these guys? Would she have to fit a second date in before the next competitor's slot? Or would she skip one of the first dates? And if skipping became the answer, then what would she do about her rotation of sources—push it back, as well, to keep the sequence between FranticDate, Dedicated Metro, etc.?

I was much better off, really. I'd already decided which man to target—Jason. I could invest all of my thoughts and energy into figuring him out. In fact, I'd sketched out a perfect conversation just that morning, ready to ferret out specific information on Ekaterina Ivanova.

I'd waited until I was shelving books near him. When he looked up, I said, "Things are really busy around here. Lots of new users. I guess grad students must be getting really busy, with the end of the term so close."

Okay, so it wasn't my most graceful conversational gambit. It sounded a bit like one of those games where you have to get your teammate to say a key word—*Password,* or *Taboo,* or one of those things. Still, I had his attention.

"Nice dress," he said, and I almost melted in front of his grin. "Is the library having a costume party?"

I tugged at my lace cuffs and cursed Evelyn under my breath. "This is something new we're trying. To make the collection come alive."

Before he could reply, someone rang the bell at the coffee counter. It was probably just as well. I'd seen the look in his eyes. There was confusion there. Confusion, and just a spark of pity. Great foundation for a romance.

But better than a mama's boy who needed to be surgically separated from his cell phone. "I'm sorry," I said to Melissa. "Better luck next time."

She sighed. "Yep. I'll have to start reviewing the next candidates." She had a stack of responses to her most recent

Washington Today ad. She brushed her hands, as if she were shaking off excess flour. "Enough about that, though. Are we still on for yoga tomorrow?"

"I don't know," I said. I hated going to yoga with Melissa. She was a lot more flexible than I was, and she was somehow able to listen to the instructor at the same time that she levered her body into impossible twists and turns.

"You know you'll feel better after you go to class."

"I'm worried about leaving Neko."

"You went to the library all day today. You came over here. What could he get into tomorrow that he couldn't do today?" I shook my head, still looking for a way out. "Come on," she urged. "Rock, paper, scissors?"

We'd settled disputes with the game since we were in elementary school. "All right," I said, reluctantly. We counted together, touching our right fists to our left palms. "One. Two. Three." I went for rock, but she chose paper.

"Paper covers rock," she said, laughing. "Yoga it is."

"Best two out of three!"

"Don't be a bad sport. I'll meet you at the studio tomorrow."

I gathered up my purse and followed Melissa to Cake Walk's back door. "I should have gone for scissors."

"Yeah, yeah. Don't be late."

I stepped into the alley, but then I turned back to look at her. She was framed in the doorway, her overalls dusted with flour and her hair ruffled from a full day's work. "Do you think I'm crazy?" I asked. "About this whole witch thing?"

She shook her head, and her smile was the same one I'd known since third grade. "You might be crazy, but this 'witch thing' doesn't prove it. I'm not exactly sure what's going on, but we'll figure it out. You might want to pick up some more tuna on the way home, though. Spare Stupid Fish for another day."

It was strange, I know. I should have been panicked about having Neko in the house—I mean, it's not every day that a girl conjures up a half man, half cat with a better fashion sense than she can ever dream of having.

But Neko just wasn't frightening. I should have been worried about his magical powers, about what he could do to me, to the house, to all of Georgetown and the world, but I couldn't be. Not when he got so aghast at the notion of my reusing a tea bag. Not when he was horrified that I would wear flats with an above-the-knee dress. Not when he had actually hissed in dismay at my Peabridge costume.

Strange things were happening, but they weren't frightening. Not terrifying, anyway. And besides, I was never going to work another spell, so none of it really mattered. Only a fool would play with magic, I had told myself all afternoon. Only a naive idiot.

"No more magic," I said to myself as I walked down the cobble-stoned Georgetown street.

If only I had listened to those words of witch-free wisdom.

I sat across from Gran and waited for her to finish pouring me a steaming cup of tea. I'd skipped out on the library for the afternoon, telling Evelyn that I needed to return Gran's car to her after moving in. I just hadn't mentioned that I was handing off the keys in the middle of the Four Seasons lounge.

It wasn't my fault. Gran had suggested that we meet for an afternoon snack, her treat. I couldn't very well refuse—the woman *was* my only living relative. Besides, I'd heard great things about the hotel's precious sandwiches and delectable sweets; I wasn't going to pass those up. After Gran had invited me, I'd taken a moment to phone Melissa, offering to do some advance work for Cake Walk. Who knew—maybe the Four Seasons served some treasure that Melissa just needed to perfect and make her own, with a jazzy name and a reasonable price. I was willing to take a hit for the team.

So far, my little afternoon escapade had not been disappointing. Our waiter had presented us with a compartmentalized box filled with glass-stoppered bottles of tea leaves. Gran and I had inhaled our way through the choices, from pear oolong to lavender Earl Grey to apricot pekoe. I had finally chosen the oolong, reveling in the dark amber brew that now perfumed the air like some rare elixir. Gran offered me sugar, which I declined, but I accepted a drop of cream.

Okay. So I'd lied to Neko on the night of his transformation. I did like cream in my tea. But just a bit, and I never kept the stuff in the house. I didn't use much of it on my own, and it always went bad before the carton was empty. Nothing stinks up a refrigerator as much as spoiled milk products.

Besides, even if I'd had cream on hand the other night, I wouldn't have shared it with the cat-man. I didn't want to do anything to bring out the feline side of his personality. That just creeped me out. The night before, I'd come home from meeting with Melissa to find two voles and a mouse stretched out on my front porch, their tiny corpses lined up like a magical offering.

Neko. I'd already decided not to mention him to Gran. Not Neko, not Montrose, nothing at all about that strange night. She'd only worry about me, and since I wasn't going to be working any more spells, there was no reason to put her through that.

A waiter swooped by our table and set down a tiered tray. I could make out some cucumber sandwiches (crusts neatly trimmed from impossibly thin slices of white bread). There were also tiny bites of curried chicken salad on glazed walnut bread, and a dollop of egg salad with feathery dill on pumpernickel. I would leave the egg for Gran—it was her favorite—but I could never get past the smell. I helped myself to smoked salmon on lemon brioche.

"I really appreciate your getting away from the library," Gran said. "I just wish you hadn't changed out of your new outfit. I wanted to see it. I'm sure it's darling."

I took my time chewing a pale orange bite. After I swallowed, I looked down at my neat A-line skirt. An A-line skirt that I'd never wear to work again. An A-line skirt that Jason Templeton would never have the opportunity to admire—even from a distance, much less from the up-close-and-personal view of the sometimes tricky side zipper. "I can't wear those things in public, Gran. The skirt has honest-to-God hoops, and the quilted petticoat looks like something out of a museum."

"The stays must make you stand up straight, though. You've always needed a reminder about your posture."

Thanks, Gran. I love you, too.

I settled for "Before I forget—here are your keys. I left the car with the valet."

Gran set them on the table between us. For just a moment, it seemed that she put them there to keep them available, like an escape hatch. In case one of us needed to flee the scene. How strange was that? I chased the thought away by asking about her board meeting. She had just come from her monthly session with the concert opera guild board of directors.

"It was fine, dear."

"Fine?" Something was definitely wrong. Gran could

talk about the opera board for hours—long detailed stories about the volunteers who performed above all expectations, or the prima donna sopranos who arrived at the theater expecting special treatment that wasn't to be found anywhere outside of New York's Metropolitan Opera.

"Yes, dear, fine." She glanced around distractedly, as if she were trying to find a waiter. A buffer. "Do you need more tea?"

I looked down at my still-full cup. "Um, not yet, Gran." Now I was beginning to get a worried.

"Jane, will you make me a promise?"

Whew. So that was it. Just another one of Gran's promise binges. She had me going there for a moment. "About what?" I asked.

"I can't tell you yet."

"What?" I started to ask, but then I remembered my manners. "Pardon me?" I heard the sharpness, barely hidden under my voice.

"I'm going to ask you to do something, and you aren't going to be very happy about it. Promise me, though, that you'll do it. It's very important to me. More important than anything I've ever asked of you before."

Wait a minute. This was more than the usual Gran request. This time, she wanted to bind me before I even knew what was at stake. What was going on?

Suddenly, all the bits slipped into place. Gran's nervousness. Her luring me with afternoon tea. The "fine" concert opera guild board meeting.

Uncle George.

Uncle George wasn't my real uncle. He was a friend of

Gran's, her oldest friend. For decades he'd taken her out on dates—the only grown-up evenings she'd had the entire time that I was growing up. Uncle George and my grandfather had known each other in elementary school, and George had stepped in to help out around the house when my grandfather died.

Truth be told, I'd never liked the man all that much. He'd pulled quarters out of my ears for way too many years. I mean, it was one thing to be amazed and giggly when I was five years old. But when I was fifteen? And he had jowls—honest-to-goodness jowls just like a bull mastiff. They wobbled beside his mouth when he talked.

But he made Gran happy. In fact, he was the one who had gotten her interested in concert opera. She said that he made even the longest board meetings bearable; he was the president.

And now, it seemed that he was finally ready to move their relationship "to the next level." Uncle George was going to ask Gran to marry him. It made sense. I had finally secured a real house through the Peabridge, and even though Scott was out of my life forever, it was pretty clear that I wouldn't need to move back home with Gran.

I wondered if she would wear a white dress. I mean, *I* didn't have any trouble with that—I'm hardly a conservative person. Something tea-length, maybe? With a small bouquet of sweetheart roses? We could even have the wedding in the Peabridge gardens, use my cottage's kitchen to serve up punch and wedding cake. I was sure Evelyn wouldn't mind. She'd welcome the opportunity for publicity.

"Jane?" Gran asked. "Do you promise?"

I smiled, now that I knew we were on safe territory. Before I could say anything, though, the waiter materialized again. He swept away the sandwich tray and set in place another tiered wonder—this one packed with little bites of dessert. Even in the midst of my reluctance to promise— for form's sake, mind you—my mouth watered at the sight of the coconut-dusted scones, the bite-sized lemon-meringue pies and the cherry-crowned pistachio financiers.

Gran smiled at the treats, as if she were a child on Christmas morning. I almost thought that she was going to clap her hands. "Look, Jane! All of my favorites!"

"Gran—"

"Here. Let me serve you." She spent a century selecting treasures, maneuvering them onto my plate with hands that showed every single year of their age. Okay. So, she was still nervous. What was going on here?

She bit into a tiny raspberry tart, and I watched her jaws move as she polished off the treat. "What?" she asked me, when she realized I was staring. "You can't be full already?"

"Gran, why did you bring me here? What did you want to ask me?"

She set down her plate and met my eyes for the first time since we'd been seated. "Promise—"

"Gran, I promise. You know I'll help you plan your marriage to Uncle George. *I* think it's wonderful that you've finally decided to get married."

"Get married!" Gran was loud enough that several other tea-patrons turned to stare. "What are you talking about? Who said anything about marriage?"

"Well, why else would you bring me here? Why would you be going on and on about this great promise I'm supposed to make, about your incredible secret?"

Gran laughed. It was the deep laugh that I'd heard since my earliest childhood—the one that carried her through my toddler tantrums, my grammar school superiority, my high school rebellion. The sound carried relief, but also a hint of desperation.

The more she laughed, the more disgruntled I became. Okay, so she probably wasn't going to get married. She and Uncle George didn't need to change their relationship now, after years of their friendship working just fine. But the idea wasn't *that* outrageous. She didn't have to act as if I were some clown, sent solely to entertain her. I plopped a cocoa-covered miniature truffle into my mouth and let the bittersweet chocolate melt its comfort over my tongue.

"Jane," she said, when she could finally draw a breath. "I'm so sorry. I didn't mean to mislead you."

"You did, though," I said, and even I could hear the sulkiness in my voice. I sat up straighter and pushed my shoulders back. "What's going on, Gran?"

"Promise—"

"Fine! I promise! I'll do whatever you're going to ask me to do."

She nodded her head, finally satisfied with my pledge. "There's someone who wants to meet you."

"You want to set me up on a blind date?"

Gran's smile was small, almost wistful. "Not at all, dear." She took the napkin from her lap and folded it into a precise rectangle. She set it beside her plate, as if she were through with tea. "The person who wants to meet you is a woman. Her name is Clara. Clara Smythe."

Smythe was Gran's last name. And Clara had been Gran's sister. Great-Aunt Clara had died decades ago in a car crash, just a month before my mother was born. That was why Gran had named my mother Clara, and it was a terrible irony that my mother had also died in a car…

"Clara?" I made it a question.

Gran nodded. "Clara. Your mother."

The room had suddenly become too warm. I wondered why they couldn't control the temperature better in a public space. I felt as if a giant fan had sucked all the air out of the room. I stared at Gran, unable to process her words. I realized that I was tapping my butter knife against the table, and I set it beside my saucer, lining it up precisely with the edge of the table.

"My mother." My voice didn't sound like it belonged to me. It was a little voice. A child's voice. A voice that was swirled in a cotton candy of hope, spoiled with the sour dust of fear. "She's dead."

Gran shook her head. "She isn't, dear. She never was. That was a story that we told you—that she decided I must tell you—when she left."

"When she left…." I knew that I should say something more, that I should be thinking faster than I was. But my brain seemed stuck in neutral. I could hear my thoughts revving, faster and faster as they chased each other.

My mother was alive. My mother had left me. My mother had let me think that she was dead for all these years. *Gran* had let me think that my mother was dead for all these years.

As I tried to think of something to say, something to ask, something to jolt me back onto the ordinary path of being, the waiter appeared from nowhere. "And how are we doing here?"

I looked up into his false smile, and I could not think of the right response, the polite words that everyone knew.

"We're fine," Gran said.

"More tea?"

"No, thank you."

The waiter nodded professionally and transported over to the next table. I looked into Gran's face. "What happened?"

"Your mother was very young, dear. She had no idea how much responsibility a newborn would be. She tried—she really did. But she just couldn't do the job."

Job. I'd been a job. For one insane moment, I pictured my mother punching a time clock, her hair wrapped up in a bandanna, her face weary from long hours on the graveyard shift.

"So she just abandoned me?"

"Jane, dear, she left you with me! That's hardly abandonment. She knew that I could take care of you, that I could give you everything you needed."

"Except the truth!" I heard how loud I'd become, how melodramatic, but I couldn't stop myself. "I should have known the truth! You should have told me that my own mother thought that I was too much trouble—"

Gran cut me off, a clear sign of just how upset *she* was. "She was sick, dear. She was lost." For one horrible moment I thought that Gran was going to cry. I had *never* seen her cry, not ever. She swallowed hard and touched the corners of her mouth with her napkin, and when she spoke again, her voice was even. Quiet, but even. "Your mother had a drug problem. She stayed away from the stuff while she was pregnant—that's how much she loved you. But after you were born… And when your father left…"

"So he left, too? He wasn't in the car crash?"

"There wasn't any car crash, Jane." Gran shook her head. "There was never any car crash. No one died. I've sent your mother letters through the years, told her how you're doing. She's asked to meet you now. She's ready."

She was ready? Well, that didn't mean that I was.

I'd gotten used to having no mother a long time ago. All those Mother's Day art projects in school, all those parent-teacher conferences where I had to explain to the other kids why my grandmother was there instead of my mother and father. I'd filled out endless forms, striking out *parent* and writing in *guardian*.

But now, to find out that it was all a lie… And my own grandmother was the biggest liar of all….

I stood up very carefully, grateful that I had stuck to pear oolong and forgone the champagne that had been an option on the menu. "The valet will get your car for you, Gran."

"Where are you going, dear?"

"Home." Away from here. To a cottage filled with witches' books. To my gay feline familiar. To the colonial dresses that had become my new uniform. To the sudden wreck of my life.

"At least let me drive you there." Gran reached for her handbag.

"I'd rather walk," I said. "I need some fresh air."

I heard Gran call the waiter. I heard her start to negoti-
ate paying for our treats. I heard her call out, "Jane, you
promised!" She was torn, frantic.

I only started to cry after I left the hotel, pounding the
heels of my black suede pumps against the sidewalk.

7

The yoga instructor spoke in a voice that she meant to be soothing: "Remember, Downward-Facing Dog is your friend. Ease into the stretch. Push your heels toward the floor. This pose is restful. Soothing. Relaxing."

Relaxing, my ass. My arms trembled, and my hamstrings felt like they were roasting in one of Melissa's ovens. I glanced over at my supposed best friend who was gazing at a point on her yoga mat, blissed out in the perfection of her pose.

The yoga instructor said, "All right, now. *Hop* your legs up to your hands. *Hop!*"

Yeah, right. Somewhere on her mantle, Gran has a trophy that I won for Best Hopper, when I was in preschool. My life as a bunny was long over. I straggled my right foot forward and tried to look jaunty as I dragged my left one into alignment.

"Let's move into Warrior I," the instructor said, as if she honestly believed I had all the position names memorized. I sneaked a look at Melissa to figure out what we were supposed to do, and I spread my legs into the expected triangle. As the instructor recited the rest of the exercise, I let my mind drift.

My mother was still alive. *My mother.* The woman that I thought had loved me. She was alive and well and could have come back to me at any moment, at any point in the twenty-five years that had passed since she walked away.

And now she wanted to see me.

I kept replaying my conversation with Gran in my head. I heard the words, over and over, like an old vinyl album skipping and repeating.

What had Gran been thinking? Had she realized how shocked I would be? She must have—that was why she'd staged the afternoon tea. She had wanted me in a public place, a place where I couldn't throw a tantrum, where I couldn't say words that I might later regret.

Even as I tried to build the case against her in my mind, I knew that I wasn't being fair. She was my Gran. She loved me. She had taken me to the Four Seasons because she wanted her revelation to be special, to be happy.

My mother was still alive. My *mother.*

"Jane," the yoga instructor said. "Raise your right arm. Look out over your fingertips. Flex your legs more. Activate your right leg."

I gritted my teeth and squatted lower, but the motion proved too much for my poor out-of-shape body. I staggered sideways, narrowly missing the woman on the next mat. I caught Melissa's quick smile, but she smoothed it away when I glared at her.

The instructor's voice remained calm. She spoke to the entire class, but I knew her words were meant for me. "If you ever find an asana too challenging, remember that you can assume the Child's Pose."

Sounded like a good idea to me. I folded myself onto my mat, sitting on my heels and stretching my arms in front of me. I tucked my head down and tried to focus on my breathing.

Child's Pose. I was a child. My mother's child. My mother was still alive.

Enough! Yoga was definitely not for me today. (Was it ever?) As the instructor started to move the class into a series of sun salutations, I rose up out of Child's Pose. I collected my mat, not even bothering to roll it into a tight cylinder.

Both the instructor and Melissa looked at me questioningly. "Cramp in my foot," I said.

The instructor started to offer me a bottle of the overpriced water that she sold from a minifridge at the back of the studio, but I shook my head and mouthed to Melissa, "I'll wait in the hall." She looked torn, but I shook my head. "Stay," I enunciated silently.

I limped out to the hallway, exaggerating my supposed foot cramp like a teenager trying to get out of gym class. I dropped the act as soon as I closed the studio door, and I slumped against the wall to wait for the dogs and warriors and children to finish up their class.

I thought about lighting up a cigarette.

I don't actually smoke. I never have. I can't stand the smell of cigarettes in my hair. But there have been times when I wanted a cigarette as a prop, as an image. I wanted to lean against the wall like a weary ballerina, staring down the hallway as I struggled to bear the burden of my recent knowledge. I would look wan and brave, with wisps of my hair just curling beside my high-cheekboned face. My collarbones would jut out like wings as my delicate wrist rose, as my lips pursed one last weary time to take a deep, mentholated drag, and the cigarette tip glowed vermilion in the darkening hallway.

Yeah, right. I'd probably cough like a patient on a consumption ward, and my eyes would tear up, and my mascara would run.

By the time Melissa joined me, I'd had time to select another vice.

"Mojito therapy," I said.

"What?" Her face was flushed with her yogic success. She went on as if I hadn't actually spoken. "I went from Bow to Camel today! I could feel the energy flowing through me, down my arms and legs, all at the same time!"

I tried to remember which was Bow and which was Camel—I think that Melissa had just accomplished the back bends that the springy, popular girls had always shown off in third-grade gym class. I fought the urge to ask what Mary Lou Retton was doing these days, and I repeated, "Mojito therapy. Now."

Melissa finally heard the dire note behind my words. "What's wrong?" she asked. "Your foot wasn't really cramping, was it?"

I shook my head. "I'll tell you all about it when we've got drinks in our hands. You've got limes? And mint?"

"Of course." Melissa shrugged and tossed her yoga mat over her shoulder. She'd rolled hers into a perfect cylinder and sheathed it in its nylon bag. I felt like a naughty pre-schooler beside her, too slovenly even to have picked up my toys. "Oh," Melissa said. "I brought one of these for you."

She passed me a fluorescent-pink flyer. I recognized the logo for the yoga studio centered at the top of the sheet. In delicate script, the page announced a special weekend series on "hot yoga." Participants were expected to bring their own towels (three, recommended) and water supply. I looked at Melissa for a long time before I crumpled the paper and crammed it into my bag. "You have got to be kidding."

"Rock, paper, scissors?"

"No way." She must have heard the vehemence in my tone, because she didn't even try to argue. Instead, she struck off down the street, leading the way to the canal towpath that formed the shortcut to Cake Walk.

Melissa made short work of the walk. Opening up her back door, she slung her yoga mat into the corner and dug in a drawer until she came up with kitchen shears. She waved me toward a tangle of potted herbs in the tiny side yard, and I found the mint without any problem. Ah, sweet therapy. If the mojitos didn't work their magic, we might have to move up to the big guns: deep-dish pizza, with pepperoni and black olives. That would still leave Ben & Jerry's in reserve with its pints of last-ditch salvation.

Breathing deeply of the fresh-cut mint, I returned to the

bakery. Melissa was setting a gigantic net bag of limes on the counter. "You've got sugar?"

"Yep." I felt proud of myself. I was just like a regular homeowner.

"And rum?" She glanced dubiously at her cooking supplies; she kept rum for the Devil's Nips that she made when she was feeling particularly devious. I swallowed hard; I could taste those liquored-up chocolate truffles now.

"I've got half a bottle at home. That should be enough."

"Should be?" She arched a bemused eyebrow. I wish that *I* could arch an eyebrow. I wasn't certain I could harness "bemused" for any amount of money. "Sounds like some serious therapy you're contemplating."

"You don't know the half of it."

She nodded and wrapped the mint in a paper towel, adding it to the limes in a tote bag. She glanced around the kitchen and started to turn off the light, but then she shook her head and turned back to the industrial-size refrigerator.

She pulled out one of her heavy pottery serving plates and set it on the counter. When I glimpsed the treasures beneath the plastic wrap, I felt a warm flush of joy. Melissa *did* understand how serious this was.

"Almond Lust!"

"Only the best for you," she said. I loved the shortbread concoction, and my mouth watered at the thought of the rich chewy caramel and dark Valrhona chocolate that cradled sliced almonds. I started to lift the corner of the plastic wrap, but Melissa playfully slapped my hand away. "Patience!"

"But there are three bars!"

"One for each of us, and one for Neko, right?"

Neko. Well, that was one thing to be said for my grand-mother's informational bomb. It had driven all thoughts of the strange cat-man out of my head. Thoughts of my, um, familiar came spiraling back, and I wondered how I could have forgotten about my life as a witch so quickly.

"Right," I said. Suddenly those mojitos sounded med-ically necessary.

It didn't take us long to walk to the Peabridge. I was glad that the library was closed when we passed by—there was no need for anyone there to see me in workout clothes, carrying my bedraggled yoga mat and the makings of tropical drinks. I started to dig in my bag for my keys, but the door swung open before I could find them.

"Good evening," Neko said, and he bowed to Melissa and me. My ingrained manners took over enough for me to in-troduce them. Melissa shot me a sharp look as I turned toward the kitchen.

I knew that expression. She was sizing up Neko for a spot on the First Date roster. *Oh, girlfriend,* I almost said out loud. *You are going to be so disappointed.* There was more to Neko than the tautly muscled torso carved beneath his black T-shirt, more than the exotic slant of his eyes beneath the oh-so-touchable buzz of his hair. So much more, but we women weren't going to see any of it. Not that there was anything wrong with that.

I glanced toward my bedroom door, but it looked un-touched. It seemed like a second safe day for Stupid Fish. At least, I could hope so.

As Melissa and Neko traded pleasantries, I marched into the kitchen and got straight to work. I opened the left cabinet and reached for the rum on the top shelf. Not there. I checked the middle shelf. No luck. I glanced at the bottom shelf, but I knew I wouldn't have put the alcohol there.

I tried the second cabinet without any greater success before I remembered that I had put all the liquor beneath the sink. After all, I didn't have that many cleaning bottles left by the time Melissa and I had made the cottage livable, and I didn't want visitors to see my alcoholic stash and conclude I was a lush.

Okay. I didn't want *Jason* to see my liquor and think that I was just a hard-drinking party girl. Our first date was already scripted in my mind—I was going to brew him a nice hot cup of tea one evening when we had worked late at the library on some difficult research project. I'd save the hard stuff for our second date. Or for Bloody Marys the morning after.

I pushed aside a woefully depleted fifth of gin and reached past sculpted bottles of Kahlúa and Baileys. The rum was at the back of the collection, and I was pleased to discover there was even more of it than I'd remembered. "There," I said. "Now, if I can just figure out where I put my pitcher…"

"The one with the fish on it?" Neko asked, popping back from his chat with Melissa. He produced the oversized item from a cabinet as if he'd lived here all his life. Which, come to think of it, he might have. I had a lot of questions for the guy. Questions that I'd be ready to ask, just as soon as the drinks were mixed.

"Thanks," I said. Melissa started to help with the mojito preparation, but I waved her over to the tin kitchen table. "Both of you, sit down. I'll do this."

"I can't wait anymore, though," Melissa said. "Tell me what we're treating with the mojitos!"

"Treating?" Neko purred, and I could see interest waft over him like the scent of salmon. He'd ignored my instructions to sit down. Instead, he had taken over preparing the limes. After watching me roll one across the counter, hard, to release the juice inside, he repeated the process with the rest of the fruit. He moved his fingers like a pastry chef kneading dough. A distant look came into his eyes, as if the motion provided him with a distinctly sexual frisson of pleasure. As if he were a cat.

I shook my head and began to bruise the mint. I spoke as I worked, telling Melissa and Neko about my meeting with Gran. Both reacted appropriately, gasping in surprise at her revelation (or, in Neko's case, hissing).

Years of practice let me eyeball the correct amount of mint, along with sugar, the juice from Neko's limes and sparkling water. I poured in a healthy amount of rum, then added more when Neko cast a critical eye. I started to dig for a wooden spoon in the container on the counter, but Neko placed a utensil in my hand. I stirred absently, looking from one friend to the other, as I concluded my tale of woe: "And so, I left. I needed time to think. That's why I couldn't finish yoga class."

"Mmm," Neko said. "Cat Pose. It's perfect for tightening your abs." As if to illustrate, he flexed his taut belly.

"I'll drink to that," Melissa said, eyeing him appreciatively.

I poured us each a tall glass. The mojito was icy cold as I
swallowed, but the rum warmed my woefully untaut belly.
Already, I could feel myself relaxing, opening up. The mint
was sweet-sharp against the back of my throat.

"Mmm," Neko said. "You put in extra lime. I like them
like that."

I swallowed another healthy dose before I asked, "How
do you do that?"

"Do what?" His eyes were sly as he met mine over his
glass.

"Know about mojitos. I mean, you've been in my
basement for a while, right? Frozen as a statue?"

He licked his lips and glanced over at Melissa, as if he
were wondering what he could say in front of her. Fine
time for him to decide to be circumspect. "Go ahead," I said.
"She's my best friend. She already knows about you. At least
as much as I do."

Melissa nodded and drank from her own glass. She must
have been thirsty after yoga class; her drink was already half-
gone. I refilled it and topped off mine. Hmm. I must have
been thirsty, as well.

Neko shrugged and said, "It's part of the Covenant. The
power of witchcraft." He spread his hands a precise distance
apart in the air, and I couldn't help but picture him as an
interior designer, describing the parameters of my living
room just before he told me I had no fashion sense and
everything I owned must go. "The Covenant is always there,
for those of us who are sensitive to it. When I was put into
stasis by—" he hesitated only slightly, but I caught the ripple
"—the person who owned the books downstairs, I was

current on everything known to every member of our Coven. As soon as you awakened me, the Covenant was reenergized. It flowed through me, and it filled in all the gaps in my knowledge."

"So the witches know about mojitos?" I asked, and the question seemed silly enough that a bubble of laughter rose inside me.

"At least one of them does. Or one of their familiars. It only takes one for all of us to have the information." Neko reached out for the fish pitcher and stirred it carefully before refilling my glass. Melissa accepted more, as well. "Different witches specialize in different things. We familiars transmit the specialized information that we learn. It's our job to explore as much as we can."

I remembered what Montrose had said. Neko had been awakened on the night of the full moon. He was free to go anywhere he wanted. Anytime he wanted. He could explore a hell of a lot.

Melissa interrupted before I could say anything. "So how does this all work? How do you help Jane with her spells?"

Neko raised a single eyebrow—he could challenge Melissa in the "bemused" department. "I help her channel her power. Whatever she needs. I can't work the magic on my own; the power has to come from her. I'm sort of like a magnifying glass. Or Batman's Lucius Fox. Or James Bond's Q. Or—"

"We get it," I said, washing down my annoyance with another healthy swallow of mojito. Like I was going to be some sort of suave superhero, saving the nation's capital from threatening villains. Yeah, right. Me, and my well-chewed fingernails. My freckles. My unruly hair and glasses.

"So can I go downstairs and look at the books?" Melissa was really into all this. She jumped up from her kitchen chair, but she had to steady herself with a hand thrust out against the table edge. Maybe I *had* been a bit too generous with the rum.

"Sit down!" Neko cried. "Here." He topped off her glass again and saw to mine before he said, "I'll bring one up. Won't be a minute."

I started to protest, but the mojito therapy was working its own magic, mellowing me out so that I didn't really care to argue. Neko was out of the room before I could explain what a bad idea it was for him to bring anything magical upstairs. Well, I wasn't going to read any spell from the *Compendium* again. And I *certainly* wasn't going to light any beeswax tapers. I'd promised Montrose. And my life was complicated enough without adding to the witchcraft quotient.

Neko trotted back into the kitchen, and for a moment, I thought he was empty-handed. He certainly hadn't lugged the *Compendium* with him. Instead, he set a small book on the kitchen table. It was no larger than a paperback volume of poetry. It was clearly old, though; the cover was bound in leather. Gold letters were stamped on its surface.

"A Girl's First Grimoire," Melissa read, and she burst out laughing. "What is that, like *Pat the Bunny* for the witchy set?"

Neko struck a pose. "You are *too* funny, girlfriend."

Melissa turned to me. "So what do you do? Just read from the page?"

I looked at Neko, but he merely gave an elaborate shrug.

His job might be to help me work magic, but he wasn't about to answer all my questions. I could practically hear him whistling his innocence. "I'm still not totally sure," I said. "Montrose said that the candles I used were important—they were pure beeswax. Also, I touched my forehead, and my throat and my chest before I read. And I ran my fingers under the words."

"Ran your fingers…" Melissa sounded amazed. Frankly, so was I. I mean, I must really have some sort of power, right? If my touching a page could make something come magically to life? Melissa shoved the grimoire toward me. "Read from this one!"

"I can't! I promised—"

"Come on! It'll be like a Ouija board! You remember when we used that at my ten-year-old birthday party."

"I remember that you moved the pointer. You made the board say that John Goodnight would be the first boy I ever kissed."

"John Goodnight," Neko crooned, and I swore as my cheeks flushed. There was something provocative about the way he said the name, and I suddenly wanted to show him that he was wrong, that I wasn't the Goody Two-shoes girl that he seemed to think I was.

I stepped up to the table. I would show Neko. I could read from a silly leather-bound book. I wouldn't light a candle this time, wouldn't touch my rapid pulse points. I wouldn't run my fingers beneath the words, and I definitely wouldn't speak them aloud.

Neko smiled and opened the book, apparently to a random page. I squinted at the letters, but they seemed to shift in front of my eyes. I started to put my fingertips beneath them, but I pulled back as if the parchment burned when I remembered my promise to Montrose. Neko handed me the wooden stirrer from the mojito pitcher, giving it one quick wipe against a towel.

Feeling more than a little silly, I teased out the words on the page, saying them to myself:

"Glamour, glamour, magic bind
Vision twist and veil unwind
Wrap my face in power hidden
Spark a love from man unbidden
Tie him to me ever more
Lock him up with grimoire's lore."

And then there was that flash of darkness, more astonishing than the first time, because I had specifically worked to avoid the spell. I bit off a shriek and caught my breath against my teeth before I whirled around to face Neko.

"It couldn't work!"

"It did." He smiled and looked pointedly at my hand. I wasn't holding the wooden spoon that I expected, the ancient utensil that had been nibbled by the garbage disposal in my old apartment. No, I was holding a smooth piece of wood. A dowel, really.

A wand.

"What the hell is this?" I asked him, and Melissa jumped at the anger in my voice.

"What?" Neko asked, trying to look innocent. "It's just a little something I picked up while I was out and about this afternoon." But even he could not carry off the happy-go-lucky charade as a loud knock sounded at my cottage door.

This time, David Montrose was dressed in casual clothes. In fact, he looked like he had just stepped out of a Lands' End catalog spread. His dark brown hair was ruffled, just enough out of place to prove that he was not overly vain. His slacks were a charcoal-gray, the perfect contrast to his light blue button-down shirt. His sleeves were rolled up, displaying the corded muscles of his forearms. As before, though, his eyes were dark, his pupils were expanded by the nighttime, or by the wild ride he'd taken to appear on my doorstep. "Miss Madison," he said, and the formality of his words contrasted with his easy-going appearance.

I looked down to see that I'd brought my glass to the door. My empty glass. Where was a good slug of rum when you needed one? "Would you like a mojito?" I asked, because I couldn't think of anything else to say.

Montrose strode past me into the living room. "I thought we'd reached an agreement."

"We did! I didn't work a spell." I thought of the flash of darkness. "Well, I didn't mean to." I remembered the electric tingle that had rippled down my arms. "Um, I'm not even sure that it worked." Montrose just stared at me. That blue shirt really did contrast with his eyes, really made his face stand out. "I don't even know what it was supposed to do!" I found myself saying, and I felt like I was going to my first confession, blurting out all sorts of sins that I hadn't even committed, just so that Father Brennan would smile kindly and grant me absolution.

"And *that* is precisely why you should have some guidance. Some training." He sighed and gestured toward the basement door. "You might think that this is all *Bewitched* and *Charmed,* but I can assure you that it is not. There are consequences for your behavior."

"My behavior! What about Neko! He's the one who made this happen. He's the one who gave me the stick—"

"Neko." Montrose raised his eyes to the kitchen doorway, where my familiar stood next to my best friend. The cat-man managed to look unabashed, as if nothing out of the ordinary had happened—as if nothing out of the ordinary could *ever* happen when he was around.

Melissa seemed a bit more shocked—and intrigued. Again, I knew that expression. Now that she'd recognized the impossibility of snaring Neko, she was measuring David Montrose against her entire pool of First Dates. She was calculating his net worth, determining where he would stand in her ongoing home-run derby. She didn't understand, though. She apparently didn't remember that Montrose was a warder, that he was a cosmic policeman. That he was here to monitor me and what I did.

In a flash, she ducked back into the kitchen, and before I could say anything else, she returned with a pottery plate in hand. "Lust?" she asked, and she managed to look bashful as she peered up at Montrose through glistening eyelashes.

He actually blushed, which made Neko gasp with delight. "Who is this?" Montrose turned to ask me, indicating Melissa with a cautious nod of his head.

"My best friend. Melissa White." I sent her a glare and a vehement shake of the head behind Montrose's back. "She's a baker," I added, as if that could erase Melissa's come-hither glance. "Almond Lust is her specialty. Look, I had a really crappy day, and she brought the bars over, and we decided to make some drinks, and she asked about the library downstairs, and Neko brought up one of the books."

I realized that I was rambling, and I forced myself to take a deep breath. Montrose nodded, as if he accepted my explanation of what had happened, but then he turned to glare at Neko. The cat-man was suddenly fascinated by his empty glass. "Whoops!" he said. "Time for a refill!" He dashed back into the kitchen, leaving Melissa alone in the doorway.

I crossed over and took the pottery plate from her, placing it on the coffee table and waving everyone toward the hunter-green couches. It was obvious that Montrose wasn't leaving any time soon, and I decided I'd rather sit on an overstuffed cushion than stand to face an angry warder, especially on a mojito-filled belly, without any dinner to speak of.

Montrose followed my lead, sitting beside me with a casual sense of command. Melissa was forced to settle on the other couch with Neko, who joined us with a full glass. Montrose waited for both of them to grow still before he turned to me.

"This has got to stop," he said. There was no room for argument, not even the protest that threatened to laugh past the lime taste at the back of my throat. "You don't understand. Witchcraft is powerful. The surges that you released from the house tonight could be felt for miles."

"Felt?" My stomach did a flip-flop.

"By warders. And other witches." Montrose waved toward the door, toward the darkened colonial gardens that surrounded my home. "And by the creatures that seek them out."

I rubbed away goose bumps from my arms as I raised my chin defiantly. "Now you're just trying to frighten me."

"I hope that's what I'm doing." Montrose reached for my glass and set it on the table. One part of my mind noticed that his hand was warmer than I expected it to be. His fingers were smoother, too, not the rough flesh that I anticipated, given his gruff tone. Another part of me noted that he took care to place the glass on a slate coaster, protecting my coffee table from the evils of water rings.

"Listen," he said. "We can end all this right now. The Covenants grant priority to any witch who actually possesses the materials—books, runes, crystals. You don't have to take advantage of that presumption, though. If you'd like, you can give back everything in your basement."

"Give it back?" Even saying the words felt wrong.

"The Coven would gladly accept the return. As it is, they

will likely contest your ownership, but things move slowly in Hecate's Court."

Hecate's Court. He made it sound like traffic or small-claims court. I laughed uneasily, overwhelmed by the strangeness of all this.

"Jane," he said. "This is serious."

Jane. He'd called me by name.

And all of a sudden, I was looking at Mr. David Montrose, Hecate's warder, a little differently. He wasn't a bully who'd come into my home to make me feel bad for fiddling with another person's property. Instead, he was a protector. He was a teacher. He was one of the good guys.

Neko snorted, and the moment was ruined. Montrose turned to glare at my familiar. "Laugh all you want," he said to Neko. "But will you report to Hecate's Court when the dispute over ownership begins?"

Neko squirmed for a moment before looking away. I glanced back at Montrose, only to find that I couldn't break his gaze. His eyes were brown, the color of dark chocolate. They were flecked with green, though, specks of color that gave them depth. All of a sudden, I was aware of the small creases around those eyes, the lines beside his mouth. He had a shallow cleft in his chin—just a hint of a flaw to balance a face that might have been too pretty otherwise. I could tell that he had shaved that morning, but chestnut whiskers pricked his skin.

And for just a moment I imagined kissing him. I envisioned the feel of those whiskers against my cheek, and then the soft touch of his lips. I thought about his hands, those marvelously warm, smooth hands, moving down my arms, then one palm cupping the back of my head as he pulled me closer. I imagined my own fingers grabbing at his hair, closing around his curls.

"So," Montrose said, and the spell was broken. I was back in my living room, sitting rigidly on my couch. I stared at the mojito glass on the table, wondering just how drunk I must be. After all, I didn't know the first thing about Montrose. I certainly didn't know him like I did Jason Templeton—how could I even think of letting the warder supplant my Imaginary Boyfriend?

Wait. No one was supplanting anyone. Montrose was here as a warder. He was here to teach me about my magic, to make sure that I didn't break any bizarre astral laws, to help me keep the strange possessions that appeared to be mine. I might *think* that I was attracted to him, but that was probably just my old habit of developing crushes on men in power. I'd had my first crush on my fourth-grade social studies teacher, Mr. Solomon. And a monstrous one on my freshman literature professor. And a killer infatuation with my first boss for a summer job, at the Springfield Public Library.

Whew. That was a close call. My entire career as a witch might be ruined if I let myself have a crush on my warder.

My warder? *My* career as a witch? What was I thinking?

Apparently, I had made a decision. I was going to learn about this witchcraft stuff. I was going to find out what powers I had, and I was going to explore how to use them.

"So, what now?" I asked. I watched Melissa lean closer. I recognized the expression on her face as one of confusion. She couldn't know all the thoughts that had just careered through my head. Besides, I probably looked pretty dazed myself.

Neko, though, was bouncing up and down on the couch. He looked like a little boy who had just been told that he was going to celebrate his birthday, the Fourth of July and Christmas, all in one day. "Yes!" he exclaimed. "We are going to have *so* much fun!"

"What?" Melissa asked. "What's going on?"

David looked at her, then at me. "Are you going to tell her, or shall I?"

I swallowed, surprised to find my throat so dry. "I'm going to learn about this." I ran the next sentence through my head before I said it aloud. "I'm going to learn how to be a witch."

David nodded, and I watched Melissa swallow a dozen questions. "First things first," he said. "No more alcohol."

"For tonight?"

"For good."

Melissa laughed and said, "Well *that's* not going to happen."

I glared at her. After all, I wasn't exactly a lush. I always knew exactly how much I was drinking, and I made a decision for every separate glass. I looked over Melissa's shoulder into the kitchen. Toward the empty bottle of rum. Toward the wand sitting on the counter. Well, I usually make a decision. When my familiar isn't pouring with a heavy hand.

"It will," David said evenly. "If she wants to learn more."

All of a sudden, it seemed important for me to stake a claim here. I mean, I'd spent eight years with Scott, with him telling me what to do and when to do it. I wasn't about to let some new man, some *stranger*, take charge of my life without putting up a fight. Even if he did know more about witchcraft than I did.

"I won't drink when I'm working with you. I won't drink when I'm being a witch."

Neko's guffaw sounded like it was from a sitcom laugh track. "As *if* you're the one setting the rules!"

I scowled at him and turned to David. "I'm serious," I said. "It's not like Melissa and I get drunk every night. But I can't let this witchcraft thing take over my entire life."

"This witchcraft thing," David repeated, and he shook his head. "You don't understand—"

"And I'm not going to, if you set rules that change who I am." I was arguing with him like a Shakespeare comic heroine, hoping to match my Beatrice wit to his Benedick scorn. "I won't let you lock me up in a convent."

A convent? Where did *that* come from. No one had said anything about a convent, about sex, about any other restrictions. We were talking about a few drinks. My face reddened as I continued to stare at David.

I don't know what it was. Maybe it was my struggle to cool my burning cheeks. Maybe it was my sudden determination. Maybe it was just that the hour was getting late, and David was ready to go back home, or wherever it was that he stayed when he wasn't waiting for me to work some errant spell. But he nodded and said, "Very well."

"Very well?" Neko squeaked, which was a good thing, because I wasn't certain what David had just agreed to.

"Very well. You may have a drink, or two. But not when you're working magic. And not when we work together."

I extended my hand, as if we had just negotiated some major business deal. My lips curled into a wide smile, but I wasn't sure why. Maybe it was the mojitos talking, but I thought that it was something more. I thought that I was proud of myself, proud that I'd said what I wanted and stuck to my guns until I got it.

David took my hand and pumped it three times in a classic business handshake. I couldn't help but look down at our fingers, and when I tried to glance back at his face, I couldn't meet his eyes. "We'll start tomorrow, then," he said. "After dinner."

"After dinner." I sounded as if I accepted invitations for witchcraft training all the time.

David nodded and stood up. He had almost opened the front door—his hand was on the latch—but then he turned back. He moved quickly, like a shepherd dog closing in on a rambling, errant sheep. I watched in surprise as he lifted one of Melissa's confections from the pottery plate on the coffee table. He took a bite, and his teeth flashed white against the shortbread and chocolate.

"Mmm," he said, chewing carefully and swallowing. "Lust, indeed." I glanced at Melissa and saw her jaw drop, but it was my face that flamed with embarrassment. David's eyes met mine. "Until tomorrow."

"Until tomorrow," I echoed, and I closed the door after him. I took a moment to compose myself before collapsing into Melissa and Neko's arms. Surrounded by their excited squeals, I wondered why they were cheering. Was it for me, because I was a witch? Or for me, a friend who had outwitted a demanding guest? Or for me, a completely exhausted and more than a little intoxicated homeowner and librarian and friend?

What did it matter? They were my friends, and they were happy for me. Almost happy enough not to complain that we were out of mojitos.

9

Someone had emptied an ashtray into my mouth. Probably the same someone who had pounded my forehead with a ball-peen hammer. The same someone who had placed ten-thousand-kilowatt lightbulbs outside my bedroom window.

I moaned and rolled over, pulling my pillow on top of my head. My comforter slipped onto the floor (who had tangled it into such a massive knot while I slept?) and the chilly air immediately raised gooseflesh on my arms and legs. I swore and reached down for the quilt. My hand closed on empty air. I stretched farther, but found nothing. Resigning myself to do battle with the evil someone who had sabotaged my sleep—if only to regain my comforter—I sat up in bed.

The clock screamed eight forty-five in angry red numbers.

Eight forty-five.

I needed to be at work in fifteen minutes.

I swore again and threw myself into the hallway. One

glance into the living room brought back all my memories of the night before. Had we really mixed another pitcher of drinks? Had we substituted vodka for rum? And frozen orange juice concentrate for lime juice? Screwdrivers, with mint, washing down two remaining Lust bars and not much else for supper? My belly trembled at the thought.

No time to rue the damage.

I splashed icy water on my face and began to attack my furry mouth with a generous swoop of Colgate. I made a face as I scraped the bristles across my tongue.

"I wondered when you were going to wake up," Neko said, and I swallowed half of my toothpaste in surprise.

"Eye i'nt oo ake ee?"

"What? Sweetheart, are you still drunk from last night? I can't understand a word you're saying."

I spat into the sink and whirled to shake my toothbrush in his general direction. "Why didn't you wake me?"

"You needed your beauty sleep. After all, you're going to be working with David Montrose from here on out, and I'd hardly be a good familiar if I didn't make sure that you presented at your very best." He smiled slyly and gave me an appraising look. I could only imagine the glamour that he beheld, with my hair standing out at all angles and tooth-paste foaming at the corners of my mouth.

"I have to be at work in fifteen minutes!"

He glanced at his sleek wristwatch. "Ten, now."

"Arrrr!" I grabbed for a hand towel and wiped my face dry. My hairbrush caught in my tangles and I forced it through the knots as I pushed past Neko into my room. I slammed the door and offered up a silent thank-you to

Evelyn's foresight in establishing our latest get-out-the-patrons effort. At least I wouldn't have to figure out what to wear. My colonial costume beckoned from my closet. *Fashion Central, here I come.*

I tugged open a dresser drawer and fumbled around for underwear. One clean pair remaining. I cast a dagger glance toward the hallway.

"Neko!"

"Yes?" He was clearly standing just the other side of the door. I jumped at the sound of his voice so near and cast a reflexive eye toward Stupid Fish. The tetra was swimming in his tank, oblivious as ever. I sprinkled in a pinch of fish food and reminded myself that I needed to change his water. I glanced at the clock. Five minutes to nine. No fresh water today.

"Neko, you're supposed to help me, right?" The question came out through clenched teeth as I pulled my panties into place and struggled with the hooks on my bra. Honestly, my clothes fit me better last fall. Last fall, when I was still engaged to Scott. Last fall, before I'd taken solace with my best friends, Ben and Jerry. And about a million pitchers of mojitos. And another one, last night, of minty screwdrivers. Don't think about it, I told myself, swallowing hard.

"Yes?" He made his answer sound like a question, and I could picture his head turned to the side as he measured out what I was asking.

"What about with things other than spells? I mean, if I don't have time to study the books downstairs *and* do things around the house, could you help me with chores?" Chores? I sounded like Gran. I tugged my hoops over my head and jerked them into place around my hips.

"What did you have in mind?"

The quilted petticoat settled over the hoops with a few brisk tugs. I jerked on my jacket, momentarily flustered by its fitted back and shortened flare around my hips. The cotton chintz was smooth under my fingers, but I didn't waste time admiring the floral design. "Laundry!" I called out to Neko as I grabbed my neckerchief.

"Laundry?" His skeptical tone made it sound like a foreign word.

"You know, washing machine, dryer? Little fabric softener sheets that smell like mountain meadows?" I whirled back to my bureau. My dress might be colonial, but I was still wearing contemporary shoes and panty hose. I could see the run in the first pair before I even pulled them out of the drawer. I couldn't risk Jason glimpsing any slovenly behavior on my part. After all, he might drop by the library any time.

"You want me to do laundry?" Neko sounded scandalized.

"I want you to help me so that I have time to study the books downstairs." I tried to sound reasonable. "Time to be the best witch that I can be." That sounded like an army slogan. Was there an army of witches? The uniform had to be better than the one I was wearing now.

The second pair of hose looked fine until I worked my fingers down to the right toes. There were three little scabs of nail polish, each blocking a run. As I tried to maneuver my toes around the polish, I managed to tear open the entire leg.

"Where?" The cat-man was no fool. He was wary of accepting this new responsibility. I didn't blame him.

"Up by Dupont Circle. There's a laundromat on P Street. You can take a cab there and back. My treat." Third time was the charm—my last pair of panty hose actually made it onto both feet. I tugged at the waistband, trying to stretch the hose higher, and I sighed when I realized that I might need to graduate to the dread "Q" size. I grabbed my mobcap and plopped it onto my unruly hair before I opened my bedroom door.

"You'll throw in coffee?" Neko bargained. "I have to have something to sustain me while I wait for the clothes."

I lugged my hamper into the hallway before closing my door and locking it behind me. I turned back in time to catch Neko's blatant disappointment that Stupid Fish would be beyond his reach. "Fine. One venti coffee. Or latte. Or steamed milk. Whatever you want." I dug in my purse for a crumpled five-dollar bill. "Here. And there are quarters in the pottery bowl, for the washing machine." I gestured to the kitchen counter. I was about to open the front door when a thought occurred to me. "You *have* done laundry before, haven't you?"

"I'll check with the Coven," he said.

"Neko—"

"They knew how to make a mojito, didn't they?"

Well, I couldn't argue with that.

The Presbyterian church on the next block began to toll the hour, and I rushed around to the front of the Peabridge. I was digging around in my purse as I climbed the three stone steps. I had to have a lipstick in there somewhere. It was too late to do full makeup, but Gran always said that lipstick made a woman look put together.

Gran. I hadn't spoken to her since leaving the Four Seasons. Her name had come up on caller ID both at home and at the office, and I'd heard four of her messages: "Jane Madison's grandmother," but I hadn't called her back yet. I still wasn't sure what I was going to say. I didn't know what I wanted to do about Clara. I had enough going on in my crazy, mixed-up life without that problem to solve.

My fingers closed on a tube of Cover Girl. I squinted at the bottom of the barrel. Pick-Me-Up Pink. Was that an offer to put out? Or a plea for someone to brighten this already hideous day?

"Good morning, Jane!" I looked up to find myself face-to-face with Harold Weems, our all-purpose janitor, maintenance man, security guard and—apparently—greeter. Usually, Harold was too shy to mumble a hello. This morning, though, he was holding the door open for me. I was more than a little surprised as he looked me over, studying my outfit from head to toe. After all, we'd both been dressed to the colonial nines for a week now.

He sported stockings and emerald breeches, with an embroidered waistcoat and a close-fitting frock coat. A tricorn hat, currently tucked under his arm, completed the ensemble. He nodded earnestly as I approached and said, "That skirt is a lovely shade of brown."

I glanced down at my costume, incredulous. When I looked up at Harold, I was surprised to see him blushing. I said, "Um, thank you?"

He blinked and swallowed hard. His face was usually pale, but now it flushed nearly crimson. The strands of his hair were stringy across his scalp, and for just a moment I worried that he might suffer a heart attack right there on the Peabridge steps. He blurted out, "I really wanted to say that you look nice today, but I know that I'm not supposed to say that. You know, with harassment laws and everything."

I glanced over my shoulder, just to make sure that he hadn't been put up to this by someone else. Was he making some sort of joke? Could he have seen me tearing around the corner from the cottage, frantic about being late, yet again? But no, he was smiling shyly when I looked back at him. "Thank you, Harold," I said again, palming the Pick-Me-Up to apply as soon as I got inside.

"Are those new glasses you're wearing?"

I pushed my old tortoiseshell frames higher on the bridge of my nose. "Um, no. They're the same ones I've always had."

"Maybe you got your hair cut?"

This was getting creepy. "Nope. Same old me. And, as always, I'm going to be late, so I really need to get inside."

"Oh. Sure." Harold stepped back as I walked past him, but I heard him catch his breath. Almost like he was excited to see me.

I flipped on the power button to the espresso machine as I crossed to my desk. Once there, I palmed on my computer and waited for it to run through its start-up routine. On my chair, I found a pink "While You Were Out" note, meticulously completed. Jane Madison's grandmother had phoned at 8:57 that morning, asking me to return her call. The message had been taken by HW. I glanced back at Harold and caught him staring at me across the library lobby. He started and shook his head, as if he were just waking up after some strange dream, but then he waggled his fingers at me with a goofy grin across his lips.

It wouldn't have surprised me if he spouted verses about my beauty, caught up in some Forest of Arden fantasy where I was Rosalind. Or maybe I had just read *As You Like It* once too often. Utterly puzzled, I waved back. I waited until he headed downstairs to his maintenance closet before I returned to my desk.

Seven reference questions, a dozen brewed lattes and three explanations of my costume later, I still hadn't called Gran back. I knew that I needed to talk to her. I needed to come to grips with Clara.

Clara. I couldn't call her my "mother." I couldn't think about her as my mother, because my *mother* was a beautiful woman with flowing red hair and porcelain skin. She was surrounded by banks of clouds, and she sighed softly whenever she thought of losing me, of being torn from me in the terrible car crash that had taken her life.

My "mother" was not a selfish woman who had ignored me for twenty-five years, only to come back and ruin my life just as I was finally getting things under control.

Yeah, right. Totally under control. Every girl who agrees to private tutoring in witchcraft has her life under control.

Private tutoring. Starting with dinner tonight. I fumbled in my desk and dug out a container of Advil, swallowing two and wishing my hangover headache would go away.

The more I tried to avoid thinking about Gran and Clara, the more I worried about David, Neko and the collection of books on witchcraft in my basement. As much as I couldn't believe that I had let Neko fool me into working another spell, I was more amazed that I had agreed to have dinner with David. Maybe he had a point there, about not mixing alcohol and spellcraft.

Friends don't let friends work magic drunk.

What *was* the spell that Neko made me read? "Wrap my face in power hidden; Spark a love from man unbidden."

Love from man unbidden? I glanced back at the front door, to the site of Harold's bizarre morning greeting. Harold, who had never shared two words with me.

No.

It couldn't be.

I could not have cast a love spell on poor, helpless Harold Weems.

My heart clenched tight inside my chest, and I sucked in my breath. I needed to get away from my desk. I needed to get out of the library. Now.

I glanced at the clock on my computer and saw that it was not even 10:30 a.m. I couldn't go home yet. I couldn't even really take a break.

I did the next best thing. After collecting my purse from its locked desk drawer, I gesticulated wildly to get Evelyn's attention. When she nodded across the lobby, I half walked, half ran to the restroom at the back of the Peabridge. I slammed closed the door to one of the stalls and thumbed on my cell phone.

Melissa took four rings to answer, and then her voice was as heavy as her Mocha Mud Bars. I suspected that things were busy at Cake Walk that morning, and if she felt anywhere near as terrible as I did after our night of mojito therapy… I got right to the point: "The spell worked."

"What?"

I hissed into the phone, even though I knew that the other stalls were empty. "The spell. The one I did last night. It worked."

"What are you talking about?"

I told her all about Harold, about his questions. When she told me that I must be imagining things, I thought about my first coffee patron of the day, Mr. Zimmer. The sour octogenarian had been coming to the Peabridge for decades. He never ordered coffee; he disapproved of our launching the espresso bar in the lobby. But he had asked for one that morning, *and* he had left me a two-dollar tip. By the time I finished recounting the details, my voice had squealed into Mickey Mouse's supersonic range. I raised my free hand to my mouth and started tearing at a ragged cuticle with teeth that were close to chattering.

"Okay," Melissa said, and I could hear her cash register chiming in the background. "So what are you going to do about it?"

"I'm going to wring that man's neck when I get back home."

"That man Neko? Or that man David?"

As soon as she said David's name, I thought of the strange moment that had passed between us, the instant where I had thought of him as a very kissable best friend. A best friend who was taking me to dinner that night. "Neko," I said immediately.

"Sounds like a plan. As for your so-called problem, I don't

think you need to worry. Let the men bask in the glory of your smile. Let *them* be the ones to drag around after *you* for a change. You deserve it, after everything you've gone through in the past year."

"It's just so strange. I've never been the pretty girl at the party before."

"You're always the pretty girl, Jane. Sometimes you just forget to use all your assets. Look, I've got to go. I have a batch of cupcakes coming out of the oven in about two minutes, and three regulars just walked in."

I let her go, even though I wanted to pump her for more information about my so-called assets. Emerging from the stall, I took a moment to stare at myself in the bathroom mirror. My skirt was a lovely shade of brown. Yeah. Right. The costume made me look like Old Mother Hubbard. At least I didn't have a poor dog waiting for me at home. Just a cat-man, who I was going to skin at the first available opportunity. A love spell! What was he thinking?

I sighed and dug around in my purse. Maybe I could do something to repair the damage of a short night of sleep and too many mint-tinged drinks.

In the bottom of the bag, I found a banana clip that I hadn't used for months. I rubbed purse dust from it and twisted my hair off my neck. It took me three tries to get the clip in at the right angle, but when I covered it all with the mobcap, I was actually surprised at the difference it made. I'd gone from looking like someone's overworked scullery maid, to looking—just a hint of a shadow of a suggestion—like a long-necked country-fresh milkmaid.

Encouraged by the transformation, I scrambled some

more in my purse and found an ancient eyeliner. The green-blue tinge made my eyes look deeper; I added a bit more at the outer corners to give the appearance of a wide-awake librarian. A daub of Pick-Me-Up Pink completed the transformation, at least as much as I was able to do in the confines of the Peabridge restroom. I took a steadying breath and headed back to my desk.

Where I found my Imaginary Boyfriend sitting in a chair. My Imaginary Boyfriend. And me, with a beauty enhancing spell firmly in place. My heart started pounding so hard that I could barely breathe.

He stood as I approached, grinning and extending his hand for a friendly, professional handshake. A handshake that might have lingered for a moment longer than strictly necessary. I thought. I hoped. "Evelyn said that you'd be back in a moment," he said.

"Evelyn was right," I answered sunnily, but I fought the urge to wrinkle up my nose. What a stupid thing to say.

Jason smiled again, though, easy and confident as ever. "You know what?" he asked, and continued before I could say anything. "Those costumes are starting to grow on me. At first, I thought they looked silly, but the more I see of them, the more I think they're a good idea." I caught his eyes straying to the lace that edged my bodice.

My bodice. My Imaginary Boyfriend was staring at my bodice.

Maybe I wasn't going to murder Neko tonight, after all. Maybe I was going to buy him a nice salmon steak instead, a reward for a well-worked spell.

Jason cleared his throat, and I remembered that I was a

librarian first and foremost, long before I was a witch. "I'm looking for some information," he said, "and I know it should be easy to find, but I'm just having no luck. I need to know how far Chesterton could ride in an average day on horseback, and then how fast he could make it back to North Carolina when he first heard that George Junior had typhus."

"Not a problem," I said. "Have you looked in Graumman's study on colonial transportation?"

"Graumman?"

I smiled and led my Imaginary Boyfriend into the stacks.

The day flew by. After I helped Jason, there were three more patrons who had obscure questions, interesting research problems that kept me busy for the better part of the afternoon. Twice I came back to my desk to find Harold standing too close. I received another call from Gran, but I really was too busy to answer, and I let it go to voice mail.

I didn't have time to take a break for lunch, and my feet ached as I finally headed down the garden path to my cottage at the end of the day. My heart was soaring, though. Jason thought that I looked good in my costume. Even Harold's bizarre attention had made me feel special.

The front door was unlocked when I got home. I could see my laundry piled on one of the couches: panties tucked in discreetly beside jeans, some knit tops, a couple of pullovers and pajamas. My towels were fluffy and still warm. I ran a hand over the stack and excavated a couple of items, holding them up to make sure that nothing had been shrunk to Barbie size.

Perfect. Neko had managed the laundry, without even a hint of the disaster that I now realized I'd been expecting.

"Jane?" I heard his voice call from the kitchen. "Is that you? We were just waiting for you to get home."

"We?" I said, crossing to the kitchen door. Had David arrived already?

No. Neko was seated at the table with a stranger, a stunning specimen of a human male. The visitor had the body of a diver—a well-muscled torso and chiseled arms that spoke of endless hours in a gym. His chestnut hair had perfect blond highlights, and his eyes glinted with a sea-blue that had to come from contact lenses. He stood as I entered, and his capped teeth nearly blinded me when he smiled. He was gorgeous. He was the cover of *Men's Health,* and he was sitting here in my kitchen.

"Neko was telling me all about your cottage. I hope you don't mind that I came by for a cup of tea."

And with those two sentences, spoken with a delicate dollop of affectation, this Adonis let me know that he would never be attracted to me, or anyone else of my gender, witchcraft or no witchcraft. I shook his hand gamely and learned that his name was Roger, and that he worked in the spa next door to the Laundromat, and that he had helped Neko when the washing machine overflowed, and how had *anyone* thought that dish soap would be a good substitute for laundry detergent?

Neko looked at me from his seat in the kitchen, and I could read the expression in his eyes without any magic at all. He wanted me to like his new friend. He wanted me to be pleased with the toy that he had brought home. And he wanted me to overlook his purposeful misuse of dish soap, consider it a minor amusement in the free-range life of my familiar. I was beginning to understand why most witches kept their assistants under lock and key. "Well, thank you, Roger," I said. "Thanks for helping poor Neko out."

Neko's grin was bright enough to light up the entire house. "He did more than that! When we got back here, the phone was ringing. I was still fighting to get the key out of the lock, but Roger got to it in time."

With a flash of premonition that had nothing to do with my roaming familiar or the magical books gathering dust in my basement, I knew that all the wonder of my day was about to come crashing down around my shoulders. "Who was it?" I asked.

"Your grandmother," Roger said, confirming my suspicion. "She seemed really surprised that a man answered here, but she left a message. She said that you and Clara are supposed to meet at Cake Walk on Saturday morning at eleven. Your calendar was sitting there on the counter, so I could see you didn't have anything else planned. It's all set up, and she says she won't take no for an answer."

10

"I'm sorry I'm late!" I was apologizing before the hostess had finished ushering me to our table. David Montrose stood as I arrived, and he placed his hands on the back of my chair in that strange gesture that conveys that a man is ready to assist a woman, but also feels possessive.

Not that I was complaining. He was back to his dark suit look, with a blindingly white shirt, and a conservative silver-on-black tie. I glanced down at my own outfit and was grateful that Neko had talked me into the microfiber one-piece dress. And the chunky green glass necklace that played off my hair. And the narrow-heeled slingbacks that were killing my feet.

"Actually," David said, "you're right on time." He glanced at his watch. I had left mine behind, in deference to this dinner that was more than a regular everyday meal. But less than a date. A lesson? A new beginning?

I surreptitiously took a deep breath and ordered my flip-flopping belly to settle down. Fortunately, the waiter chose that moment to scuttle up to the table. "Would madame like a cocktail?"

I cast a quick glance at David and hated myself for doing so. Would I like a drink? Of course. Make mine a double. But I had made a promise. If we were working tonight… David nodded and took the lead. "I'll have a martini," he said.

"Vodka gimlet," I countered, and the waiter nodded before scurrying off toward the kitchen. "So," I forced myself to say, confronting the alcoholic bull by the horns. "We're not actually working tonight."

"Not in the sense that you mean. We're getting to know each other better. You're learning to trust me. To trust yourself and what you can be."

His smile was disarming. I looked around the restaurant and wondered how much time he had spent selecting the place. When Neko had told me that I was meeting David at La Chaumière, I was excited, pleased enough that I momentarily forgave Roger for being my social secretary.

La Chaumière was a Georgetown staple; it had been around for more than thirty years. It was known for its fine French food and its fabulous service, but it was supposed to be relaxed, comfortable, almost like a country inn. I could imagine a warm hearth in the front room and lavish guest beds above, complete with fluffy down comforters and 400-count cotton sheets.

Sheets. I blushed. This was a restaurant in the middle of Washington, D.C. I'd better get my mind out of the bedroom and back to work.

Because whatever David Montrose said, this dinner *was* sort of work for me. If I was going to believe him, if I was going to accept the strange new job I'd undertaken, then I'd better accept that everything about David was business. He was my mentor, my teacher. My warder.

The waiter came back with our drinks, along with menus. "To new beginnings," David said, lifting his glass. I touched mine to his and repeated the toast, feeling the words thrum down my spine like musical notes.

New beginnings, I reminded myself. Like a new school year, the start of junior high. Like that terrible, awkward time when you looked up in seventh-grade history class and realized that you were the only girl in the room, and that odd-shaped white thing on your desk must be one of those athletic cups that you'd heard about, and that if you wanted it off your desk you were going to have to be the one to touch it, and that all the boys were going to laugh at you, and then all the boys *were* laughing at you, and it was only the second day of class, and the teacher wasn't even there yet, and, and, and…

Oh. Maybe that was only *my* experience with new beginnings.

I dove for my menu and started studying it as if it were the most fascinating thing written since George Chesterton's private diaries. Not that I had personally found those diaries so fascinating, but Jason had, and so I'd honed my passion for them. Passion…

Another sip of the gimlet. A grown-up's mojito, if you really think about it. I resisted the urge to drain the glass. I could handle this. I was an adult.

I looked at the first courses and saw that they had onion soup. French onion soup, by definition. One of my favorites. I considered ordering it, but then I heard Melissa whispering in the back of my head. Certain foods were *not* first-date foods. French onion soup. Spaghetti. Pizza. Anything that had a tendency to become long and stringy and drippy and embarrassing.

As I heard her admonitions, I wondered what Freud would say about them. It certainly sounded as if she were warning me off from more than luscious foodstuffs, trying to keep me from another whole range of messy activity. Spare me from the embarrassment, she would certainly say.

But who was I to argue with D.C.'s queen of First Dates? I sighed and decided to pass on the soup. Mesclun salad for me, with a classic vinaigrette. And while the pork loin sounded divine, it was served on a bed of tagliatelle. Tagliatelle. Worse, actually, than spaghetti, because the long flat noodles could hold more buttery sauce, could splatter more mess on an unsuspecting diner. Dover sole, then. With rice.

The waiter came back to take our order, and he attempted to complicate things. They had three specials for the night, and each sounded better than the last. But the tuna scaloppine was served with spinach (a definite no-no; it *would* get caught in my teeth.) The trout was a no-man's-land of potential bones, evil slivers just waiting to stick in my throat and embarrass me into requiring Heimlich assistance at the table. And the roast lamb was served with cherry tomatoes (did I even need to think about where the seeds might fly?).

I smiled at the waiter and ordered with Melissa-bred confidence. Mesclun and sole.

"Very good, madame. And for you, monsieur?"

"Onion soup, to start, and the pork with tagliatelle. And—" David turned to me "—if it's all right with you, we'll have a chocolate soufflé for dessert?"

Chocolate soufflé. An item I'd never ordered in a restaurant because I was too afraid of the "leave a minimum of forty-five minutes for preparation time" note on the menu. I ran through a list of Melissa's potential objections—it wasn't stringy, saucy or explosive—and said, "That sounds lovely."

"And wine?"

Without hesitating, David recited a bin number. The waiter nodded his approval and sidled off to the kitchen.

Leaving David and me at our table.

Alone.

Where were Melissa's Five Conversational Topics when I needed them? I started to raise my fingernails to my teeth, just for a quick gut-settling gnaw, but then I remembered where I was. I folded my hands in my lap instead, even managing to resist the urge to drain my gimlet.

David smiled easily and passed me the bread basket. Selecting a slice of baguette was practically therapeutic as he said, "So? How was your day at work?"

For just a moment, I thought that he was asking me about the library, that he was expressing an interest in colonial education, millinery of the eighteenth century or crop rotation for gentleman farmers.

Then, I realized his true intent. "It worked," I said. I glanced around at the tables closest to us. No one seemed to be listening, but I still leaned closer to David and whispered, "The spell worked."

He nodded in silent encouragement, and I told him all about Harold's unexpected attention, about the almost-laughable interest that he'd shown in my skirt. While that didn't surprise David, my mentioning Jason did. And old Mr. Zimmer. And the three other men who had paid me a surfeit of attention that afternoon.

The waiter interrupted to bring out a bottle of wine. David engaged in the entire tasting game, but he downplayed each step. He looked at the cork, swirled the straw-colored liquid in his glass a few times and took a single, abstemious swallow. He nodded to the waiter, who filled my glass, completed David's, then disappeared.

I took a sip and smiled approvingly at the full taste of the pinot gris. Much cleaner than the oaky chardonnays that I'd had before. Simpler. More straightforward.

Then we were back to my day as a witch. I gathered from the questions that David asked that it was unusual for a spell to have the strength of the one that I had cast. I shouldn't have been able to bring all of those men into my snare. I shouldn't have enchanted each and every one of them.

Somewhere during the telling, the waiter brought our appetizers. I only wasted a moment looking at David's soup with longing. Fortunately, the bright greens in my salad satisfied my taste buds. And I didn't have to worry about the Gruyère strands that tested David's cheese-sawing abilities. Not that the challenging soup made him look silly. It actually made him seem more…human. Less threatening. Just a regular guy eating a regular meal.

"So," I said, as we waited for our main courses.

"So."

"How long have you been doing this?"

"Warding? All my life." I waited for him to elaborate. That took three bites of baguette, a sip of water and another of wine. But at last, he said, "It's not going to be easy for you to accept all this information at once. I'll give you answers, but—for a while at least—you're going to have to accept these things on faith."

"Try me."

He took a deep breath, but was interrupted by the appearance of our entrées. The waiter put my plate down on the table and spun it a quarter turn, counterclockwise, so that the fish was best displayed against its lemon-and-caper sauce. David's pork was beautiful on its bed of treacherous, sauce-laden pasta.

"Bon appétit," David said, and he picked up his knife and fork. The knife and fork that he was using European-style, I noticed. He took a bite (sparing his suit from unsightly splashes of tomato and olive sauce) and chewed carefully before meeting my eyes. "Warding is…a family occupation. My father was a warder before me, and his father before him. I'm the oldest of three boys, and so I became a warder. My middle brother is a stockbroker, and my youngest is an experimental filmmaker, living in Toronto."

Well. That made the Montrose family seem downright ordinary.

"There are about two dozen of us warders here in D.C. One for each witch in the metropolitan area." And *that* made it all sound like a census survey. "We warders begin our training when we're children. For simplification's sake, you can think of us as students at a boarding school. We go to work with other warders, to learn from them."

"Like an apprentice." *That* was a system familiar to me. In colonial America, there were still apprentices and journeymen and masters, all learning their trades.

"Exactly."

"But what do you do when you're not watching me? I mean, what did you do before I worked that first spell?"

A dark memory flickered across David's face, and he took a sip of wine before answering. "I warded another witch until last year."

"What happened last year?" I asked softly, imagining some terrible magical battle, a beautiful young witch fighting desperately for her life. I pictured David struggling to rescue her from an evil sorcerer, grimacing in pain as he absorbed one magical assault after another.

"I was fired."

"What?" I was so surprised that I practically shouted the question.

"I was fired. My witch decided that I was too conservative. Too restrictive."

"Fancy that," I said before I could stop myself, and I was rewarded with a glare. I hurriedly asked another question, before he could match words to his expression. "So you were just sitting there…where? Waiting? Collecting astral unemployment?"

David grimaced at the word *astral*. "Let's just say I was on assignment."

"On assignment?"

"A detail."

"Doing what?" His evasiveness triggered every librarian instinct in my blood. I wanted to get to the bottom of this.

"I was working for the Court of Hecate, all right? I was reviewing valuable documents, storing them in proper places so that future generations can access the wisdom contained therein."

I stared at him in surprise. "You were a file clerk!"

"I—"

"There's nothing to be ashamed of." I cut him off, even though I wanted to laugh. My proud, domineering warder had been filing papers for the past year, alphabetizing page after page. Or scroll after scroll. Whatever.

As if he could read my mind, he said, "There was more to it than that. I provided physical protection for the Court's meeting places. I searched for lost and stolen artifacts. And I remained on call to any witch in the Coven who needed my assistance."

"Did you train them, then, the other witches? Like you'll train me?"

"No. Most of you are trained by your Caller."

You. I was a witch. The words still sounded impossible inside my own skull. I swallowed hard and forced out a whisper. "What's a Caller?"

"An older witch. One who senses strength in a new generation. One who calls you to your new powers."

"So it's not hereditary?" My thoughts flashed to the topic I'd been avoiding all night, to Clara, whom I was now supposed to meet on Saturday at Cake Walk. Curse Roger and his willingness to poke his nose into my bare-paged calendar.

"Usually, it is. Hereditary in the mother's line. But it doesn't always pass, not even from a strong witch to a first daughter. A Caller senses the seeds of power and encourages it in a young girl." He looked me directly in the eye. "Is your mother a witch?"

I started to say, "My mother's dead," because that was the way I had answered questions about Clara my entire life. But she wasn't dead. She was alive and well and ready to see me after a quarter century. Was that why she'd finally come back? Did she want to tell me that she was a witch? That I was? "I don't know," I finally said. "I haven't seen her since I was four years old. My grandmother raised me."

David nodded. "And is *she* a witch?"

"Gran!" I laughed out loud at the thought. "Absolutely not." David just looked at me. "She's a little old lady. She drinks Earl Grey tea. She sits on the board for the concert opera. She's my *grandmother,* for God's sake."

"Precisely." He reached out and rested his fingers on my wrist. As with the night before, I was surprised by how smooth his fingertips felt, how much warmth flowed from him against my pulse point. "She's your grandmother. And you came by your power from somewhere."

I pulled away from him and disguised my discomfort by stuffing my mouth with sole and rice. This was just too strange, I thought as I chewed. Too bizarre. Gran was not a witch. She couldn't be. I would have suspected something all these years. I swallowed. "Is there any other way?" I asked, and my voice sounded impossibly small.

David nodded, and I thought that the glint in his eyes just might be sympathy. "There is. Sometimes the witchcraft skips generations. Every once in a while—in a very, very rare while—it appears spontaneously. But there hasn't been a wild witch in the eastern Coven since Salem, since 1692."

"So it's not likely."

"Not likely." He shook his head and went back to his pork loin. He finished twirling the last strand of his tagliatelle as if we'd been discussing something as ordinary as pumpkins in fall. As he placed the bite in his mouth, a tiny dollop of sauce fell on his lapel. I was prepared to ignore it, but he noticed it himself and mopped it up with his napkin. He gave me a wry smile, and my heart twisted inside my chest.

So that was how it was done. You mop up the mess and move on. I consoled myself with the fact that my sole had been excellent. Before I could dwell on eating matters, I asked the question that had been percolating for days now: "So, the books. How did they get to be in the Peabridge's cottage? I mean, isn't that a strange coincidence, that I just happen to be a witch and my employer just happens to have a secret stash of spell books?"

David leaned back as the waiter came to take our plates away. When questioned, he ordered an espresso, and I—distractedly—asked for tea. The answer to my question was further delayed by the entire service ritual that accompanied that beverage: the waiter brought the little tea chest; I got to choose between a dozen flavors; and there was much shuffling of china and silverware.

Finally, David leaned forward in his chair and grappled with his answer. "The books are part of an extraordinarily valuable collection. They—and Neko, too—were brought together by Hannah Osgood. She led the eastern Coven in the first two decades of the 1900s."

"But she didn't live in the Peabridge house. I would know her name."

"No." David shook his head. "She lived up near the Palisades."

"Then how did the books get into the cottage?"

David sighed. "Hannah had seven daughters, six of whom actually had considerable power, all but the youngest, Emily. Hannah had compiled her library for her girls."

"What happened?"

"The Spanish flu. It tore through Washington in 1918. Hannah lost her husband first. And then her daughters, one by one. She tried to save them with spells, with crystals, but she fell ill herself."

"Poor thing," I whispered, feeling a ripple of pity.

"Hannah recovered her physical strength, but her spirit was broken. She renounced her witchcraft. She ordered away her warder, refused any assistance from the Coven. And when she died, all her books were missing."

"But she'd brought them to Emily's house," I said, nodding as I realized what had happened. "Emily Osgood became Emily Peabridge." I recognized the name from records kept in Evelyn's office, records that tracked the mansion's former owners.

David nodded and spread his hands wide. "It seems that she hid them away when it became apparent that her line would not survive. She'd come to despise the books, to hate the witchcraft that could not save her family. The Coven has been searching for years, but no one ever thought the books would turn up on Emily's land. No one ever imagined they'd be stored completely outside the reach of known witches."

"But why me? Why now? I mean, how did I end up living in the same cottage where those books just happened to be stored?"

David shrugged. "Magic reaches out to magic. Like magnets, jumping across space to be joined together. The books sensed your powers and influenced the world around you. Your dormant powers sensed the books."

"That's ridiculous! Evelyn let me live in the cottage because the Peabridge couldn't pay my salary."

David did not take offense at my agitated tone. Instead, he turned his hands, palm up. "I can't explain it. This isn't science. It isn't actions and reactions, like the world you've always known. If Evelyn hadn't let you live in the cottage, the books would have gotten you there another way. You might have found some colonial reference to a valuable collection in the basement. You might have chased a cat in there one day, while you were strolling through the gardens on your lunch break. In a pinch, you might have had a dream that pointed out the location. Magic calls to magic."

The thought was enough to drive me to silence. At least until the chocolate soufflé arrived.

The dessert was impressive—it towered above the walls of its shiny porcelain serving dish. The waiter maneuvered it toward our table with a satisfyingly controlled sense of urgency. I'd seen enough of Melissa's baking endeavors to appreciate the pillowy sweet, and I actually sighed as the waiter punctured the elevated crust to release a whiff of chocolate-scented steam. He poured a steady stream of vanilla sauce into the resulting crater before serving generous bowls of the treat.

One spoonful, and I thought that I would swoon.

David caught my eye and grinned. "Good?"

"Heaven."

By unspoken agreement, we were through with the witchcraft-instruction part of the evening. As we finished our dessert and I sipped the last of my tea, we discussed other things—the traditional Halloween parade that would take place through Georgetown at the end of October, the questionable quality of the first autumn apples at the Safeway up the street. We could have been friends, out to dinner after months of separation, catching up on the mundane details of our very busy professional lives.

It wasn't until David held my coat for me that we returned to the true root of our relationship. He kept the collar low enough that it was easy for me to slip my arms into the sleeves. As he settled the woolen shoulders over my own, he smoothed them into place with a comforting familiarity. "We're agreed, then? You'll continue meeting with me to learn more about your powers?"

"Of course." I realized that I'd already assumed we were going to work together. We started to walk back toward the Peabridge and home. I was so full and relaxed that I scarcely acknowledged the pain in my toes from my ill-fitting shoes. "But what sorts of things are you going to teach me? I mean, what can you tell me that Neko can't?"

David's lips pursed. "Neko is your familiar. He can

magnify your powers. To some extent, he can even focus them. But he can't channel them in the first place. There are many skills that you can learn besides reading spells."

"Such as?"

An older couple brushed past us on the sidewalk, and David waited until they were out of earshot before he answered. "You can read auras. You can tell who a person is, what they believe before you've ever met them. That man, who just walked by. He is on the board of directors of the Shakespeare Fund, and he's worrying about whether they'll raise enough money to underwrite seven productions next year, or only six."

The Shakespeare scholar in me hoped it would be seven. The new-hatched witch asked, "You could tell all that, just by walking by him?"

"My sleeve brushed his. Physical contact helps."

"So, are you a witch, too?"

He shook his head. "I don't have inherent powers, nothing as strong as witchcraft. Reading auras lets me function as a warder. The Coven gives me the power, so that I can best serve. They work a spell."

Auras. Coven. Warders. I shivered. David was talking about power. A lot of power. Power that I wasn't certain I wanted to have. I thought of Harold, hanging around my desk like an overeager puppy. But then I thought of Jason, looking me in the eye and smiling broadly as I recommended the reference source of his dreams.

Before I knew it, we were standing at my garden gate. I glanced down the path and saw that lights were on in the cottage. Neko was waiting up for me. Neko, and possibly Roger.

I turned back to David. "Thank you," I said. "For every-thing. I had a lovely time tonight."

Before I realized what was happening, he closed the distance between us. His arms came around me, pulling me in toward his chest. His lips on mine were chilled from the night air, but they thawed instantly. His fingers moved into my hair as he pulled my head closer to his, and I tasted chocolate soufflé and vanilla sauce and the deep rich coffee that had ended his meal.

It was a kiss like you read about in books. It was a kiss like the ones on movie screens, the ones that make you sink deeper into your stadium seating and lean your head back and sigh. It was a kiss that my body melted into, that made my hands grip his arms and clutch him close.

And then, it ended. He stepped back and straightened his arms. The autumn air swirled between us.

He looked down, avoiding my eyes, but then he seemed to remember some silent promise he had made. He looked directly into my face. "That was wrong," he whispered. He cleared his throat, and said again, loud enough to make both of us start. "Wrong."

"No! I mean—I wanted—" And then I fell silent, my cheeks flaming as I remembered just how much I had wanted his kiss the other night. Had that desire been in my aura? Had he read my thoughts as clearly as words on a page?

"I shouldn't have done that," he said. "I'm your warder."

"So what does that mean?" I was trying to make the best of this, but my legs were trembling so hard that I was having trouble standing.

"I shouldn't have blurred the boundaries. You're my witch. I'm your warder. We're going to work at being friends. It is too complicated for us to do anything more. Not while you're still coming into your powers. Not while you're still learning."

Of all the patronizing, controlling, master-of-the-universe, pigheaded—

But maybe he was right. I didn't know the first thing about being a witch. Okay. I knew the first thing—I could read spells in a spell book. But I didn't know the second. And I didn't even know what might be on the list for third.

"Were you reading me just now?" I asked. "Reading my aura?"

"No!" He sounded shocked. "The Coven sent me to be your warder. A warder can't read a witch unless she invites him to." My relief was almost a physical thing. I glanced toward the cottage just in time to see a dark shape jump back behind the curtains. Neko.

"Friends?" David asked, and he took another step back as if to clarify his stance.

"Friends," I said, managing a nod that felt almost jaunty.

"Get some rest, then. We'll continue with your training. And be kind to poor Harold Weems."

My lips still tingled as I worked my key in the front door lock.

11

It took half a dozen calls to Melissa to finish dissecting the night before. In between her providing baked goods to customers and my providing reference information to patrons, we worked the entire rainbow of emotions—from red anger (over Roger having the gall to make an appointment for me with Clara), to orange speculation (over what, exactly, David's kiss meant), to yellow caution (over the need to take small, precise steps as I learned more about the actual boundaries of all this witchcraft stuff), to green jealousy (over David's ability to eat both onion soup and tagliatelle without committing sartorial disaster), to blue sorrow (over that kiss, again, and whether there'd ever be another, and whether I wanted there to be another, and why my years with Scott had left me such an emotional mess), to, finally, violet intrigue (over the powers that I could harness, once I'd done a bit more study).

All in all, it was a very busy morning, made more so by

the fact that Harold Weems stopped by my desk on three separate occasions. The first time, he was carrying a small vase filled with yellow mums, a spray of brightly colored dried leaves and a curling frond of fern. "I thought that these would look nice on your desk," he'd said, and he blushed crimson.

"Thank you, Harold." For the first time, a twinge of guilt nibbled at the back of my mind. "They're lovely."

An hour later, he'd come by to bring me my mail—the mail that I had thus far managed to pick up from the library's shipping room every single day of my employment—and an hour after that, he'd stopped by to ask if I'd serve up a cup of coffee for him to sip on his break. At least I was able to give him a staff discount on the coffee.

"I've got a very busy afternoon," I said to the poor guy, trying to head off more hours of witch-inspired attention as I handed him his cup and a cardboard sleeve. I extemporized: "I'm working on a special project for Evelyn."

"What project?" he asked, perfectly reasonably.

"Umm…" I glanced back at my desk. I obviously wasn't a practiced liar, if I prepared so poorly. A flash of inspiration hit, though, as I remembered walking home with David the night before. "Foundations! I need to research foundations! Ones that might fund the Peabridge." That was it. Just like Mr. Shakespeare, who was trying to decide whether to fund another show. If I could find a handy donor or two, the library could be in the black, and I might shed my colonial garb.

"Well, good luck," Harold said. "Let me know if there's anything I can do to help."

"Mmm, hmm." I muttered noncommittally, and I crossed back to my desk. I'd have to research the collection in my basement to see if there was some sort of counterspell I could administer. I mean, poor Harold was getting more social exercise than he'd had in months, but it was only going to add up to heartbreak.

I glanced toward the second table in the reading room, the one where Jason would sit all afternoon. I could only hope that my spell had worked as strongly on him. My stomach did a somersault, and my fingers curled into fists. Jason, thoroughly bespelled. What a thought....

After all, nothing was going to happen with David. He had flat out said that it was inappropriate for him to have kissed me. And I had a lot more invested in my Imaginary Boyfriend than in my brand-new warder—months of getting to know Jason, letting him see the true me as I assisted him with his reference work. I'd spent the time to build a solid base because I didn't want anyone—myself included—to question if he was only my rebound relationship after Scott.

I was no fool. I knew all about rebound. I had carefully measured every twinge of interest that I'd ever had for Jason Templeton, making sure that it was true, pure, legitimate. Not some figment of my Scott-tortured mind.

And Jason was real. Jason was my future.

But that future might not arrive if the Peabridge was forced to shut down, despite my cut salary, my charming colonial clothes and the latte bar that perfumed the lobby. Foundation money. That really wasn't a bad idea.

Rolling up my proverbial sleeves (my overdress fit too

tightly around my forearms to permit the literal action), I dug into Google, refining set after set of search results to track down potential donors. This was the type of research project I loved—one lead ran into another, and I was swept along with the pleasure of learning new things. I was interrupted a few times by patrons, but my enthusiasm did not flag. My printer started to hum as I churned out pages from likely prospects. Some even included grant applications online.

It was midafternoon by the time I'd finished my information gathering. The stack on my desk was impressive, if I did say so myself. I glanced toward Evelyn's office and contemplated telling her about what I'd done, but I figured that it was still such a long shot that there was no reason to raise her hopes. I slipped the materials into a white Tyvek envelope; I'd follow up tomorrow, when I was fresh.

Of course, the rest of my library work had hardly disappeared while I was doing my independent study. I glanced at the massive carts beside the circulation desk. We'd had a number of patrons in for the morning—it seemed as if each person who had walked through the door had carried his own weight in books, returning them to our collection.

Well, no time like the present to get started on reshelving. Besides, Jason would arrive at any moment. He should see me busily working, not waiting for him like some lovesick puppy. Squaring my shoulders, I wrestled one of the heavy wooden carts toward the back of the stacks.

I've never been a big fan of shelving. It is actually a lot of work. It's amazing how many books are on the very bottom row of the collection, or the very top, and how many neighboring books can slip sideways during a one-month checkout span. Inevitably, I end up breaking finger-nails (when mine are long enough to break; maybe there's a reason that I routinely chew them to the quick).

Today's job was made more challenging by the fact that I had inadvertently chosen the Death Sled. The Sled was our oldest shelving cart. One wheel locked intermittently to the right, periodically pitching the entire cart to the side with a lurch strong enough to pull a poor librarian's arms from their sockets. When using the Sled, I'd been known to grunt like Maria Sharapova at Wimbledon.

But today I was determined to keep those grunts to myself. I strongly suspected that Harold was lurking nearby, ready to leap forward with a helping hand if he sensed my slightest need. And right now, I didn't want to see the man. Not until I'd figured out some way to recall my spell. Or, at the very least, dilute it.

I finished shelving all the books on the right side of the cart. The last two were destined for bottom shelves in the collection. I knelt down to place the first one, and then I stretched to the next rank of shelves to shove the other one in place. My heel, though, caught the hem of my petticoat, and I heard the fabric start to rip. Swearing a most un-colonial oath, I tried to hop forward, to free my foot. Un-fortunately, that only succeeded in throwing my weight against the Death Sled, where one of my long, ruffled sleeves snagged a corner. True to its name, the book cart chose that moment to leap forward at an impossible angle.

Out of the corner of my eye, I saw a patron standing in the path of the Sled. I threw my hip against the cart, hard, using my full body weight to yank my sleeve free and set the Sled off course. That fine football tactic, however, only upset my fragile, hem-bound balance. As I tumbled to the floor, my mobcap went flying, and my glasses were knocked askew. The Death Sled, weighted on only one side because of my industrious—if unbalanced—shelving, teetered precariously for the longest minute in the history of library science before it crashed to the ground, sending treatises, essays and bound manuscripts flying.

I waited until the crash had stopped echoing through the stacks before I pulled myself to my knees. I was blinking like Rip Van Winkle awakened from a nap, and I fumbled to straighten out the earpiece of my glasses, to get the lenses settled back on my face.

On the bridge of my nose, to be exact. The bridge of the nose that was now at hip-level to the rest of the world, as I knelt by the wreckage of the Death Sled. Hip-level. Or, to be more specific, crotch-level.

With a sickening swoop in the pit of my stomach, I recognized that khaki crotch. Even without my glasses properly placed, I knew the crisp cotton fabric. I'd spent enough days staring at it across the library. I'd wasted enough daydreams about the package behind it, about the manly gifts of my Imaginary Boyfriend.

Jason.

Jason Templeton.

The man who now cleared his throat and took a single, polite step backward.

"I'm sorry!" I gasped, finally forcing my glasses back on my nose. My embarrassment crisped the back of my neck.

At the crash of the cart, people had come running—Evelyn, Harold and at least two other patrons.

Harold stepped forward and righted the Sled. Evelyn started to collect the books, clicking her tongue over them as if they were naughty children. The patrons stared at me as if I were some sort of freak—I mean, what sort of librarian sends books crashing to the floor in the middle of a quiet afternoon of study?

Jason was trying to keep from laughing. "I'm sorry," I said again. "I didn't mean—"

"Are you all right?" Harold interrupted, taking advantage of the situation to reach for my forearm and haul me to my feet.

"Harold!" Evelyn said, as if he were responsible for the chaos I'd created. "This cart is dangerous! Someone might have been hurt. Can you fix the wheel?"

Even though he was besotted by my spell, Harold managed to turn to his direct supervisor. "Sure thing," he said.

"Well, take care of it now, so that this doesn't happen again."

Harold looked at me solicitously, but I assured him that I was fine. I raised my voice to let the others know, as well, and it took only a few minutes for the patrons to return to their work. Evelyn shook her head and went back to her office.

That left me with Jason. With Jason of the Impeccably Pressed Khakis. The khakis that I had just studied much too closely. "I'm sorry," I said for a third time.

"I don't think you have anything to apologize for."

"I've never done that sort of thing before."

"What? Knocking over a book cart?"

"No. Kneeling—" I realized that I did not have a dignified way to complete my sentence. "Yeah. That's what I meant. Knocking over a book cart."

"No blood, no foul." Jason shrugged, and his smile was blinding enough that I nearly forgot my mortification.

I don't know what possessed me. Maybe it was a bounce back from my grimoire spell. Maybe it was the wild confidence that had fueled my morning of foundation research. Maybe it was the realization that it was time to move this relationship forward, time to push Jason from the Imaginary category over to Real. But I heard myself speaking before I had even thought through the words in my head. "I've been wondering," I said, and my voice was calm and collected, as if I spoke to dream boyfriends every day of my life, "would you like to come over for dinner on Friday?"

"Friday?" For just a second, he looked surprised.

Had I been too forward? Had I been too bold, to propose the first night of the weekend? Um, that would be *tomorrow* night. Had I ruined my entire romance before it even had a chance to start?

He shook his head. "My schedule is crazy this semester. I have office hours on Friday afternoon. Then I go to dinner with Ekaterina. It's a standing thing—wind up the workweek, you know?"

"Oh!" I said, cursing the Russian ballerina princess. It made sense that he'd see her after office hours. If she was his star grad student, he probably had to give her a lot of support, a lot of personal attention.

"Any other night, though," Jason was saying. "Any week-night, I mean."

Any weeknight. He was offering me any night, Monday through Thursday. Any night we could wrap up our work here at the library and head out to my cottage. I could send Neko packing (lucky for me that my familiar was free to roam), and I could whip up a little something special....

"Thursday!" I said, like a drowning woman who had just found a raft.

He grinned. "Like a week from today?"

"Um, yes." Like a week from today. An entire week. What was I thinking? Was the power of an Imaginary Boyfriend so strong that he could make me forget the days of the week? Romeo and Juliet had an easier time planning their balcony trysts. "Exactly like that."

"What time?"

"Eight?"

"Eight." He nodded and treated me to another one of his grins. "Where do you live?"

That's right! He didn't know! He didn't realize that my home was so close to the library. I told him about the cottage, and he was suitably impressed.

"All right, then," he said. "Next Thursday, eight. The cottage in the garden." He took a step toward me. For just a moment, I thought that he was going to kiss me. Me. The librarian standing like an idiot, with twisted glasses and a rucked up colonial skirt. I took a step toward him, which made him move away.

"I—" he said, then gestured toward the shelves be-hind me.

"What?" I asked, trying to hide my confusion.

"I was going to get an atlas."

"An atlas?" I might never have heard of the word before.

"From that shelf over there. Behind you."

"Oh! An atlas!" Of course. I was an idiot. That was why he'd come over here in the first place. Why he'd been in range of the Death Sled. I stepped to the side. "I need to get back to my desk, anyway."

"I'll see you next Thursday, then."

I was dialing Melissa's phone number before I sat down at my desk.

12

Melissa replaced the pot of Caramel Karma coffee on its heating element and gestured toward the canisters of loose tea, silently asking me if I wanted my preferred form of caffeine. I shook my head. As it was, I was almost bouncing off the ceiling. Eleven-fifteen, and Clara had not yet made her appearance.

"Go on," I said, and I could hear the nervousness in my voice. "Who knows when she'll get here? Tell me about last night's dating game."

Melissa glanced at the red-X'ed calendar and sighed. "This one was a *Washington Today.*"

I grimaced. The magazine was known for its funky articles about D.C. life, but its restaurant critics were more discerning than its personals editor. Most of the men Melissa had met through the ads had grossly overstated their qualifications. I'd encouraged her to stop using the silly thing—married men looking for action on the side, shrimpy self-professed giants and "fit" poster boys for obesity clinics were not going to make Melissa happy. (Not, I hasten to add, that there's anything wrong with short or fat men—just short or fat men who lie about their status to unsuspecting, openhearted bakers whose biological clocks are ticking louder than Big Ben.)

"So," I said, fiddling with a packet of turbinado sugar. "What did this one say?"

She looked up at the ceiling, as if the ad were printed there. "Single white male, thirty-eight years old, brown hair, green eyes."

"Thirty-eight!"

"That's what he said," she replied grimly. "I thought that I could make the age difference work. After all, we all know that women are more mature than men."

I gave her a look that told her *exactly* what I thought of that logic, but I waved a hand to get her to go on. She continued to recite: "Gourmet chef in brown paper package. Can spice things up with salsa or cool them down with raita. Take a chance and feed your curiosity today."

I frowned. "A little gimmicky."

"Come on. I'm a baker. He should have been perfect for me."

"And?"

"Who knew that McDonald's is experimenting with recycled brown paper bags? And that they actually offer a raita burger?" I shook my head as Melissa went on. "Only in major metropolitan areas, but still. And a salsa burger? Did you know that they're testing them in the southwest right now?"

"This guy owns a McDonald's?"

She nodded grimly. "Thirteen of them. He's a franchise king. A graduate of Hamburger University."

I couldn't keep from laughing. "You've always said not to be too snobby about things like education."

"Want a coupon for a free Big Mac? I have several."

I swallowed hard. Poor Melissa, with her childlike preference for plain burgers. That special sauce would all be wasted on her. "But how was he, aside from that?"

"There wasn't any 'aside from that.' Our conversation was all-McDonald's, all-the-time. Oh, except for one thing. The *thirty-eight* was a typo."

"A typo?"

"He *meant* to say forty-eight. At least, that's what I'd imagine, given his appearance. Or maybe he's a youthful fifty-eight."

"So, there you were, having drinks with a fifty-eight-year-old McDonald's franchisee…."

"At least I had the good sense to plan this one for drinks only. He begged me to join him for dinner, but I told him I already had a commitment. If anyone ever asks, I was helping you bake a tres leche cake last night. You needed it for a work colleague's birthday."

"Tres leche. Birthday. Got it." I shook my head and started to consider the value of yet another this-isn't-worth-it-why-are-you-pushing-so-hard-to-find-the-man-of-your-dreams speech. Before I could work out a new angle, though, the door to Cake Walk opened.

And a woman walked in.

I recognized her from the photographs that Gran kept

around the house. The old ones, of course, since my grand-mother had not seen fit to update the collection, intent as she was on keeping me in the dark about Clara's continued existence. Not that I'm bitter, or anything like that.

She had red hair. She clearly had exploited the skills of Lady Clairol, but if the shade was even close to natural, I could see where I got the russet highlights in my own hair. Her eyes were hidden behind giant sunglasses, as if she thought she was a movie star tragically misplaced along the C & O Canal in Georgetown. Her skin was pale, a shade or two lighter than my own, and she seemed to have covered up suspected freckles with a heavy coat of makeup. Her neck was starting to sag, and her chin was softened by hints of age.

Hints of age, and the wages of hard living, I thought uncharitably.

I wondered what her eyes looked like behind those absurd sunglasses. Were they the same as mine? Did she have the flecks of gold that made the hazel seem deeper than it actually was?

"Mrs. Madison?" Melissa asked, finally breaking the spell.

"Smythe," she said, drawing out the *y* into a long vowel, just like Gran did. Of course. She wouldn't use my father's last name. She'd left him behind, like she'd left me. Like she'd left Gran. "Clara," she corrected herself before she extended her hand to Melissa.

My best friend smiled as if she always hosted my long-lost, drug-fiend relatives on a slow Saturday morning in the bakery. "I'm Melissa White," she said, shaking hands firmly. "And I'm sure you've realized that this is Jane."

I stood there, trying to remember what to say. Had Miss Manners ever written a column about reuniting with parents who had abandoned you? With parents who lied to you for a quarter century, and then decided to come back into your life? I'm sure there was some specific etiquette; I just didn't know what it was.

Once again, Melissa came to my rescue. "Why don't you two take a seat, and I'll bring some coffee." She flashed Clara the smile of a professional hostess. "Cream? Sugar?"

"Thank you. I appreciate the offer, really I do, but I don't drink coffee."

Melissa sent me a sideways glance that was meant to carry an entire conversation, like smoke signals across the high plains. "Tea, then? We've got a variety of flavors."

"Oolong?"

Melissa's smile grew broader. She knew my favorite when she heard it. "With just a bit of cream?"

"Exactly!" Clara looked as if she might clap her hands together in joy. Or relief. I couldn't help but steal a glance at those hands, and I was strangely relieved to see that they were completely different from my own. Her fingers were thick. Short. Stubby. But the nails were the same—bitten to the quick.

I silently promised to take care of my own nails once and for all. Neko would certainly help me with a manicure. Roger, Neko's newfound Adonis, had to offer them at his salon. Roger. The man owed me, after getting me into *this*.

Melissa waved us over to the two-top in the corner, the table that provided the most privacy in the small shop. Clara waited until I sat down; then she took her seat. At first, she put her hands on the table, entwining her fingers, but then she shifted them to her lap. I imagined them clenching and unclenching as our silence stretched out. As if she'd only just remembered that she was wearing Hollywood glasses, she peeled them off, folding them carefully before returning her hands to her lap.

Bingo. Hazel. Gold flecks. More bloodshot than I hoped my own were.

"Jeanette," she said.

"What!" I couldn't help myself. She didn't even remember my name.

"Jane!" She blushed crimson—the same telltale flush that I suffered through every time I was embarrassed. "I'm sorry, Jane."

"Why did you call me that?"

"It's your name. The name I gave you. Well, your father and I."

Her voice was deeper than I'd expected, as if it had been sanded down by too much whiskey and too many cigarettes. She spoke in short, sharp sentences, reinforcing that she was every bit as nervous as I was.

I supposed that should have made it easier for me. I should have realized just how much we had in common, how much we both were suffering. After all, I'd read my Shakespeare. I knew how grateful mothers were when they found their lost children. In *Winter's Tale,* Hermione's reunion with Perdita was joyous; it finally awakened the entire mourning kingdom. But I didn't feel joyful. I didn't feel grateful. I felt more as if I'd like to exit, pursued by a bear. Anything but continue to sit here and make small talk.

"Gran always called me Jane."

Clara pursed her lips. "She would. She never liked the name Jeanette. She thought it was fussy. She even made me put 'Jane' on your birth certificate, but I've always thought of you as Jeanette."

Gran was right! I wanted to shout. Melissa spared me the need to reply when she carried our tea over to the table. She used one of her cork-backed trays, and she shifted mugs, hot water, tea strainers, loose tea and cream with the ease of familiarity. The coup de grâce, though, was the platter of Sugar Suns, iced lemon cookies that always made me smile. "Thanks," I said, but she disappeared behind the counter before I could beg her to sit down and join us.

Clara and I busied ourselves with our tea. She liked it much weaker than I did; I almost asked her why she didn't just wave her tea strainer over the steam that rose from her mug. But I heard the words before I said them, and knew that they would sound too snarky. I settled for passing her the cream and taking odd satisfaction that she took more than a "bit." She added a downright dollop.

"So. *Jane.*"

I wanted to click my tongue and roll my eyes and toss my hair in a perfect approximation of teenaged frustration. After all, Clara had been exempted from dealing with me when I was stuck in those terrible years. Thrusting down my annoyance, I settled for stating her name in the exact tone that she had used. "Clara," I said, and I watched her shift back on her chair.

"I'm not surprised that you're angry with me," she said. "My counselor said that you probably would be."

"Your counselor?" I did not like the idea that Clara had been talking about me with strangers. I mean, I'd gone out of my way not to talk about her. Even Melissa hadn't heard the constant monologue inside my head, my ceaseless questions about what Clara wanted, why she was returning to my life now, what she would be like, what all this would *mean?*

"She's my...I guess you'd say that she's my spiritual advisor." Clara smiled for the first time since entering the bakery.

I bit off a Sun ray and let the sugary frosting mingle with the tart cookie on my tongue. I chewed a few times, remembering Gran's constant admonitions not to wolf my food, and then I said, "What religion?"

Clara lifted her chin as if I'd challenged her. "The Universal Family of Light."

Uh-huh.

So, she belonged to a cult. I immediately pictured her in a white robe, offering up all her worldly belongings to some wrinkled old man in a loincloth. Clara was waiting for a response, and I dug deep into the civility well. "I don't think they mentioned that one in catechism."

She smiled ruefully. "And I'm sure your grandmother didn't bring it up."

"Leave Gran out of this! She wasn't responsible for teaching me about your church!" I was surprised by the strength of my reaction, by my need to protect Gran.

Especially, a voice whispered at the back of my mind, when Gran had not protected *me.* She hadn't given me the facts that I needed to know; she hadn't told me about Clara in the first place. It was as if she'd sent me out on a first date without any prior discussion of birds, bees or the wayward hands of teenaged boys. She'd left me vulnerable, and I hated the feeling.

"I didn't mean to criticize your grandmother," Clara said. "It's just that she's never approved of the Family."

"What sort of things do you believe?" I asked, because I needed to say something, and I didn't want to dwell any more on Gran and her role in this whole strange reunion.

"We believe in the harmonic balance of the world. We believe that there are some places that are holy, sacred wells where the powers of the ancients can still be felt. We believe that there are certain perfect structures that can bring us enlightenment and power, by bringing our own warped bodies and minds into proper alignment."

"Structures?" I asked, because that seemed like the only concrete word in everything she had said.

She nodded and fished for a gold chain that had slipped inside her blouse. When she pulled it out, I could see a perfect quartz crystal. "Structures," she repeated. "Crystals to guide our meditation. To show us the ways of balance. To heal."

Crystals.

My biological mother believed in crystals. Had I just stepped back into the 1970s without any warning? I looked around wildly, hoping that Melissa would bail me out, but she was helping a customer at the counter.

But there was something about Clara's words, something that reminded me of dinner with David. Power. She was interested in the hidden power of the world around her.

"Are you a witch?" I asked, before I'd even thought about the question.

"A witch?" She blinked, confused.

"You know. The powers that you're talking about. Do you work spells? Do you channel power that way?"

Clara's face shut down just a little bit, and she let her crystal slip back beneath her blouse. "I'm not kidding about this, um, Jane. It's very important to me. I'm not just making it up to be strange."

"No!" I heard how loud my voice was, and I swallowed before continuing. "No, I didn't mean to say that. It's just that..."

"Just that what?"

"I've become interested in witchcraft lately. I thought that maybe I'd gotten that interest from you." Okay, so it sounded lame. But it was practically the truth. Even if it did sound like I'd been spending my time browsing the stacks in a library. Not working spells. Not summoning familiars. Whatever.

Clara shook her head. "No. No witchcraft that I know of in my past. Although I think that there are times that I've been more than a little possessed."

I wondered if I should ask her for details, but the question seemed too intrusive. Instead, I stared out the window, watching a handful of sycamore leaves drift to the sidewalk. The silence stretched out between us until it was something palpable. Something uncomfortable.

"Did you—"

"Your grandmother—"

We both started at the same time, then we both insisted

that the other speak. I finally gave in to her and completed my question: "Did you ever come to see me? Did you ever watch me when I didn't know you were there?"

She shook her head. "At first I didn't want to. I was too busy worrying about where I was going to get my next fix."

There. She'd said it. In plain English. She'd wanted her drugs more than she wanted me. More than she even wanted to *see* me. I felt myself shut down. My shoulders hunched up around my shoulders, and I started to chew on my thumbnail.

"Don't do that," she said, reaching out to pull away my hand.

"Don't tell me what to do!" I was surprised by the intensity of my anger. I jerked my hand back as if she had burned me.

"You've got such beautiful hands," she said, folding her own in her lap. "They're from your father's side of the family. Mine were never much to look at."

I folded my fingers into fists. Childish, I know, but I didn't want her to look at them anymore. I didn't want her to see the chewed fingernails.

"Jane," she said. "I know that I've hurt you. I know that this all must be a huge surprise."

"Do you? Do you know that?" I dared to meet her eyes—mirrors of my own. "Do you know how many times I wanted you to come back? How I hid your picture beneath my pillow? How I talked to you late at night when I knew no one else could hear?"

"I did what I thought was best," she said. "I knew that I wasn't strong enough to help you. To give you everything you needed."

"Maybe that was true when you left, but it's been *twenty-five years!* You must have found the strength at some point."

"I did. Or I thought I did. I stopped using sixteen years ago, after I woke up in a city hospital without any memory of who I was or how I'd gotten there. It took me a few years to get my own life back. When I first contacted your grandmother, though, she said that you weren't prepared to see me, that it would be too disorienting. You were starting high school. It was a difficult time."

I flashed back to an image of me at fifteen—gawky, ungainly, absolutely unsure of myself. From day to day, I'd change from a loving, immature child to a haughty, tantrum-throwing teen. I wanted to go on dates, but I was afraid to. I wanted independence, but I was terrified of being on my own. I couldn't have handled my biological mother's disclosure. Not then.

"I always asked about you, though," Clara said. "I always wanted to know how you were doing. Your grandmother should have—"

"Don't you *dare* tell me what Gran should have done!" Again, my flash of anger overwhelmed me, confused me, too. After all, I *was* angry with Gran. Why should I protect her? She was the one who had kept this secret from me. This was her fault, hers and Clara's together. They had ganged up on me from the moment I was born.

"Jeanette—"

"My name is Jane!"

"Jane, I'm sorry. I didn't mean to upset you."

"I'm sure you didn't." I scrambled for my purse. "Look, I just remembered that I have a meeting to get to. At work."

"On Saturday?"

I nodded, trying to think of something, anything, that would get me out of Cake Walk. "Big cataloging meeting. We're going over acquisitions for the next year. All the staff. All day." I stood up and pushed my chair up to the table. "I'm sorry that we couldn't spend more time together. I'm sorry."

I saw Melissa's concerned glance, but I faked a smile and a wave, and mimed that I would pay her later for the tea and cookies. I grabbed my shawl and flung it around my shoulders with a panache that beat Clara's glasses, hands down. She stood, but I was already halfway to the door.

"Jean—Jane! I'd like to see you again."

"Oh yes," I said. "We'll do that. I don't have my calendar, though. Call me, and we'll get together. Very soon."

My fingers fumbled with the doorknob, and it took three tries to get the door open. I heard Melissa call my name as I finally wrenched it free. I half turned and waved again. "Staff meeting!" I called before I fled onto the cobblestoned street.

I did not let myself think about Clara's eyes, those eyes that were the same shade as mine, those eyes that were welling up with tears as I fled home to my cottage, to my books of witchcraft, to the life that I had carved out without any mother to call me by someone else's name.

13

Melissa set her right fist against her left palm. "One, two, three," she said.

Scissors.

I tried to fold the "paper" of my flattened hand into a rock, but she closed her fingers around mine, sawing hers in a time-honored motion. "Scissors cut paper."

"Yeah, yeah," I said, none too happy. "I know. I *will* see Clara again. I promise. It was just too much—the cult thing, and the crystal, and the way her eyes were exactly like mine."

"That was a little creepy, wasn't it?" And that's when I knew that Melissa would let this thing rest. She'd let me figure out how to meet Clara again, on my own timetable.

For now, though, we had bigger fish to fry. So to speak. As it were.

Jason Templeton was arriving for dinner in four short hours.

I'd taken the afternoon off work, and Melissa had stepped up to the plate with the unprecedented act of closing the bakery to come to my aid. We'd spent the better part of the past week—when we weren't dissecting every second of the disaster that had been my reunion with Clara—planning a menu.

Against Melissa's advice, I'd decided to go with a colonial theme. Eighteenth-century delicacies. Things that would show that I was an intellectual woman, not just an infatuated librarian.

The problem was, tastes had changed a bit in the past 200-odd years.

I hadn't had any trouble finding sample menus. The Peabridge had a huge collection that covered kitchens, gardens and foodstuffs, along with countless diaries from housewives, butlers and more than a few men of the house.

I'd spent the better part of Monday plowing through them, reaching up to run my fingers through my unruly hair, consistently forgetting that I wore a satin-ribboned mobcap. I'd spent Tuesday selecting the best candidates, winnowing the possibilities down to a meager half dozen possibilities. I'd spent Wednesday writing lists of ingredients, organizing the recipes so that I could cook them most efficiently and creating detailed flowcharts of what needed to be accomplished when.

And I'd spent Thursday freaking out and wondering if this wasn't the biggest mistake of my entire romantic life.

We were talking about *Jason Templeton,* after all. The man who was supposed to sit at my table, eat my cooking, stare into my eyes and realize that we were destined to be together forever.

The man I was meant to spend the rest of my life with. The man who was going to make me forget Scott Randall and his controlling, manipulative, debasing, two-timing ways forever.

I took a deep breath and looked down at my menu one more time. I wasn't an idiot. I wasn't about to serve the twelve courses that would have been standard in colonial times. I wasn't going to offer a half dozen meats, as if this were the Hardy Lumberjack Buffet. I'd keep things simple.

Peanut soup (don't knock it if you haven't tried it—it's really pretty good). Lamb chops (substituting for the mutton that most colonialists would have enjoyed. Have you tried to find mutton in a store these days?). Peas—Thomas Jefferson's favorite vegetable (it was late in the season to find fresh ones, but Dean & Deluca, the gourmet grocery in the heart of Georgetown, had finally obliged me—for a price). Sweet potato and pecan muffins—already baked by Melissa. And, for dessert, a pear tart.

There. That wasn't so complicated. Any girl could do it.

My kitchen already looked like a battleground. Every horizontal surface was colonized by herbs and spices. The ingredients for the soup huddled by the toaster. The spices for the lamb mustered by the sink. Fresh peas in the pod assailed the tin table. (I could not believe how many I'd needed to buy to make sure I'd have enough once they were shelled and cooked down.) The tart looked like it would command the most attention; flour already powdered the countertop, and sugar threatened to dive onto the floor.

Before I could implement my master plan of attack, the front door opened, and Neko waltzed in. My dry cleaning was draped over his arm; I had remembered just in time that I wanted to wear my pleated skirt.

Neko stopped in the doorway to the kitchen, his eyes widening in shock. "You girls better have a *lot* of alcohol planned."

Alcohol! Wine! I hadn't even thought of wine. What sort of hostess would I be if I didn't have wine for my guest?

What fit the meal? I ran through a list in my head. Thomas Jefferson had been a Francophile; he would have drunk something French—a fine burgundy, most likely. What about George Chesterton? Did I know his wine preferences? Maybe a claret? What the hell *was* a claret, anyway? And would it go with lamb?

"Neko!" I said, reaching for my wallet. "Please, go buy some wine. Two bottles. You can go to the store down on M Street. They'll help you choose something right. Make it French. And bold." I gave him a twenty and watched disbelief twist his face. I extracted another bill from my wallet and folded his fingers around it. "Go on! The wine will need time to breathe!"

Neko pocketed the cash. "I'll just put your skirt in your closet," he said.

"No!" I shouted. Melissa jumped at the vehemence of my reply, but Neko wasn't surprised. "You are *not* going into my room. You are not getting anywhere near Stupid Fish." I had managed to change the tetra's water the weekend before, but not without slapping Neko's hands on three separate occasions. "Drape the skirt over the couch. I'll hang it up when I'm done here."

He shrugged and set down the garment, catching it twice

when the plastic wrap threatened to slide to the floor. "Can't blame a boy for trying."

"I can very much blame the boy," I said. My patience was wearing thin. I glanced at the clock. Four hours till Jason arrived. Four hours to make everything perfect. "Please, Neko. Go. And don't stop off at Roger's. There isn't time."

Neko pouted, but he left.

Four hours *definitely* wasn't enough time for Neko to visit Roger. I'd gone to the salon with my enabling familiar on Sunday afternoon, still trying to recover from the fiasco with Clara. I'd decided to get my nails done. Roger had convinced me to splurge on a pedicure to go along with the manicure I'd already chosen. He'd seduced me with scented lotions and heated towels, and I had luxuriated in every second of the treatment.

And I'd been astonished to realize that Neko and I had wiled away an entire afternoon in the marble-and-chrome temple to self-indulgence. It was too easy to lose track of time there. Too easy to slip away from responsibility, from the details of daily life.

"So, are you going to begin with the tart?" Melissa's question tugged me back to reality.

"Yep," I said, and I took a deep breath. "The crust first, right?"

"Right." Melissa came to stand beside me. It really was brilliant for me to choose a baker as my best friend. She made all these little details fall into place.

We had decided to go with a gingersnap base—no chance for me to ruin a traditional pie crust by adding too much flour, or by kneading for too long. Besides, the smell

of the ginger would brighten the entire house, *and* gingersnaps were a colonial favorite. Melissa walked me
through the details—placing the store-bought cookies (hey,
a girl has to take a few shortcuts) into a plastic bag, crushing
them with a rolling pin.

It took a surprisingly long time to break them all into
perfect crumbs. I was beginning to think that I should have
bought one of those premade graham cracker crusts. After
all, who was going to know the difference?

I would, I chided myself, quickly regaining my senses.
And Jason would. He would know that our Founding
Fathers (and Mothers) did not have graham crackers. He
would know that my meal was not authentic. All the cachet
that I hoped to gain with my scholarly feast would be lost,
held hostage by stupid cookie elves.

Besides, once the gingersnaps were crushed, the rest of
the crust was easy. I added sugar and shortening and pressed
the resulting mixture into a pan.

"There," Melissa said. "Now you want to blind bake it
for ten minutes."

"Blind bake?" I asked, picturing a trio of mice in dark
glasses.

"Without the pears. So that the crust gets done."

Right. I knew that.

I put the crust in the oven, set the timer and turned back
to my friend. She was collecting the last of the dusty
peapods from the table. The vegetables themselves were
glinting in a bowl, fresh and inviting as summer.

"How did you do that?"

"What?"

"Shell the peas? I was busy over here, and you were giving me advice the entire time. It's like magic!"

"You took long enough to press the crust into the pan." She smiled to take the sting from her words. "And speaking of magic, when do I get to see the books?"

"You saw them. Neko brought up the grimoire the other night."

"I mean all of them. When do I get to see the collection?"

"It's not like I'm keeping it a secret or anything." We crossed through the living room, and I turned the key in the basement door's lock. I'd replaced the lightbulb at the top of the stairs, so we didn't need candles to light the way.

Melissa exclaimed when she reached the bottom. I still hadn't found time to put the books in order. Truth be told, I was a little afraid of them. I'd thought of asking Neko to get the collection in shape, but I wasn't sure what I'd end up with if I put him in charge. Besides, David's story jangled at the back of my mind. The books were part of Hannah Osgood's estate. They weren't really mine. They'd have to be returned to their rightful owners at some point.

"They're incredible!" Melissa said. "Just *smell* them!"

She was right about that. They did smell amazing. Leather, parchment and a hint of ancient dust. That was the scent that had roped me into libraries in the first place— the magic of the written word, separate and apart from any special powers.

"May I touch them?" she asked.

I shrugged. "Might as well. They've definitely been handled in the past."

She ran her fingers along the spines on the nearest shelf before pulling out one of the larger volumes. Letters were picked out in gold on the cover, and I craned my neck to read along with her: *"Elemental Magick."*

She supported the volume with her left hand as she opened the cover, taking care not to spread it too wide. "On water," she read. "On its summoning and its banishing."

"Great. If the basement starts to flood, I'll have somewhere to turn."

"You just can't find good plumbers these days." We both started to laugh, but were interrupted by the triple chirp of my electronic timer up in the kitchen. "Crust is done," Melissa said, leading the way upstairs.

I reached for the timer as she opened up the oven. She took a half step back and said, "This oven runs hot."

"I set it for 350."

"I see that. It's probably cooking at around 400, though. Maybe a little higher."

"Does that mean I can't make the tart?"

"No, it'll be fine. Just turn down the temp. Cook it at 300 on your dial, and check it after about three-quarters of the time." The things I didn't know about baking.

The rest of the afternoon flew by. Under Melissa's instructive gaze, I sliced the pears and layered them onto my gingersnap crust. I coated them with a honey glaze so that they wouldn't oxidize, and then I baked them in my too-hot oven. As Melissa had recommended, I checked the dessert early, and I removed it just as the first hint of caramel color appeared on top.

It was a damn good-looking tart, if I did say so myself.

Melissa returned the ingredients to their respective cupboards, and I moved on to the peanut soup. I sautéed celery and onion in a stockpot, marveling that my kitchen—*my* kitchen—could smell like a real home. In a bowl, I combined milk and flour to make a slurry that would thicken the final soup. I added chicken broth to my savories and let it come to a slow boil, and I scooped a cup of chunky peanut butter out of its jar. When I had finally scrubbed the excess peanut butter from my knuckles, I set the entire project aside; I'd finish it at the last minute.

That venture went so well that Melissa let me mix the spice rub for the lamb on my own. I read the recipe three times before I measured out the ingredients. Salt, of course, and freshly ground black pepper. Fennel. A pinch of cinnamon, which would have been a treasured rarity in colonial times.

I took the fat chops out of the refrigerator and rubbed in the spice mix. I kept getting distracted by the burgundy polish on my fingernails. Burgundy polish. *My* nails. Almost like I was a grown-up.

The whole time that I was working on the lamb, Melissa kept reading from the witchcraft book, which she had carried upstairs with her. "You can use this thing to clean earth from surfaces."

"Pity we didn't have it when we were cleaning this place the first time." I returned the spices to the cupboard, trying first the top cabinet, then remembering that I'd chosen to keep them next to the stove. Easy access. It all made sense, if I could only remember my rules.

"And you can freshen the air to make it healthful."

"Great. Just think if that book got out in public. Glade would be right out of business."

"You're not taking this very seriously."

"I am," I said, frowning. "I've seen exactly what I can do. Did I tell you that Harold has taken to laying out the newspaper for me in the mornings? He has it waiting at my desk, all neatly turned back to the engagement announcements."

"No!"

"And he stops by at least three times every day. Sometimes I worry that he's going to wake up from his trance, and he'll just stare at me with horror."

"You're not fair to yourself. Spending time with you wouldn't be so horrible."

"I worry that I'm getting used to having him there. Just the other day, he diagnosed a computer problem—one of those blue screens of death. He walked me through some weird menus that he got to through the function keys."

"Good man to have around."

"Yeah. Right." I looked at the production I was putting on for Jason, and I felt a little guilty. I still hadn't found a counterspell for Harold. But I hadn't looked that hard, either. I'd been too busy playing Colonial Martha Stewart. Besides, Jason was smitten with my spell, as well. Jason, and old Mr. Zimmer, and a dozen other men who frequented the library. If I liberated Harold, would I have to liberate all of them? Including my Imaginary Boyfriend?

Squelching an icky feeling in the pit of my belly, I glanced at my cooking notes.

Peanut soup—done, except for the last-minute pulling together.

Lamb chops—ready to broil.

Peas—ready to cook in a small saucepot, while the lamb finished in the oven.

Pear tart—stunning, if I did say so myself.

"Hey," Melissa said. "I think this is actually going to go okay."

"You say that as if you had doubts."

"Um, you? Cooking? Colonial fare?"

I started to splutter, defending myself, but even I couldn't make the argument sound real. Melissa laughed and walked into the living room, collecting her jacket from the couch where she'd thrown it upon her arrival. "Going so soon?" I asked her.

"Soon? It's almost 7:00."

"Yikes!" I had completely lost track of time. As had Neko. I was certain that he'd stopped by Roger's. I started to mutter under my breath, but Melissa read my mind. "Don't worry. He'll be home soon."

"How do you know?"

"The salon closes at seven on Thursdays."

"And how do you know that?"

"Neko told me the other day. I guess he didn't mention it to you? He decided to have Roger over tonight."

"He *what?*"

"Don't worry. He said they'd stay in the basement. He said you'd never even know that they were here."

I was torn between tearing out my hair by the roots and screaming at the Fates. Everything was going to go wrong. I just knew it. "Relax," Melissa said.

"Easy for you to say. You wouldn't be quite so content

if you were suddenly planning on entertaining your Imaginary Boyfriend while your gay familiar got it on with the salon guy downstairs."

"It's all going to be fine," Melissa said in the voice that a perfect nanny uses on her fractious charges. "Some day, you and Jason will laugh about this."

"And if we don't?" I asked darkly, opening the front door for Melissa to leave.

"Then you'll know that he wasn't actually the right man for you. Spell or no spell." She smiled sweetly and ducked outside before I could swat at her. She was a fine one to talk, with her Mama's Boy and McDonald's Owner and who knew what other romantic treasures waiting in the dating wings.

I closed the door and hurried off to shower before the men converged on my cottage.

14

"Ja-ane..." Neko's voice echoed from the living room. I checked my teeth in my bedroom mirror one last time, making sure that nothing green and embarrassing had lodged between them. I ran my fingers through my unruly hair—at least I wasn't wearing a mobcap—and pulled the bottom of my blouse down over my skirt. I lifted my arms so that the hem rode more normally. Leaning over to adjust my bra, I jiggled back and forth to even things out, and then resisted the urge to tug the blouse down one last time.

"Ja-ane! He's at the front of the garden!"

I flung open my bedroom door, scarcely taking the time to close and lock it behind me. For one fleeting moment, I wondered what Jason would think as I led him back here, as we were clinched in the throes of passion, and I needed to dig my key out of my pocket. What kind of freakish woman locks her own bedroom door?

What kind of slut sleeps with a guy on her first date? Even a perfect guy. Even an Imaginary Boyfriend.

I'd changed my sheets, though, just in case.

Wishing that I had invested at least one blouse-tug's worth of time into hunting down a breath mint, I hurried into the living room. "Okay, guys. Downstairs, now. We all need our privacy."

"Don't we?" Neko purred, raking me with his almond eyes.

Roger clicked his tongue against his teeth. "A-plus on the manicure, sweetheart, and the blouse works wonders for your décolletage, but we have *got* to do something about that hair."

"What's wrong with it?" I asked, panicking.

"Nothing," Neko said immediately, splaying a possessive hand across Roger's well-muscled chest. "Nothing at all."

But Roger would not be hustled into silence. "It's just a few inches too long. Too boxy. You have got *cheekbones,* darling, if you'd just learn how to show them off."

A knock at the door saved me from more belated makeover advice. "Get downstairs!" I hissed, starting to run my fingers through my hair again. Would that help, though? Or would it hurt? What if I ruined any possible emphasis on my cheekbones? "Now!"

I never should have let Neko bring Roger back. I should have taken the late wine delivery and sent them packing for the evening. I should have splurged on dinner for both of them, somewhere in Georgetown. Better yet, somewhere on Capitol Hill, all the way across town. Somewhere with atrocious service, so that they'd take at least three hours to eat their food.

There was another knock at the door—this one more insistent. Showtime. As the basement door clicked closed, I took a huge breath that I intended to be calming. And then, I greeted my Imaginary Boyfriend.

"Jason!"

He was perfect. He'd traded in his khakis for gray flannel slacks that managed to look casual and special all at the same time. His sweater picked up the gray, but wove the color into a swirl of blue and green, leaving ample golden highlights to enrich the glints in his curls. His hair was mussed, like that of a little boy who had forgotten to bring a comb.

And he was holding flowers.

Honest to goodness flowers. A mixed bouquet of bright autumn colors—zinnias and gerbera daisies and dahlias and one late sunflower splash. Scott had bought me precisely one wrist corsage in all the years that we had dated. He'd always said that flowers were a waste of time because they only died. Died. Just like romance, when it's left unfed.

"They're beautiful!"

He smiled shyly. "I saw them, and I thought of you. 'There's rosemary, that's for remembrance.'"

A man who read Shakespeare. My heart clenched, and I pulled up another part of Ophelia's speech. "'And pansies, that's for thoughts.'" A shiver swept my spine. Of course, I was quoting the words of a madwoman, a woman insanely in love with a man who did not return the affection. Not a good omen. I shook the rest of the words out of my skull, ordering myself not to dwell on fennel. Or rue.

"Come in," I said, ushering him into my living room. I

finally remembered my best hostess manners. "May I get you a cocktail?"

"Sure. What have you got?"

"You name it, I've got it." I finally took the flowers from him—an awkward motion that resulted in his stepping forward, my jumping back, his easing away from me and my leaping to catch his arm to keep him from toppling over the coffee table.

When we were both standing steady and the flowers were in my hands, I managed to smile, turning my head to the side in an attempt to remind him that I was waiting to serve him a drink. "Um, Scotch, then," he said. "On the rocks."

Hmm. I shouldn't have been so glib about my household bar. "No Scotch. Bourbon? Or anything clear?" Except for rum. I hadn't restocked after the last mojito-therapy night. "Or wine? I have wine!"

He laughed. "Wine sounds perfect."

"Please, have a seat," I said.

"Let me help you."

I immediately pictured the clutter on my kitchen counters. I'd read that there were two things you never wanted to witness being made: sausage and legislation. I'd add another thing to the list: a cozy dinner for two. "The kitchen is tiny," I lied. "I'll be back in just a minute."

He shrugged, and I retreated into the battle zone. Of course, you could see it from the living room. He'd know that I'd lied about the size. I wanted to smack myself on the forehead, but that would have ruined the bouquet.

Bouquet. Flowers. For me.

My heart was doing strange flip-flopping things in my chest, and I was having trouble remembering to breathe. Wasn't that one of those things that your body was supposed to do for you automatically? Keep your lungs moving in and out, without your consciously reminding it?

I opened the drawer to the left of the sink, searching for the corkscrew. None to be found. I *knew* that I kept it there—that was one thing important enough that I wouldn't lose it in my kitchen. I pulled open three other drawers. I stopped and decided to put the flowers in water while I worried about the looming wine disaster.

No vase.

Well, that's what pitchers were for. The mojito one. With fish on the side.

Okay. So the flowers were going to live to see another day, but where had the corkscrew gone? Had Neko made off with it? He'd threatened to come upstairs every half hour, just to keep an eye on Jason and me. To make sure that my Imaginary Boyfriend didn't take advantage of me, he'd said. Maybe stealing the corkscrew was part of his master plan.

I wanted to be taken advantage of. Here. Now.

I took a deep breath and resigned myself to crossing the living room, to knocking on the basement door, to calling downstairs and asking where my conniving familiar had hidden the corkscrew.

"Is everything all right?" Jason called from the living room.

"Fine! Just fine!" And then I saw that it *was* all fine. Neko had followed my instructions to the letter. He had left the bottles of wine on the counter, and he'd opened the first one to breathe. The corkscrew was sitting on the counter, the cork standing guard beside it like a loyal infantryman.

I contemplated taking a solid slug from the mouth of the bottle, but I told myself to wait. I'd be a *lady* tonight. I'd sip delicately.

I poured with a heavy hand.

"Here we go," I said, returning to the living room and raising Jason's glass like the Olympic torch.

"Thanks," he said, taking it from me. "To new beginnings."

I thought that I'd never draw a full breath again. "To new beginnings," I whispered, clinking my glass against his and barely managing to take a sip.

"I always think of the autumn as the start of the year," Jason said, nodding toward the darkened garden outside my windows. "The beginning of the new school year. Meeting new students. Launching new projects."

Oh. So maybe *he and I* weren't beginning anything new. My cheeks flushed, and I didn't know whether to blame the wine or my presumptions. Just for good measure, I took another sip. I wracked my brain for something to say, something witty and endearing and entertaining.

Normally, I don't have any problem talking. I can go on and on; I can be the belle of the conversational ball. Something about Jason, though, left me speechless. It might have been the sight of his fingers around the stem of his wineglass—long fingers, sensitive ones. They looked as if they could work any manner of magic, grimoires or no.

It might have been the light glinting on his eyes. His

eyelashes were really long—longer than any guy should have. I'd never noticed that before, in the daylight of the library. Everything was different here, in my cottage, alone, together. At night.

A loud thump came from the basement.

"What's that?" He looked at the floor, as if it might open up beneath his feet.

"Um, my cat?" Was I asking him, or telling him? "My cat," I repeated. "He's downstairs."

"This place has a downstairs?"

"It has a basement."

"And you keep your cat down there?"

Yeah, what was I? Some heartless wench imprisoning a helpless animal? "No, no, I just put him down there for tonight. I was afraid that you might be allergic."

"Oh, no. I love cats. You can let him out."

Fat chance. "No!" I realized that I sounded too stressed. "I, um, I gave him a treat when I put him down there. He gets really nasty when I interrupt him when he's playing with his...treat."

Jason shrugged. "Maybe I'll see him later, then."

"Maybe."

Well, that was the end of one fantastic conversational gambit. Hopefully, Jason would forget about my phantom house cat before long. There was another thump from downstairs, but we both pretended not to hear it.

"So," I said, "I thought that we'd start with some soup." If I couldn't wow the man with my words, I'd reach him through his belly.

"Sounds great. Is that what smells so good?"

Ah, he was a silver-tongued devil. I answered breezily, as if I spent every day whipping up three-course dinners for two. "That, or maybe the pear tart I baked earlier."

"Wow! You *are* domestic, aren't you?" His praise was like a warm wash, flooding me from head to foot. "You work at the Peabridge all day. You cook in the evenings. What other secrets do you have up your sleeves?"

If he only knew. I'm a witch, I could say. Now *that* was a conversation starter, for sure. Instead, I went for the more traditional "Why don't you just make yourself comfortable in here while I—"

"That's ridiculous," he said. "I'm not going to sit here while you wait on me all night. I won't take no for an answer. Let me help. Or—" he shrugged, and his grin was positively boyish "—at least let me watch. You probably don't want me touching anything. I'm dangerous in a kitchen."

I wasted a split second making the calculation. I could leave him out here, listening for the Neko serenade from below, or I could let him into the kitchen. The directions for the peanut soup really were straightforward. I could risk finishing it, even with the man of my dreams as my audience.

"Well then, come on in."

And he did. He sat next to the counter as I reheated the celery-and-onion mixture on the stove. He watched as I retrieved chicken broth and the milk-and-flour combination from the fridge. He turned his head to the side as I produced the cup of peanut butter.

I felt like I was on some cable-channel cooking show,

demonstrating technique for a crowd of impressed guests. Since Jason and I weren't doing so well on the small-talk front, I decided I might as well fill him in on the cooking process. "So, now I just pour in this chicken broth, and I wait for it to boil."

"You look so intense when you do that."

Intense. I was trying to keep from splashing broth onto my low-cut blouse. I should have thrown on an apron, but I didn't want him to think that I was some 1950s house Frau.

"Wait a minute!" he said, and his tone was so sharp that I almost stopped stirring the soup. "Peanut soup. Pear tart." He spun back to the counter and found the basket with the muffins, the ones that Melissa had baked earlier in the day. "Sweet potato and pecan muffins! Thomas Jefferson! You're making Thomas Jefferson's favorite meal."

He got it. He understood. It was as if I'd reached out to him through a code, a secret language, and he'd deciphered everything. He truly understood me. "You figured it out!"

"Then that means that you've got mutton for the main course! And peas. You must have peas somewhere."

"In the fridge. And, um, lamb, not mutton."

"I don't even know who *sells* mutton these days," he said.

"Exactly!" We laughed, and for the first time that evening I felt confident that I might—I just possibly, conceivably, potentially might—make this whole Imaginary to Real transition happen.

When our shared laughter had finished, he looked away. He cleared his throat, as if he were about to say something, but his eyes fell on the book. *Elemental Magick.* Melissa had left it on the counter, beside the pear tart.

"What's this?"

"Oh, nothing." I would have slipped it out of his hands, tucked it away out of sight, but my fingers were coated with the peanut butter that I was trying to coax from the measuring cup. Somehow, I didn't think that Julia Child ever had these problems.

"It looks ancient! It's certainly from before my dates."

His dates. Colonial America. The field that I specialized in, at the day job that he knew all too well. I thought quickly and forced a bright smile. "It's from before my own, also. I'm branching out a bit. Taking some library continuing education courses."

"And they let you keep rare books in your kitchen?" He lifted it with a scholar's reverence, easing open the cover to peer inside. "What sort of program lets you do that?"

"It's not really a program," I hedged. "It's more like independent study." I finally managed to get the peanut butter out of the measuring cup and into the soup, but I didn't back up quickly enough to escape the resulting *plop.* My blouse was drenched.

"Dammit!" I swore without thinking. I grabbed for a dish towel and tried to mop the worst of the damage from my cleavage. It was hot, but not bad enough to burn me. The fat from the soup would stain the fabric, though. At least it was black. That was part of the method to my fashion madness—stains were virtually unnoticeable on my wardrobe.

"Are you okay?" Jason looked up, but he didn't move toward me.

This was why I'd wanted him to wait in the other room.

This was why I hadn't wanted him to watch me cook. I was embarrassed to find hot tears rising behind my eyes, embarrassment spilling over.

"Hey," he said, setting down the spell book. Well, at least I'd distracted him from the magic. He still kept to his half of the kitchen, though. He must be mortified that he was wasting an evening on a klutz like me. "Don't worry about it," he said.

"I'm sorry! I didn't realize that it was going to splash all over."

"I wouldn't have, either. I'm totally helpless in the kitchen. I can't even fix myself a turkey sandwich."

Chagrined by my own incompetence and thinking that I would have done better to order in two turkey sandwiches from Subway, I was horrified to feel two huge tears escaping down my cheeks. I suddenly remembered watching him with Ekaterina in the hamburger joint. She had been crying then. She had looked gorgeous, despite her tears. I would *not;* I knew that. I would look like a goggle-eyed carp. The thought of my red nose and swollen eyes was terrifying enough that it immediately desiccated my tear ducts.

"And besides," he said, before I could find a way to maneuver the conversation around to Ekaterina, before I could find out something more about the ice ballerina, "I've been standing over here trying to figure out how to tell you something."

I took a deep breath. This could not be good. Something that he had to think about. Something that he had to debate. Something that worried him. Something that kept him all the way on the far side of the kitchen. "What?"

"I'm allergic to peanuts."

My rush of relief nearly made my knees buckle. In one panicked flash, I'd imagined much worse. I'd suddenly expected him to tell me that he was married. That he and Ekaterina had two perfect children and a Labrador retriever named Molly. That he secretly lusted after *Neko* and had only accepted my dinner offer because he'd seen my familiar lurking about the cottage. That he had agreed to come to dinner because he was involved in a sociological experiment that measured what hopeless, awkward, plain women find attractive about accomplished, gorgeous, entertaining professors.

He just couldn't eat the food that I'd prepared.

"No problem!" I turned off the burner with a precision usually reserved for aborting missile launches.

"I'm sorry. I should have said something when you first took out the peanut butter, but I was so surprised."

"I didn't exactly give you a chance."

"But you planned everything, and now I've ruined your colonial menu."

"The proportions would be off, anyway. Now that I'm wearing half of it." I managed a bemused shrug.

He laughed, and I joined him after only a few heartbeats of hesitation. Then he said, "When you told me you'd locked up your cat because you thought I might be allergic, I almost said something about this stupid peanut thing, but I figured, what are the chances that you'd serve them?"

I glanced at the bread in Melissa's basket. "How are you on pecans?"

"Just fine."

"And gingersnaps?"

"Not a problem."

"And lamb?"

"My favorite."

"Peas?"

"The finest of all the legumes."

I grinned. "I think we're still in business, then."

He finally took a step closer, as if he'd realized that he would not actually collapse from the peanut infestation on top of the stove. "You know, you have a beautiful smile."

I looked down, unable to meet his eyes. That shy glance let me realize that my Miracle Bra was outlined perfectly against my soaking blouse. I shrugged, but the fabric didn't move. The silence was stretching to something uncomfortable, so I reached for a feeble joke. "You must say that to all the girls."

"It's the truth." He reached out and touched my chin with his finger. With gentle pressure, he made me raise my eyes. I was suddenly preternaturally aware of my smudged eyeglasses. "I notice you at the library every day I'm there."

And then he kissed me. Jason Templeton kissed me. Standing in my kitchen, surrounded by herbs and spices and the makings of poisonous peanut soup, Jason Templeton kissed me.

I'd like to say that it was the finest kiss I've ever experienced. I'd like to describe how he made me feel, what he did to my swooning body. I'd like to explain how this kiss was like no other I'd ever known, that it was better and deeper and more meaningful on a hundred different levels.

But all I could think was that I was covered in chicken

broth and standing dangerously close to a cupful of potent allergen, some of which was certainly still on my fingers. I could kill him, then and there. I could send my Imaginary Boyfriend into anaphylactic shock and spend the rest of my life explaining to the police that I'd never meant to harm him, that it had all been Thomas Jefferson's fault.

I waited for Jason to come up for air before I took a step back. "I'm a mess," I explained, when he looked confused. I managed a steadying breath and transformed it into a laugh. "Here. I'm going to turn on the broiler so that we can cook the lamb. You must be starving." As I suited action to words, he grinned wolfishly and pretended to lick his lips. "For food!" I said, laughing and playfully pushing him away, but taking care to use my noncontaminated forearm. "I'm just going to change into—"

"Something more comfortable?" He was totally irresistible when he grinned.

"Something a little dryer. I'll be back in just a moment."

"Don't take too long. I might try to work those spells in *Elemental Magick.*"

"Be my guest," I said, laughing and shaking my head. I hurried across the living room, managing to palm the key to my bedroom door and open it smoothly.

Once the door was safely closed, I collapsed against it, fighting down a fit of giggles. Jason Templeton had kissed me. He had stood in my kitchen, put his arms around me and kissed me.

I was *so* over Scott Randall. I was on my way to true love and eternal happiness. Melissa had her First Date system, but I had knowledge and planning and foresight. I'd had the courage to ask my Imaginary Boyfriend to dinner, and now everything was, um, slipping into place.

I stripped off my blouse and tossed it into the corner of my closet. I could deal with it tomorrow, have Neko take it to the dry cleaner to see if it could be saved. For tonight, though, what would I put on?

Casual T-shirt, right out. Clingy crop top, would have been perfect about ten pounds ago. Sheer oxford-cut to accentuate curves, ideal—except that the middle button had an annoying tendency to pop open. I was not about to limit my options for the evening by applying a safety pin for protection.

Slinky wraparound that tied on the side. Yes. That was perfect. It said, I am sophisticated, yet fun. It said, I am available, but I'm not an utter slut. It said, you want me, you know you really do.

I was slipping the garment from its hanger when I was interrupted by the most piercing Klaxon I'd ever heard.

15

Chaos.

Complete and utter chaos.

The piercing whistle continued as I stumbled into my living room, frantically wrapping my new blouse around my still-damp bra. The door to the basement was gaping open, and Neko was standing beside Roger, crowding the way to the kitchen. I plunged past them, terrified about what I would find.

Smoke billowed out of the oven in greasy black clouds. The uninterrupted shrieking was the smoke detector, letting me know that my house was on fire. And Jason was standing on the far side of the kitchen, looking like a deer trapped in someone's headlights.

When I moved into the cottage, I had told myself to get a fire extinguisher. Melissa had suggested it on that first day, but we'd forgotten when we were at Target, buying all our cleaning supplies. She'd already told me the brand to get, the one that would be useful on grease fires. The one that could have saved me now, if I'd remembered.

I could barely think with the smoke detector's constant shrieking.

I grabbed for a dish towel, taking a hurried moment to wrap the cloth around my hand. Reaching for the oven door, I tried to open it quickly. The motion felt silly, helpless, like the softball throw that had made me the laughingstock of third-grade gym class. Steeling myself (and filling my lungs with too much greasy smoke), I tugged the door open. And then I realized my mistake.

Oxygen feeds a fire.

I grabbed for the mojito pitcher, full of water and flowers. Before I could throw the entire thing into the oven's maw, Neko knocked the container to the floor, sending the flowers flying. "Not on a grease fire!" He managed to convey the same horror he might have expressed if I had proposed wearing white shoes after Labor Day.

He was right. "Smother it!" I exclaimed, finally remembering my one summer at Girl Scout camp. Drop and roll. Well, I didn't have a fireproof, outdoor sleeping bag at the ready, but I recalled the principle. "Roger!" He was closest to the couch in the living room. "The throw!"

He somehow figured out what I was saying, even above the penetrating scream of the smoke detector. Damn that thing! It should have some sort of wall switch, so that I could turn it off and deal with an actual emergency without going deaf in the process.

Roger tossed me the blanket—his overhand throw was more girlish than my own. I wasted a few moments shaking it out, hoping it would cover more area. Then, I hurtled it toward the oven.

In theory, that should have worked. The blanket should have smothered the flames and cut off the oxygen that was feeding them. Everything should have been fine, and I should have earned my Fire Safety merit badge.

Except the blanket had been made out of something flammable.

The greedy flames crackled as they grabbed hold of the material; for one short moment, the fire was actually louder than the smoke detector. Then, the flames began to work their way down the throw, onto the linoleum floor, where the ends of the blanket trailed after my imperfect toss.

"Jane!" Neko's voice rang out, sharp and clear over the shrieking detector. I turned to him in panic, wondering just how long we had before the floor caught along with the walls. This cottage was ancient; it had to be as dry as kindling. And Jason was still on the other side of the oven, still frozen into place.

Neko called my name again, and this time he sounded strangely calm. My excitable familiar might have been summoning me to a discussion on the merits of beige over ecru, for all the emotion in his voice. I realized that he held a book in his hands. *Elemental Magick*.

It was open to a page in the middle. A page that I was willing to bet Neko had not chosen at random.

I crossed to him.

He leaned in toward my side, putting his mouth right

beside my ear. He held the book in front of us, and his fingers rested lightly beneath the words. "Take a breath," he said, and I did. "Now exhale. Again. Exhale. Calm yourself. Take another breath. Deeper. Exhale. One more time."

He sounded perfectly centered, perfectly calm, as if we did this exercise every single day. In a flash, I was reminded of Melissa's yoga teacher, the woman whose constant droning about breathing and holding postures and reaching for the quiet inside us made me fall asleep in Corpse Pose.

"Very good," Neko said, and now I could listen to him and hold his words separate from the screech of the smoke detector, apart from the crackle of the flames that wanted to take over my kitchen. "Now, take your right index finger and touch your head to offer up your pure thoughts. Touch your throat to offer up your pure speech. Touch your heart to offer up your pure belief." I did as he said, and each time my finger landed against my flesh, something thrummed deep inside my mind. I felt as if I were in the middle of a child's game, suspended on a string stretched between two tin cans. Power vibrated around me, through me, in me.

"Now," Neko said, "read the words." I started to argue. There were strangers around us, people who did not know about my powers. "No," he said, his voice still given over to that eerie calm. "Read. The rest will follow. Read."

And so I read.

"Good and evil, loss and gain
Flame is savior, flame is bane
On a bitter winter night
Fire might preserve a wight

Flames unbound can lead to ruin
Lives destroyed, possessions strewn.
Learn the power of the fire,
Note its strength within the pyre.
Tame the flames by calling other
Powers of the world to smother
Balance water, air and earth
Push back fire, salvage worth."

For a moment, nothing happened. After all, it couldn't be so simple. Who was I to think that I could control one of the four elemental forces of the universe? Me—Jane Madison? A librarian who couldn't even make a single date work out? A witch who didn't know the first thing about her powers?

But then, I saw a shimmer in the air. It was a curtain surrounding the flames. I sensed the pure essence of water, *knew* it with my witchy senses. It looked like a waterfall made up of the finest droplets possible, suspended in the middle of my kitchen. I poured my thoughts into the curtain, summoning up all of the tingling power that I'd ever felt and transferring it into the wall of water.

I was terrified by the whoosh as the fire consumed the sheer liquid conjuring, but that sound was immediately dampened by a sudden heaviness in the air. The weight of the atmosphere in my kitchen had doubled, trebled. It felt like the pressure was dropping before a hurricane; I was crushed beneath the airless weight of a ferocious weather system, the kind that made old bones ache and migraines blossom. Its pressure smothered the remaining flames, beating them out as if they were trapped beneath an invisible flame-retardant blanket.

Sparkling dust coalesced from the heavy air. It fell like gritty snow, sifting down on the already-cooling remnants of the fire. It was like a pulverized earth, volcanic stone exploding into the tiniest fragments imaginable. The dust drifted down in silence, catching the light in the room, sparkling like a million diamond shards. It ensured that no whisper of flame survived.

The fire was out.

But the smoke detector was still shrieking. I grabbed one of the kitchen chairs and dragged it across the room, so that I could step up and retrieve the battery. Neko moved like my shadow, and I put a hand on his shoulder to steady myself before I climbed onto the seat. It took three tugs to get the plastic case off, before I could reach the nine-volt battery. My fingers slipped twice, but I finally wrenched the power source free.

The silence was so sudden that I wondered if I'd been struck deaf. But no, I heard Jason's slacks rustle as he finally stepped forward. I heard Roger breathing deeply as he tugged his tight T-shirt down over his six-pack abs, which had been on display after whatever basement romp the fire had interrupted.

And I heard Neko whisper, "Okay, Jane. We're all done here." Then he stepped back and raised his voice for everyone to hear. "What *are* we going to do with you, Jane? Three alarms are fine for a chili cookoff, but they really put a crimp in a boy's love life."

I was still standing on the chair. My knees were turning to jelly, though, and it seemed as if I hadn't filled my lungs since Neko had told me to take those cleansing breaths. I reached out for his shoulder, but he stepped away, gesturing toward Jason.

And my Imaginary Boyfriend finally moved to my side. "What the hell is going on here?" He sounded more frightened than angry. I leaned on him a little more heavily than strictly necessary as I stepped down, but he didn't get the idea. He didn't sweep me off my feet and carry me into the next room, lay me down on the couch and fan my flushed face with fathomless concern.

Instead, he stared at my stove as if it had been possessed. Then, he turned those disbelieving eyes on me.

Before I could muster a response, Neko stepped forward. He cocked his head to one side, executing one of his perfect single-eyebrow arches. I knew that he was evaluating Jason's every move, measuring out every drop of manliness my Imaginary Boyfriend had to offer. When Neko presented his hand to Jason, he kept his wrist just lax enough that there could be no mistaking his intentions. Or, rather, his preferences. "I'm Neko," he said. "And you must be Jason. Charmed." My familiar turned to me and grinned. "Yummy."

Jason shook the offered hand, but he looked at me in confusion. He blinked hard, and I was reminded of a child waking up from a too-long nap. He started three different questions before he settled on "What just happened here?"

I worked a spell in front of you. Just a little something I've been working on in my spare time. Witchcraft, you know. It's all the rage in library circles these days.

I sighed and said, "I don't know. It must have taken longer for the blanket to smother the fire than I thought it would."

"But you stood there." Jason pointed to the spot that Neko and I had occupied. "I watched you. You read from that book, and the fire went out."

"I must have panicked." The explanation sounded lame, even to me. "While I was waiting for the blanket to work. I'd been reading about the fire spell before you got here—my subconscious must have grabbed at straws."

"*Something* happened when you read those words. I couldn't see clearly—it was like there was some silvery curtain or something. But the fire died down."

"Silvery curtain?" I looked at Neko, desperate for help, but he only gave an elaborate shrug. "It must have been something in the blanket. Some strange chemical reaction when it came in contact with the flames."

Jason shook his head, but he didn't really have an option, other than to accept my explanation. After all, it wasn't like any ordinary, everyday, red-blooded male was going to believe in magic. He let himself become distracted enough to nod toward Neko. "And where did *he* come from?"

"Downstairs?" I said, and realized that it sounded like I was asking a question. "Downstairs," I repeated firmly.

"With your cat?"

"Um, there is no cat. There's only Neko."

"Only!" Neko repeated, and he sounded scandalized.

"Well, Neko and Roger," I amended, gesturing toward the sculpted stylist, who was now fully clothed. "Neko's my, um, tenant. He lives in the basement. Roger is his friend."

"And you said you had a cat because?"

Because I didn't want you distracted by the thought of the passionate man-man love being made one floor below us, I thought. I didn't say that, though. I just sort of shrugged. Roger stepped forward and saved the day. "So, that old blanket trick really works? I thought it was just something they told you about in Scouts."

And when had *he* ever been a Scout? Nevertheless, I could have kissed the man, deflecting attention like that. "Apparently so."

There was a knock at my door.

I should have expected it. By the time I crossed into the living room, I knew who would be there. Not the fire department, dispatched to save the day. Not Dan Savage, ready to research another exciting "Savage Love" sexual-advice column with the plethora of men in my kitchen.

"David!" I said, as my warder swept into my living room. I tried to make it sound like I was surprised to see him, even as I worked to convey a hidden message, a mental telegraph. I wanted to tell him to get out of my house and let me get my dream date back on track. I settled for the more direct use of speech. "I was just about to finish cooking dinner for my guest."

"I'm sorry to interrupt," David said, barely playing along enough to sound civil. He strode directly into my kitchen.

I took a deep breath and began the unavoidable introductions. "David, I don't think that you've met Roger, Neko's friend." The men exchanged somewhat wary handshakes. "And this is Jason Templeton." I sighed and gestured toward my Imaginary Boyfriend. "Jason, this is David Montrose. He's the, um, mentor I mentioned earlier. The one who is guiding my independent study."

Jason glanced at *Elemental Magick* as he offered his hand.

The book now looked perfectly harmless, resting on the countertop where Neko had placed it after our fire-dowsing. "David," he said, offering his hand.

"Professor." David shook, but his voice was flat. It barely warmed when he turned to me. "Jane, we need to talk."

"Can't it wait?"

"No."

"Look," I said, and I must have recovered from the shock of everything, because I could feel anger shortening my breath. "This has not been my dream night, okay? First, I almost burned the pear tart because the oven runs hot. Then, I came close to poisoning Jason with peanut soup. As you can see, the oven caught fire while I was preheating the broiler. I do not have time to talk to you, David. Not tonight."

If I had not known better, I would have said that a smile tugged at David's lips as I cataloged my catastrophes. He managed to sound sincere, though, when he said, "There are just a couple of details that we need to work out. Tonight. There are some problems that have come up with your…independent study, and I would hate for the *administration* to get involved." As if to emphasize his words, he laid a protective hand on my elbow.

Jason stepped forward, glancing at that hand, and then at my face. "Look, Jane. Maybe I *should* head home."

I shrugged off David's grasp in annoyance. "But we haven't eaten!"

Neko looked at the lamb chops on the counter. "I wouldn't trust the oven," he said helpfully. "But I've heard that lamb tartare is considered a delicacy in some parts of the world."

Jason looked repulsed, either by the notion of eating raw lamb, or the thought of spending another minute with me. "You probably *should* get someone to check that oven. We'll do this again, though. Sometime soon."

"But I baked a pear tart!"

Jason glanced at it with barely masked horror, as if he believed it might fly from the countertop and attempt to choke him. "And I'm sure it's wonderful. Look, you can bring it into the library tomorrow. I'm sure you could sell slices to go with lattes. It would give a real colonial feel to the library."

"Jason—" By now he had edged around David and made his way past Neko and Roger. His hand settled on the door latch. I crossed the living room, trying to pretend like I was the perfect hostess, like this sort of thing happened all the time, and didn't we all just love the quirkiness of it?

"Thanks for everything, Jane. The… Well, the glass of wine was great."

"Yeah," I said miserably. "Thank you for the flowers."

I resisted the urge to look at the trampled blossoms spread across my kitchen floor. I'd like to think that Jason would have kissed me good-night if we hadn't had a full audience watching from the kitchen, but somehow, I doubt he would have. I closed the door and leaned my head against it. One deep breath was not enough. Nor two. Nor three.

I was going to have to face them all some time. I steeled myself and turned around.

David was just slipping his wallet into his back pocket, and Neko was palming several bills. "Right," my familiar whispered, but I think that he intended me to hear. "Roger and I will have a 'late supper.' At Bistro Bis. On Capitol Hill." He winked and put his hand on Roger's shoulder.

They slipped past me, closing the door quietly behind them. I came to stand beside David, surveying the wreckage in my kitchen. "Well," he finally said. "At least you weren't frivolous about using your magic this time."

"I'd pretty much run out of other options." Even though I was tired, even though I was embarrassed, even though I wanted to sob about the mess I'd made of my perfect date, I somehow found myself smiling.

The entire thing was absurd. Magic on a first date. My gay familiar making loud thumps from downstairs. My culinary talents stretched to their maximum extension.

At least I didn't have to pretend for the rest of the night. David already knew I wasn't perfect. He already knew that I wasn't the ideal girlfriend. He already knew that I made mistakes—and plenty of them. I could relax around him.

"Come on," he said. "Let's go."

"Where?"

"I'll take you out to dinner. We'll get something safe. Something cooked in someone else's kitchen."

I started to protest, but then I looked around. My kitchen looked as if the Battle of Agincourt had been fought across its tiled floor. The mess from making dinner had sifted into the debris from extinguishing the fire. I should clean it up as best I could and then tumble into bed.

Before I could say anything, though, I realized that I was truly exhausted. The adrenaline from working my spell had pumped away, and I was left with a bone-weariness that could only be partially ascribed to ruining my date with

Jason. I looked into David's guileless face, recognized his offer for the kindness that it was. "Thank you," I said. "I'd like that. Very much."

16

The next day, I conferred with Melissa, and she suggested that I bring the pear tart to Gran's apartment. It's a good thing that she remembered my social calendar—I had completely forgotten that I was supposed to help Gran with a little party she was hosting for the concert opera guild board of directors.

A soiree, she called it. They were putting the finishing touches on plans for their Harvest Gala, their biggest fundraising event of the year. With only two weeks left until the fete, there wasn't much to be done, but the board members enjoyed each other's company, and Gran never passed up a chance to use her fine china.

A gathering of operaphiles was not my first choice for a Friday-night date, particularly since I was still exhausted from the night before. David had rewarded my hard work by taking me to Paparazzi, a late-night Italian restaurant down by the canal. The waiter had rolled his eyes at my order of baked ravioli, but he had conceded that the kitchen was still open despite the relatively late hour. I had not even realized that the pasta came with mozzarella cheese—stringy, baked mozzarella cheese—until after I ordered, but I decided to take my chances. After all, this wasn't a first date, so Melissa's food rules did not apply.

David and I had talked until they threw us out of the place—at nearly one in the morning. We'd avoided witchcraft and Jason Templeton, managing to fill in a couple of hours of light conversation about favorite foods, treasured childhood books and dream vacations.

My late-night activities had made for a long day at the office—a day made longer by the arrival of a thin envelope from one of the foundations I had queried about grants. That envelope contained a parsimonious half sheet of paper with a form letter that had been photocopied so many times the words were scarcely legible. I made out the message, though. The Peabridge could not expect any funding from the Institute of Library Preservation.

Oh well. There were more fish in that sea. Twelve more, in fact. I tried not to let myself get depressed. After all, Eleanor didn't know that I was trying to track down grants. I didn't need to admit my failure to her.

By the time evening rolled around, I resorted to a Starbucks latte with an extra shot of espresso just to keep awake. No, I don't drink coffee. But lattes are medicinal.

Especially when I hadn't seen my grandmother since I'd run out on her at the Four Seasons. At least we'd spoken on the phone several times in the past few days.

Ostensibly, I was invited to this meeting as the Voice of Youth. (I could hear a chamberlain introducing me at the Gala: "Miss Jane Madison. The Voice of Youth." Smattering of applause as I swept into the ballroom wearing a stunning gown and tiara.) The entire board wanted my opinion about what "You Young People" thought about the Harvest Gala. Apparently, We Young People all think alike, act alike and donate to charities alike.

Would You Young People mind paying for your drinks at a cash bar? (Yes, and we'd be more inclined to donate if we felt indebted to the guild for our liquor.) Was it sufficient to have wine and soft drinks, or was the hard stuff mandatory for You Young People? (Not mandatory, but "spirits" would loosen a lot of wallets.) Should the dress code be strictly black tie, or would that frighten off You Young People? (They should label it black tie; people would wear what they had in their closets.)

I'm not sure why I got to make all the decisions, but it made Gran happy for me to help out. Besides, where else was I going to get such excellent counseling on my love life?

"Wonderful to see you," Uncle George said, kissing my cheek after I let myself in the front door. "Doesn't that tart look delicious! And homemade? That's where you've gone wrong, Jane dear. You should advertise your baking skills more. *They* will help you find a good man."

If he only knew how my cooking had worked the night before. Or that Melissa was still frustratedly single, despite being a baker extraordinaire. He only meant well, though. "Thanks, Uncle George."

"Your grandmother is in the kitchen."

I thanked him again and threaded my way through the gathering in the living room—a dozen opera fans whose average age was higher than the freeway speed limit. What did it matter, the advice that I gave at these meetings? Concert opera just did not attract young listeners; I could not think of a single person my age who went.

In fact, with a few exceptions—Bugs Bunny cartoons or the *Marriage of Figaro* scene from *The Shawshank Redemption*—I could not think of any opera that was familiar to my peers. Certainly none that would make them fork over thousands of dollars to support the arts.

I sighed. If I could find a few enthusiastic opera lovers, I might be able to identify someone to help support the Peabridge. I'd been upset enough about the morning's rejection letter that I'd crumpled it and tossed it into my wastebasket. *That* led poor besotted Harold to hurry across the lobby and ask me if anything was wrong with the way he'd delivered my mail. It had taken nearly half an hour to reassure him, although I think that part of that time he was dragging his feet, purposely staying on to have a few more minutes to bask in the glory of my presence. Yeah. Right.

And I need hardly add that Jason had not shown up at the library that afternoon. Not that he ever did on Fridays, but still. He could have called. To make sure that I was all right. That I hadn't burned down anything else.

"Jane, dear! Why so glum?" Gran looked up from the counter, where she was pouring coffee into a monstrous silver pot.

"Nothing, Gran." I brushed a kiss against her cheek,

noticing how flushed she was in the close heat of the kitchen. "Let me take care of that."

"What a beautiful tart! To what do I owe the pleasure?"

The greatest disaster of my dating life, I thought of saying. That would only worry her, though. "I had the pears sitting around, and I thought you'd enjoy the treat."

"How sweet of you!" Gran nodded toward a pink cardboard box. "You'll put my store-bought cookies to shame."

Her cookies *were* shameful, but not because she bought them in a store. If she'd stopped by Cake Walk, for example, she could have had any number of toothsome treats. Instead, Gran insisted on buying from the Watergate Bakery. The name was prestigious, but the sweets hadn't been updated since Nixon was a boy—there were plenty of pink ladyfingers and a passel of green leaf-shaped cookies, all of which crumbled into dusty remnants when you picked them up.

Gran and I made small talk as I sat down on the floor, reaching back into the deep cabinets to retrieve her china cups and saucers, along with the dessert plates that were her pride and joy. She had polished her silver earlier in the day; the dessert forks gleamed on the countertop.

When everything was ready to be carried into the other room, Gran laid a hand on my arm. "I'm so sorry, dear. I heard that things did not go well when you met your mother."

For one brief moment, I thought that Melissa must have phoned Gran, must have filled her in on the unhappy reunion. I quickly realized, though, that Clara had done the dirty work herself. She'd probably called my grandmother straightaway, reporting on all of my perceived shortcomings.

"Yeah, well…" I shrugged and tried to figure out an explanation. Not an excuse, mind you. I didn't have anything to excuse. Just a reason why things had not gone as Gran had hoped.

"Your mother felt just terrible, dear. She worried that she'd put too much pressure on you, that she overwhelmed you with too much information all at once."

I shrugged again, feeling like a teenager who had lost the last vestige ability to communicate with her elders. If I weren't careful, I was going to be reduced to a vocabulary consisting entirely of exasperated sighs, eye rolls and deep grunts. I made myself say, "I think that too much time has gone by, Gran. If we were ever going to find a way to talk to each other, it had to be years ago."

Gran's lips thinned into a grayish line. "We're never so old that we don't need people who love us."

"Gran, that woman doesn't love me! She doesn't even know me! At most, she loves the *idea* of me, a perfect little girl that she tragically lost so many years ago."

My grandmother shook her head. "I don't expect you to understand, Jane. You've never had children, so you don't know what it's like." That's right. Let's turn this conversation into a referendum on my floundering love life and nonexistent children. Gran went on, though, obviously unaware of how much her words bothered me. "You can't imagine how it feels, Jane. A mother is always connected to her children. She always feels the bond that once fed them, nourished them, kept them safe and sound—"

Gran would have gone on (was she really waxing eloquent about the umbilical cord, or was there something else she was getting at?) but she started coughing. She made a terrible noise, deep and wheezing, as if her lungs were melting inside her chest.

"Gran!" I said, throwing an arm around her waist to support her. She felt so frail, so tiny. For one terrible moment, I realized that my grandmother was old. Not old as in she-liked-opera. But old. Old as in she-was-going-to-die-someday. Old.

Her face turned crimson with the exertion of her coughing, and she turned away from me. I didn't know whether she was trying to hide her weakness or just keep her face away from the counter, the cups and the food. The motion, though, only served to make her look more vulnerable.

I grabbed a glass and filled it with water, but she waved me away. By then, she was able to snag great shuddering breaths in between coughs. Tears pricked at the corners of her eyes, but I wasn't sure if she was crying from emotion or physical effort.

When the coughing finally died away, she accepted the water, sipping it slowly. After emptying the glass, she set it firmly on the counter. She gathered up her apron and used the hem to wipe at her eyes. She turned to the sink and washed her hands, lathering them up like a surgeon getting ready to enter the operating room.

"Gran!" I said, when she started to pick up the saucers as

if nothing had happened. "How long have you had that cough?"

"It comes and goes."

"Comes and goes! It sounds like you've got pneumonia!"

"It's allergies. You know, the changing seasons always get to me."

I knew that spring always got to her. Spring, and its pollen. My grandmother had never had a problem with ragweed, or mold or burning leaves. As if anyone still burned leaves in the fall. "You've never had problems in September before."

"I'm *fine,* Jane. Just fine." She patted my hand and turned to the door, only to draw herself up short. "If you really are worried, though, there is one thing you can do, dear."

"What?" I would do whatever she asked. Run out to the drugstore. Phone her doctor's emergency line. Take her to the hospital.

"Make me a promise."

"Gran!"

"Promise me that we'll go to the Smithsonian next Saturday. A week from tomorrow. The Natural History Museum, like we used to visit when you were a little girl."

"Gran, I haven't—"

"Promise me! The three of us will go—you, me and your mother."

I wanted to say no. I wanted to tell her that I had work to do. I wanted to make up some hot date, or some important library meeting, or some absolute need to wash my hair.

But her coughing fit had frightened me. My grandmother wasn't going to be around to extract promises forever.

And, I had to admit, there was a teeny, tiny part of me that wanted to give Clara one more try. After all, she was my biological mother. And we'd spent less than an hour together. Her whole cult thing couldn't possibly be as alarming as I'd made it out to be. And she certainly couldn't be as into crystals as she'd seemed.

"All right, Gran. Next Saturday."

"Wonderful. We'll meet at the elephant. At ten."

The giant bull elephant was in the building's rotunda; it greeted thousands of amazed tourists every single day. I had marveled at him when I was a little girl, inventing long, involved stories about his elephant wife and elephant children, and their happy lives in the African bush. Father, mother, perfect kids. Life was simple back then.

"Now you bring in the tart, dear. We'll serve it out here." Then my grandmother swept into the living room, apologizing for her delay and serving up coffee, tea, tart and crumbling cookies.

I found myself sitting next to Samuel Potter, an old friend of Uncle George's and the newest member of the concert opera guild board. "So, Jane," he said. There was a glimmer in his eye, and I suspected that he pulled coins out of his own granddaughters' ears. "Do you come to these little get-togethers every month?"

"Oh, no. Only when I can help with the Gala planning." That sounded wrong, as if I thought there was something wrong with opera, or with the board gatherings. I added, "I'm usually too busy at work."

"And where do you work?"

"At the Peabridge Library."

"Is that part of D.C. Public?"

I knew two things by the way he asked the question. First, he was a librarian, or someone he knew was one. We librarians were all hip-and-happening folks; we dropped *Library* from the names of major systems because we all knew what we were talking about. I had once dreamed of being a reference librarian at New York City Public, until Melissa told me that I sounded totally affected, phrasing it that way.

The other thing, though, was more important: My magic spell was still working. I recognized the expression on Mr. Potter's face; I'd come to know it well over the past couple of weeks. He was nowhere near as smitten as poor Harold Weems, but Mr. Potter was attracted to me. Not in an icky, dirty old man way. Rather, in an avuncular way. I thought that he might buy me a box of salt water taffy, or invite me to an ice cream social. And there was a part of me that was pleased to have that effect on him.

I really had meant to ask David about that spell. About ways to soften its effect, or to withdraw it altogether. I'd forgotten, though, the night before. We'd had too many other things to talk about.

Withdrawing from the only good memory of the night before, I smiled at Mr. Potter. "No, the Peabridge is a private library. We specialize in colonial America."

"Ah! I've walked by your place! You're over by the university, right? In the heart of Georgetown?"

I agreed that we were. Mr. Potter told me that he took his

dog for a walk near us almost every evening. The shih tzu had actually belonged to *Mrs.* Potter, but poor Lucinda had passed away about six months before. She was the one who had been a librarian, a cataloger. She'd always loved the profession.

"I'm sorry that I didn't have the chance to meet her, Mr. Potter."

"Aren't you a dear." He patted my hand. "She spoiled that silly dog as if it were her own flesh-and-blood baby. We were never blessed with children."

So much for his pulling coins from his granddaughters' ears. Now I wanted to pat *his* hand. He shook his head, though, as if he were well-accustomed to changing his mood by force of will. "So tell me, dear. What do you do at the Peabridge?"

"I'm a reference librarian by training." Because I was at the board meeting of an arts society, I felt compelled to add, "But I've become involved with development lately." Development. Not fund-raising. I'd picked up the lingo in the course of drafting my grant applications.

"Have you now? What sort of projects are you working on?"

"I've started to apply for grant funding. We've got several specific projects that we want to take on, cataloging our collection of manuscripts, developing a system to track all of our ephemera."

"Ah… My Lucinda would have loved to talk to you about those things. When we lived in Indianapolis, she got our little opera library in order. She organized all of the sheet music, along with the archives of programs, production notes…"

"She sounds like a very interesting woman. Dedicated, too."

"She would have loved the Harvest Gala," Mr. Potter said. His eyes started to look sad again, but he speared a bite of pear tart into his mouth. "Oh! This is wonderful!" He smiled at me conspiratorially. "Much better than those nasty cookies from the Watergate."

I laughed out loud, and then I needed to make up an explanation when Uncle George asked me what was so funny. I didn't want him to think that I disrespected Gran's choices, even if she did woefully misjudge baked goods.

The rest of the evening passed quickly. Gran led the review of plans for the Gala. Ticket sales were strong. The reach-out program to local universities seemed to have worked; there were more young people (everyone turned to smile at me) than the guild had seen in years. The caterer was an opera fan himself, and he was upgrading the hors d'oeuvres as a donation to the guild. The silent auction was organized; a fussy-looking woman sitting on the chaise longue had agreed to print out the bid sheets on her home computer.

In fact, the meeting would have been perfect, if Gran had not succumbed to two more coughing fits. The first one left her surrounded by her fellow board members, each trying to help in perfectly ineffective ways, passing over glasses of water, trying to fan her with napkins, patting the backs of her hands. The second fit must have given her some warning; she said that she had something to check on in the kitchen and escaped before it grabbed hold completely.

I followed her out of the room, trying to avoid setting off an alarm among the guests even as I moved quickly. The spasm wasn't as bad as its predecessors, and Gran caught her breath quickly. "Silly me. I must have swallowed something wrong."

"Don't play around with this, Gran. If you're still coughing tomorrow, I want you to phone Dr. Wilson."

"He doesn't want to waste his time with the likes of me. Especially on the weekend."

"You're not a waste of time. You're his patient."

She made a noise that sounded like "Pshaw."

"Gran," I said. "Come on, now. Promise me. You're the only grandmother I'm ever going to have, and I don't want to see you suffer like this for no reason."

She smiled at the mock warning tone in my voice. She'd used it often enough on me. "Fine, Jane. I promise."

By the time we returned to the living room, the meeting was breaking up. I collected another round of compliments on my pear tart and a handful of avowals that I would make some lucky man an excellent wife. I had my cheek pinched by Mr. Potter, and I submitted to a slobbery farewell from Uncle George. It took half an hour to gather up the china and wash it, another half hour to return all the finery to its properly appointed cabinets.

As I slipped my coat from the hall closet, Gran rested her palm against my cheek. "Thank you, dear. I don't know what I'd do without you."

"You'd do just fine, and you know it. Besides, I enjoyed the meeting. I think the Gala is going to be wonderful."

"I certainly hope so." She smiled. "It's late, sweetheart. Why don't you just go sleep in your old room?"

Gran had kept my bedroom set up, almost as a shrine. It had last been decorated when I was sixteen years old. Although I had torn down the Daniel Day-Lewis and Ralph Fiennes posters and taken the high school yearbook photos from the frame of my mirror, I couldn't do anything about the Barbie-pink color that I had once thought was the height of sophistication. I'd tried to convince Gran that she should convert my bedroom into a home office, but she just laughed and reminded me that she didn't work from home. And I have to admit, a part of me was pleased that everything was just the way I'd left it.

Of course, I couldn't sleep in Gran's apartment. I had to go home and feed Stupid Fish. I had to make sure that Neko had not gotten into any trouble. I had to start organizing those books in the basement; there were several spells that David had mentioned the night before that seemed intriguing.

Besides, Jason might have called.

My life was much more complicated than Gran needed to know. I laughed as if I thought she was joking about my spending the night. She sighed, but saw me to the door. "Now, you aren't going to take a bus at this hour are you?"

"Of course not, Gran. I'll take a cab."

"I can give you money."

"I don't need your money." I patted my purse. "I've got my own."

"Promise!" she insisted.

"I promise!"

My fingers were still crossed as I walked out the door of her apartment building and headed up the street. I went two blocks north, up to Calvert, so that there was no possible way for her to see me getting onto the 42R. My timing was good. I only needed to wait five minutes, and I got a seat at the front of the bus. I wondered if I could find a spell to make all of my transportation endeavors work so flawlessly.

17

I stared out the window of the yoga studio, cursing my choice of "scissors" that had succumbed to Melissa's "rock." Unaware of my thoughts, the instructor was saying, "Today, we're going to work on inverted poses. We'll start with a supported shoulderstand."

I wondered if our colonial fathers had ever considered using the asana, instead of placing people in public stocks for humiliating punishment. Taking a deep breath, I met Melissa's game smile. "I love this," she whispered to me. "I feel so strong when the energies shift to my head."

Strong was not the word I would think of. *Silly,* maybe. *Foolish. Completely and utterly out of balance.*

The yoga instructor was undaunted. "The pose is called Salamba Sarvangasana. It is extremely important that you do it properly. You must not turn your head to either side, or you risk serious neck injury. You can use a blanket if you'd like, folded once on top of your mat, but don't give yourself any more padding. You can hurt yourself badly with this posture."

Okay, now I was getting a little afraid. There were more qualifications for contorting my body than there were for working magic. It sounded like the instructor was doing her best to keep from being sued. I imagined my legs, kicking up into the posture. I saw myself toppling sideways, knocking over Melissa to my right and sending her falling into the next three students. I envisioned myself in a hospital bed, tied to one of those strange triangular bars that looked like an oversized instrument from a giant child's music class. I saw the bandages wrapped around my head and neck, turning me into a classic mummy.

I sat back on my heels.

"Come on," Melissa whispered. "Just try it once. It's easier than it looks."

"Easier for you," I muttered. But then, I stopped to think. Since my last yoga class, I had accomplished any number of new things. I had worked successful spells. I had begun a campaign to keep the Peabridge alive. I had faced Clara. I had even kept from chewing my fingernails—sure, my nail polish was chipped from use, but I had not gnawed it off since Roger had given me my manicure.

No silly supported shoulderstand was going to get the better of me.

And I did it.

I followed the instructor's words, and I did it. My legs moved into the air as if they had a power all their own. The pose felt out of balance, but I shifted my hands higher on my hips, providing a little more support for my lower back. I tucked my chin in closer to my chest, and I felt my spine stretch and relax, just like the instructor had said that it would.

Melissa was right. It *was* easier than it looked. And the energies did shift to my head. I felt them, just as I had felt the power of my magic when I extinguished the fire in my kitchen. There was a distinct hum, a definite buzz as my body realigned itself.

I should remember this, I told myself. I should draw on this when I'm working with David.

The instructor had us hold the shoulderstand for a few more minutes before she walked us through a supported headstand. Salamba Sirsasana, for those of us who wanted to add to our Sanskrit vocabularies. Not that I'd remember that name after I left the studio.

We took up stations along the wall as the instructor assured us that many students needed the security of a vertical surface. In fact, she pointed to a patch of wall where the paint was a half-shade lighter than the rest, and she admitted that she had put her own foot through the wall not two weeks before.

Maybe that should have intimidated me, but it had the opposite effect. If my instructor had not perfected the pose, then how could I expect my own attempt to be flawless? I might as well try.

The headstand was harder than the shoulderstand—it *hurt*. I felt as if the crown of my head was going to break open. But then the instructor reminded us to take as much weight as we could on our arms, to transfer our balance outward.

People around me were falling down, and I got distracted more than once, but each time I was able to try again. I finally managed to hold the pose for a full minute, and then the instructor decided it was time to move on to our closing sequence.

As we stretched and balanced before settling into corpse pose, I could not keep a smile from my face. I had conquered the inverted poses.

Okay, that might not have been a very yogic way of thinking about things—"conquering" was probably not the central metaphor that I should use when talking about peace, meditation and harmony between body and mind. But I knew what I meant.

As I practiced my deep breathing and blanking my mind to conscious thoughts, the instructor walked around the room. She approached each student with lavender oil on her palms, making small adjustments to our necks and shoulders. When she lengthened my spine, she leaned close to my ear and whispered, "Excellent job today, Jane."

Well, maybe she didn't. I'd never heard her compliment anyone like that during class. I'd never heard her make any purposeful noise to break up the meditative silence. But I could sense her approval in her fingers.

"Really!" I said to Melissa as we walked away from the studio. "I could tell that's what she believed. For once, she didn't think that I was wasting my time there. She was proud of me."

"She's always proud of you," Melissa said, shrugging. "You're the only person who thinks you should be perfect the first time you try anything."

"I don't think I should be perfect!" I met Melissa's smirk, and I corrected myself. "I don't *always* think I should be perfect. I should just be more flexible than I am. I should be able to stretch more."

"And you do. Over time."

I started to argue, purely out of habit, but I realized that Melissa was right. Yoga *was* getting easier. Even Downward-Facing Dog—I had enjoyed the stretch instead of feeling like my calf muscles were about to tear loose from my bones. Or tendons. Or ligaments. Or whatever my muscles attached to.

I was spared needing to reply because we'd reached M Street, the main drag of Georgetown. We were supposed to meet Neko on the corner. He was going to join us for mojito therapy.

Roger had gone out of town for his sister's big-deal thirtieth birthday party, and Neko was sulking because he hadn't been invited. I didn't think that my familiar truly wanted to wander the wilds of West Virginia, attending long-scheduled family events as the ho-mo-sex-you-al companion of a hometown boy, but I hadn't said anything. I understood that Neko had wanted to be *invited,* even if he didn't actually attend. I just didn't think it would do any good to tell him how miserable he would likely be. Or to point out that he'd only known Roger for a couple of weeks. Or to mention that he was squandering his ability to roam free from our book collection if he only used it to moon after Roger. I bit my tongue.

We found him on the corner, leaning against a streetlight. He sighed as we approached, the deepest sigh I'd ever heard from someone who wasn't a teenage girl. Anyone passing on the street might have thought that the poor man had just learned that he was suffering from some terminal disease. "Hey, Neko!" Melissa said. We'd already decided that our best strategy was to ignore his despondency.

Another sigh, even deeper. Entire wind farms could be fueled if he went on like this. "Hello."

This wasn't going to be easy. Melissa tried, though. "You should have seen Jane in yoga class! She mastered the inverted poses."

He gave me a wan smile that might have broken my heart if I'd thought for a second that he was truly suffering. "Wonderful."

We moved down the sidewalk, avoiding the early revelers who were starting their big nights out in Georgetown's trendy restaurants and bars. Amateurs, Melissa called them. People who wanted to see and be seen.

Passing by the plateglass windows of Sephora, I was amazed by the number of women buying cosmetics on a Saturday evening. Hard to believe, but I'd never been inside the place. I knew that it was a high-end cosmetics emporium; I'd seen the ads and walked by the classy black-and-white storefront. But when I was with Scott, it seemed silly to spend all that time and effort making myself beautiful for my own fiancé. And since he'd dumped me, I hadn't had any reason to splurge.

I shrugged and said. "Can you imagine spending hours shopping for makeup?"

Neko sighed. "*Roger* could spend hours shopping for makeup." He made life as a spendthrift sound downright noble.

Melissa started to retort—I knew that she would say that she had never spent more than five minutes at the drugstore selecting a lipstick. And I suspected that Neko would bite back with something unkind. I was desperate to avoid sniping between the two of them, so I said, "Well, *I* want to see what they've got."

I grabbed both Neko and Melissa by their hands and plunged inside, only to be stopped by the first display. TARTE, said large letters. I picked up a bottle of Clean Slate and read the ingredients. "Here, Melissa. This should sound familiar—avocado oil, rosemary, hibiscus oil."

"I wouldn't know whether to cook with it or put it on my face."

"Roger uses hibiscus oil." Wistfully, Neko picked up the makeup base and read the rest of the label, barely summoning the strength to return it to the counter.

"But Roger isn't here now," I said, deciding to take a firm hand with my lovelorn familiar. I wasn't totally heartless, though. I knew that I'd have to do something to distract him. "I'm going to have to rely on *you* to help me."

"Me?" Neko perked up at that, but then he remembered that he was supposed to be drowning in the slough of despond.

"You."

"What are *you* looking for?" Melissa sounded incredulous, and I tried to flash her a warning look over Neko's bowed head.

"A new image. A new me. I've got fingernails for the first time in my adult life. I remembered to put on Pick-Me-Up-Pink lipstick every morning last week. I have to do *something* to brighten up my colonial wardrobe. And there's certainly a lot to choose from here."

When I'd started cranking out my explanation, I had no idea what I would say. I didn't even know what half the things *were* in the store; I'd certainly never applied them to my body before. But the more I thought about it, the more I wondered why I shouldn't go on a shopping spree. After all, my brilliant foundation idea looked like it was going to be a bust. I wasn't likely to shed my Martha Washington look anytime soon. I might as well do all I could to freshen up my appearance. Especially if I ever hoped to regain Jason's attention, after the Great Indoor Barbecue Fiasco.

"Come on, Neko," I said. "What would you suggest?"

"Mojitos. Extra rum."

"I'm serious!"

"So am I," he said mournfully.

"We'll make the mojitos," I promised. "But first you have to help me choose some makeup."

Nothing. I was having flashbacks to the babysitting I had done when I was twelve, to my desperate attempts to get an overtired five-year-old to pay attention to dinner and get ready for bed.

Melissa wasn't helping. She had wandered down the counter, studying the rest of the Tarte line. I watched her pick up a palette of eye shadow and flip it over so that she could read the price tag. It must have been pretty steep; she practically slammed it back into its Lucite holder.

Well, fine then. I wasn't going to waste the rest of my evening trying to orchestrate fun for the whole gang. "Okay," I said. "I'm just going to buy this eyeliner, and then we can go." I chose the purple one. Purple has always been one of my favorite colors—that must go back to my Barbie dream-girl days.

"You're not going to buy the plum!" Neko could not have sounded more scandalized if I had suggested stripping bare and performing a bump and grind under the chic store's pinlights. A dozen heads swiveled in our direction.

"Um, no," I said, blushing a color only a shade lighter than the offending eyeliner. "I just meant that I would buy this brand."

Neko took the pencil from my hand and eased it back into its container. "Step away from the plum. It would bring out all the red in your face. You need something green. But not too green. You don't want to lean toward sallow. Green-blue. Like Roger's eyes…"

And for a moment there, I'd thought we were making progress. Melissa rolled her own eyes. "Look," she said. "I'm heading down to the bakery. I'll make the mojitos. Come down when you're finished here."

I nodded, not quite ready to give up on revivifying Neko. I was certain that we'd be fine for the rest of the weekend if I could just make him forget his vacationing love for five straight minutes. Consecutive minutes. Whatever. "Go on," I said to Melissa. "Just don't forget to—"

"Add extra lime. I know."

I gave her a finger wave as she ducked out the door. She actually shook her head when she got out to the street, as if she were clearing away a physical residue of froufrou girli-ness. I thought of a Labrador retriever puppy shaking off rain-drops.

"Green-blue," I prompted Neko. "Help me find something."

"It doesn't really matter."

"All right then." I strode over to the Cargo display. "I'll go with this Casablanca palette. Mmm. Caramel lip gloss."

"Caramel?" Neko's shriek actually stopped a transaction at the cash register. He swept over to me and covered my hand with his own. "If you get the caramel, you will absolutely look like a corpse. It will bleach every hint of color that you have in your cheeks."

I bit back a smile as Neko led me down the row. "Here," he said. "You need something more pink. A little sheer. No glitter."

His hands moved as if he were dealing blackjack. Before I knew it, I was holding foundation and blush, pressed powder and loose. He passed me a pair of eyeliners and a tube of mascara. Seven lipsticks—they were all just too luscious to pass up he assured me—and three different bottles of nail polish.

With each category of cosmetic, Neko became more of the man I knew and—well, not quite loved—but expected. He offered bitter criticisms of some products. "Can you *imagine* who buys that? She'd have to have the skin of an elephant and the coloring of a 300-year-old witch. Oh. Present company excepted." I bit my tongue and kept from pointing out that I had a few years left before I hit the three-century mark.

He was on a roll. "Orange? Who needs orange lipstick? There isn't a woman alive who would look good in orange lipstick." My favorite was when he checked out the sample of glittery body powder. He shook the powder puff against its ornate cardboard box with an expert flick of his wrist before he highlighted his collar bones with the faintest hint of gold sparkles. "Stunning!" he pronounced himself.

"Enough!" I said, figuring that we had done sufficient retail therapy. "I can't buy all this stuff."

"Why not?"

"Fifty dollars is my limit. I'm just a working librarian, remember?" The Peabridge might be paying my rent, but I didn't have a stash of hundred-dollar bills for all Neko's treasures.

"There are *ways*," he countered, waggling his eyebrows in a manner that suggested something utterly unethical. Or at least immoral.

I was afraid to ask if he meant shoplifting or peddling my own pitiful body to pay for the wares. "David Montrose would have you turned back into a cat statue faster than you can blink if he even heard you make that suggestion."

I watched him contemplate retorts. One even bubbled to his lips. But he thought better of his words and settled for a shrug. "Well, you have to get the eyeliner. And the nail polish. The stuff you have on is working wonders. You really need it to remind yourself not to gnaw."

He made me sound like a rabbit, but I decided not to take offense. Instead, I said, "And we'll add the blush. I'll get lipstick another day—stay with Pick-Me-Up-Pink for a bit longer."

He gazed wistfully at the products we were abandoning. "Can't we just add the foundation?"

"Nope."

"The Tarte Clean Slate?"

"You are incorrigible! It would cost half my budget. No."

He pouted. "I can't be held responsible for the damage if you don't take my advice."

"No one is holding you responsible for anything. And there won't be any damage. Besides, if I spend all my money here, I won't be able to get my hair cut."

"You're getting your hair cut?" I might have told him I was giving him a pony for his birthday. He clasped his hands and held them close to his chest. "You're having Roger cut it, aren't you! Tell me that you are! Tell me that you'll let him do it! Please, please, please!"

"Yes!" I said, laughing.

"Then I forgive you for getting my hopes up here." He fondled the mascara and bid it farewell with one last sigh.

We paid a small fortune for my three new cosmetics, and I let the salesgirl put my loot into a cute bag. Neko prattled on about the choices that we'd made, debating the considerable merits of blue-green over green-blue. At least he'd recovered from his heartbreak.

Melissa greeted us at the back door to Cake Walk. She already had the drinks made, and she was sipping from her own well-iced glass. We followed her upstairs to the Snuggery, her name for the cozy one-room apartment on the townhouse's second floor. She raised her eyebrows at Neko's streaming commentary about her throw pillows, her coffee table, her breakfast nook and the color of her walls. I shrugged when she gave me a questioning look, but we both knew that it was better to ignore his transition from moping and lovesick to hyper and designer-obsessed.

"So," she said, when we were gathered on her couch and matching love seat. "When am I going to see you work some of your magic, Jane?"

I wriggled deeper into the pillows and sipped from the mojito she had just passed me. "Not tonight. I promised David I wouldn't combine alcohol and magic."

"You've had one sip."

I looked at Neko. He shrugged elaborately. "My lips are sealed," he said, taking great care to lock them with an invisible key.

"Well, I don't know. I mean, I don't have a lot of skills yet. If you want to fall in love with me at first sight, then great, I've got that covered. Or if you want to set your kitchen on fire—I know how to handle that."

"It doesn't have to be anything big."

"Neko?" I asked, uncertain of what I should try.

"How about that candle?" He gestured to the three-wick monster that Melissa had centered on her coffee table. I knew that she lit it for a few minutes each night, using it to calm her thoughts before she went to bed.

"I don't know the spell for lighting it." I tried to hide the exasperation in my voice.

"Well, I do, silly. That's my job, remember?"

I stuck my tongue out at him. Of course I knew that was his job, but I wasn't exactly sure how all this worked. He grinned and moved closer to me, pressing his leg up against mine in a comforting way. When he spoke again, his voice was soft, quiet enough that Melissa would not be able to make out his words. "I'll tell you the spell. You just repeat after me. This is a fire spell, in the same family as the one you did on Thursday. Do you remember how to start it?"

I nodded, glancing at Melissa to see if she thought I was nuts. She was staring in rapt fascination, but she didn't seem ready to call the men in white coats. Yet. "Four deep breaths," I said to Neko. "Then I touch my head, my throat and my heart."

"Perfect," he said, and he settled even closer to me as I went through the routine. I felt the same thrum that had risen earlier in the week, the tingling energy that had released itself into water and air and earth. "Now point to the first wick," he said. I did. "And say after me…

Candle light, candle bright
Wick kindle, bring sight."

Well, that was simple enough. I repeated the words, but I couldn't keep from gasping when the first wick blossomed with golden light. The vibrating power inside me ratcheted down a notch.

Neko nodded. "Go ahead, then. You can do the other two."

And he was right. I could. I repeated the little rhyme, pointing at each wick. Obediently, they also bloomed with little tongues of fire.

I felt calm inside when I had finished. I knew that I had spent some energy, but I was not at all exhausted. In fact, I felt a little as if I had successfully completed a supported headstand, the same rush of pleased success. "Salamba Sirsasana," I whispered, wondering how I had remembered *that* phrase.

"What?" Melissa asked, finally pulling her eyes away from the candle.

"Nothing," I said. "I was just remembering something else."

"That is amazing," Melissa said, clearly not listening to my answer. Instead, she was craning her neck, checking her candle as if she thought I might have worked some sleight of hand with smoke and mirrors. When she looked up at me, there was a hint of awe in her face. "What happens now?"

I glanced at Neko.

"Now, you feed us something," he said. "Do you have any tuna?"

Before Melissa could think about searching her kitchen, I gave her the real answer to her question. "Now we wait for David Montrose to appear. He'll read me the riot act and tell me what I've done wrong."

But I was mistaken. David did not arrive. And, when I finally gave up waiting for him and drank the rest of my mojito, I realized that I was just a little bit disappointed. Not as disappointed as Neko, though, when he found out that Melissa's cupboards were bereft of canned-fish products.

I poured a second drink and reminded myself that I did *not* want to see my warder when I was working new spells during cocktail hour. And for a few minutes, I even believed myself.

On Monday morning, Evelyn was waiting for me beside my desk the instant I arrived at the library. "Just a second," I said. "I'll turn on the latte machine."

"This is more important."

More important than the precious aroma of Colombian Roast filling the lobby? Evelyn had always insisted that I prepare our coffee service first thing; we could lure early-morning researchers that way. Besides, if we were ready to serve them right when the doors opened, we were more likely to get their repeat business before they finished their library work.

I locked my purse into my desk drawer and straightened to look at her. Deep lines cut beside her lips, making her face look even more jowly than usual. I was sure that Neko would know some cosmetic fix, but I didn't have the courage to suggest such a thing. "Is everything okay?" I asked, apprehension twisting my stomach.

"Come into my office."

Gulp. This was serious.

I followed Evelyn into her glassed-in office, shutting her door as she took her seat. She was wearing a brown-and-green tweed suit, with a large, loose weave. The colors weren't terrible on her, but the cut was far too boxy. More advice that I'd absorbed from Neko. More advice that I wouldn't share.

Evelyn nodded her head toward one of the guest chairs. I sat down, but I did not lean back. Something told me not to get too comfortable. "What?" I finally asked.

"Saturday night, something came to my attention, and I spent all day yesterday trying to figure out the best way to discuss it with you."

Saturday night. She had been strolling by Cake Walk, and she had looked up to see me light the candle in Melissa's apartment, without benefit of match or Zippo. Or she had watched Neko and me frolicking in Sephora. Could she have stopped by the cottage while I wasn't home? Oh my God—had she stumbled on the collection of books?

That must be it. She had discovered the trove of witch books. She had found the valuable leather and parchment, noted its complete and utter disarray. Even if she weren't furious with me for keeping the collection a secret, she must be angry that I had done nothing to preserve the rare tomes.

Every fiber of my being wanted to explain. I wanted to tell her all about my witchcraft experiences, let her know that I completely understood the responsibility that had fallen into my lap. I wanted to say that I would never harm the books, and that I *would* get them into some semblance of order, and that I was only using my powers for good and not for evil.

I mean, putting out the fire in my kitchen had been good, hadn't it?

The fire in my kitchen. Oh no. Was *that* what she was upset about? Had she heard that I'd invited Jason over for dinner? *Had he complained to my boss?*

"Evelyn, I can explain."

He'd been my Imaginary Boyfriend for almost a year, I would tell her. I'd watched him every day that he'd come in. I knew his study habits. I knew his writing style. I knew everything about him, and I knew that he and I would be perfect together. Once he got around to recognizing the same. Once he thought to ask me out.

"I can't tell you how embarrassed I was," Evelyn said, shaking her head. She really should think about getting her hair cut. That length was just so unflattering, the way the ends of her hair curled under right beside her jaw. Of course, if she colored it, instead of leaving it that mousy gray…

Wait. Evelyn was embarrassed? What had Jason said that embarrassed *her?* I was the one who should be mortified. Just what had he told her?

"Whatever Jason said, I can explain, Evelyn. Just let me tell you the whole story."

"Jason?" Her lips thinned.

Should I have called him Professor Templeton?

Evelyn said, "You mean Justin. You don't even remember the man's name."

Justin. Justin? I hadn't invited any Justin over for dinner. I hadn't ignited my oven for any Justin. I could hear Neko's snarky voice whispering, *Ignited your oven? Is* that *what they're calling it these days?* I tried to tamp down the smile at the corner of my lips, but I wasn't really successful. If Evelyn was upset over someone called Justin, then my Jason had not spoken to her. He had not complained to my boss, had not told her that the pyromaniacal librarian she had living on Peabridge property had attempted to work a spell in front of him. Had *actually* worked a spell which, from Evelyn's perspective, just might be worse.

Well, thank God for small favors.

"I'm sorry," I said. "Justin?"

"Justin Cartmoor." I must have looked blank, because Evelyn gusted out a sigh. "Justin Cartmoor? The executive director of the Library Foundation."

Oh.

I didn't even bother to make my words into a question. "He told you I applied for a grant."

"He assumed that I knew all about it. He told me that he was terribly sorry, that if he'd known we were interested earlier in the year, he might have been able to do something. I had no idea what he was talking about, of course, and so I made a fool out of myself, trying to get details about what I'd allegedly done."

"I'm sorry," I said, and I really, truly was. "Evelyn, it was just an idea I had. I thought that if I could line up some grant funding, then we wouldn't have to wear our costumes. We might not have to turn the library into Starbucks, just to keep going for another year."

"Jane, I was horribly embarrassed. It looked like I have no idea what my employees do. It looked like I don't keep track of our day-to-day operations, or—worse—that I'm a forgetful old…old…*biddy!*"

Tears were starting to build up in her eyes, and her voice had grown thick. My belly twisted, and I caught my breath. I had never intended to cause anyone *harm*. I really had thought that I'd be helping—helping me, of course, but also helping Evelyn and the Peabridge.

"Of course you're not a biddy, and anyone who would imply that is absolutely insane!" The words came out a bit more vehemently than I'd intended, but they made Evelyn smile. I took that as a good sign and carried on. "The applications were totally a spur-of-the-moment thing. I spent a morning putting them together." Hmm. That might not reflect well on me—it made me sound like I'd gone off half-cocked. Oh well. In for a penny, in for a pound.

"Applications?" Evelyn said, stressing the plural.

I nodded, suddenly wary, but I knew I needed to come clean. "Thirteen of them."

"Thirteen!" She looked out the windows of her office as if she expected the Inspector General of Grant Applications to be waiting for her, black briefcase and bad suit at the ready.

"Those were only the strongest leads. For historic collections. And original materials. Like ours. There are lots of other possibilities. That. I. Can. Follow up on later." I ended in a rush, realizing that there would be no "later."

Evelyn shook her head. "Jane. Jane, Jane, Jane." When she finally looked at me, though, her face had relaxed. I thought that there might even be a hint of a smile behind her powdered cheeks. "Jane, you are an excellent librarian. You really have a flair when it comes to research, and I am often amazed at the obscure details that you're able to come up with in our collection. You are personable. You are flexible. You understand customer service."

Any other time, I would have preened at the compliments, but I knew there was some giant *but* coming.

"But—" There it was. "But, you are not a fund-raiser. You aren't trained in development. We have board members who specialize in that, people who have retired from successful careers working with some of the largest nonprofits in the country." She leaned back in her chair. "The Library Foundation is one of the 'big guys.' Applications to them should include complete records of our finances and plenty of graphs, charts about our past, present and future needs. If we're going to ask them for money, we need to make sure that we've dotted every single one of our i's and crossed each of our t's. It's a tremendous job. Much more than any one of us should take on, on our own. And even so, the Peabridge is likely below their radar screen."

I felt as if I had shrunk to the size of a munchkin. Smaller. To a fairy. A gnat.

What had I been thinking of? I walked by one guy on the street, found out that he was thinking of donating money—to a theater company—and I believed that there were thousands of dollars just waiting to be taken?

"I'm sorry," I said, and now I was surprised to hear tears in my own voice. "I only wanted to help. I thought that I'd surprise you, that you'd be happy—"

"I *am* happy, Jane. I'm happy that you care enough about the Peabridge to have tried. And I'm happy that we understand each other going forward. We'll wait for a few years. Get our collection under control. Once we're running a little more smoothly, we can try to go after the big grant people. All right?"

It wasn't all right. I wanted to ask how we were going to get our collection under control without additional funding, without qualified cataloging help. But Evelyn knew the situation as well as I did. Better. I wasn't going to teach her anything she didn't already know. I nodded. "All right."

"Thank you." She nodded.

I pushed back my chair and crossed to the door. When my fingers touched the knob, Evelyn said, "Oh, one more thing." I froze, afraid to turn around. "Justin was quite impressed with the essay that you wrote. He said that you were clearly passionate about your work, that your true librarian interest shone through. He was particularly taken with your quoting that line about Prospero's books, and how you tied it in with the magic of learning."

Well, that made it a little easier to head back to my desk and face another workweek. But I wasn't any more enthusiastic about getting the latte machine set up.

I had ground the first batch of coffee beans when Harold came through the library doors. Great. Frosting on my Monday-morning cake.

"Did you have a wonderful weekend?" he asked. "You deserve the very best."

Poor guy. I looked into his eyes and saw the patient trust and loyalty of a basset hound. "Yeah, Harold. I did. I helped my grandmother out with a party on Friday night and then I mostly hung out with friends. How about you?"

"Well, my mother needed a ride to her bridge club." That's right. I'd forgotten that Harold lived with his mother. "I brought along a book to read, instead of driving back and forth. The ladies there were really nice. They offered me treats, but all they had were those nasty cookies. You know, the pink-and-green ones? From the Watergate Bakery?"

I actually laughed out loud, and I was rewarded with the first pure, unworried smile I had seen on Harold's face for a long time. "I know those cookies," I said. "My grandmother loves them." I added freshly ground coffee to the paper filter and set the first batch of drip coffee to brew. Harold liked his black, although he sometimes treated himself to one of the sugar packets at the end of the counter. "What book are you reading?"

"Oh, nothing interesting."

"You never know." I smiled, amused by his hangdog look. "I'm interested in a lot of things."

He blushed, and I wondered if he was reading the secret erotic diary of some desperate Victorian lady. He looked carefully to either side before he replied, *"Linux for Dummies."*

He looked so uncertain when he said it that I wanted to assure him that the *dummies* part was a joke, that he didn't have to be dumb to want to learn. Especially about Linux. *I* barely knew what Linux was—some sort of computer operating system, a gold standard with geeks who managed computers. "Do you program computers, Harold?"

I didn't think it was possible for anyone to blush more.

The strands of hair that he had carefully combed across his bald pate looked as if they might catch fire from his embarrassment. "Not yet," he said. "But I want to."

I remembered the day that he had fixed my computer, pushing it past its annoying blue screen of death. "I'm sure you can, then. Especially if you're willing to spend your weekends reading up on the subject."

"You don't think it's stupid? For me? I mean, I've never been to college." He lowered his eyes, suddenly overcome with bashfulness. "Like you have."

Ach! What had I done working that spell? Sure, I'd gone to college, but so had most women in the world around us. Certainly Evelyn had. And Marie, our intern in the mail room. Harold was putting me on a pedestal, and I had no right to the special treatment. Oh well, I might as well see if I could use my power for good. "If there's one field that you *can* break into without college, it's likely to be computers. Take Bill Gates—he never got his degree."

Well, that might have been a little overly optimistic. I mean, how many billionaires dropped out of Harvard? I thought that I should temper things a bit. "You might want to look into some of the technical schools around town. Or one of the community colleges. An associate degree may open just the doors you want."

"An associate degree," he repeated the words as if they were a mantra. I'd better watch what I said, or he'd be filling out college applications right in front of me. A quick beep let me know that the coffee had finished brewing, and I gratefully filled a cup for him, ready to send him on his way.

"Thank you," he said gravely. "You make the best coffee I've ever tasted."

"That's very nice of you to say." I made the best coffee. Right. He hadn't even tested this batch. All I'd done was grind the beans, put them in the filter and let the machine work its magic. Still, I supposed it was a nice sentiment. I said, "I'd better get back to work." I nodded toward Evelyn's office. "I don't want her to think that I'm slacking off."

"Who could ever think that of you?" Harold sounded astonished. So this is what it felt like to have a knight in shining armor, ready to ride to one's defense. Poor guy. He took his coffee and shambled off to the front door.

Before I could return to my desk, another patron approached the coffee counter. "Mr. Potter!" I said, recognizing Uncle George's friend from the opera guild.

"Good morning," he said, tipping an invisible hat. "And how is the Peabridge's grant-writing phenom?"

I tried not to make a face. "Not the best, Mr. Potter."

"What's wrong?"

I gave him the sanitized version of the story—the funding just wasn't going to come through this year, but we had high hopes for the future—and then I asked if I could make him a coffee. "A small mocha would be wonderful, dear."

"Whipped cream?"

"What's a mocha without whipped cream?"

I laughed and agreed and got to work making the chocolate-and-coffee mixture. Mr. Potter took advantage of the time to look around the Peabridge lobby. "You've got a beautiful building here, don't you?"

"It was converted from a residence nearly fifty years ago. The architects did a wonderful job at bringing in light."

"My Lucinda would have loved this place. She always said that her spirits rose, just by standing near books."

I smiled. "I know what she meant. How's her dog?"

"Oh, Beijing is doing fine."

I passed him his mocha, and he took a tentative sip, relying on the generous serving of whipped cream to keep from burning his mouth. "Ah," he sighed. "As perfect a mocha as I've ever had."

"We aim to please," I said.

"I never would have expected to find a coffee bar in a library."

"Well, you know. We try to make up budget shortfalls wherever we can."

"How much revenue can coffee possibly generate?"

"You'd be surprised," I said. "Besides, our budgetary needs are relatively modest. A thousand here, a thousand there, and we might be able to get started on cataloging our colonial recipe books."

A smile crinkled the corners of Mr. Potter's eyes. "I'd better stop in for a mocha more often, then."

"I'll look forward to seeing you."

Then he was gone, off to his widower's life, with Beijing and whatever else he had for company. I turned my attention to wiping down the milk-steaming nozzle. When I looked up, I was astonished to find Jason Templeton standing at the counter.

Jason Templeton. Flashing the perfect Imaginary Boyfriend grin.

"Good morning."

"It's nine o'clock!"

He looked confused, but then he said, "And it can't be a good morning at nine o'clock?"

"You don't come in until nine-thirty."

"My morning class was canceled today. Founder's Day. The students are supposed to attend other lectures on the deep inner meaning of higher education in our country. Most of them are still sleeping off the weekend, though."

I was hearing the words, but I wasn't truly processing them. Jason was here. In the Peabridge. Talking to me as if I hadn't incinerated dinner in front of him the week before. As if I hadn't worked magic.

"I brought you something," he said, and he handed me a white plastic bag.

Jason was here in the Peabridge *and* he'd brought me a present.

"What is it?" It was light, whatever it was. And it squished when I clutched the bag close.

"Open up and see."

Marshmallows. A bag of giant marshmallows.

"I—" I started to say, but I couldn't imagine how I'd complete the sentence.

"I thought that you could use them, if your oven catches fire again. I should have brought graham crackers and chocolate bars, as well." I laughed, and he shook his head. "No! I should have brought you another blanket to replace the one that burned. That was really quick thinking, to smother the flames."

There we were. He'd decided to completely ignore the

magic spell. Well, wasn't that what I'd told him to do? Hadn't I insisted that the strange sights had been miscon-strued in the panic of the moment? I felt a strange mixture of disappointment and relief. I wanted him to press me for information about my witchcraft and yet, I was thrilled that he was willing to make light of the Great Lamb Chop Debacle.

"Well," I said. "Once a Girl Scout, always a Girl Scout." I gestured with the bag of marshmallows. "And I can use these to bake banana boats over an open campfire." Quick. Think of something else to say. Before he walked away. "I'm sorry that you had to leave so quickly Thursday night."

He looked uncomfortable, as if I'd chastised him for bad behavior. "I didn't want you to go to any more trouble on my behalf. And things *were* getting sort of strange with your tenants appearing out of nowhere and your ex showing up and all."

Scott? What did Scott have to do with anything? Scott was in England with his new lady-love.

"Oh!" I said, finally understanding. "David!"

He nodded. "I know that you called him your mentor, and I understand how that works. It's always strange when professors start seeing their students, isn't it?" Just how much did he know about *that,* I wondered? But first, I had to make him understand that David wasn't my ex.

"I imagine that *is* pretty strange, but David and I have really never been romantically involved." Our one kiss didn't count. He and I had agreed on that.

Jason looked unconvinced. "You can't tell me there

wasn't *something* going on there. I got definite possessive vibes from that guy."

I remembered David's insistence that he and I needed to talk, that we needed to discuss the fire spell. "He can be pretty pushy, but it's just that he takes his study seriously. And he thinks that I should, too."

Jason shrugged. "If you say so."

"So."

Okay, that was stupid. I know that it was stupid. I don't know what possessed me to say it. But it just popped out, before I could stop it. Throwing good impressions after bad, I said, "I don't suppose there's any chance that you'd come over for dinner again?"

That surprised him. What was I thinking? I trapped the guy in a corner of my kitchen and nearly burned the house down around him, then I asked him back for dinner? Right. He might be willing to forgive me one disaster, but what idiot would put himself on the line for a second attempt on his life?

"Actually, dinners are sort of hard for me. You know, as the term gets going at school…"

"Oh, I understand," I said. My stomach swooped down to my toes, and I tried to remember to keep a smile on my lips, to pretend that I couldn't feel my heart shattering inside my chest.

"But if you were free for lunch? My treat?"

"No! I mean, no to your treat. But yes to lunch. Of course. Yes."

He wasn't rejecting me! He wasn't trying to avoid me! He wanted to eat lunch with me!

He took out a slender black calendar from his briefcase. "Hmm," he said. "This week is crazy, with Founder's Day changing courses around. How about next week, though?"

"Next week's fine. Name the day." If I had anything on my calendar, I'd move it.

"How about Wednesday? We could meet at, say, noon? At La Perla?" Italian. That would make Melissa-approved first-date ordering a challenge, but I'd manage it. For my Imaginary Boyfriend, I'd manage anything.

"La Perla," I said brightly. "Noon on Wednesday."

"It's a date, then."

A date. He actually said the word *date*. He started to turn away and walk toward his usual research table. "Jason!" I called, unable to let him go quite yet.

He came back to the coffee counter, a smile quirking his lips. "Jane."

"Um, what if I need to phone you? You know, if Evelyn calls a meeting or something and I'm going to be late. Can I get your number?"

"Oh. Sure." He dug a pen out of his briefcase and looked around for something to write on. I started to tell him that I'd grab a pad of paper from my desk, but he picked up one of the cocktail napkins from the counter. "Here you go. It's my cell. I'm never home, so it's useless to try to reach me there."

He smiled and handed me the number. Ten digits. Ten consecutive steps toward making my dream come true. A kiss that I scarcely remembered, a silly gift of marshmallows, a lunch date for next week and now a phone number. That was clearly progress, anyone would have to agree.

As I watched him settle in at his worktable, I resisted the urge to call Melissa. I would never have been able to keep the teenage squeal out of my voice as I told her that I was ready to drop the Imaginary category.

Jason Templeton had asked me out on a date and then he'd given me his phone number. He'd taken the first step over the border into the delicious, terrifying, exciting, breathtaking territory of Boyfriend-land.

19

"All right, Gran. It's a quarter after. Can we go now?"

"Jane," my grandmother said, and I could hear annoyance in her voice. I wasn't sure, though, if that emotion was directed at me, or at Clara, or at the small children who were dodging around us, intent on seeing every square inch of the stuffed elephant in the center of the Natural History Museum's rotunda.

I looked toward the front doors of the museum, wondering if I could have missed Clara in the crush of people. By arriving right at opening time, at 10:00 a.m., Gran and I had been caught up in the melee of families, the mothers and fathers and screaming, anxious children, all eager to get a glimpse of the museum's fossils and skeletons and other exotic displays of the natural world.

I'd never understood why families *start* at the Natural History Museum. Most kids were fascinated by the collection. Didn't that make the museum a more likely target for the afternoon, then? Drag the kids to the art museum in the morning, make them study the delicate application of paint by the Dutch masters, or the effects of atmosphere in Impressionist paintings.

Then, reward them in the afternoon, by taking them to see the suspended blue whale or the rampaging tyrannosaurus rex or the live insect zoo. (A live insect zoo, by the way, sponsored by Orkin. No one could say that our government didn't have a sense of humor.)

Instead, I was willing to bet that half these children would be weepy and/or hyperactive by the afternoon, and their one real chance at learning art history while still in elementary school would be ruined. But who was I to say anything? No one had asked me *my* opinion.

"There she is!" Gran said, and her relief was as loud as the horde of rampaging kids who had just discovered the elephant's tusks and were debating whether the pachyderm could throw them up to the balcony with one toss of its head.

Clara swept up to us, as breathless as she had been in Cake Walk. She was wearing the same movie-star sunglasses, and she raised the same hackles on the back of my neck. "I'm sorry," she said. "I had to read my runes before I came over here this morning. The spread took longer to interpret than I'd planned."

I slung my purse over my shoulder and started to head toward the door. Runes. Clara's runes were more important to her than I was.

"Jane!" my grandmother called.

I stopped. This wasn't fair. Gran shouldn't have come. If Gran hadn't been here, I could have been as rude as I wanted to Clara. As rude as she'd been to us, leaving us waiting for her. Waiting for fifteen minutes. For twenty-five years. But with Gran standing at the base of the giant elephant, I couldn't very well turn around and walk away. I'd be offending the one woman who had loved me un-conditionally, who had nurtured me and raised me, even when my own mother abandoned me.

I took a deep breath and turned back around. When a troop of Cub Scouts started to shriek their excitement over the dinosaur exhibit, I moved back toward Gran and Clara, so that we wouldn't have to shout to make ourselves heard.

I set my teeth and tried to keep my voice civil as I asked, "And what did the runes have to say?"

I must not have succeeded in the civility department, because Gran gave me a sharp look. Clara, though, seemed thrilled by my interest. "I used my jade runes," she gushed. "They're often the best at depicting matters of emotion, Jeanette, family, love, relationships."

"Of course," I said, icily ignoring the oversight about my name.

Gran glared at my superpolite tone, but Clara went on, oblivious. "I drew a fork spread, because we seem to have reached a critical point in our relationship. Decisions have to be made."

Oh, don't they.

No, I didn't say it out loud. But I thought it very, very clearly. Clara chattered on, utterly unaware of my scorn.

"The first rune of a fork represents the first possible outcome. I ended up with Ken."

Ken. Like Barbie and? I had no idea what Clara was talking about. Even Gran seemed a bit put out, and she started to look at the banners over the different museum galleries. I sensed that she was trying to find something to distract Clara, to rein in her rampant enthusiasm over bits of green stone.

"I'm sorry," I said, feeling some bizarre need to fill the silence as Clara paused for breath. "I don't know what Ken means."

Clara swept off her oversized sunglasses for the first time, and she blinked at me. Once again, I was struck by the color of her eyes. My eyes. And when I glanced at Gran, a shiver crept down my spine, for I realized they were her eyes, as well. Any stranger looking at us would know that we were three generations of the same family. Three women in a long line.

I thought again about what David had said, about how witchcraft typically descended through the mother. Could there be some truth to that? Was it possible that I came by my powers legitimately? Did my mother's use of runes have the same magical base as my working spells?

"Ken," Clara said, obviously unaware of my introspection. "It looks like an arrow, a less-than sign. It stands for light. For knowledge." She pursed her lips in a rueful pout that almost made me smile. "I don't draw Ken very often."

I wanted to tell her that I knew the word then. Shakespeare had used it in his long poem, *The Rape of Lucrece:* "'Tis double death to drown in ken of shore."

I suspected that I knew what he'd meant. You can see salvation, but you know that you're never going to reach it. Just as I could see the family that I'd never really known, I could see the mother who had abandoned me when I was a child, but I was never going to find comfort in her arms.

Grudgingly, I asked, "What other ones did you draw?"

Gran looked at me in surprise, as if she suspected that I was mocking Clara. I was able to turn an honest smile to her, though, and I was rewarded by her glance of relief. Clara answered, not at all aware of the silent conversation that had passed between Gran and me. "Gebo was the next one, the second possible outcome."

Gebo. Okay, Shakespeare never used that word. "Um, I don't know that rune," I said, but I was curious enough that I forgot to sound snotty.

"It looks like the letter X. It stands for a gift. It's a positive sign, because the giving of a gift enriches both the person who gives and the person who receives. But it's a complicated one, because additional bonds are built with gifts. Debts are created."

"Or paid." I said the words without thinking, but I knew that they were true. Clara looked at me directly for the first time since she'd arrived in the museum.

"Or paid," she repeated, and she nodded slowly. I could almost see the wheels spinning inside her head, and I wondered what connections she was making, what lines she was drawing between what she'd said and what she thought.

Maybe—just maybe—there *was* something to these runes. After all, two months ago, I would have said that the notion of witchcraft was ridiculous. If anyone had told me that there truly were familiars or magic wands made of rowan wood or fires that could be extinguished by chanting some words, I would have laughed and asked them what book they were reading. Or what they were smoking.

But witchcraft was real. And maybe Clara's jade tiles were, too. "What was your third rune?" I asked.

She flashed me a huge smile. "With the fork spread, the third rune is the critical factor. The one that determines which possibility will come to pass." She looked from me to Gran, then back at me. "My third rune was Berkana. It looks like a *B,* but the loops are triangles." She looked down at her short, stubby hands, suddenly—amazingly— shy. "It stands for household. For family."

And there it was. I could hear something in her words, something that I hadn't heard before. Not in her rush of ex- uberance here by the elephant. Not in the crazy words she'd spouted at Cake Walk.

Clara wanted this to work. She wanted to build a rela- tionship with me, to strengthen the one she had with Gran. She wanted to find the family that she'd walked away from, that she'd abandoned so many years ago.

This couldn't be easy for her. Every time she looked at me, she must see opportunities that she'd lost. I must remind her of my father, of her youth, of all her mistakes.

"So, that's why I was late. You can see why I needed to finish the reading." She sighed and looked around expec- tantly. "Now, where are the crystals in this place?"

Okay. Well, I might have a glimpse of understanding into Clara's soul, but she was still weird. I mean, I was coming to believe in witchcraft, and I might ascribe some form of power to her strange jade stones, but I certainly wasn't about to embrace every form of New Age hocus-pocus that crossed my path.

Gran shook her head, but there was a hint of fondness at the corners of her lips. "They're upstairs, dear."

Dear. That's what Gran called *me*. I felt the scrabble of a green-eyed monster at the edge of my thoughts.

I was adult enough to know that Gran could love two of us at once. She could call two people *dear*. Hell, she called Uncle George dear half the time. But it was different when she directed the word to Clara. It felt as if Gran was taking something away from me.

"Let's go, then!" Clara started to soldier off to the nearest flight of stairs.

"Clara!" I called, and needed to repeat myself to be heard above the noise in the rotunda. "I think we should take the elevator."

"Oh." She turned back and gave me a curious glance. "If you really need to."

I looked at Gran, but Clara didn't seem to get my point. Gran did, though. And she took exception to my trying to protect her. "I'm *fine*, Jane. I can walk up a silly flight of stairs."

But they were long flights. Two of them. And Gran was breathing heavily by the time we got to the top. "Let's just look out at the crowd from up here," she said. She didn't fool me. I knew that she wanted to catch her breath.

And then she started coughing.

It was the same cough that she'd had at her apartment, but now it seemed worse. Much worse. Her face flushed crimson as she fought for breath. I started to put an arm around her shoulders, intending to help, but she shrugged me away. Frantic, I looked around for a bench. Without touching her, I directed her toward the stone surface. Still coughing, she collapsed onto the seat.

"Mom!" Clara said, sitting beside her. "Are you all right?"

"She'll be fine," I said, but I didn't really believe myself. "She was coughing like this the other night."

After what seemed like a lifetime, my grandmother finally got her breathing under control. By then, the color had drained from her face, and her lips were thin gray lines. Clara hovered next to her. "Mom, you look terrible."

I was torn between snapping at Clara for her lack of tact and agreeing with her assessment. Gran gave a wan smile. "Just what a mother loves to hear from her daughter."

Again, that green-eyed weasel burrowed beneath my heart. Gran should be directing words about love to me. I was the one who'd been there for her, for years. I was the one who'd helped her at the party the other night, who had listened to her coughing then. Which reminded me… "Gran, did you call Dr. Wilson?"

She patted my sleeve, as if I were the person who needed to be comforted. "There was no need, dear. I'm fine."

"Mom, you didn't sound fine just now," Clara said. Again, I pushed down my frustration with her. After all, she was on my side in this. I knew that. It was hard for me to admit, but I knew it.

"I'm feeling better already," Gran said, forcing a ghastly grin. She insisted on getting to her feet. "Now, where are those crystals?"

Shrugging and exchanging worried looks with Clara, I followed my grandmother into the minerals display.

I had been to the National Museum of Natural History approximately 5,347 times, counting school field trips. Every single time, I visited the minerals and gemstones. Every single time, I was bored out of my skull with the display, except for the Hope Diamond.

And it wasn't even the Hope itself that interested me. It was the myth that surrounded it—legend said that disaster would befall every one of the stone's owners. The Hope was the largest blue diamond in the world. A billion years old, it was the size of a baby's fist, and it glinted balefully on its velvet display. It was sheltered behind bulletproof glass, set inside vault doors. Rumor said that the treasure was lowered into the ground each night, stored in a secure safe dozens of feet below ground level. A line stretched around the viewing gallery as scores of museum visitors waited for their chance to ooh and aah over the cut stone.

But Clara could not have been less interested. Instead of waiting to see the Hope, along with the Star of Asia, jade carvings and other valuable pieces of jewelry, Clara was immediately drawn to the minerals. Not the gemstones. The boring, ordinary, workaday minerals.

She stopped in front of a display case and stood transfixed, as if she were reading all the secrets of the universe. I stepped up beside her and saw a bunch of rocks.

"Pink kunzite," she breathed.

"What?"

"That one. The dark pink one. With the black streaks going through it."

I saw the stone that she was talking about. It was pretty enough, but nothing special. I might have seen rocks like it in the cheap jewelry stores along Wisconsin Avenue in Georgetown.

"The pink of the stone reflects the heart. Unconditional love. Mother love."

She hesitated for a moment before she looked at me, but I wouldn't meet her gaze. Instead, I looked behind us for Gran. She was sitting on one of the benches, across the gallery. She caught my concerned glance, but when I started to take a step toward her, she waved me back to the display. Her expression was clear: she did not want me drawing attention to her. She wanted me to stay with Clara.

Who seemed not to have noticed my distraction. "But there's violet in there, too," she was saying. "Violet is the sign of the higher mind, Je— Jane. Of wisdom."

I rolled my eyes. Runes, I was able to accept. They were a way of working human experience into the world around us, sort of like my spells. But crystals were just *bizarre*. They were a bad joke, and I was the butt of the story.

Again, Clara was oblivious to my skepticism. She pointed at the rock. "And see those striations? They're a sign of rapid transmission of energy. When things change, after having stayed the same for years."

Come on. Was she making all of this up? Would she have said the same thing about the chunk of fool's gold in the next case? Or the—I craned my neck to read the label— elongated tetrahexahedral copper crystals next to them?

Clara could go from display to display and make every single thing we saw be about family and love and hope and renewal. That still didn't explain the fact that she'd ignored me for a quarter of a century.

Yet, even as I started to work myself into my abandoned-by-my-mother rant, I realized that twenty-five years was not actually all that long. Sure, it was most of the time that I'd been alive. But it was nothing compared to the timeline of the rocks around us. Hell, it wasn't even all that much compared to Gran's life.

My grandmother had been abandoned by Clara and still found room in her heart to love.

Shouldn't I be able to do the same? Wouldn't Gran want me to show off the lessons that I'd learned from her?

As if she knew that I was thinking about her, Gran began to cough again.

I could tell that something was different this time. Something was worse. The coughs sounded like they were coming from the bottom of her lungs, as if her entire body was seizing up each time her throat constricted. Staring across the gallery, I watched a handful of people look in Gran's direction, then look away, as if they were embarrassed by her infirmity.

I ran toward her bench, falling to my knees in front of her. I grabbed her hands in mine, but then I tumbled backward. Her palms were burning. Her fingers were powdery and dry, and I knew that she had a dangerous fever.

The coughing continued, soggy, threatening. It hurt my ears to hear her laboring so hard, and I scrambled in my purse for a Kleenex. Gran took my linty offering and pressed it to her lips. When she took it away, she wasn't quick enough to fold it over, and I saw that it was flecked with crimson.

"Clara!" I cried. She looked up from her precious kunzite. "Call 911." She looked at me without understanding. "It's Gran," I screamed. "She needs a doctor now!"

Gran would have protested, but she couldn't get enough air. By that point, a crowd had gathered around us. A balding man, his brow creased with worry lines, was digging in his pocket, flipping open a cell phone. I saw him press three digits, and I nodded, turning back to Gran. "You're going to be okay," I said.

Then, everything spiraled out of control.

I was vaguely aware of the museum guards, appearing in their blue uniforms. They moved the curious onlookers away, redirected the crowd's attention to the glinting treasures in the display cases. My Cell Phone Samaritan hovered nearby, looking at his watch and then his phone and then his watch again. One of the guards spoke into her walkie-talkie, enunciating our location clearly and professionally.

There was a gurney, and two uniformed paramedics. They helped Gran onto the platform and eased her back. They elevated her head, to help her breathe. They slipped plastic tubing over her head, issuing instructions loudly, firmly. Gran tried to explain that she was fine, that she didn't need their assistance, but they ignored her. They started the flow of oxygen, adjusted it, adjusted it again. They put a blanket over her, tucking it in beside her arms, her legs. She was smaller than I'd ever imagined she could be.

The EMTs raised up the gurney and started rolling it toward the elevator. I trotted beside Gran, babbling words that I meant to be soothing. She looked at me over the oxygen mask, and her eyes—my eyes—were wild and frightened. As the elevator door closed, I saw that Cell Phone Samaritan was hovering outside. I called out thanks, and he nodded. The doors closed.

I turned back to Gran, and I realized that Clara was beside me, closer to Gran's head. The paramedics were going about their business, checking the flow of oxygen, taking Gran's pulse, being professional.

An ambulance waited in the half circle of driveway at the back of the museum. A crowd of tourists had gathered around, staring at us as if we were some sort of special historical reenactment designed for their viewing pleasure.

The EMTs brought the gurney up to the back door of the ambulance. Like clockwork, the legs collapsed against the ambulance floor, and the crew eased the rolling surface into place. The nearest paramedic said, "Only one of you can come with us." I looked at Clara. She looked at me.

I opened my mouth. Closed it. Looked at Gran, whose eyes were shut.

"Go," Clara said, and she put her hand in the small of my back. Tears exploded down my cheeks. Clara looked at the EMT. "Where are you taking her?"

"George Washington. Twenty-third and I."

"I'll meet you there." Clara stepped back, already turning toward the street to hail one of D.C.'s ubiquitous cabs.

"Wait!" I cried, and the paramedic hesitated as he reached for the heavy ambulance door. "Do you have money?" I called out.

She nodded. "I'm fine. Don't worry. I'll see you at the hospital."

The door closed, and the ambulance started, and the siren sang out, and the EMTs chanted to my grandmother that she would be fine, that she shouldn't worry, that everything was going to be all right.

20

By the time we reached the George Washington Hospital emergency room, I had a greater appreciation for Indy 500 drivers. I'd never thought about how much they accomplished as they were enveloped by teeth-shattering sound, taking tight corners with g-forces that would make an ordinary human's face stretch like a cartoon character's. Or maybe it only seemed that way in the back of the ambulance.

The EMTs handled the gurney professionally when we arrived at the hospital. They hopped down from the back of the ambulance as if they were performing some well-rehearsed ballet. I scrambled after with minimal regard for how ridiculous I looked. I followed the EMTs through the rubberized doors into the confusion of the emergency room.

One advantage of traveling by ambulance—we got priority treatment upon arrival. Gran was wheeled into an examining room, and a doctor called out the count as she was transferred to a bed. The EMTs folded the straps back onto their conveyance, snapped out some medical information to the treating physician and then they were gone.

Before I could get their names. Before I could even thank them.

Clara joined us quickly; her cabdriver had made excellent time getting across town. We both worked to stay out of the doctor's way as we craned our necks for a better view.

The doctor slipped off the oxygen apparatus and listened to Gran's chest. She was already protesting that we were making a big deal out of nothing; she insisted that she was just a little tired, that she hadn't slept well the night before. She said that she always had a cough, that she had allergies, that there was absolutely nothing wrong with her and that she was ready to go home right now.

The doctor agreed with everything she said, but he did not stop his exam. He shone a light onto the back of her throat, and he peered into her nose and ears. He spent a lot of time applying the bell of his stethoscope to her back, and he repeatedly urged her to take deep breaths. Only the slightest of frowns told us that he was not pleased with what he heard.

He took Gran's temperature, tested her reflexes, checked her blood pressure and asked her any number of personal questions about her diet, elimination and daily life in general.

Gran got increasingly snippy with the doctor, insisting that she was well. When he started to feel the glands under her neck, she announced that that was the last straw, and she started to jump down from the examining table. The half breath that she took prior to jumping triggered something inside her lungs, though, and she was off and running on another coughing jag.

This one was every bit as bad as the last she'd suffered at the museum; however, the doctor did not seem surprised. He passed Gran a Kleenex and only nodded when it came away from her lips splotched with red. He made some cryptic scribbles on his clipboard and waited for the coughing spasm to pass before he told Gran that she would get to stay at the hospital for a few days.

Double pneumonia. Likely viral in origin. Given the tenderness on her left side, she had probably cracked a rib with her coughing. She needed Tylenol for her fever and an IV to combat her severe dehydration. X-rays would tell us more and confirm that she had nothing more dire—like the terrible word *cancer* that my mind kept spinning away from.

Actually, dehydration was causing the medical staff their greatest concern. A phlebotomist fussed over Gran's birdlike arms, telling her that he could scarcely find a place to stick his needle. He hovered as he started administering fluids, chiding her as she explained that she just hadn't been thirsty.

A nurse watched as Gran swallowed her Tylenol. Personally, I felt like crying with relief when I heard the drug of choice. Tylenol. Just like I could buy at the CVS. There was something tremendously comforting about that, about the fact that I could pronounce the name of the treatment Gran was given. It wasn't mysterious or terrible or threatening.

The doctor convinced Gran to lean back and relax, and

Clara and I stepped out to complete the admissions paperwork. That's when things got a little, um, interesting.

The admissions nurse was a large African-American
woman. She wore brightly colored hospital greens, those
shapeless clothes that were designed for maximum comfort
and easy cleaning. Around her neck hung an amber
pendant; I could just make out flecks of Jurassic life suspended in the orange stone.

Clara gasped when she saw the jewelry. "When was the
last time that you had that thing cleansed?"

The nurse blinked at her. "We're allowed to wear jewelry,
ma'am. Studies have shown that necklaces pose no threat
to patient health. Now, if you could just complete these
forms, indicating the patient's name—"

"No!" Clara said. She was loud enough that several
people in the waiting room looked up from their zombie
states. "I don't mean germs. Any idiot can take care of
germs." I winced. Surely under the circumstances, it wasn't
a good idea to call health-care providers idiots. Clara bulled
forward. "I mean the negative energies that you've collected."

Negative energies. I could see the nurse parsing the
words. Her eyes narrowed, and I knew that she must wonder
if Clara was some sort of raving loon. The nurse—R. N.
Lampet, I saw from her nametag—started to vocalize three
different retorts to Clara, but then she seemed to decide that
she was better off addressing her comments to me. "If your
grandmother has insurance other than Medicare, we'll need
that information here—"

Clara was not willing to be put off that easily. "Your

amber is exposed to some major negative energy here. All of the pain in this hospital. All of the fear. Listen to me— I am a trained vibrational consultant, and I'm telling you that you need to cleanse that thing, before it affects your entire body."

"Trained vibrational consultant?" The disbelief in Nurse Lampet's voice echoed across the waiting room. I heard two different people snicker. So wonderful that we were able to brighten the morning for other people here in the emergency room. How nice that we were able to ease their own fears and concerns, give them a moment of amusement.

"I'm sorry," I said to the nurse, mortally embarrassed. "If you just give me the clipboard, I'll see what I can do."

R. N. Lampet nodded. "Just make sure you take *her* with you."

Miserably, I dragged Clara to a pair of plastic chairs. "I'm not making this up, Jeanette. Jane!" She corrected herself as I uncapped the ballpoint pen. "That woman needs to place her amber in the open air. Keep it free from human contact for at least a fortnight. Burying it in the earth would actually be best, especially if she can find some undyed, virgin wool to wrap it in. I've got some at home. I should bring it when we come back."

"You do that, Clara."

Something about my tone silenced her. I'm not quite sure what it was—the way I had to force my words through my clenched teeth? The way I barely restrained rolling my eyes?

Clara sat silently while I filled out sheet after sheet of information. Any known allergies. Any prior hospitalizations.

Any prior surgeries. Any current medications. I knew all of the answers.

When I had reached the fourth page of the admission forms, Clara said, "You do know that I love her, don't you?" Reflexively, I looked toward Nurse Lampet. "Not her! Your grandmother."

I took my time signing my name at the bottom of the form, taking care to print my relationship to the patient in large, accusing letters. Granddaughter. There, in black and white. A concise declaration of Clara's failure. Only then did I look up at my biological mother. "I know that you think that you do."

Clara's lips narrowed. "I fully admit that I made mistakes, Jeanette."

"Jane."

She ignored me. "I lost years, which I'll never be able to get back again. I didn't expect you to come running into my arms. I knew that you were an adult, that you've found your own way in the world. You make your own decisions. But I'd always believed that your grandmother would have taught you her greatest lesson—to keep an open mind."

Low blow.

I pictured Gran in the examining room, surrounded by ominous medical paraphernalia. What would she think if she heard us squabbling out here? She certainly had not intended any of *this* to be the result of our morning visit to the Smithsonian.

Gran had forgiven Clara. Couldn't I?

I sniffed and ran a hand down my face, as if I could scrape away the confusing mixture of emotions sparked by Clara's words. "I need to give these forms back. And I have to make a phone call."

"Tell that nurse that I'll bring her my black tourmaline solution when I come back tomorrow. That won't be a perfect fix, but it will extend the life of her amber by at least a few months."

I shuffled across the room and dropped off the forms. Nurse Lampet looked at me with pity, shaking her head as she reviewed the paperwork. When everything was pronounced to be in order, I dug into my purse and found my cell phone.

I stepped outside the hospital doors to make my call, forcing myself to take a trio of calming breaths. I punched in Melissa's number from speed dial. I could only hope that she had baked a batch of Triple-Chocolate Madness that morning. Nothing else was going to get me through the rest of the day.

Melissa didn't have any Triple-Chocolate Madness, but she brought along the next best thing—an entire pan of Butterscotch Blessings. The creamy flavor of the butterscotch blended into the oatmeal base, and the chocolate drizzle over the top provided a perfect bittersweet balance.

I ate half a dozen of the things.

But anything eaten in a hospital doesn't count, we all decided, as we kept Gran company in her room. Personally, I was just pleased that I had set aside the temptation to chew my fingernails to the quick. That Sephora nail polish really *did* work wonders.

Melissa passed around the pan of Blessings one more

time before she leaned back in her chair. "So, ladies," she said. "This whole hospital thing is not the *worst* thing that has happened this weekend."

Clara's eyes widened. "What could be worse?" she asked. She and I had fallen into a respectful, mutual silence. I needed to think about what she'd said. Not the part about the black tourmaline cleansing—that was total hogwash. But the rest of it would take some time for me to process.

Melissa grinned. "My date last night."

I laughed out loud. For years, I had been regaled with Melissa's tales of dating woe, but Gran and Clara were in for a treat. My best friend spread her hands out in front of her, as if she were presenting a tray of perfect drop cookies. "Last night was one for the record books."

"He was a FranticDate?" I asked, but then I laughed at the confusion on Gran's face.

Melissa nodded, taking a moment to clarify: "It's a Web site, Mrs. Smythe. I filled out a questionnaire, and a bunch of guys filled out the same questionnaire, and a computer matches us up with our soul mate."

Gran snorted. "A good square dance at the church did better for my husband and me. We didn't need any computer."

"Maybe I'll add square dancing to my list," Melissa said. Honest to God, I didn't know if she was kidding.

"So?" I said. "What's this guy like?"

"According to the computer, he's a doctor."

"Ohhhh," we all said, as if we'd just excavated some sacred relic from an ancient civilization.

Clara asked, "What else did you know about this man before you met him?"

Melissa ticked points off on her fingers. "Doctor. Prefers city loft to mountain cabin. Prefers Chinese food to burgers and fries. Reads *Popular Science,* not *People.* Favorite color, yellow."

"Melissa…" I said. I thought I could see where this was going.

She shook her head and held up one more finger. "Oh. And he's five feet six inches tall."

Melissa was five feet six inches tall. In her stocking feet. Not that she was a stickler for height in a prospective mate, and not that she spent a lot of time walking around in stiletto heels, but all the same…

Clara asked, "So how does this work? The computer spits out his name and you just call him up and invite him over for dinner?"

Melissa shook her head again. "Not quite. We exchanged e-mail a few times, using anonymous e-mail addresses that the computer set up for us. You know, in case he's an ax murderer. Then we talked on the phone. He sounded like a nice guy—really interested in giving back to the community, energized by finishing up medical school. We agreed to have dinner down in Chinatown. At Eat First."

Gran looked confused again. "It's a Chinese restaurant," I explained. "With a menu that goes on about a thousand pages."

Clara said, "And? How was the charming doctor?"

But Melissa was not one to be rushed. "I got there first. Jane, you'll appreciate this. I actually changed out of my work clothes. I had on a jersey skirt and a cable-knit sweater. I brushed my hair. I *even* put on lipstick."

That told me more than Melissa would ever convey to Gran and Clara. She had put on makeup for this guy. She had liked him. A lot. I nodded to let her know that I understood what she was telling me.

"I got to the restaurant first," she repeated. "They seated me, and I started to look through the menu. I'd had a busy day at the bakery, and I hadn't had a chance to eat lunch. I was *starving.*" In honor of Melissa's suffering, I helped myself to yet another one of the Blessings.

"Three different men came up to my table. Who knew that Eat First could be so popular for first dates? For first *blind* dates. The third guy seemed nice enough, and I almost decided to say that I *was* Penelope, and that I did, in fact, play the piano, and that I was—surprise, surprise!—waiting for George. But that wouldn't have been right."

We all shook our heads. It *wouldn't* be right. Even if it was the perfect fodder for a sitcom.

"Then, Michael-the-doctor came in. He walked directly over to my table, and he sat down before he said hello. He held out his hand across the table, and he said it was a pleasure to meet me."

"And?" I asked. I felt as if I were on a roller coaster, and the car had ratcheted its way up the steepest hill.

"If he was a half inch over five feet, that was because he was wearing elevator shoes."

"No!" Gran gasped.

"Cross my heart," Melissa said. "His body was strange— sitting at the table, he was normal height, but standing up, he was just about eye-level with my, um, chest."

Gran shook her head, determined to be the voice of

wisdom in these things. "But surely you wouldn't let a little thing like height get in the way of an otherwise perfect romance?"

"It wasn't the height," Melissa said. "It was the lying about it. And even if that wasn't enough, the real fun started when we got ready to order. No beef, because he doesn't eat red meat. No seafood, because you can't trust any restaurant's refrigeration. In fact, no meat at all, because it could be cross-contaminated—yes, that's the word he used—*contaminated*."

"Well," Clara said. "There are lots of good vegetarian options in Chinese restaurants. I frequently enjoy Chinese because it helps me to keep my aura balanced. The harmonic—" She caught herself and swallowed hard. "So what did you order?"

"At first, I thought I'd try the General Tso's Tofu. But I was informed that it would be a nightmare for my arteries. No, not just a nightmare. I was treated to an entire discourse on arterial plaques and the demon that is the American diet. That ruled out fried rice and lo mein. And don't even get me started on the Buddha's Eight Treasures."

"What?" I asked. "He has a problem with water chestnuts?"

"Baby corn. You can never be sure that child-labor laws weren't broken in its harvesting."

I leaned back in my chair, feeling utterly defeated. "So what did you end up with?"

"An order of steamed cabbage wontons and a side of brown rice."

I laughed. "At least it couldn't take you very long to eat.

You could make it back home with plenty of time for a real dinner in the peace and quiet of your own kitchen."

"And that, my dear best friend, is where you would be wrong. Michael-the-doctor is a proponent of natural digestion."

Even Clara was taken off guard by that one. "Natural digestion? As opposed to what? Swallowing a bunch of enzymes and jumping up and down?"

"Nat-u-ral di-gest-ion. Chewing each bite fifty times." Melissa took on a tone as if she were reciting the good doctor's words. "Complete chewing promotes the release of hormones, digestive enzymes and gastric juices specific to the food being chewed. Chewing also lets the food become covered with saliva."

"And you actually made it through a plate of cabbage wontons?" My fascination and horror were blended in equal amounts.

"I made it through three."

"Three plates?"

"Three wontons. I couldn't, um, stomach any more."

"What a horrid little man!" Gran exclaimed.

"But why did he choose Eat First, if he had so many problems with their menu?" I asked.

"Can you think of any place he might have liked more?"

Clara started laughing. "And let me guess. Your part of the dinner bill—"

"Came to eight dollars and twenty-three cents. Tax and tip included. Ten percent tip, because they stopped filling our water glasses after the first hour."

"The first hour!" I whooped. "How long were you there?"

"Three and a half hours," Melissa enunciated grimly.

We all exploded with laughter. Three-point-five hours, one order of cabbage wontons and a bowl of rice. Plus waiting. Plus lying over height. Plus the lost opportunity to pose as piano-playing Penelope for George. "This may be your best blind-date story yet," I said.

"You are a cruel and heartless woman," Melissa countered. She glanced at her watch. "Look, I have to get going. There's always a rush at the bakery on Saturday afternoons."

Clara stood and stretched. "I'll walk you out. I want to get a bottle of water. Anybody else need anything?"

Gran and I demurred, gave our goodbyes to Melissa and then were alone in a room that was suddenly too silent. After an awkward moment, I reached toward her. "Can I shift that pillow for you?"

"It's fine," she said. I tugged at it, anyway. "Jane," Gran said, and I knew that her warning tone was about more than the pillow.

"What?"

"She's trying."

"What do you mean?"

"I can see how impatient you are with your mother. It's written across your face, every time she says something."

"Most of the time she's saying something weird!"

"She's every bit as nervous as you are. She wants this to work."

"She's got a strange way of showing it." I knew that I sounded like a brat, but I couldn't help it. I tried to think of something a bit more mature to say.

Fortunately—or not—Gran filled the conversational gap. "Make me a promise, Jane."

I sighed. "What this time?"

"Promise me that you'll come up to the Farm."

The Farm. A Connecticut farmhouse just outside of Old Salem. It had been in the family for years. Gran's sister and two brothers always got together there the third weekend in October. They brought their kids and grand-kids; the place absolutely swarmed with aunts and uncles and cousins. There were two huge rooms in the attic, a Girls' Room and a Boys' Room, and assorted outbuildings were pressed into service as guest cottages.

"Gran, you know I hate the Farm."

"You loved it when you were a little girl."

Of course I did. When I was a little girl, we spent the entire weekend running around, playing practical jokes on each other. We ate apples that we picked fresh from the trees in the yard. We lit a giant bonfire. We stayed up talking until the darkest hours of the night, pretending that the thumps we heard from the boys' dorm were ghosts haunting the hallways.

Now everyone was settled down. The last time I'd gone—seven years before—I had explained to thirteen different relatives that Scott and I were going to get married someday. Someday soon. He loved me. We just weren't ready to settle down. But we would be. I knew we would be.

I could hardly face all of them now. Alone. Still unmarried after all that time. Without a likely candidate on the horizon.

"Gran—"

"Jane, I don't make many requests of you." She didn't? What world did *she* live in? "But your mother is going to be there. And I want you to come, too."

I looked at her, pathetic in her hospital bed. They had dressed her in one of those embarrassing cotton gowns. An IV needle threaded into her arm, and her papery flesh looked bruised. Plastic tubing draped around her neck like some avant-garde excuse for a necklace. A machine by her head pulsed a bright red light every time her heart beat.

"Okay, Gran," I sighed. "I'll go to the Farm."

"You can bring along a friend."

Like *that* would help. Melissa had to run the bakery. And Neko… Let's just say that he wouldn't quite fit into the Farm aesthetic. Still, I managed a smile. Gran was trying to make this easier for me. "Thank you. I'll see if I can think of anyone to ask."

21

Neko said, "Tell me again what you're looking for?"

I waved my hand at the stacks of books surrounding us. "I don't even know, really. Something that will help my grandmother. A spell that I can work for her to get better faster. Something to help her breathe more easily. To keep her fever down."

I'd spent the entire day at the hospital, but I was too tired to sleep. After climbing in bed at midnight, I'd stared up at the ceiling, telling myself that I really needed to get my rest. When the digital clock flashed 3:00 a.m., though, I'd given up.

When I'd snuck into the living room, Neko was instantly awake, calling out from his makeshift bed on one of the overstuffed couches. I hadn't heard him come in from his dinner with Roger; that was a sign of how distracted I'd been. I'd made us a pot of chamomile tea, and we'd discussed the relative merits of standard undershirts versus A-shirts. (According to Neko, Roger had a distressing tendency to wear the latter. I didn't want to know more.)

We'd retreated to the basement when I realized that I just wasn't going to get any sleep that night. If anything, the books were in greater disarray than when I'd first discovered them. I had personally thumbed through the shelves a couple of times, studying titles and bindings, and I suspected that Neko had been prowling around during the days, when I was at work. I really needed to make the time commitment to getting them in order.

Right. After Gran got out of the hospital. After the opera guild's Harvest Gala. After the trip up to the Farm.

"How about crystals?" Neko asked.

"What!" I hadn't mentioned Clara to him. What possible good could it do to tell my familiar about her oracular harmonic-convergence-centering crystal-cleansing?

"All the best witches use them." Neko looked around the basement. "I know there's a box in here somewhere."

"You have got to be kidding." Were the crystals really another link between Clara and me? More proof that my family had magical roots?

Neko blinked. "I never kid. Not about magic, anyway. It's not in my nature to joke about my essential raison d'être."

I sighed. Far be it from me to question my familiar's essential raison d'être.

Neko crossed the basement, peering into the darkest corner. "Let's see. I sensed it when you first awakened me. I could feel all of the power in the room—that's one of the first things they teach us, to take an inventory of our surroundings."

"Who is 'they'?"

"The Coven." Neko looked at me as if I were either insane or heinously stupid. "Maybe you're too tired to think about this tonight. If you want to go back to bed, I'll see if I can find the crystals, and we can talk about them in the morning."

Neko being solicitous was almost as annoying as Neko being fashion advisor. I shook my head. "Okay, so the Coven teaches you to take an inventory each time that you're awakened."

"Right. And when you awakened me, I was standing there." He moved back to the reading table, where he'd crouched as a cat statue. "And I felt the harmonic vibrations—"

"Oh, come on!"

"What?" Neko looked totally innocent.

"Harmonic vibrations? Next thing, you'll be telling me that you're a trained vibrational consultant."

"And when would I have found the time to do that? I'm just a familiar, you know. And Hannah Osgood locked me away in 1919. They've only been training vibrational consultants for the past thirty years or so."

I shook my head at his matter-of-fact tone. "What about black tourmaline?" I challenged him, thinking of Clara's offer to cleanse Nurse Lampet's amber. "Did you sense any black tourmaline solution when you woke up?"

"Right," Neko scoffed. "Like I'd actually fall for that 'black tourmaline' stuff. I didn't join the Coven yesterday, you know. It's only the most gullible fools who get taken in by 'black tourmaline' solution. You might as well waste your money on eye of newt."

So there. Even if Clara *was* a witch, she'd been conned by a beginner's trick. I didn't know if that made me feel better or worse.

"Aha!" Neko pounced on a pile of books with the vigor of a tabby going after a mouse. He picked up half a dozen volumes, one by one, setting them aside and shaking his head. And there, underneath the disarray of parchment and leather, was a wooden box.

With a grunt, Neko picked it up, but he sneezed as he brought it to rest against his chest. "Dust. Someone should really get this place cleaned up."

"I thought that was your job," I said, hoping to deflect a little of my guilt.

"I don't do windows," Neko said. "Or dust. Or vacuum. Let's get this thing upstairs, where the light is better."

I followed him out of the basement, unable to resist looking over my shoulder a few times. I don't know what I expected to see. It wasn't as if the books were going to come to life on their own. They weren't going to fly across the room, placing themselves on the shelves in order.

Neko grunted as he set the wooden chest on the coffee table. I sat beside him on the couch and studied the thing. It had looked heavy in Neko's arms. It was about two feet on a side, entirely made of wood. I could make out a pair of corroding brass hinges on the back and a metal hasp along the front. A bar of polished wood held the hasp closed.

The surface of the box was scarred, as if someone—or something—had sharpened its claws against the surface long ago. I looked at Neko, but his well-manicured nails did not seem up to the destructive job. He met my eyes. "Well, go ahead."

"Go ahead?"

"Take out the wooden bar. Open the thing."

"What is it?"

"Open." He sighed and rolled his eyes, as if he were waiting for me to finish trying on a new blouse.

I set my jaw and pushed on the wooden bar. It was surprisingly difficult to get moving. I grunted and tried again. "Son of a—" I said, as I ripped one of my fingernails.

"Ah, ah, ah!" Neko said, playfully stopping my foul language.

His admonition wasn't enough to knock me silent, but my fingers were. I had torn a fingernail. Me. The girl whose nails had been bitten to the quick for so long that I'd forgotten what it felt like to break one. Inordinately pleased with myself, I attacked the wooden bar again, and it finally started to slip. I banged it with the heel of my hand a few more times, and it fell free from its brass hasp.

I made short work of opening up the box. Inside, there were a half dozen nested trays, suspended on a complicated system of brass hinges and struts. The container reminded me of a tackle box, but it must have been built in the days well before plastic. Built in the days before glowing fishing lures, as well, for that matter.

But my ancient wooden tackle box was filled with treasures, nonetheless.

Each tray was broken into dozens of velvet-padded compartments, and each of those cells contained a separate stone. There were rocks that were readily classifiable as crystals—jagged shards with regular angled sides. There were other stones, as well—some beads that looked as if they'd been rubbed smooth by countless fingers, a handful of spheres, each polished like perfect marbles.

"What *are* these things?" My voice was thick with wonder as I reached out for the nearest stone.

"Neko, aren't you obliged to warn her before she touches the Spinster Stone?"

I jerked my hand back and bit off a surprised cry, managing to smother another like I was swallowing a hiccup. Even before I turned toward the kitchen door, I recognized David Montrose's voice. "Don't you knock anymore?"

"I did. You must not have heard, because you were down in the basement. I let myself in and helped myself to some tea."

He saluted me with his mug of chamomile. I cast a wary eye toward my front door. I could have sworn that I'd locked it before I went to bed. "You did," David said, as though he were reading my mind. "You locked it. It's standard practice, though, for a warder to be able to open his own witch's locks. It can come in handy if she's ever in any real danger."

"I guess witches don't feel any great need for privacy."

David shrugged. "I guess not. Not from their warders, anyway." For just a moment, I was reminded of the David Montrose who had appeared on my doorstep that first night, after I'd awakened Neko. That man was cold and angry, domineering in his possession of specialized information. Not the same man who had taken me to dinner at La Chaumière and Paparazzi. Not the one who had answered the rest of my questions with good humor. Not the one who had kissed me and retracted that promise.

David grinned, and the expression helped him to slip back into the new and improved warder that I'd come to like. "So you've decided to move on to crystals?"

"I told Neko that I was looking for something to help my grandmother." I summarized Gran's illness.

David nodded. "You've shown some affinity for spells. But working with crystals is completely different. Most witches aren't able to work both areas."

"I think I might manage." I looked at the box again, at drawer after drawer of empowered stones. "I think my mother has an affinity for crystals."

If David understood how much effort it took for me to call Clara my mother, he didn't say anything. Instead, he came to sit beside me. "Let's see what you can do, then." He reached into the box and shifted the layers to get to the bottom one. His fingers ranged over the divided compartments, alighting first on one stone, then on another.

I glanced at Neko. He was watching David curiously, turning his head slightly to the side, as if he were trying to discern some meaning behind my warder's actions. As David finally selected one stone, Neko nodded minutely. I reached out my hand for the rock, and Neko leaned close to me, as he had when we cast the fire spell in my kitchen.

David set the stone on my palm. "Tell me what you feel."

It was a clear crystal about half the length of my index finger. I turned it around in the light, looking for striations or other markings, but there was nothing to distract from the stone's simple perfection. If not for its weight and its cool touch, it might have been made of plastic. I examined its facets and found nothing, no distinguishing marks, no surface features.

I started to feel silly. I mean, here it was, the middle of the night. I was a grown woman, looking for a magic token to help my sick grandmother. What did I think this was? Some sort of fairy tale? I closed my hand over the stone and looked at David. "What?" he asked.

"Nothing! It's a rock."

Neko shifted closer to me, and I sensed that he was disappointed in my response. I craned my neck to look at him, but his attention was locked on the crystal closed inside my fist. I took a deep breath and tried again. "It's clear. It's heavy, for its size."

"Very good," David said, and I could tell from his tone that he meant it. "How does it feel?"

I took a deep breath and forced myself to concentrate. After all, the spells had worked, even if I had first thought that their singsong rhymes were absurd. "It doesn't have a feeling," I said after a long pause. "It doesn't have an emotion of its own. Instead, it's like a magnifying glass. It makes other things more intense." The more words that I strung together, the more confident I became. "Yes! That's it! It enhances other feelings. It's making me more sure of myself right now!"

"Precisely." I had not realized that my eyes were closed until David spoke. I popped them open to find that he was smiling at me. "That's clear quartz in your hand. An excellent specimen of it, too. It's an amplifier, a strengthener of your existing thoughts. Try this one."

He dug around in the box again, extracting a rounded stone. He took the clear quartz from me and filled my palm with the new specimen. This one was pink, with black stripes arcing through it. It was completely smooth, as if it had spent years in a rock tumbler.

I folded my fingers around it and closed my eyes. This one had a definite…flavor. A power. It was soft. Gentle. It made me think of Gran. Of Gran tucking me into bed at night when I was a little girl. I remembered something that Clara had said at the museum that morning—it already seemed so long ago! The pink crystal there meant family.

"Love?" I said, trying to distill the sensations into a single word.

"Yes," David said, and he pitched his voice low, as if he were reluctant to disturb the balance I was building with the stone. "It's called rhodosite. It eases stress. Heart-ache."

My eyes snapped open. Exactly what did he know about my heart? Just how much did he know about me?

If he was surprised by my reaction, he gave no sign. Instead, he dug around in the box again. This time, the rock that he gave me was a translucent dark green. I thought that it might be jade, except it didn't have any milky quality. When I peered closer, I saw a sheen across its surface, as if it had been dusted with the finest glitter imaginable.

I folded my fingers around it and reached out for its meaning. The stone felt…positive. Beneficent. I smiled as the word unfolded in my mind. This stone was designed to do good. It was designed to bring about positive changes. I took a deep breath and tried to extend my powers further around it. It thrummed. Like the energy I had harnessed through the spell books, the crystal vibrated. The power moved up my arm, and it settled in my chest. In my heart. My lungs.

I breathed as deeply as I could, thinking fleetingly that my yoga teacher would be proud of me. As I exhaled, the crystal's warmth stayed behind. It made my torso glow.

I was vaguely aware of Neko leaning against me. I remembered his steady force, his focusing of my witchy power, so unlike his manic fashion and makeup advice. Without opening my eyes, I reached out for his magical anchoring. I felt it in the air between us, a path into the heart of the stone. I gathered together the energy inside me, and I plunged deep into the green crystal.

Then I realized how the stone could help Gran. It could hold all of the energy I felt. It could relay power to *her* heart, to her lungs, to her weary, ailing body.

All it took was my recognizing the possibility, and then I was siphoning off healing power from myself, pouring it into the crystal. I streamed in all the warmth, the comfort, the vibrating strength that had coalesced in my own body. The green rock drank it up; the shimmering glitter became energized with my thoughts. The crystal was a battery, a bank; it stored all the power I could give it.

"That's enough," David whispered, and his words startled me back to consciousness.

I hadn't been dreaming, precisely. I hadn't fallen asleep. No. I'd been meditating. I'd been harnessing the power of my mind over my body, as if I were mastering my yoga instructor's Corpse Pose.

I opened my eyes and stared at the crystal on my palm. "What is it called?"

"Aventurine. It's a quartz, as well. But one that focuses healing." David reached into the wooden box and pulled out a velvet drawstring sack. "Here."

I was exhausted. I had no idea what he expected me to do with the sack. Neko finally took my hand and tilted it gently so that the stone rolled into the bag. As my familiar tightened the silk ribbons, David nodded. Neko tucked the sack into a pocket that rested over his right breast.

"You can give it to your grandmother tomorrow."

"No." I tried to protest, but I could barely manage a whisper. "She's sick. She needs this tonight. I'm family. They'll let me in."

"It's practically morning, anyway, and she has Western medicine for now. The IV they put her on is doing more than even this crystal can. When you give it to her tomorrow, it can start the long work of healing, of strengthening."

I shook my head and tried to get to my feet. I only succeeded on the third try.

I was as weak as a kitten. I felt as if I'd run a marathon. As if I were a single pat of butter spread over an entire baguette.

A baguette. Melissa should bake baguettes for Cake Walk. She could call herself a bag lady.

I giggled at my own joke. I felt drunk, as if I'd downed an entire pitcher of mojitos without benefit of any food.

Come to think of it, a mojito would be good about

now. "Neko!" I said. "Mix some drinks! The magic wand is in the drawer!"

Neko looked disconcerted, but David only pursed his lips. "Come on, Jane. It's time for you to get some sleep. Let's get you ready for bed."

I took a step and started to stumble. I covered really well, though, by catching myself on the sofa. I folded my hands in front of me, trying to project an image of determined innocence. Dorothy Gale bound to confront the Wizard of Oz. When I spoke, however, my voice cracked, and I came off more like Margaret Hamilton, the Wicked Witch of the West. "Is that an invitation, big boy?"

I'm pretty sure that Neko snickered, but by the time I swiveled my eyes toward him, he was studying his fingernails. David shook his head and said, "Just doing my job."

It took both of them to walk me down the short hallway. My legs didn't want to cooperate—my feet kept dragging against the floor. It was a good thing I still had my bunny slippers; I could have ended up with some terrible splinters otherwise.

When we got to my bedroom, David took my key and unlocked the door. The three of us started to stumble forward, when I saw the moonlight glint off of Stupid Fish's aquarium. "No!" I said. I flailed around to push a hand against Neko's chest. "You can't come in here!"

David followed my line of sight, and he turned to look at Neko. My familiar shrugged elaborately, as if it had never crossed his mind to invade the piscine privacy of my bedroom. David said, "I've got her from here."

Neko's disappointment would have made me laugh, if

the room hadn't suddenly started to spin like a Tilt-A-Whirl. Somehow, Neko disappeared. David got me over to my bed. I collapsed backward onto the mattress, closing my eyes as calliope music filled my skull.

I felt David's hands on my feet, slipping off my precious bunnies. He sat beside me on the bed, and I sensed his fingers untying the knot of my bathrobe around my waist. He eased me into a sitting position and slid the robe from my shoulders. I was vaguely glad that I was wearing my faded men's pajamas—top *and* bottom.

Somehow, he got me underneath the covers. My pillow was perfectly centered under my head. The sheets were cool against my bare arms, and the comforter was heavy across my body. "Go to sleep," he said, and he passed his hand over my forehead.

There must have been something magical about the motion, because I was suddenly unable to open my eyes. "David?"

"Hmm?"

"What happened?"

"You used new powers. I let you go deeper than you should have. I felt the strength of your love for your grandmother, and that swayed my judgment. Get some sleep. You'll be fine when you wake up."

"David?"

"Hmm?"

"You're different now."

"Different?"

"Than the first night. You scared me then."

For a long time, I thought that he wouldn't answer. I

thought that I had fallen asleep, but my brain didn't quite know it. I thought that I was imagining our entire conversation. But then he spoke.

"That first night, I didn't know who you were. I came here as a warder, trying to protect resources that were in danger."

"And then?" It took all my strength to pull out the two words.

"I met you. I did some research. I became the warder you wanted me to be—you *needed* me to be. So that you would listen. And learn."

There was something wrong about that. Something that didn't quite make sense. I started to put more words together, to ask another question, but David passed his hand over my forehead one more time. "Sleep, Jane. We'll talk more later. Sleep."

And I did.

22

Gran was staring listlessly at the television set when I arrived at the hospital. Her bed had been cranked up so that she was sitting upright. Her pillow, which had probably once been situated to cradle her head, had slipped down her back, making her look cramped and uncomfortable. Oxygen flowed through tubing that nestled under her nose.

"Good morning, Gran!" I pasted a cheery smile on my face.

"Hello, dear." She sounded cranky and tired, and if she were a toddler, I would have prescribed a long nap. I was a bit surprised that I wasn't more tired myself, but I had awakened refreshed and recharged, completely energized by my working with the crystals.

I tried not to let my good mood get burned off by Gran's frown. "How are you today?" I asked, in a voice that might have been appropriate for a grown-up on *Sesame Street*.

"I hate it here," Gran said.

"You'll be home soon," I reassured her.

"I can't get any sleep because the nurses constantly come in to take my temperature, or adjust my oxygen or read my blood pressure. The man next door was moaning all night, and the woman on the other side of that curtain had her grandchildren visiting until ten o'clock. Grandchildren! In a hospital!"

I reminded myself that Gran didn't mean me. She was only complaining about someone else's brats. I renewed my smile. "I've brought you a present!"

Gran seemed about to make another tart observation, but then curiosity got the better of her. Her hazel eyes, so like my own, even if they were bloodshot just now, looked inquiringly at me.

I handed Gran a small box. Neko had helped me to find it in the basement. It just about filled my palm, sitting high, with a row of hinges on one wooden edge. It looked ancient and delicate, but solid at the same time, the sort of box that Romeo might have used to give a ring to Juliet.

"What's this?" Gran asked. "You shouldn't have gone to any trouble. Not for me. Not just because I have a little bug."

"Open it!" I urged. I wanted to see her reaction. I wanted to see if my crystal would work.

Still fussing, Gran lifted the box's lid. For just a moment, she didn't know what to make of the contents. I'd nestled the aventurine on a bed of soft velvet. "What's this?" Gran asked again, but now her voice was filled with tetchy curiosity.

"Just something that I found. Something that I thought you'd like. Maybe you can use it as a worry stone, rubbing it when you feel stressed."

Gran looked at it dubiously. "Your mother has always been a big one for worry stones." I stored away that interesting tidbit of information.

"Well, Gran, maybe I got more from her than I knew," I said.

Gran drew in a deep breath, as if she were going to reply, but she only triggered a coughing fit. Like the others, this one shook her entire body, turning her face purple, and clenching her fingers into claws. Helpless, I handed her a Kleenex, but then all I could do was wait. And wait. And wait.

When over a minute had passed, and she was still hacking painfully, I threw caution to the winds. I snagged the jewel box from Gran's sheets, where she had set it when the spasm began, and I upended it onto her withered palm.

Her fingers curled around the stone by reflex. Her eyes closed as she sucked in more air. But she stopped coughing.

She sank back on her pillow, eyes still shut, as she breathed shallowly. Perspiration stood out on her forehead, but I did not want to disturb her by wiping it away.

"Do you want me to get a nurse, Gran?" I asked, when it seemed certain that she had completely conquered the cough. This time.

"No, dear. Not right now."

Surprisingly, Gran's voice sounded stronger than it had when I arrived. She must have heard it, too; her eyes flew open. "No, dear," she said again. "I'm actually feeling a little better."

I helped her to sit up straighter in bed, and I adjusted her pillow so that she no longer looked like Quasimodo's frailer cousin. When she was settled, she smiled at me, and it was the patient smile I remembered from my childhood. My heart quickened, and I glanced at the aventurine, only to find it still hidden in her fist.

"There is one thing, dear, if it wouldn't be too much trouble."

"What, Gran? Anything!"

"I wasn't hungry for dinner last night, but some applesauce would be lovely now. Some applesauce, and maybe a hard-boiled egg?"

"I'll see what I can do," I said, moving toward the door. When I stepped into the hallway, I glanced back and saw that Gran was absentmindedly rubbing the aventurine with her thumb. Color had come back into her lips, and her breathing was easier. I almost skipped down the corridor in search of a healing woman's breakfast.

"You are totally falling for him!" Melissa's amusement over the telephone line was so extreme that I looked up to see if any of the library patrons could hear her.

"I am not!" I whispered into the handset.

"You are. You used to talk about Scott exactly the same way. You were going to wear the such-and-such dress to please him, you were going to see the whatever-it-was movie because you thought he'd like it."

"That's ridiculous! I certainly didn't wear my faded plaid pajamas because I thought David would like them."

"You know what I mean."

I did. But Melissa was totally, completely, one hundred percent wrong. *Jason Templeton* was my Imaginary Boyfriend. I mean, Boyfriend. No longer Imaginary. Jason. The man I had watched for the past nine months. The man I had dreamed of. The man I was going to lunch with in less than an hour. Just to clarify my arguments one more time, I said to Melissa, "I do not have feelings for David Montrose. He's like my *boss*."

"And you've never heard of interoffice romance?"

"He's my *mentor*," I said priggishly. "He has a moral and ethical obligation to show me the way toward being a proper witch."

"And he's really, really hot." I could imagine her grinning, leaning against the counter in Cake Walk.

Well, that's what I got for calling my best friend in the middle of the workday. I should have known that she'd give me a hard time. And I did *not* need to be traumatized today. It was time for me to leave, to meet Jason for lunch at La Perla. I said, "I'm not even going to dignify that with an answer." Melissa only laughed. "I'm hanging up on you now! I'm going back to work!"

I was laughing, too, by the time I returned the phone to its cradle.

Sure, David was a viscerally attractive guy. But he was totally off-limits. I mean, it would be one thing if we were peers, if we were walking into the relationship on equal footing, both understanding who we were and how things work.

But he was light-years ahead of me in the witchcraft department. He understood all of that magic stuff; he knew how to harness powers that I could only imagine. Exhibit A was the healing crystal that he had guided me in making for Gran.

Besides, a nagging voice whispered at the back of my mind, he had changed himself to be with me. The more I thought about that, the more creeped out I was by the information. I mean, how many times had I changed myself to be with Scott? And had it worked out well?

I mean, had I really thought that I was going to develop a love for Italian cinema just because Scott had one? And what had I been thinking when I'd started in on the collected works of Tolstoy? Just because Scott said that they contained the sum experience of the human condition, why had I thought they would speak to me? And we wouldn't even begin to talk about my professed love of ice hockey. There were some things no girl should ever be forced to pretend.

And yet, things were different with David. He had readily *admitted* changing himself to be with me—a clarification that I'd never made with Scott. And David actually seemed happy to have done it. He seemed…content.

Before I could twist myself into any more emotional pretzels, I dug my purse out of my desk. A quick check in my compact mirror for makeup flaws, a dash of lipstick, confirmation that nothing terrible had sprouted between my teeth…. I popped a mint into my mouth and headed to the library's front door.

That was one thing I could say about working at the Peabridge. The pay might be terrible, and I had to listen to way too many choruses of "Marian the Librarian" when I told people where I worked, but I had freedom when it came to my personal life. That morning, I had mentioned to Evelyn that I had an appointment over the lunch hour, and she had merely nodded, telling me to make up the time whenever I could.

And Jason Templeton was certainly worth making up a little time.

I smiled as I got to the doors, thinking of the date that awaited me. I could actually call it that. *He* had.

I looked down at the outfit that had taken an ungodly amount of time to assemble that morning. Black wool skirt. Formfitting cashmere sweater (of course, also black). Black tights. High-heeled pumps. A necklace of chunky green beads that I knew set off my eyes. I tried not to think of the mounds of clothing on my bed, the rejects from the morning's dressing marathon that would only have to be returned to their hangers.

I also tried not to think of my colonial costume, crammed into a garment bag and hanging over the chair beside my desk. I'd have to change back as soon as I returned from lunch. Even now, I suspected that Evelyn would give me the evil eye if she saw me out of uniform. I took a deep breath and headed out into the autumn chill.

"You look beautiful today!"

Dammit.

"Thank you, Harold." I had hoped to sneak out without encountering my lovestruck friend, but he was holding the door for me with all the formality of a Beefeater at Buckingham Palace. I slipped outside so that the fallen leaves on the doorstep wouldn't blow inside the lobby.

"It looks like you have an important meeting," Harold said.

"I have a d—" I stopped myself. I'd been cruel enough,

binding the poor man's love with that cursed spell. I didn't
have to rub in my lunchtime destination. I searched my
mind, frantically trying to find another word that started
with *d*, something other than *date*. "A dentist appointment!
Yes!"

"You seem really excited about it."

I did, didn't I? "Oh, no. It's just that I thought I was going
to forget it, and I've had it written down on my calendar
for months, you know, since the last time I went. I filled out
the little postcard thing, and they sent it to me as a reminder,
but it seems like I always have to reschedule anyway." I heard
myself rushing through my explanation, trying to justify my
enthusiasm and digging myself a deeper and deeper hole.
"I really hate the fluoride treatment, but I love it when I
get a new toothbrush. The last time, all they had were
orange toothbrushes, so I've been stuck with that, but this
time, I'm going to get a good color. Like purple. I love
purple. It's my favorite color."

Oh my God. I had gone insane. I was standing here
outside the Peabridge Library, babbling about purple toothbrushes.

"Mine is blue," Harold said.

"Blue! *Great* toothbrush color. Second favorite! Gotta
run! Don't want to keep the dentist waiting!"

Someone should just shoot me now.

Jason was waiting for me when I finally arrived at the
restaurant. He had managed to secure a table in a corner,
tucked into the back. I was a little disappointed. I liked the
idea of sitting behind the restaurant's lace curtains, of
watching the traffic go by on Pennsylvania Avenue. Maybe

someone would see us, someone I knew. They would wave and smile as they realized I was on a lunch date. They would call me during the afternoon, to ask about the absolutely gorgeous man who had been eating with me, the one with the blond curls and easy grin, who seemed to be hanging on my every word.

No one would see me now that I wasn't sitting at a table in the window.

When I took my seat, however, I realized that Jason had actually chosen well. Within our little nook, it seemed that we were the only people in the entire restaurant, the only people in the entire world.

"I'm sorry I'm late," I said, fiddling with the beads on my necklace.

"Traffic can be bad."

"Especially at lunchtime." Great. Brilliant conversation. This was terrible. It was as if I'd never seen Jason before, as if we'd never even spoken to each other.

The waiter came to take our drink orders. "I'll have a glass of Chianti," Jason said. "It's cold outside," he justified to me.

"And a Chianti for me, too," I said, following my Imaginary Boyfriend's lead.

No, I reminded myself. He wasn't Imaginary anymore. He had asked me out. He had brought me cute gifts (the marshmallows were still inside my desk drawer)!

Flustered by the seismic shift in our relationship, I gave the menu a ridiculous amount of attention. The entrées were all too heavy for lunch. The salads were too fussy. Pasta, then. Not long pasta, though. I'd never live it down with Melissa if I dripped linguine down my front. (Not to mention the dry-cleaning bill I'd get for my cashmere sweater.)

Tortellini, then. Bite-sized. Self-contained. No hidden dangers.

"Do you want to start with some garlic-cheese bread?" Jason asked.

My heart exploded in my chest. Garlic-cheese bread. You only ordered garlic-cheese bread if you really knew the person you were eating with. If you trusted them. A first date could never order garlic cheese bread, but a Boyfriend could.

"I'd love to," I said.

The waiter came back to the table, bringing the blessed fruit of the vine. He took our orders (Jason chose the lasagna al forno) and then he disappeared.

"So," Jason said.

"So," I echoed.

An ambulance went by outside, and its siren kick-started my brain. I took a sip of wine and dove into my story. "You would not believe the weekend that I had!"

I told him about going to the Natural History Museum with Gran, about how she had collapsed. I somehow managed to make it a funny story, stressing the bits that had not been at all amusing at the time—the way the Cell Phone Samaritan had blinked at the closing elevator doors, the way the ambulance had careened around corners. I told him how Melissa had come to the hospital with her But-terscotch Blessings, and how my grandmother had become the most popular patient on the floor.

Of course, I left out some parts. I didn't mention that I

was estranged from my own biological mother. I didn't tell him about my late-night crystal training session with David and Neko. I didn't say that I had created a healing charm in the privacy of my own living room, and I overlooked announcing that I seemed to have an affinity for crystals that was at least as great as my ability with spells.

I didn't tell him that my grandmother seemed to have some sensitivity to magical power—the same as Clara. As I.

But I entertained my date. Jason seemed intrigued as he dug into our garlic bread with gusto. So much had changed, he commented, since George Chesterton's time. Health care then was a nightmare of tinctures and ointments. I found myself agreeing, even going so far as to volunteer my time researching treatments for typhus, to learn more about how Chesterton's son had been cured of the deadly disease. After all, I *was* a librarian, and if my skills could help my Boyfriend…

Scott had never asked me for help.

By the time our pasta arrived, I was much more relaxed. I asked Jason how his work was going, about the current semester and the classes he was teaching. I laughed when he told me about one of his students—the one who thought that the colonists should have purchased their arms from the Soviet Union on the black market, so that they could have overwhelmed the British that much sooner.

"The Soviet Union?" I asked, incredulous.

"Well, he knew that the Soviets preceded today's Russia."

"What *do* they teach in high school these days?"

"A question that I ask myself every single day," Jason said, shaking his head. "I'm actually thinking of setting up a new project for next semester. You probably won't believe this, but I got the idea from the Peabridge."

"From us?" I felt a flush of pride. Or maybe that was my second glass of wine.

"When you started wearing your costume, it really changed everything for me. It made my reading come alive—it was as if the history was happening right then. George Chesterton could walk in the door at any moment."

Damn. Evelyn had been right.

Jason went on. "I'm thinking of having the students put together their own outfits. Use quill pens. Do some laundry the colonial way. Anything to actually experience the time period, to realize how different things were two hundred years ago."

"Don't you think that sounds a little…beneath college students?"

He smiled at me across the table. "Is it beneath you?"

"Well—I—" I tried to picture a roomful of college coeds, all wearing hoops and petticoats and sack gowns. I expanded my mental view, imagining Ekaterina the Ice Ballerina in a mobcap, grading essay exams with a quill pen dipped in red ink. "Do you think your grad students would go for it? I mean, I only met Ekaterina once, but *she* certainly didn't seem the type—"

"Ekaterina?" Jason looked surprised. He obviously had not thought through his grand hands-on scheme. Then, he shrugged. "She wouldn't need to join in. She specializes in nineteenth-century. Early suffrage movements."

"Yes!" I was surprised to hear myself say that out loud.

Must have been the Chianti. But I had told Melissa that Ekaterina was a proto-feminist controlling bitch the first time I'd met the Russian Ice Queen. I'd known it from the moment I'd laid eyes on her perfect brow.

Jason blinked, then smiled slyly. "It wasn't Ekaterina I was thinking of when I came up with the idea."

I twirled the stem of my wineglass between my fingers, suddenly shy. "Oh?"

"It was you." He leaned forward, settling his hand on top of mine. "Jane, I have to admit that there's something about seeing you dressed up that way."

I tried to laugh, but no sound came out. "I bet you say that to all the girls who try to poison you with peanut soup."

He shook his head. "I'm serious, Jane."

I couldn't believe it. Jason—my Boyfriend—was attracted to me in my colonial costume. It *must* be the love spell that I had worked, the words I had read from the grimoire.

He went on. "You'll probably think I'm crazy, but when I look up from my research, and I see you sitting at your desk, wearing your stays and that lace bodice…"

Oh. My. God.

The waiter came to take away our plates. "Dessert?" he asked. "Coffee?"

Jason looked at me, and I managed one short shake of my head. Jason said, "Just the check, please."

It was my turn to say something. Anything. "Sometimes, the lace itches."

Oh, that was great. Brilliant. The hottest words that anyone had spoken to me since Scott Randall first told me what he wanted to do in my Barbie-pink bedroom, and all

I could think to say was that I itched. I deserved to be alone until the day I died.

"I've made you blush."

"I just don't think of quilted petticoats as a turn-on."

"When you wear them, they are."

The waiter returned with the check before I could stammer out another embarrassing reply. Jason pulled out his wallet and dropped some money on the table. I started to reach for my purse, but he waved my hand away. As the waiter returned, Jason asked him, "The restrooms are downstairs?"

"Yes, signor."

I recognized Jason's grin. I remembered it from years before, from when Scott still thought about long afternoons of romance. Somehow, miraculously, I matched that goofy smile with one of my own.

Trying to pretend that I had just discovered my own need to freshen my makeup, I followed Jason down a narrow flight of stairs at the back of the restaurant.

Melissa was never going to believe this. She would never believe that I had shared garlic-cheese bread with my Boyfriend on our first official date. And she would certainly never believe that said Boyfriend found my colonial dress sexy. And there was absolutely, positively, no possible way that she was going to believe that that Boyfriend had led me down the service stairs toward the restrooms, only to sweep me into an alcove underneath those very steps.

I didn't even believe that it could happen to me.

Until I felt Jason's hand on the back of my neck. Until I felt his lips on mine.

Was this what I had missed the other night? The kiss that

I had managed to overlook, because I had been stupidly obsessing over the dinner I was about to ruin?

Okay, so it wasn't the best kiss in the world. How could it be, with us standing up in a poorly lit alcove beneath the stairs of an Italian restaurant during a busy lunch hour? I worried that I wasn't into it enough, that I wasn't leaning against him the right amount. I was afraid that my feet would slip on the linoleum floor.

But Jason managed to distract me from the flaws in the setting. The touch of his palms on my back did that. And the realization that he was gliding his hands around to my front. That he was slipping his fingers under the straps of my bra. My black lace bra. The one that I had hooked up that morning, chiding myself for wishful thinking.

A door opened behind us. I heard a woman's heels on the hard floor, heard her quick gasp of indrawn breath as she saw us. "Well, I never!"

Well, lady, I never did, either. But I sure as hell wouldn't mind doing it again.

Jason, though, was stepping away from me. "I'm sorry," he said, as the woman's heels clomped above us.

"Don't be."

He brushed back a strand of my hair. "I shouldn't have done that. You must think I'm some sort of animal."

"I think you're something, all right." I hoped that my smile indicated exactly what I thought he was.

There was more traffic on the stairs, another woman coming down. What was this, Grand Central Station? Trying to find something to do while she walked by, I glanced at my watch. "Ach! I have to get back to work!"

"So soon?"

"Evelyn thinks that I'm at an appointment. I need to get back to the reference desk." I started to sigh, frustrated that I hadn't managed to win the lottery and retire from my day job forever.

"I should let you go then." He trailed a finger along my jaw, and I almost melted into a garlic-fragrant puddle.

"I'll be changing clothes," I said when I could breathe again. I felt more than a little foolish, but I was rewarded by another one of Jason's wicked grins. "Once I get back to the library. I'll be wearing my costume." He actually moaned as he kissed me. I whispered as we pulled apart from each other: "But I'll think of you as I lace up my stays."

And I did.

Cheeks flushed from the walk back to the office, eyes bright with untold secrets, I pulled the linen strings extra tight. And I thought of Jason's touch all afternoon, as I researched medicine of the eighteenth century, an obscure founding father and the father's even more obscure son.

"Jane, I just can't get over how wonderful you look with-out glasses."

"Gran, was I really so terrible before?"

I was beginning to wonder. I'd received nothing but compliments since I'd picked up my contact lenses four days before. Neko had watched as I made faces in the bathroom mirror, inserting the lenses and taking them out until it seemed natural to poke my fingers in my eyes. He'd sniffed when I set aside my eyeglasses. "They were the wrong shape for your face anyway."

Now he told me.

Even David Montrose had noticed—and commented on—the change during our training sessions. We'd met three times in as many days. He had wanted me to focus on crystals rather than spell books, once I'd explained that Clara and Gran both seemed to have an affinity for them.

He thought that we should explore their magic, try to figure out whether they were the true source of my own power.

We hadn't come to any solid conclusions, but I'd learned a lot more about chalcedony, bloodstone and natrolite than I had ever thought possible. (Chalcedony stimulates maternal instinct among other things. I decided that I might want to make a gift to Clara.)

The training sessions had been intense, all the more so because I was constantly distracted by thoughts of Jason. My Boyfriend had not phoned during the week, and I'd constantly fought the temptation to dial his cell. I'd hoped that he would add a research session or two to his library schedule during the week, but I'd been sorely disappointed. I kept reminding myself, though, that the university was hurtling toward midterms. Jason was probably busy counseling students. Still, I sulked for the second half of the week, reading and rereading the research notes I'd prepared.

Maybe that was why I was so determined to make the Harvest Gala a success. Perhaps I was depressed over Jason's failure to phone. Or I was just desperate for a break from studying crystals with David. Or, just possibly, I wanted everything to be perfect for Gran.

She had been released from the hospital two days before, but she was still on strict instructions to get plenty of rest and limit outside activities. It had taken every ounce of my persuasive capabilities to convince her to stay home during the Gala. In the end, I think that it was actually Uncle George who made her believe that the possible risk of a relapse wasn't worth it. He'd said that he wanted to spend many more Harvest Galas with her.

Gran's eyes had teared up, and she'd finally agreed to stay in bed. Somewhat surprisingly, Clara had offered to spend the evening with her. Now I stood in front of both of them, feeling for all the world as if I were about to head out to my high school prom.

Earlier in the evening, I'd started to force my newly trimmed hair into some sort of updo for the grand event, but Neko had talked me out of that. Just as he'd convinced me that I couldn't wear my classic little black dress, as I'd long intended.

Well, if I hadn't wanted his advice, I probably shouldn't have told him that the event was black tie. He had immediately decided that I simply *must* wear autumn colors. I'd assured him that there was not a single shade of orange or yellow that would complement my coloring, and he'd reluctantly agreed. But then, he'd dragged me into some little boutique, a tiny hole in the wall that he'd apparently discovered during his daily neighborhood rambles.

I had to admit that the dark green shantung sheath he picked out was stunning. It was shot through with a hint of gold, just enough to make the eye take notice. I'd never had the courage to wear a strapless gown before. (I won't even bother explaining the lingerie lessons I was given by my familiar. Suffice to say that Victoria's Secret can accomplish miracles. Even on short notice.) Fortunately, Gran had already agreed to foot the bill for my finery.

"Now, don't forget to place my bids at the silent auction,"

Gran reminded me for the 432nd time. "And try to mingle with the new people. Make them feel at home."

"And don't forget to be home by midnight, or your coach will turn into a pumpkin," Clara added in a grave tone.

Gran frowned at her, momentarily distracted from her list of dos and don'ts. "Do you need money for a cab, dear?"

"I'm fine," I said, brandishing the little gold handbag that Neko had insisted I buy to complete my outfit. "But I really should be going."

I still needed another fifteen minutes of grandmaternal advice, including instructions on the frequent reapplication of lipstick and a reminder to keep my hair brushed. By the time I finally escaped, I wondered if I should just give up and head home. After all, it was the getting-dressed-up part that had been fun. The event itself was bound to be a disappointment, as I tried to remain vivacious and witty with the over-seventy crowd.

But I knew that Uncle George would report back to Gran. And I *had* promised to place her silent auction bids. Not to mention the fact that I felt pretty wonderful wearing my ball gown.

Ball gown. Who would have ever thought that Jane Madison, Librarian, would own a ball gown? Whether I was lucky or the green sheath did its job, I had no trouble hailing a cab right outside of Gran's apartment building.

The Gala was being held in the St. Regis Hotel, just a couple of blocks from the White House. As the taxi pulled into the small circular driveway, a shiver tiptoed down my spine. I paid the driver while the uniformed doorman waited to assist me out of the cab. Fairy lights reflected off the lobby's turquoise and gold coffered ceiling, and I blinked, trying to figure out where I was supposed to go. Another uniformed attendant glided to my side. "May I help you, madam?"

Madam? Me?

I couldn't help but answer with a British accent—it just seemed like the appropriate thing to do. "Yes, please. The Concert Opera Harvest Gala?"

"Of course, madam," he murmured. "Right this way."

Rather than point to the door on the far side of the lobby, he walked me across the inlaid floor. I murmured my thanks as he left me framed in the ballroom's ornately carved double doorway.

The Gala seemed to be in full swing, or at least as full a swing as the evening was likely to achieve. A surprisingly good jazz band filled the stage at the end of the room, energetically playing something that was actually danceable. At least a dozen couples were taking advantage of the parquet floor.

Rectangular tables had been set up around the edges of the room, pushing up against heavy gold-brocade curtains. Each table had a green-shaded accountant's lamp, directing light onto a beautifully printed silent auction form. As I sidled along the wall, I could see that several bids had already been entered for many of the prizes. Deciding that I should keep my promise to Gran early, I wrote in her bids on the appropriate sheets, taking especial care with her first pick, a landscape painting by local Impressionist artist, Bill Schmidt.

The bar was set up against the near wall of the room, and a few people were waiting for drinks. Next to the bar was a towering display of desserts; even from my vantage point, I could make out perfect mini-eclairs, a glistening croquembouche and wave after wave of individual fruit tarts.

Feeling strangely anonymous without my glasses, in my grown-up dress with my grown-up hair and my grown-up clasp handbag, I secured a glass of champagne from a passing waiter. Alas, once I had my drink in hand, I slipped back into the trauma of every party I had ever attended anywhere in my life. I didn't know anyone. I was terrible at making small talk. No one was ever going to ask me to dance. I'd never even heard of most of the operas that were the bread and butter of this crowd.

I made another circuit of the room, upping one of Gran's auction bids that had already been countered, and then I retreated to the corner farthest from the band. I wished that I could lock myself into a stall in the ladies' room until the evening was over.

I considered it a success that I made my champagne last for an entire jazz number. When a too-attentive waiter took my glass away on his silver tray, I practically sprinted to the bar to secure another flute. After all, it wouldn't do to have my hands empty. People might think that I wasn't enjoying myself.

That second drink, however, only made things complicated. Just as I was feeling the first heady tickle of the champagne, a flock of waiters descended on the room, passing enormous trays of sinfully tempting appetizers.

The first that came my way was a deconstructed Peking duck—slivers of duck served with shreds of crisp pancake and a drizzle of hoisin sauce, all presented on porcelain Chinese soup spoons. The food was delicious, and I managed to eat it without leaving behind unsightly streaks of Pick-Me-Up Pink. But then, I was left holding a spoon in one hand and a champagne glass in another.

And I realized I was really hungry.

Other waiters sailed by. There was a tantalizing tray of miniature frenched lamb chops, their curved bones serving as the perfect handhold. Another tray of grilled pear slices with blue cheese melting on top. A third of roast beef tenderloin, sliced paper thin and presented on caraway flatbread.

But not a single server was collecting used soup spoons. If I had planned better, I would have eaten the other treats first, then gone for the Peking duck. Having gone out of order, I was stuck without fingers for the finger food. (In theory, I could have put down my champagne glass, but I never actually considered that as an option.)

Just as my stomach actually gurgled a protest, I heard someone say, "May I help you with that spoon?"

I turned around, relieved that one of the tuxedoed staff had finally noticed my predicament. I found myself face-to-face with Samuel Potter, the owner of the shih tzu named Beijing. "Mr. Potter!" I said, surprised to find a person instead of a waiter. No, I knew that waiters were people, too. But you know what I meant.

Much to my embarrassment, he took my spoon, and my now-empty glass. Within seconds, a waiter materialized to relieve Mr. Potter of the burden. I started to make a snappy complaint, but I decided that the Harvest Gala was neither the time nor the place.

Mr. Potter kissed my cheek gallantly. "You look ravishing, dear."

I flushed, even as I wondered at the strength of my grimoire's love spell. How many weeks had passed since I had first worked it? How long could my witchcraft hold? And why had I repeatedly forgotten to ask David about the spell? I'm sure I would have remembered at some point in the past week, if he hadn't been plying me with tray after tray of dusty rocks.

I remembered that I needed to reply. "It's certainly kind of you to say so, Mr. Potter."

"And are you enjoying yourself?"

"Absolutely. The Peking, er, Beijing duck was excellent."

Mr. Potter's laugh boomed across the room. "My Lucinda used to do that all the time. One of our neighbors owned a yappy little *Beijingese,* if you listened to my wife—you know, those lapdogs with the dark little faces and fluffy bodies."

"I've always thought they looked like mops," I said.

"Precisely!" Mr. Potter laughed again. "Lucinda also irritated the smile off my cousin, an anthropologist, by always referring to *Beijing* Man, no matter how many times he explained that the evolutionary find was made well before we became politically correct in our pronunciation."

"And how is Beijing the shih tzu tonight?"

"Home alone, and probably howling at the window. He

hates to be abandoned." For just an instant, a frown crossed Mr. Potter's face, and I regretted having reminded him of his loss. Before I could think of something to say, though, the jazz band began an energetic swing number. Mr. Potter's face cleared, and he said, "May I have this dance?"

He sounded so formal that I almost wondered if I was supposed to have a dance card. I wouldn't put it past those opera people to perpetuate the tradition. Ordinarily, I'm afraid of embarrassing myself on a dance floor, but the poor man looked so smitten. And I *was* wearing my new green silk dress. And I *did* have the perfect haircut. And new contact lenses. "I would love to, Mr. Potter."

I felt like a child, being led out to the middle of the parquet surface. I wondered if Mr. Potter would let me put my feet on top of his, matching him step for step, as if I were a little girl. Instead, he clasped one hand firmly to my waist and offered me his palm. We shuffled awkwardly for a moment, trying to find the beat of the music. As he stumbled left and I leaned right, I wondered if I had a dance spell hiding in my basement, a few magical words that would lend us even a faint semblance of grace and beauty.

We staggered around the floor, Mr. Potter muttering the count beneath his breath. We never quite found the rhythm projected by the band, and we certainly didn't mesh with each other.

But none of that really mattered. The entire time that we were demonstrating how not to dance, Mr. Potter was beaming. He looked from me to his fellow opera fans, then back to me. He maneuvered us so that we were standing directly in front of the band. He was *proud* of me. And proud of himself for being with me. And I was pleased that I could make him happy.

I wished that my grandfather had lived longer.

As if summoned by that thought, Uncle George was waiting for us at the edge of the dance floor when the band finished its number. His applause was partially for the musicians, but he tilted his head toward me in an amused acknowledgment of my supposed dancing skills. Or, at least, my social skills. I laughed and kissed him on the cheek.

"Jane," he said. "You look stunning." He clapped his hand on Mr. Potter's shoulder. "Sam, you old dog. You were quite a sight out there." Uncle George winked at me, and I grinned in response.

Mr. Potter said, "Jane, your grandmother must be so proud of you. Not only are you accomplished in a noble profession, but you're willing to fritter away a weekend night with us old farts, in support of a good cause. What a pity that Sarah couldn't be here tonight."

Sarah. I never thought of my grandmother as "Sarah." I never thought of her having any life separate from being my grandmother.

Mr. Potter turned to Uncle George. "Have you heard about the holdings in the Peabridge Library, George? They have original manuscripts dating back to the seventeenth century."

I smiled at Mr. Potter's enthusiasm. He had the vigor of the newly converted whenever he mentioned libraries. I said self-deprecatingly, "Not that we could find anything if we needed to."

Uncle George shook his head and waved one hand about vaguely. "Surely you've got them all arranged by Dewey

Decimal number, or something like that? I remember learning those numbers when I was just a boy. Always liked the 920s. Biography."

"I was an 800 girl, myself. Literature." And a touch of 133, I added silently. Witchcraft. Before I could say something aloud that I might regret, I surged ahead in the conversation. "But we don't use the Dewey Decimal system in our library. If we did, all of our holdings would be under the same few numbers, for American Colonial History."

"Ah!" Uncle George said, as if I had explained some secret of the universe. I saw that his attention was being drawn across the room. Anything, I supposed, to escape a discussion of the joys and beauties of library science. Either that, or he was actually taking seriously his role as "host" at this soiree. He made polite excuses and crossed the room to talk to a potential donor.

"So," Mr. Potter said. "No Dewey Decimal. What do you use instead?" He seemed so interested that he ignored the three waiters who converged upon us with silver trays of appetizers. I snagged a lamb chop and a napkin, operating on the assumption that I needed to make up for time lost to both the Peking duck spoon and the dance floor.

I managed one quick bite of the most succulent meat I had ever tasted before I said, "We've pretty much invented our own system."

Mr. Potter breathed in, as awed as if I had told him we were constructing an atom bomb in the basement. "Just like that? Without guidance from anyone? You must be so proud of yourself!" I could hear echoes of his love and respect for his lost librarian wife in the question.

I smiled gently. "I wish. I've never been fully trained as a cataloger."

"Like my Lucinda was," he said, and sighed.

"If we had the money, we would hire someone like her tomorrow. Good catalogers are worth their weight in gold."

Mr. Potter looked out over the dance floor, his face gone soft and vague. I wanted to know what he was remembering, what private jokes, what secret love. A pang daggered just beneath my heart, and I wondered if anyone would ever miss me as much as he missed Lucinda.

I took another bite of lamb, trying to fill the silence with some sort of normal life activity.

"Jane Madison. I didn't know you were an opera fan."

I knew the voice before I turned around. Before I finished chewing. Before I swallowed. Before I thought about the animalistic awkwardness of clutching a lamb bone in my supposedly delicate well-manicured hand.

"Jason," I choked out after I had gulped down the partially chewed bite in my mouth.

He was stunning. He wore a tuxedo that had clearly been tailored specifically for him. His glistening linen shirt shone against a scarlet cummerbund. As my eyes lingered, I realized that the red was shot through with gold—a perfect complement to my own silk dress. The satin stripe on his pants accentuated the long line of his legs, and I felt myself melting right there.

Mr. Potter cleared his throat.

"Oh! Jason Templeton, this is Samuel Potter, one of the board members of the concert opera guild. Mr. Potter, Jason is—" I started to say "my Boyfriend," but I couldn't bring myself to say the words. Not in public. Not in front of another man I had snared with my love spell. "Jason is a professor at Mid-Atlantic. He uses our collection regularly."

"The best in the city," Jason said. "For *my* purposes, the best on the entire eastern seaboard. And the reference librarian is the finest in the profession."

I blushed.

The band struck up a spirited waltz. "I'm sorry, Mr. Potter," Jason said. "May I steal Jane away for this dance?"

The older man looked disappointed, but only for a moment. "Of course. I should mingle with the crowd, anyway. The role of a board member, you know." He turned to me, though, before he walked off. "Thank you, Jane. This has been a most memorable evening."

"Thank *you*," I said, hoping that Gran would be proud of me. I glanced around, desperately hoping that I could find a waiter to take my nasty lamb bone, now wrapped in a napkin.

"Here," Mr. Potter said, just before stepping away. "Let me take that for you."

"I couldn't—"

"Now, don't keep your young man waiting." He took the napkin and waved me toward the dance floor. Once again, I felt like a child, spitting out my gum into an adult's hand before a meal. But Mr. Potter smiled, and I turned away. To dance with "my young man."

Jason guided me toward the floor with a hand on my waist. My heart was beating so hard that I could scarcely breathe. If Neko had found me a dress one bit tighter, anyone could have seen the pounding inside my chest.

And Jason proved to be everything in a dancer that Mr. Potter wasn't. His arms around me were strong, confident. He guided me about the dance floor, not in any showy way, but in a manner that convinced me—and apparently everyone around us—that he knew what he was doing.

Where had a man his age learned to dance? My peers had mostly managed to shuffle back and forth at the occasional bar mitzvah, or we had jumped up and down at school dances in high school. I would never have learned ballroom dancing myself if it weren't for Uncle George and some misguided Arthur Murray lessons that Gran had insisted on giving me for my Sweet Sixteen.

But who was I to question my Boyfriend waltzing me around the dance floor of the Harvest Gala?

I finally recovered enough presence of mind to say, "What are you doing here?"

"The opera folks contacted the university about this fund-raiser. They said they wanted to build town-gown relationships. The head of the history department is a big opera fan, so he bought tickets for everyone—to help us bond as a department, he said." Jason nodded toward a cluster of people in the far corner of the room. I darted a glance and saw that Ekaterina was anchored in the middle of the circle. Well, any department head that brought me my Boyfriend could bring the Ice Ballerina, as well, I supposed. Jason asked, "But what are *you* doing here?"

"My grandmother is on the board. Sarah Smythe. She's the one who thought it would be a good idea to build up the guild's relationships with universities."

He smiled, and I suddenly felt faint. "I suppose I should

meet her and thank her for getting me here. For letting me see you. I should have phoned you this past week, but things have been insane. I have an article due on the fifteenth. You know—publish or perish."

I took a breath, the first time I'd filled my lungs since turning around to see Jason. So that was why he hadn't phoned. He'd been busy with work. Nothing more ominous than that. Everyone got busy. I did, myself.

"Which one is your grandmother?" he asked.

"She's not here tonight. She's still recovering from her pneumonia."

"What a shame," Jason said, pulling me in closer as he led us through a graceful spin. "I'll have to meet her another time."

And that's when it hit me. The perfect plan. After all, I'd already promised Gran that I would go to the Farm. And she had said that I could bring someone. And after my little, um, makeout session with Jason beneath the stairs at La Perla, it was time to see just how far my Boyfriend was willing to follow me....

I took a deep breath, closed my eyes and leaned in closer to Jason's ear. "Come with me to my family reunion."

He almost stopped moving, right there, in the middle of the parquet floor. Not exactly the reaction I had hoped for. Nevertheless, he recovered his dancing legs quickly, and he asked in a careful voice, "When is it?"

"The third weekend in October. Two weeks away. We get together up in Connecticut, at our family farm. Gran will be there, and a couple dozen cousins and aunts and uncles."

"The third weekend... That's Historical Politics."

"Excuse me?" I knew that my family had a lot of issues, but I'd never heard anyone phrase it quite like that.

"The Historical Politics Society of America. The 'trade association' all we history professors belong to. They always have their annual meeting the third weekend in October."

"Oh." I knew that I shouldn't feel so disappointed. I mean, five minutes before, I'd never even considered asking Jason to join me. I looked up to find him staring across the dance floor, looking at his historical political colleagues. He was probably imagining the raucous time they'd have, discussing Hegelian dialectic and Cartesian dualism over endless beers in the hotel bar at the conference.

He pulled me a little closer to his chest, his fingers spreading more broadly across my back. "This reunion thing. It's for the whole weekend?"

"Friday afternoon until Sunday afternoon."

"I wouldn't be able to make it up there until Saturday. I can't get out of a commitment Friday night. I could drive up and meet you there, though."

I knew that the music was playing. I knew that other couples were dancing around us. I knew that Jason was holding me close, waiting for me to say something.

I knew that my entire world was opening, expanding, like the moment that a theater curtain flies up and a play begins and all the possibilities are spread out on the stage, just waiting for the audience to discover them.

"That would be wonderful," I finally said.

Suddenly, I thought that he would kiss me. There. On the St. Regis ballroom dance floor, with his arms folded around my perfect green silk dress, as he looked down at my new-cut hair and my manicured nails, into eyes not obscured by glasses.

But the band stopped playing. The waltz ended, and everyone started to clap. Out of the corner of my eye I saw movement, and then Uncle George was standing by my side. "Jane!" he exclaimed. "Your grandmother's bid on the Schmidt painting has been overwritten. You should take a look and see if she wants to pay more."

"Okay," I said, wishing that he would disappear, that he would take all of his concert opera cronies and enter suspended animation, that he would leave me for even one more minute with my amazing, stupendous, incredible Boyfriend. My Boyfriend who was joining me at the Farm. My Boyfriend, who was going to redeem me after years and years of aunts and cousins questioning how I could possibly remain single for so long.

"I'm sorry," Uncle George said, half turning toward Jason. "I didn't mean to interrupt."

"Not at all, sir," Jason said, inclining his Greek-statue head. "In fact, I should get back to my friends." He still held my hand, though, and he squeezed my fingers gently before he started to walk away. "We'll talk more at the library next week, Jane. I can't wait to see what you've found for me about the apothecary trade. That's the last piece that's missing from my article."

"I'll have it for you at the circulation desk on Monday morning."

I felt like I was speaking code in front of Uncle George. *And I'll see you at the Farm,* I meant.

"Wonderful," he said. Then he smiled and was gone, scarlet cummerbund, impeccable tux and all. Uncle George needed to remind me three times before I was ready to cross the room and check on Gran's silent auction bid.

My Boyfriend was going to meet my family. At the Farm.

24

"Jane, you're just not concentrating," David said, collapsing back on the couch and sighing with frustration.

"I'm trying!"

"No, you're not." He picked up the pink fluorite crystal that was centered on the coffee table. He'd explained numerous times that it was supposed to help focus my thoughts. I was supposed to be able to see through it, to channel my energies as I worked a spell.

I glared at the stone. "I just don't think that my strength is with crystals."

"Your mother's seems to be," he said in a perfectly reasonable tone.

Neko had the good sense to cringe at those words. He'd heard enough of my rants about Clara to know that mentioning her was not about to make me more pliant to the warder's wishes.

"And if *Clara*—" I gave a definite emphasis to her proper name "—had bothered to train me, then maybe all this witchcraft stuff wouldn't be so hard to pick up now. Maybe I'd be ready for a teacher, if a decent one could be found around here."

David sucked in breath to reply, but he visibly caught himself before he could say something that he'd regret. Neko winced, stood and stretched. "Perhaps if I made you both a cup of tea…"

David looked toward my familiar, annoyed. "We don't need tea. What we need is a bit less self-pity and a bit more concentration."

Neko positioned himself precisely equidistant between us and shrugged. "It seems to me that at least one of us needs a nap. Awfully cranky tonight, aren't we?" He minced into the kitchen before David or I could ask just who was supposed to be the tired one.

I leaned back against the couch's cushions, exhaling sharply to get my stupid bangs out of my eyes. I'd never had a problem with my hair when it was just one long tangle of curls. I closed my eyes, suddenly too exhausted by the whole training process to focus on the room around me. Not that I needed a nap. Really.

"Neko," I called. "A cup of tea *would* be wonderful."

He didn't answer, but I heard him bang the kettle against the sink.

David took another deep breath and said, "I'm not meant to be a trainer, you know. I'm here to protect you. To keep you safe. I only started to teach you about your powers because you seemed so completely lost."

I didn't bother opening my eyes. I was almost too weary to say, "Fine, then. Don't teach me anymore."

He was silent for a long time, and I wondered what expression was on his face. We'd worked together twice since the Harvest Gala and at both sessions, he'd complained that I wasn't applying myself. I wasn't quite sure what he wanted me to accomplish. I thought it was extremely unlikely that I'd hurtle from being Jane Madison, Meek and Ordinary Librarian to Jane Madison, Super Witch, practically overnight.

Besides, I had important things on my mind. Like my Boyfriend. And our looming weekend at the Farm. I'd only seen Jason once since the Gala, to hand over my apothecary research which—if I do say so myself—he had declared invaluable. Now he had me digging up historic midwife's records; he believed that Chesterton and his wife might have lost twins before young George was born. That loss might modify how scholars had traditionally viewed the stoic farmer—and Jason might glean another career-advancing article.

"You don't understand." David interrupted my scholarly distraction, using a weary parent's tone of voice, as though I were an unruly toddler.

"Explain it to me, then." I forced myself to sit up and open my eyes. "Tell me what I'm missing. Tell me why this is so important. There are about a hundred other things I'd rather be doing, you know. I was supposed to be at yoga tonight with Melissa. And I should be packing for the weekend. I leave tomorrow morning."

"I know."

I heard his disapproval, as loud as a bonfire crackling.

"And what's that supposed to mean? Are you telling me that I shouldn't go to my family reunion?"

"I don't have anything against your family." He laid out his answer very precisely, with just the faintest emphasis on the last word.

Jason. I never should have mentioned that Jason was coming to the Farm.

Well, David Montrose had passed up his chance. After all, David was the one who had stood outside my cottage and kissed me good-night before deciding that it was better off for both of us to stop our "relationship" before it began. I certainly wasn't asked what *I* preferred.

Not that I would ever trade Jason for David. Perish the thought.

I *knew* Jason. I'd spent almost an entire year observing his every move. All the time that he'd been my Imaginary Boyfriend, I'd memorized his preferences, his quirks, the endearing little things he did that made my heart twist inside my chest.

I didn't know David well enough to get worked up about him. He didn't make me tongue-tied. He didn't make me question every word, every thought I had in his presence. There was no chemistry with David. No rush of flirtation. He was my warder, plain and simple.

And he was acting as if he was in charge of every aspect of my life. Including my love life.

Neko slunk in from the kitchen, carrying a tray laden with teapot, mugs, butter cookies and a pitcher of cream the size of Montana. He poured oolong for all of us, then doctored his own, adding a quick dollop of tea to a mugful of cream. He blew on the lukewarm mixture and sipped daintily. When he finally noticed that David and I were studiously avoiding looking at each other, he pursed his lips and asked, "Are we having fun yet?"

"I'll be having fun tomorrow afternoon. When I'm in Connecticut." I crossed my arms over my chest. I knew that I was acting like a petulant teenager, but what else could I say? David brought out the worst in me. If he was going to act like my schoolteacher, I was going to regress to the worst of my student days.

Predictably, David sighed in exasperation and set down the mug that he had just picked up. "You know, we don't have to do this, Jane. You can just hand over all the books downstairs. Let the Coven take charge, and you won't have to worry about them anymore. The crystals, too. The Coven would be thrilled to have the entire collection."

Neko slammed his own mug onto the table, letting some of his ecru-colored drink slop over the top. "Stunning advice," he hissed, glaring at David. I was reminded immediately of the black cat that Neko once had been, and I wondered what he would look like if he actually attacked in his feline form.

David answered my familiar, but he looked directly at me. "It's not 'advice,' Neko. It's merely a statement of fact. The Coven hasn't interfered so far because I've convinced them that a valid witch has possession of the materials downstairs." He pointed at my familiar. "The fact that Jane was able to awaken you is an indication that—at some level—the magic accepts her. I assure you, though, that the Coven is getting rather curious about the situation. They're growing impatient. They want to meet Jane, know her capabilities. And they want to know exactly what is in that collection. I can't put them off forever."

"Dammit, David! I'm not asking you to!" I responded more loudly than I'd intended. "All I'm asking is to be left alone until after my family reunion. Is that so much? The books were missing for decades. Can't I take one more weekend, for myself?"

David sighed. "You can take one more weekend."

Surprised by my sudden victory, I sank back onto the couch and hid my gloat behind a swallow of tea. As I thought about Neko's hissed concern, though, it occurred to me that there was more at stake here than I had imagined at first. "David?"

"What?" He sounded every bit as annoyed as I had felt.

"If I did give back the books, what would happen to Neko?"

David looked at the young man who sat in the chair beside me. Neko, for his part, studiously avoided both of us, apparently discovering endlessly fascinating patterns on the surface of his drink. When David answered, his voice was soft. "He goes with the materials. He's the familiar for the collection."

"Not for the witch? Not for me?" I was stunned by how much David's words hurt. As annoying as Neko might be, as frustrating as he was, I had become accustomed to sharing the cottage with him. I had just assumed that he was meant to help me. To stay with me.

"If the collection is yours, then he is yours. But if you reject the collection, then he'll go with it to the next witch who has the power to transform him."

Neko wouldn't meet my eyes.

I wondered if he was thinking about this cottage that he'd come to call home. Or the fish market down on Thirty-first Street. Or the cream that he'd taken to buying in quart containers. Or Roger. Or me.

I sighed. "Fine," I said. "I'll make a serious effort with my witchcraft after I get back from the Farm. But I really don't have any choice about this weekend. I promised Gran."

"And Jason," Neko added helpfully, stealing a butter cookie from the tray. So much for his everlasting loyalty as I made sacrifices to protect him from strangers.

I watched David stiffen at my Boyfriend's name. "What?" I said to him, and I was surprised to hear that my one-word question was a shout. "What can you possibly have against Jason Templeton?"

David eyed me steadily. "Do you really want me to answer that question?

His smooth certainty infuriated me. "Yes! I am sick and tired of your coming in here and posturing every time his name comes up. This isn't some kind of contest between the two of you. Jason Templeton has nothing to do with you, Scott!"

I was so deep into my tirade that it took me a moment to realize my mistake. The name of my ex-fiancé hovered in the air, taking on a life of its own, assuming every bit as much form and substance as Neko possessed.

And in the end, it was Neko himself who broke the charged silence. "Well now," he said. "Isn't this uncomfortable?"

"Shut up, Neko," I said. I turned to David, whose face

had set in a perfect, implacable mask. "Seriously. Jason has nothing to do with you. He is completely separate from your world. From witchcraft. From warding."

"My job is to keep you safe," David said. His voice was so flat that it might have come from a million miles away.

"And how can Jason possibly be a threat? Do you think that he's going to come in here with a stake, or a silver bullet or, or, I don't know, whatever kills witches?"

"Of course not." David set his answer perfectly in the center of the room, the words as smooth and polished as if he'd spent a lifetime carving away any hint of an offensive note.

"And is he a threat to my powers? Do you think that he'll suddenly decide to burn the books downstairs? Or steal my crystals? Or stab Neko?"

"I have no reason to think that he will." David sounded like Mr. Spock; he had stripped out every last vibration of emotion from his voice.

"So you think that he'll steal everything in the basement? Hide it away from the Coven? Sell it to the highest bidder on the magic black market?"

"No."

I stood and gestured toward the door. "I think that we're through with this conversation."

David stared at me for a long time. I watched the muscles in his jaws tighten, as if he were biting back words. He reminded me of the David that I'd met the night I awakened Neko. The dark David. The angry David.

Gone was the man who had changed himself to appeal to me, and in his place was a man doing all that he could to test me. He was Petrucio, cracking his whip to tame my rebellious Kate. It seemed like he was *trying* to alienate me. To distance me.

And he was being remarkably successful.

He set down his mug and stood. He brushed his hands down the front of his slacks, as if he were shedding invisible crumbs. He looked at Neko for several heartbeats. My familiar gazed back, his almond eyes as distant and remote and unblinking as a cat's.

"Very well," David said. "No more training."

I waited for him to finish, and when he did not, I made my voice as firm as I could and said, "Until I get back from the Farm."

"No." He shook his head slowly. "No more training from me at all. Things have become too confused. Too confusing. I had hoped to avoid that, but I can see that I was not successful."

He held out his hand, as if we were concluding a business meeting. I stared at it, not offering my own. "You're kidding, right?" I finally said. "You want me to think about what you've told me tonight. You want me to realize that I need you, and then get back to witch school like a good little student. Right?"

He did not answer. I looked to Neko, but he gave me no further guidance. His gaze was pinned on David, as intent as a cat stalking a broken-winged bird.

I tried again. "So, do you want me to apologize? Is that it? I'm sorry, and I want you to be my teacher again?"

David's voice was perfectly even. "I don't want anything of the sort. I want you to be content in your life. I want you to know who you are and what you are. I want you to be balanced, so that you can find all your natural power and strength. Jane, I want you to be happy."

"And your walking out of here tonight is going to make me happy?"

"In the short term," he said, his voice so dry that he might have been lost in a desert.

I said, "And in the long term?"

"In the long term, the Coven will take care of you. They'll provide you with a proper trainer. Someone who is used to teaching witches. You don't need to be afraid. They'll be fair about everything. They won't test you until you're able to show your true potential."

He made everything sound so reasonable. So sane. So utterly, perfectly normal. "And if I can't learn from the Coven's teacher?"

"Then they'll take back the books."

"And Neko?"

He nodded, not sparing my familiar a glance. "And Neko."

Before I could even begin to figure out a response to that, David crossed to the front door. "Enjoy the Farm, Jane. But be careful. And apply yourself when you come back here. Work *with* your teacher."

Then he was gone.

My warder was walking down the garden path outside my home. I stared after him until he turned the corner of the library, until he was out of sight. Until he was clearly not coming back again.

I sat down on the couch and stared at Neko. My belly ached, and I realized that I was dangerously close to tears.

I felt like David and I had just broken up. We'd never been going out, and now we had broken up. Hell, we had shared *one kiss,* and now I was parsing every word of his conversation, trying to figure out what he had meant, why he had spoken, what did he mean when he said….

I *knew* this feeling. I remembered it. It had swooped over me when Scott phoned from London that last time. I had lived with it for those long days after my beloved fiancé had told me that we should see other people. That he had started to see someone else. That he wanted his ring back.

But why should David Montrose make me feel that way? Especially when our fight was about the *real* love of my life, my Boyfriend, Jason?

I gulped the last of my tea as if it were a vodka shot, closing my eyes. Actually, I could use some vodka. Or mojitos. Was it too late to call Melissa?

I looked at my watch. Ten-thirty on a school night. It was too late to get started with mojito therapy.

I closed my eyes and collapsed back on the couch.

"Burning," Neko said, breaking the silence at last.

"What?"

"Burning witches. Stakes are for vampires, and silver bullets are for werewolves."

"Gee. Thanks," I said. "I guess."

"Anything I can do to help," he said. "More tea?"

I shook my head and heaved myself upright. It was time to go to bed. Cut my losses for the night.

Tomorrow would be an all-new day. I would get up early to pack. I would take a cab over to Gran's apartment. We'd drive up to the Farm. I would get ready for Jason to arrive on Saturday. And I wouldn't have to worry about witches or warders or familiars until after the long weekend was over.

25

It was still dark out when I attempted to leave the next morning.

Attempted. It took me three tries to actually get out the door. First, I forgot my keys to Gran's apartment. Then, I left behind my carefully hoarded bag of Sephora cosmetics. Then, I forgot the box of condoms that had languished in my night-stand for nearly a year, a present from Melissa to celebrate my so-called freedom from Scott, once he had broken off our engagement. I had not looked favorably on the gift at the time, but now I allowed a spiral of excitement to uncurl in my belly at the thought that they might—finally!—be put to excellent use.

Neko hovered close as I made my way out the front door for the third time. "Don't make too much noise while I'm gone," I told him. He nodded, looking for all the world like a teenager being left home alone for the first time in his life. "I left some food for you in the fridge."

"Salmon?"

"No. Chicken." He sniffed, letting me know what he thought of that choice. I hoisted my bag on my shoulder, fighting to free the ends of my hair from the shoulder strap. "How do I look?"

"He's not going to be there until tomorrow."

"Who?" I asked, forcing myself to sound shocked.

"Be careful, Jane," Neko said.

"Don't start sounding like David."

"For all his faults, David can be right sometimes."

"Well, not this time. I'm going to have a wonderful weekend with Jason. And when I come back, we'll straighten out this witchcraft thing once and for all." Neko kicked at a stone embedded in the garden path. "Seriously. You don't have to worry. I'm not letting anyone take the books. And I'm definitely not letting anyone take you."

He made one last half-hearted kick before forcing a smile across his face. "You aren't really going to wear your hair like *that,* are you?"

"What's wrong with—" I grumbled in exasperation and dashed back into the house. A quick stop in my bedroom to retrieve a black scrunchie, a dash into the bathroom for a mirror as I gathered up my staggered waves of hair, and then I really, truly, absolutely was ready to go. I leaned forward and kissed Neko on the cheek. "See you Sunday night."

"Ciao!" He made a big show of waving farewell.

Fortunately, I hailed a cab just one block away. Gran was

waiting in the lobby of her building, when I let myself in. She was sitting primly on one of the benches beside the mailboxes. I picked up her small suitcase, led her over to the garage elevators and we hit the road.

After a brief stop, that was, to pick up Clara. With a rush of shame, I realized that I had not even known where my biological mother was living. It turned out that Clara had rented a townhouse in the northern suburb of Silver Spring. I didn't get to see the inside, but the front of the building was unassuming: red brick, hunter-green front door, whitewashed window boxes that were currently bare.

At Gran's instruction, I got out to ring Clara's doorbell. She opened the door almost immediately, but kept us waiting nearly fifteen minutes while she ran around, collecting the last of her necessities for the weekend. I started to get irritated, but then I remembered that it had taken me a half dozen passes to gather up my own things. Like mother, like daughter? What a truly terrifying thought.

The ride to Connecticut was uneventful. I had forgotten how much I enjoyed driving, even when the vehicle was Gran's mammoth Lincoln Town Car. "Best looking car on the road," she affirmed, every time she got into it. She drove herself to the grocery store and to opera guild board meetings, but the car spent most of its time just sitting in her garage.

We stopped a few times, for food and drink and the elimination of same, but we made great time, arriving at the Farm by 1:00 p.m. As I stepped onto the wraparound porch, I was transported back to my childhood, to the years when I had loved vacationing in Connecticut. As I had when I was a little girl, I centered my feet on the great marble block that nestled in front of the door, and I touched my fingers to the house's wooden clapboards.

> "Protect me and keep me safe from all harm
> Watch o'er my family here at the Farm"

A frisson ran down my spine, and I turned to Gran, who had taught me the rhyme on my very first visit, more than a quarter-century before. "Gran," I said. "It's like a spell!"

"It's a tradition, dear," she chided. But I felt the same prickle on my neck when she repeated the words, and Clara, as well.

I gave a second look to the inset marble block. Marble. A stone long associated with physical protection. With safety. Security.

Before I could question Gran more closely, the door flew open, and relatives boiled around us. Someone took our bags, others ushered us into the kitchen. A dozen helping hands made us more sandwiches than we could possibly eat.

My cousin Leah rested her hands on her hugely pregnant belly as she looked curiously out at the car. "Where's Scott? Not able to join us again?"

Aunt Jenny leaped to my rescue. "Leah, I *told* you that Scott wasn't going to be here." She lowered her voice to a harsh whisper. "He broke off the engagement more than a year ago."

Leah laughed in fake embarrassment and waved her hand in front of her face. "Of course, of course! I have been *so* forgetful this pregnancy! They say it gets worse with each one. After three, you'd think I would have learned my lesson. My Joey is just about ready to divorce me!"

Her Joey wouldn't dare—he'd never find another woman to put up with his wandering eyes and roaming hands. I barely managed to keep from saying that out loud. Leah was exactly why I had not wanted to come to the Farm. Leah, and all my other contented, breeding cousins.

But then, I remembered my secret weapon. I forced a beatific smile to spread across my lips. I tested my tone of voice inside my head, lightened it another shade, then another for good measure. "I invited someone else to join me for the weekend."

"Who?" Leah asked. I watched Aunt Jenny crane her neck, as if she could make out a body stored in the Lincoln's deep trunk.

"My Boyfriend," I said, shrugging to show that my relationship was so steady and stable and committed that I could be casual. "His name is Jason Templeton. He wasn't able to get away from the city until tomorrow morning, but he'll stay for the rest of the weekend."

As I'd hoped, Leah pounced on my information. I spent the next hour insouciantly describing how Jason and I had met, how we worked together, how he was writing definitive articles on George Chesterton and changing colonial scholarship as we'd known it. I even managed to fit in how we had attended the Harvest Gala, making it sound as if we'd planned to be at the event together all along, instead of running into each other by accident.

Gran, bless her heart, kept silent. And Leah, true to form, continued pressing me. She wanted to know about Jason's family, his background, where he was raised, whether he had any siblings. I didn't know the answer to most of her questions (despite my most determined research as a reference librarian—that is, using Google to research Jason incessantly—I had not been able to uncover most of my Boyfriend's background). Nevertheless, I invented details on the spot. When he arrived, I'd let him know what I'd said. He could back me up.

And until Jason arrived, there were plenty of Farm traditions to take care of. Gran had mapped out who would stay in which rooms. Not surprisingly, I had been assigned a bed in the Girls' Room up in the attic. Clara was parked next to me. We lugged our bags upstairs, and Clara made a show of opening up the round window under the eaves, waving her hands to bring more air into the room.

Cousin Leah was waiting for us when we descended. "It's always so musty up there," she said. "Fortunately, Joey and I are in the White Cottage."

The White Cottage. One of the four outbuildings on the property. They always went to the breeding pairs, as if a couple couldn't go without sex for two nights in a row. I thought about the box of condoms shoved into the side of my duffel bag. Some of us had survived without sex for months. Over a year, even.

I knew that I needed to change the topic of conversation or I'd say something I'd regret, so I dredged up my last vestige of maturity and pointed to the choker that Leah wore. "That's unusual. I don't think I've seen stones like those before."

She raised her fingers to her throat as if to remind herself of what she was wearing. "Oh, this? Mom gave it to me when I was pregnant with Joe Jr. She said it's tradition for women in our family to wear it during their last trimester. Oops! You wouldn't know about that, would you?"

A hot retort rose to my lips, but I made myself look closer at the necklace. The stones were mottled, red with veins of green and white. Sard, I realized. A type of agate, often associated with safe childbirth. (Thank you, Neko, for your patient naming of stone after stone from the kit in my basement.) How long had the necklace been in my family? And what other witchy artifacts lurked here at the Farm?

"Penny for your thoughts."

I looked up to see another cousin. "Simon!" I leaped to my feet and threw my arms around him. He kissed my cheek and folded me into a bear hug. "How *are* you?"

"Wonderful. Carol and I are both great." I looked around for his wife, as petite as he was massive. "She's corralling the twins." Carol and Simon had two seven-year-old boys who must be doing their best to brew mischief around the Farm. They lived on a real, working farm in Vermont, and Simon's boys always knew more than their cousins about leaping from tall surfaces, eating inedible treasures and setting small fires to precious objects.

"What's this I hear about a new beau?" Simon asked, scratching his belly as if he'd just awakened from a nap. I launched into my Jason story, ridiculously pleased that the rumors had already spread.

In fact, I got to repeat my tale more than a dozen times, throughout the afternoon and into the evening, as I caught up with relatives I hadn't seen in far too long. By the time we were returning to the Farm from a chaotic dinner at the Clam Shack, I was having trouble remembering all the details I'd glossed onto my relationship. Was Jason one of five boys, or six? Did he have an allergy to clams and oysters, or clams and crab? Had we discussed wanting three children, or four?

Back at the Farm, I managed to secure one of the prime wicker armchairs on the porch, along with a woolen blanket. The temperature had dropped as soon as the sun went down, but we'd all suited up with jackets, gloves and mufflers. The entire family was unwilling to miss out on fresh, country air.

While the children played a rambunctious game of flash-light tag on the sloping front lawn, I leaned back in the darkness, listening to my relatives chatter into the night. Clara was quite a hit among my aunts and uncles, catching up with her siblings as if she had merely taken a long vacation.

No one seemed to begrudge her the lie that she had lived; no one resented that she had kept her very existence a secret for so long. Clara made her travels sound exotic and brave, especially as she drew out a long story about making a spirit quest outside of Sedona, camping in the Arizona desert for thirty days and thirty nights to find her true self. I found my mind wandering to that region's famous red rock, and I wondered what witchy powers my mother might have found inside herself on her retreat, what spells she might even now be working to be so easily accepted back into the family fold.

By the time I staggered up to the attic, I was drunk on family gossip, the shrieks of children and a bellyful of fried clam strips. I was asleep before my head hit my pillow.

At sunrise, I was awakened by more shrieking children on the front lawn. I could remember when I had been one of those kids, drawn outside by the early-morning mist, captivated by the crunch of dew frozen on the grass. I pulled my pillow over my head and pretended to sleep for as long as I could. Eventually, though, even I couldn't keep up the illusion, and I pulled on my wooly bathrobe and stumbled down to the kitchen.

The teakettle was always ready to go at the Farm, and I soon had a steaming cup of English breakfast to help me wake up. In short order, Aunt Jenny had taken charge of the kitchen, heating up the electric griddle and spooning out massive rounds of pancakes. Simon took over frying up a half ton of bacon, and Joey actually bothered to lug in a few gallons of orange juice from the giant refrigerator in the storage shed.

After breakfast, one group decided to head out to Old Mystic Seaport, a sort of Disneyland-on-the-Sea that recaptured the magic of the whaling industry. Another group decided to head into Salem for the annual Autumn Art Arcade, a judged show of local artists.

Pregnant Leah claimed that her ankles were too swollen for her to go anywhere; she staked a claim to the farmhouse's sunny parlor. I stayed in the Girls' Room, trying on every item of clothing I'd brought with me, brushing my hair, pulling it back, letting it go straight, applying makeup, reapplying makeup, eating an emergency doughnut, eating another, contemplating a third (and eventually giving in, but promising myself that I would not have lunch).

Oh, and I drove myself insane wondering when Jason would arrive.

As it turned out, he must have left Washington well before dawn; his boxy blue Volvo pulled into the Farm's driveway just a few minutes past noon. While I knew that one school of Boyfriend management said that I should wait on the porch for my one true love, I gave in to the Jane Madison School of No Restraint.

I hurtled down the front steps, coming to a gravel-spray stop in front of the driver's door. "Hello!" I exclaimed as Jason clambered out. I couldn't keep from grinning. Truth be told, I felt like laughing loud enough for them to hear me out on the highway.

"Mmm," Jason said, pulling me in for a kiss that was as perfect as any I could have scripted. My arms automatically went around his waist; I hardly spent any time wondering if he would think I was too forward, too passionate, too needy.

"Any trouble finding us?" I asked.

"None at all."

"And the traffic wasn't bad?"

"Oddly enough, at six o'clock on a Saturday morning, traffic is relatively light. Even around the Beltway." The laughter behind his words made my heart pound, and I tried to shake my goofy grin off my face. This was all too perfect. It couldn't be happening to me.

"Come on in!" I said, finally remembering that I was supposed to be the hostess. "Most folks have gone out for the day, but there are still a few of us here."

"I didn't mean to make you miss out on all the fun," he said, running a long-fingered hand through his unruly curls.

"I haven't missed out on anything," I said. And Jason's

smile absolutely convinced me that I was speaking the truth—as if I ever could have doubted. We climbed the steps to the front porch.

"So, Professor Man really does exist." Leah barely smiled from the top of the stairs, her pregnant belly thrusting toward us like the body of a malevolent spider.

Jason turned toward me in mock surprise. "And here, I thought that all my years of schooling were wasted. Professor Man! To the rescue!" He slid his left palm to the small of my back, and the motion ran a shiver from the top of my head to my tailbone. "Jason Templeton," my Boyfriend said, shaking Leah's hand.

"Leah Stark," she said reluctantly. I could read her thoughts as clearly as if they were words written on the parchment pages that filled my basement. She wondered how *I* could have landed a catch as perfect as Jason. She gave me another appraising glance before she stepped aside. "Well, I'd better get back to the kitchen. I promised to start the baked beans for tonight." She whirled back to Jason with all the subtlety of a tabby pouncing on a mouse. "Jane said that you were allergic to clams, but we'll have halibut and side dishes at the clambake."

Jason, bless him, didn't bat an eye. "Jane always remembers my allergies. I hope you didn't expand the menu just for me, though."

Leah rolled her eyes. "No. Most of the kids hate clams, anyway."

"They've got good taste," Jason said with a smile. He reached around Leah to hold the screen door for her as she went back into the house. I could have melted on the spot.

Instead, I remembered that Jason had never been to the Farm before. "Here!" I exclaimed, once the screen door had slammed closed behind us. "Let me show you the upstairs."

As we clambered up to the attic, I waited for him to comment on his sudden shellfish allergy. Instead, he waited until we were on the upper landing before he wrapped an arm around my waist, pulling me close and nuzzling my neck. It was a good thing that he was holding me; otherwise, I might have swooned like some silly woman in a Shakespeare comedy, tumbling back down to the ground floor.

"So," he whispered, his lips close to my ear. "Anything else I should know about myself before I meet the rest of your family?"

I squirmed, but his fingers tightened around my waist.

"I don't suppose you have four brothers, do you?"

"Nope," he said. "Only child. But maybe I forgot the Wyoming branch of the family."

"And, um, you've always wanted to have three kids?"

"I've never really done the math. But three's as good as any other number. Anything else?"

I shook my head, unable to meet his eyes. I could feel his laughter against my side. "I'm sorry—" I started to say, but he stopped me with a kiss. A serious kiss. A steal-your-breath-away-and-make-you-wonder-where-your-toes-went kiss.

"Don't be. That's what this weekend is all about, right? Building up our own fantasy world away from the pressure of work?"

And that's when I knew that I loved him. Not had a crush

on him. Not dreamed that he would replace Scott on the appointment book in my heart. Not imagined that he would sweep me off my academic feet and admire my librarian accomplishments as if they meant something in the world at large.

Love.

Quickly followed by a darting twist of guilt through my belly. I couldn't help but think of poor Melissa, struggling through her First Date hell. She was working to achieve *this*. She was hoping to experience what I had been lucky enough to stumble upon. All of her strategies, her pools of men, her hopeless, hapless first dates, they were all supposed to lead her toward this warm vanilla rush of comfort, of fun. Of love.

I'd found it, and she had not. Of course, a little voice nagged at the back of my mind, I had the benefit of the grimoire spell. But a girl had to use all the assets at her command, didn't she?

"So," Jason said, easing away from me. "I suppose you'd better show me what's up here, and then we should get back downstairs before your cousin thinks that I've carried you away."

I knocked twice on the door to the Boys' Room, just to make sure that it was empty. When I showed Jason where he'd be sleeping, he looked shocked. "I *thought*…" He trailed off, but the way his eye roamed over my sweater told me exactly what he'd thought.

My cheeks flushed, and I started to stammer. "I did, too. I mean, I'd hoped. I mean, I wanted…" I took a deep breath and forced myself to exhale slowly. "I'll see what I can arrange. There are cottages on the grounds. They're spoken for, but maybe…"

He leaned over and brushed a wayward strand of hair off my cheek. "See what you can do."

My heart was pounding by the time we got back to the kitchen, and that had nothing to do with the climb down the steep stairs.

Jason was the perfect Boyfriend. As the family troops returned from their morning excursions, Jason met relative after relative. He let himself get roped into a surprisingly brutal game of touch football on the front lawn, managing to capture one of Simon's twins and hold the boy upside down while a teammate scored the winning touchdown. He helped collect wood for the night's bonfire, securing a tiny pine cone that he pressed into my palm like a secret token. He sat on the porch with Gran, holding out his hands for her new skein of wool, admiring her knitted shawl and asking intelligent questions about her latest project.

He even carried on a spirited conversation with Clara, about whether our colonial forefathers had been capable of breaking free from their Christian indoctrination to experience a true spiritual awakening in the rugged new land of America. I think that he gained innumerable points when he proclaimed that Plymouth Rock was a symbol of all religious settlement of the New World, and that the stone beneath the pilgrims' feet was echoed in the crystal around Clara's neck.

Chalcedony, I noticed at a glance. The stone for motherhood.

If Clara caught my intent gaze, she ignored it.

My contribution for the evening clambake was a giant

casserole dish of apple crisp. Some of the cousins had brought back bushels of orchard-fresh apples that afternoon, and I had found myself grinning as I peeled and cut them, slapping Jason's fingers away as he tried to steal slices. When the kitchen timer beeped its alarm, I excused myself from the porch to remove the bubbling, cinnamon-scented dish from the oven.

And when I turned back to the counter, Gran was standing in the doorway.

"He seems quite charming, dear."

I let the fluttering joy beneath my heart burst through my smile. "He is, Gran. He really is."

"I'm surprised that you've never mentioned him before." I heard the hurt behind her words, and I knew that she was asking if I was ashamed of her. She'd always worried about my being different from my friends, growing up without the standard issue of one mother and one father.

I set the hot apple crisp on a cooling rack before looking up at her again. "Gran, it's not like that at all. This has all happened so quickly. There have been so many changes, just in the past couple of months."

"Changes?" She sat down on one of the kitchen chairs. Suddenly, I was assailed with déjà vu. I'd had this conversation with my grandmother before. We had talked about Jason, about my job at the Peabridge, about the mysterious collection of books in my basement.

I blinked and realized that we'd never had such a discussion. But we had talked throughout all my painful years of high school. Through the trials and tribulations of my first date, my first kiss, my first agonizing decision of who to invite to a Sadie Hawkins dance.

I took a deep breath, ready to share with Gran, ready to tell her about Neko, and David, and what little I had learned about witchcraft. Before I could get out the first words, though, Leah burst into the kitchen. "Oh, good," she said. "You've got the cobbler out."

"It's a crisp," I said, irrationally annoyed by her appearance.

"Crisp, cobbler, freaking brown betty. The kids are screaming for dessert. If you had children, Jane, you'd know that they really can't be kept waiting when they're excited like this. Honestly, sometimes I don't know how you single women survive."

My retort was hotter than the crisp in its casserole dish, but before I could spill out a venomous reply, Gran pulled herself up from her chair. "We'd best make sure all the little monsters get more sugar, then, shouldn't we? At least they'll work it off running around the bonfire." I flashed her a smile of gratitude and scrambled for bowls and spoons.

The crisp was declared a success, and everyone adjourned to the back clearing for the evening's main event.

The bonfire was everything that I remembered from my childhood. Flames leaped high against the pitch-black sky, sending up sparks in ever-changing patterns of light. My back grew chilled, even as my face was toasted by the fire. Someone broke out bags of giant marshmallows (Jason and I shared a fond smile), and Hershey's bars magically appeared beside boxes of graham crackers. The kids tracked down long branches for marshmallow-roasting. One of Simon's twins discovered a coveted five-pronged stick.

I learned that Jason preferred his marshmallows charred to a crisp. I learned that he liked extra chocolate on his s'mores. I learned that he could lick stray graham cracker crumbs from the corners of my mouth, in the dark, on the very edge of the fire's light. And I learned that he could protect me from the spookiest ghost stories in Connecticut, his arm hollowing out a perfect circle by his side.

As the kids fell asleep and parents began to make noises about shuffling off to bed, Simon came and sat beside me. "It's been a long time, Jane," he said, nodding to Jason, as if to include him in reminiscences.

"Too long," I sighed.

Simon held out his fist, and I automatically extended my hand. Something brass slipped from his fingers to mine. "Blue," he said.

The Blue Cottage. The one that Gran had set aside for Simon and Carol, to give them a break from their boys. The one that was nestled on the very edge of the Farm's property, far away from prying eyes. "Simon, I can't."

"Of course you can. I'll take the couch in the main house. Someone has to make sure that the boys don't sneak out too late. And Carol will be fine up in the Girls' Room."

Jason's fingers tightened on mine. I leaned forward and kissed Simon on his cheek. "Thank you," I said.

"You look happy," he replied, and he nodded toward Jason again. "Both of you."

We waited a few minutes, just for appearance's sake. Someone called for another ghost story, and there was a good-spirited debate about whether it was time to bring out a bottle of schnapps.

I waited until the singing began before I clambered to my feet. Trying to look innocuous, as if I were heading out to search for a new marshmallow stick, I eased into the darkness. Jason followed behind me, close as a shadow.

My feet knew the path to the Blue Cottage; they'd traveled the walkway often enough when I was a child. I clutched Simon's key like a good-luck charm. I felt Jason breathing behind me as I worked the lock. When I fumbled for the light switch, his fingers closed over mine, keeping me from springing the cottage into brightness.

The moonlight was enough. It puddled on the queen-sized bed, illuminating the wedding-ring quilt that had been in the family for as long as I could remember.

I barely managed to set the key on the nightstand before Jason was kissing me. These were not the sweet, promising kisses that he had stolen on the stairs. These were urgent kisses, plying kisses. They reached down into my belly, twisted me, arched me against him with an urgency I had long ago forgotten.

We were like animals, there in the Blue Cottage. We were like fairies from the woods around us, Titania and Oberon, come together in desperate forest love. Jason tugged at my sweater, peeled off my jeans. I returned the services, pulling him closer to me.

The air was chilly in the cottage, kissed by the autumn night. We dove underneath the quilt at the same time, pulling it up to our shoulders and giggling like mad children. For just a moment, I wondered what Jason was seeing. I worried that he would feel betrayed by my too-chunky thighs, that he would close his hands around my waist and realize that I was never going to be a ballerina. I was never going to be a sculpted Russian Ice Queen.

But then his hands moved with a new urgency. Even I— a woman who had been left high and dry on the sexual seas for over a year—recognized what pushed against my belly.

"Damn!" I exclaimed.

"What?" He barely pulled back.

"The condoms! They're back in the house." I was furious with myself. Embarrassed. Disappointed. Desperate. "Maybe Simon and Carol—" I started to say.

But Jason silenced me with another kiss. And when I'd abandoned the ridiculous notion that my happily married cousin might have rubbers sitting around his weekend cottage, Jason sat up. He fumbled for his jeans in the pooled darkness on the floor. He reached into his pocket and drew out a ring of keys, placing them on the nightstand. He extracted his wallet. He opened it up.

And he displayed a foil packet.

A glorious foil packet.

A foil packet that was ripped open in a matter of seconds. And put to astonishingly good use in the middle of the Connecticut woods.

26

The early-morning sun woke me up, slanting through the window shade. For one confused moment, I thought that I was back at home. I pulled my comforter up closer to my chin, only to realize that it was not my comforter.

It was a quilt.

And I was lying under it, naked.

And I was not alone.

I rolled over to find myself looking into Jason Templeton's eyes. "Good morning," he said.

"Good morning." I barely got the words out, as my heart started jackhammering away, and I regretted them immediately. What was I thinking? I hadn't brushed my teeth yet! Here, I had finally lured Jason to bed, and I was going to drive him away with clambake-and-s'mores morning breath.

Before I could figure out a way to sneak out of bed, to

redeem my breath by stealing Simon's toothpaste and rubbing it on my teeth with my finger, before I'd reconciled myself to showing Jason my bare rear end as I ducked into the bathroom, the decisions were taken away from me.

Jason's hands were firm as he pulled me close. His fingers clutched my hair. His lips found mine, as if it were perfectly natural for two people to kiss without the aid of minty fresh breath.

Which, I supposed, it was.

And I didn't regret that lesson. I didn't regret anything, as his fingers began to massage my scalp. His hands moved lower, smoothing over my bare back. I wriggled even closer to him, relishing the feeling of our bodies awakening, tangling, finding each other beneath the quilt.

Scott had never been one for morning lovemaking. He'd never wanted to linger between the sheets—he'd had too many important things to do, too many exciting people to see. I'd once proposed an entire "Pajama Weekend," where we'd do nothing but stay at home, make love and eat disgustingly fattening food, and he'd looked at me as if I was mad before laughing and "getting" my so-called joke.

But Jason… Jason was a different man entirely.

When he came up for air, he said, "And here I thought it might be strange, coming to your family reunion."

"I knew you'd fit right in," I said. And the double entendre in my innocent words made both of us laugh. "Seriously," I said, when I trusted my voice again. "I don't know what possessed me to invite you. I know it can be overwhelming to meet so many people at one time."

"At least Leah set out a welcome mat." We both laughed again. If only my spiteful cousin could see us now….

Jason leaned back on his pillow, pulling me on top of him so that my head rested against his chest. His surprisingly well-muscled chest. His perfect chest. I mean, the man was a college professor! I hadn't expected him to have the body that he had, hidden beneath his long-sleeved shirts, and his impeccable khaki pants.

As I listened to his heart lub-dubbing beneath my ear, I spread my fingers against the curve of his ribs. "This is too perfect," I sighed. I hadn't actually intended to say those words out loud. Nevertheless, they seemed right, drifting to rest in the morning cabin, settling in with the dust motes that sparkled in the sunlight. I closed my eyes as Jason started drawing designs on my back with his fingertips. "Tell me something to make it real," I said.

"What?" His voice was as lazy as his hands.

"Tell me something bad about you. A secret, or something. Something so that I'll know this isn't some fairy-tale dream."

"Something bad? You mean, other than the fact that I'm married?"

I froze.

He was joking, of course. He was teasing me. I had practically *asked* him to tease me. "Married?" I sounded stupid, but my question freed me to sit up, to gather the quilt across my chest like some censor-conscious heroine on a TV show.

"You know, Ekaterina? Marriage? I do, and all that crap?"

I knew all the words that Jason was saying, but I couldn't

make sense out of them. I couldn't make them apply to my Boyfriend, to the man I'd just slept with.

"Ekaterina?" I'd lost the ability to form sentences, to string together subjects and predicates, nouns and verbs. Even as my belly twisted, even as my fingers and toes flamed red-hot then fell icy cold, I tried to remember how to speak, how to ask what I was suddenly terrified that I did not want to know.

Jason went on, before I could piece together a coherent sentence. "You met her, remember? At Five Guys? At the Harvest Gala?" He was sitting up now, too, leaning against the bed's headboard and staring at me warily.

"I met her," I said, finally managing to make a sentence. "I met her, but you never said anything about being married."

"I told you that she was going to Historical Politics this weekend," he said, as if that explained everything.

"But you left out the tiny fact that you're her *husband!*" I was such an idiot.

He'd let me make a fool out of myself. He'd let me declare my interest in him. He'd flirted with me and joked and made me think that we had a future. But he would never, ever be there for me. He would never, ever be mine. Because he belonged to someone else. To have and to hold. Till death do us part.

I was such a total idiot.

I'd seen him with her twice. I'd watched her crying. He'd talked about her research. I'd forced myself to believe that she was a grad student, that she meant nothing to him, that she was just another woman among the hundreds of women that he saw in his professional life.

I was such a complete and utter idiot.

I threw myself out of bed, tugging the quilt with me, so that Jason was suddenly exposed. Bare. Silly.

He stared at me in astonishment. "Jane, you had to realize I was married!"

"And how was I supposed to realize that?" I said, as I scrambled for my clothes. "You don't wear a wedding band!"

"I told you that I couldn't make dinner on a weekend night." He honestly sounded aggrieved, as if *I* were the one who had lied, who had pretended to be something I was not. "I told you that I couldn't get up here to Connecticut until Saturday. I gave you my *cell phone* number."

I tugged on my pants. My bra was tangled around itself, and there was no way that I was going to stand in front of him long enough to tuck myself into its cups and clasps. Instead, I jerked my sweater over my head, slashing at my hair to free it from the tight-knit neck. By the time I had finished that maneuver, I could trust my voice with a few more complete sentences. "You never told me you were married. You never gave me any reason to believe that you were. You lied to me, Jason. You lied, and you took advantage of me."

I shoved my feet into my tennis shoes, deciding that socks were as unnecessary as my bra. Jason took a deep breath, and stood up in front of me, completely naked.

"Jane, you're being completely unreasonable!"

"I'm—" I started to say, but he cut me off.

"Come on! You had to know Ekaterina was my wife. You're the one who brought her up in half our conversations."

"But what—" My voice broke, and I needed to swallow hard before trying a second time. "What was *this* all about?" I gestured toward the bed.

"This was a break," he said. "We've both been working so hard—me, writing my articles, you, doing my research…."

Doing his research. My so-called Boyfriend thought I was nothing more than a research assistant. Well, a research assistant and an easy lay. A research assistant, an easy lay and a willing partner in adultery.

My anger was hotter than our passion the night before, hotter than the bonfire that had blazed in the back clearing, hotter than the greasy flames that had shot out from my oven on the night that Jason first kissed me.

I needed to do something, needed to move. My arms rose up, and my fingers stiffened. Power pulsed inside me, building with every heartbeat. The thrumming energy of spell-work rippled down my spine. My hair crackled, and I knew that it must halo my face.

The magic was strong, stronger than anything I had summoned before. It was greater than my fumbling efforts when I awakened Neko, greater than my mastering simple kitchen flames. I opened my mouth and heard a terrible sound, a grating laugh, a murderous glee. *I* was making that noise; *I* was gloating over this power, this strength.

Part of me was mortified, horrified, afraid to even look at Jason's aghast face. But part of me reveled in his terror. He was remembering. He was thinking back to the fire in my kitchen. He was making himself see the magic that he had denied, the power that he had convinced himself was nothing.

Nothing.

He thought that I was nothing. He had been playing me from day one. Plying me with marshmallows and Italian lunches.

I closed my eyes, but I could no longer control my rage. It spun me around, crashing my thoughts against each other. I needed to ground the force; I needed to store it away. Even thinking of dampening it, though, only made the magic surge higher. I panicked, and *that* adrenaline rush folded into the maelstrom.

My mind was moving faster than light now. Jason was frozen before me—naked, frightened. The anger, the rage, the sucking, spinning power—

"Neko!" I sent the call across space, across time. It echoed inside my skull, and yet I knew that I'd said nothing aloud. "Neko!" I called again. My familiar had been awakened under the light of a full moon; he could leave our books, leave the home we shared. He could come to me here, where I needed him. "Neko!"

"Oh, my," he said, and under other circumstances, I might have laughed at the expression on his face as he studied the naked Jason. "I know they *say* that size doesn't matter, but—"

"Help me!" I cried as the tremendous forces inside my body, inside my soul, began to rattle my teeth.

Neko glided to my side. He leaned in, barely stifling a yelp as he came into contact with my scarce-pent magic.

"No time for spells," he muttered, and he grabbed one of the sheets from the cottage floor. "Here," he said. "Bleed the power into this." He took my hand, and I felt him pull off

the worst of the heat, the core of the pressure. The power
seeped into the fabric fibers, dissipating through the warp and
weft. Then, there was a concussion, short and sharp as a car
backfiring. The sheet flashed into brightness, every thread
illuminated into instant brilliance, and then it simply disappeared.

"Again," Neko said, and he sacrificed the wedding-ring
quilt. That bulk siphoned off a little more of my rage, but
there was still too much for me to control alone.

"Again." The bed's fitted sheet. "Again." Pillows. "Again."
The towels in the bathroom. "Again." The shower curtain.
"Again." Jason's tangled clothes still strewn on the braided
rug where I had flung them the night before.

"And again." The rug itself.

Finally, I was able to breathe. I was able to look around
the cottage. I was able to see Jason, freed also, trying to cover
himself with trembling hands.

"Jane," he croaked.

"No."

I swept his keys off the nightstand before he could react,
and I sailed out of the Blue Cottage, letting the door swing
wide so that the freezing air shriveled the lying, cheating
bastard I'd thought of as my Boyfriend.

Neko followed in my wake. He was silent as we thrashed
along the wooded path, but I watched his eyes dart toward
a flash of bird wing here, a shimmer of insects there. I only
paused when we stood on the edge of the lawn, looking at
the Farm's sturdy wraparound porch.

"So," Neko said. "I take it he wasn't any good in bed?"

I burst into tears.

Neko folded his arms around me, and I buried my face against his black T-shirt. He let me cry, making a soft sound deep in his throat, which might have been a purr.

"I didn't know what I was doing," I said, when I could finally speak. But even I couldn't say if I was referring to sleeping with Jason, or to the magic disaster. Neko just made noises of agreement. "I didn't know. And David told me, and I didn't listen, and now he's going to show up, and I'll have to explain, and Leah will watch, and I'll be an idiot in front of her again, like always."

"Well," Neko said reasonably. "She can't watch if you aren't here."

"Just where am I supposed to go?"

Neko looked pointedly at the keys in my hand.

"But I can't just take his car!"

"Why else did you grab them? Besides, it didn't seem to bother you much, taking his clothes."

"But David will—"

"Oh, he won't be pleased. But taking the car isn't going to make *that* any better or worse. It's the magic he cares about. Not grand theft auto."

"David's going to kill me."

"Give him some time to calm down, then. Drive home."

"But won't he just materialize inside the car?"

"He may be a warder, but he's not a complete idiot. Would *you* try to pick out a few square feet of vehicle cruising down the highway? And attempt to materialize inside it?" I still felt dubious. *"Go,"* Neko insisted. "I'll deal with him here. I'll explain. You can talk to him later, when he's had a chance to calm down."

"And Jason? He's going to be ranting like a madman. He'll tell everyone I'm a witch."

"Not that I'm sure your family would care… Don't worry. I'll blur his memory of what happened. I'll make sure he remembers *why* you were so upset, though. Knock a little shame into him."

"Can you do that?"

"Have I failed you yet?"

Gratitude swelled in my chest, and I wiped my eyes with the backs of my hands. "Thanks, Neko." He walked me over to the Volvo and watched me climb in on the driver's side. "I owe you one." I jammed the key into the ignition.

"Just remember you said that, after you get home." He closed my door and knocked twice on the roof before stepping back to let me drive away.

It was Sunday morning; there was no traffic on the rural Connecticut roads. By the time I got to the highway, I was reliving every moment that I'd ever spent with the bastard Jason, every time that I'd looked at him in the Peabridge, helped him find a book, ordered a rare pamphlet for his studies. I remembered every word we'd ever exchanged through the long, long months when he was only my Imaginary Boyfriend. I remembered speaking the grimoire spell, and the short six weeks when I'd thought that there was something real between us. Something more than my being a tool. A research slave. And a cheap thrill besides.

I remembered the way that he'd touched me the night before. I wanted to take a shower, the hottest one that I could stand. I wanted to stand under water that made my eyes smart and my skin turn pink. I wanted to scream.

But instead, I drove.

I drove until I reached the Beltway. I drove until I turned off for D.C. I drove until I'd threaded my way into Georgetown. I drove until I reached the No Parking Any Time Towing Enforced 24 Hours zone, three blocks from the Peabridge. I left the engine running, and I locked the keys in the car. I hoped with all my heart that it would be out of gas by the time that it was towed.

I was still reciting angry imprecations to myself as I passed through the garden gate. I was halfway down the path to my front door when a man stepped out of the shadows. For one heart-stopping instant, I thought it was David, already arrived to chastise me.

I was mistaken. But my actual visitor was nearly as bad. Harold. Harold Weems. My would-be knight in colonial frock coat. As if I needed to see him now. As if I needed to be reminded that everything I did went wrong, that every idea I'd ever had became warped and twisted and ruined.

He slid to a stop in front of me, trying to catch his breath and suck in his belly, all the time smoothing back his pitiful strands of hair. "Jane, are you all right?"

"I'm fine, Harold," I said, my voice nearly a whisper.

"I was closing up the library a few minutes ago. I always take a look back here, just to make sure everything's okay, that *you're* okay—"

"I'm fine, Harold," I said again, through gritted teeth.

"No." He shook his head. "I mean, you might be fine,

but your house… Your front door was open. I've already
checked inside. Everything seems fine. Perfect. Of course,
since it's your home, how could it be anything less than
perfect?"

Oh, great. My front door. I must have plucked Neko to
Connecticut just as he was entering or leaving. Wasn't *that*
my perfect luck.

Harold rattled on. "I'm really glad that I could be here
for you, Jane. I'm really glad I could help you out. Let me
just go inside with you now. Maybe make you a drink?"

And I just couldn't take it anymore. I couldn't stand
there, in my sweater that stank of bonfire smoke. I couldn't
bear my belly aching, my legs sore from exercise I never
should have had the night before.

I planted my feet and looked Harold directly in the eye.
"I don't need you to help me, Harold. I don't need you to
'take a look' at my house. I don't need you to make me a
drink. I don't need you in my life, Harold. I release you. Go
play with your computers or read your books or whatever
it is that you really want to do, but leave. Leave. Me. Alone."

I felt a *ping* in the air between us.

Harold was shocked. His gentle eyes squinted closed, as
if I'd slapped him. He swallowed hard, started to say something, stopped and swallowed again.

But I couldn't bear to hear what he would say. I couldn't
bear to think about what I'd done to him. I was hurt, angry
and confused, and I'd just lashed out at another person—at
a *spellbound* person—for no good reason. I should have
found a way to release him from my witchcraft without de-
stroying him in the process.

Disgusted with myself, I pushed past him into the cottage. I closed and locked the door behind me.

Inside, the house did indeed look fine. Sunlight streamed in the front windows. Yesterday's mail was centered on the coffee table. A wineglass glinted in the drying rack on the kitchen counter. My bed was neatly made, the comforter perfectly centered and the pillows fluffed to perfection.

My bed.

I shouldn't be able to see my bed from the front door. My bedroom was supposed to be locked.

All of a sudden, I remembered my frantic departure on Friday morning, my multiple attempts to gather all of my belongings. Neko had asked about my hair. I'd stormed back into my room, grabbed a scrunchie.

I had left my bedroom door unlocked.

"Stupid Fish!" I cried, running into the room. I searched the ten-gallon tank, looking for the familiar tetra flash, the ripple of Stupid Fish's tail as he circled endlessly. But the tank was quiet, dim, lifeless.

Empty.

27

I was going to sit here in my basement, surrounded by books, and I was never going to deal with the outside world again.

Okay. I knew that wasn't really feasible. After I'd recovered from the immediate shock of Stupid Fish's demise, I'd grabbed a bowl of apples, a bag of pretzels and a two-liter bottle of water. That was all I had for food here in the basement. I wouldn't stay here forever, of course. I wasn't going to starve myself to death just to prove that my familiar was a lying, cheating pescivore. Or to avoid my warder. Not even to prove that my so-called Boyfriend was a conniving, manipulative adulterer.

I was just going to spend some time alone. Take some time to figure out why I always made such an idiot out of myself. Figure out what I'd wanted from Jason, and why I'd settled.

First things first.

My collection of books on witchcraft hadn't changed much since the night I'd discovered it. Now, under the full glare of overhead lights, I could see how dusty the spines were. When I shifted a few volumes to make room on one shelf, I left a dark dust-free footprint behind.

Even worse than the dust, though, was the disorganization. I'd peered at the titles for nearly an hour, and I could figure out absolutely no overall system. They'd just been shoved onto the basement shelves without regard to origin, size, subject matter or anything else.

If this were a typical library, I'd organize the books by subject matter. After all, people who came looking for one book on colonial agriculture were likely to be interested in others. The same principle should hold for crystals or runes or whatever.

I quickly found, though, that I didn't know enough about witchcraft to organize my collection that way. A peek inside the ancient leather-bound portfolio, *On Scrying and Ways of Seeing,* showed me that crystals could be used in conjunction with mirrors or pools of water. Certain crystals made visions sharper. But was scrying more related to *Reflections on Life as a Witch,* or *Using Mirrors To Increase Magical Flow?* Should it be with books about stones or books about mirrors?

As I worked through the collection, becoming more and more confused by the obscure terminology of witchcraft, bigger doubts nibbled at the back of my mind. Why had I let myself be deceived by Jason? I remembered the feeling of his hands on my back, the tickle of his chest hair against my cheek as I listened to him breathe. Had he always been lying, cheating scum? Or had he only become that way as time moved on, as he realized that I was hopelessly, helplessly in love with him? And what about my spell? Had I forced him to violate his marriage vows? No one else that I had bewitched had acted so…completely, not Harold or Mr. Potter or my newly-coffee-loving Mr. Zimmer.

Was Jason different because *I* had been in love with him?

Well, not exactly. I'd been in love with the *idea* of him. With the Imaginary Boyfriend. The perfect man who just hadn't had the chance to discover that I was the perfect woman.

I'd barely known Jason at all. That's what I'd learned up at the Farm, even before the disastrous night in the Blue Cottage. I didn't know his favorite foods. I didn't know his family (little had I realized how *much* I didn't know his family!). I didn't know what he wanted to achieve in life.

Inside my mind, I'd taken him and made him into something that he wasn't. Made *me* into something that I wasn't.

I felt as if I'd lost something at the Farm—a dream, a hope, a future. But all I'd really lost was my own pathetic image of those things. I'd let myself be deluded.

And what was *that* all about? Why had I been so willing to tell myself stories?

As I got to my new barrage of questions, I realized that I needed to stretch my legs and my back; I'd spent too much time crouching in front of bookshelves, peering at dusty spines, trying to translate strange words into comprehensible subjects.

I peered at my watch as I stood—nine-thirty.

How had it gotten so late? I'd made it back from the

Farm in good time, but it had been early afternoon when I discovered that Neko had murdered Stupid Fish. I'd spent nearly seven hours down here—practically an entire work-day.

Work. I had to go to work tomorrow.

It would be Monday. Jason would be in all morning. Sitting at "his" table in the reading room. Facing toward my desk.

I was going to be sick tomorrow. A terrible flu. I wouldn't want to infect the entire staff. I'd sleep it off and be in on Tuesday. If I could.

I practiced my phone call to Evelyn in my head, repeating myself until I sounded natural. Feeling like a sneaking thief in my own home, I crept upstairs to the kitchen. I had a brick of cheddar cheese in the fridge, and there was bread in the freezer. I made myself two slices of cheese toast, savoring the bubbled orange surface like a little kid. I washed down my comfort food with a glass of milk, phoned Evelyn, used the restroom and retreated downstairs, bringing a blanket to shield against the night's growing chill.

As I curled up on the cracked leather couch, I thought about the Farm's wedding-ring quilt. I remembered how soft the fabric had been as I pulled it up to my chin, as I spooned with Jason and fell asleep, certain that I would find him next to me in the morning. I drifted off on the couch with slow tears leaking from beneath my eyelids.

When I awoke, I lay quietly and listened for noise upstairs. Nothing. No footsteps. No water running. No chattering.

I gathered the blanket around my shoulders and crept up to the living room. Sunlight streamed in the cottage's front windows. I squeezed my eyes shut and raised a hand to protect my face. So what if I looked like a vampire? There was no one there to see me.

In the kitchen, I glanced at the clock—eleven-thirty. I'd slept away nearly the entire morning.

On the table, there was a note in Neko's slanted handwriting. He'd obviously found his way back from Connecticut, by magic or by Lincoln Town Car.

Talked to David. I'm sorry about the fish.
He'll see you later. I'm sorry about the fish.
9:00. Gran called. I'm sorry about the fish.
9:05. Melissa called. I'm sorry about the fish.
9:10. Gran called again. I'm sorry about the fish.
9:15. Clara called. I'm sorry about the fish.

Fine. *I'm sorry* wasn't going to bring back Stupid Fish. Let Gran and Melissa and Clara call as often as they wanted. I wasn't ready to talk to them yet. I hacked a chunk of cheddar off the brick in the refrigerator and went back downstairs.

And that was my pattern for the next three days. I ate when I was hungry, drank when I was thirsty. I waited to hear footsteps cross the living room and the front door close before I stole upstairs to use the toilet and gather fresh food supplies. Each time I emerged from my darkened lair, there was a fresh note from Neko, cataloging phone messages and apologizing.

My grandmother favored clustering her calls, while Melissa and Clara spread theirs out through the day. When I remembered, I updated my message to Evelyn at the office, telling her that my stomach bug was more tenacious than I'd thought at first.

Each time I returned to the basement, I slept. Hours and hours, for more time than I'd ever imagined possible. My body felt wrung out, as if someone had squeezed all of the energy from my flesh. I kept thinking of Hamlet's soliloquy—"to sleep, perchance to dream." I wasn't contemplating suicide like the Prince of Denmark, but I wasn't dreaming, either. I slept like the dead.

Every time I came upstairs, I knew that I should take a shower. I should brew a cup of tea. I should comb my hair and brush my teeth and pretend that I was a normal, everyday girl.

That required too much energy, though, and the couch in the basement always lured me back with its comfortable, overstuffed arms. I brought an extra set of sheets downstairs and tucked them into the cushions. I dragged my pillow with me.

But in the few hours that I wasn't sleeping or eating or reading Neko's increasingly agitated notes, I organized the books in my basement. After the first night's shuffling, I did what I should have done in the first place; I pulled all of them off the shelves, stacking them in the middle of the room.

Then, I sorted them by title, taking care to set each in its proper place, lining them up methodically at the front of the shelves so that they looked like some Hollywood designer's idea of a library. I looked through each volume, finding a surprising number of handwritten notes, scraps of parchment, papers filled with dozens of different handwritings.

There were objects on the shelves, as well. I uncovered a set of jade runes and another of gold and a partial set of wooden tiles. I found three different wands, each as long as my forearm, each carved out of a different type of wood. I discovered a set of three nested iron pots, all shaped like classic witch's cauldrons.

In one corner, sheltered beneath a dusty crocheted afghan, there was a wooden chest. I opened it to discover dozens of glass vials, each carefully labeled. Robin feathers. Columbine. Tortoiseshell. I glanced back at the books, wondering what sort of potions I could make with the ingredients.

After finding the first few objects scattered among the books, I realized that I needed to take care of all of the treasures. I couldn't just consign them to further forgotten life on their dusty shelves. I waited until I heard Neko close the front door one afternoon, and then I darted upstairs to find my laptop computer. It was a hand-me-down from Scott that I'd had for almost five years but never used. I plugged it into one of the basement wall sockets, fired it up and pulled up the ancient database program that Scott had loaded on it years ago.

I took great pleasure in deleting the files that Scott had stored away. In fact, I enjoyed wiping out his databases so much that I opened up his Office program. I started to delete everything there, but I paused when I found an

MINDY KLASKY

e-mail folder labeled "Amelia." Amelia had been in Scott's law school section; they'd studied together for first year and remained friends after they'd both graduated. I double-clicked on the folder icon.

It was locked; I needed to type in a password. I barely hes-itated before entering Scott's birthday, two digits each for month, day and year of birth. If I'd learned nothing else in library school, I'd learned that most people are completely unimaginative when it came to protecting their computer files.

Sure enough, the folder sprang open as if it were loaded on a spring.

If I'd expected an exegesis of criminal law, I was disap-pointed, but I managed to uncover a great deal of criminal intent. Okay, maybe not criminal. But I found myself utterly fascinated by the notes that Scott had written to Amelia. They'd had e-mail sex. They'd apparently had phone sex, too, on several nights when I'd left the apartment, hoping to make it easier for Scott to study for exams. And they'd had real sex, on numerous occasions, in the bed that Scott and I had shared.

With fingers trembling so hard that I could scarcely type, I closed Amelia's folder, and I opened the next: Birgit. Then, Cathy. Donna.

The folders read like a list of hurricanes, and each one ripped through my gut. Woman after woman after woman. Scott had flirted with all of them, lured most of them into online antics, and many of them into his bed. Our bed.

How could I have been so blind? How could I have missed the fact that my fiancé, the love of my life, the man I was going to marry and love happily ever after, had been screwing anything in a skirt?

And what did it mean that even when I was free from my philandering significant other, I had immediately sought out Jason, a man who was carved from the exact same stone?

Nauseated, I deleted all of it. The e-mail, word-procesing files, spreadsheets. I would have reformatted the entire computer hard disk, but I wanted to use the programs that Scott had installed so long ago. I wanted to use his computer, to use him, to make *something* good come out of the years I'd wasted on him.

Tears trickling down my cheeks, I reopened the database program and started to build my library catalog. I made neat entries for my witchcraft books—their titles, authors, subject matters, physical descriptions. I created records for the slips of paper that had been tucked between their pages; I made special notes about the objects I'd found.

The work took a long time, but it was mostly mindless.

And that gave me time to think. Time to cry. Time to look at the mess I'd made of my life.

Why was I so good at choosing bad men? Why did I seek out the same type, time after time? Why did I write stories in my mind, justifying them, explaining them? Why did I hang on to them so desperately?

And what was I possibly going to do with myself, now that I knew I had to let them go?

28

I thought that I was dreaming when I smelled the choco-late-chip cookies.

I'd spent four days in the basement, working feverishly whenever I wasn't sleeping. Although the room was cool, I knew that I smelled, um, somewhat less than fresh; I still hadn't brought myself to waste time taking a shower. It just seemed unnecessary. I mean, it wasn't like I was ever going to see a man, ever again. Scott had lied to me. Jason had lied to me. Even the nice guys, like Harold, were driven away by my bitchiness.

I *was* going to have to do something about food. The apples had only lasted until Tuesday. The pretzels were long gone; I'd run out of cheese the night before. I'd even resorted to eating the canned Bartlett pears that had lingered at the back of my kitchen shelves for months. I'd fallen asleep, wondering if Neko's Stupid-Fish-engendered guilt was great enough that he would run to the grocery store for me, solely on the strength of a written note. Could I trust him to bring back a pint of Chubby Hubby? Or would my favorite ice cream go the way of my poor, lost fish, right down Neko's gullet?

So, I thought that I might be hallucinating the chocolate-chip cookies.

I crept to the top of the stairs and listened carefully. The night before, I'd stayed awake until nearly dawn, finishing the catalog of my witchcraft books. I had to admit that I was impressed—Hannah Osgood had brought together quite a collection. Even though I couldn't say which were rare in the world of witchcraft, I knew that most were by different authors. Many reached back several centuries, and all were now neatly listed in my sortable, printable, one hundred percent accurate and up-to-date catalog.

Now, huddled at the top of the stairs, I smelled something else beneath the aroma of chocolate-chip cookies. Something salty and hot, a memory of childhood sick days.

I twisted the knob and eased the basement door back on its hinges.

Chicken soup. Hot chicken soup. With rice, if I remembered anything from my childhood. Easy tears sprang back into my eyes. Someone had cared enough about me to make chicken soup.

I tugged my bathrobe tighter around my waist and crossed to the kitchen, only to discover a half circle of earnest, silent women. Okay. Three women and Neko. But Neko was looking his most feminine, brushing on clear nail polish and studying his fingers as if they were works of art.

"Hi," I said, suddenly aware of just how greasy my hair must be.

Melissa stood up. "Hi," she said. "We thought you might be hungry."

"Yeah, well…" I trailed off, taking a moment to dash my palms against my damp cheeks.

Gran stepped up beside my best friend. "Why don't you go take a shower, dear? Then, we'll all sit down to a bit of midnight supper."

I glanced at the clock—11:30 p.m. I had completed another sleep marathon.

Clara rose to complete the triumvirate. "I'll make some sandwiches to go with the soup. Turkey or ham for you?"

"Turkey," Melissa and Gran both answered, before I could. They knew I didn't like ham.

"Go ahead," Melissa said to me. "Wash up and come eat with us."

Gran volunteered, "I put some clothes on your bed. You can change into them after you shower."

Neko twisted shut his bottle of nail polish and came to stand beside the others, waving his drying fingers in the air. "Don't look at me like that," he said. "I wasn't going to keep taking messages forever, you know. I had people to see. Places to go."

Fish to eat, I thought, but I didn't say it. Instead, I shut myself into the bathroom and turned on the water for the hottest shower I could stand.

Someone had been at work here, as well, and I suspected Melissa's hand. My favorite Body Shop shampoo was standing on the floor of the shower, partnered with con-

ditioner and a matching bar of glycerine soap. My toothbrush and toothpaste had been retrieved from the Farm;
they were laid out on the counter like offerings to some
goddess of hygiene. I peeked underneath the sink and
found my entire cosmetics bag, the one that I had abandoned in the Girls' Room, tucked away safe and sound.

As I soaped up a washcloth, I remembered how good a
shower can feel. I lathered shampoo into my hair and filled
my lungs completely for what seemed like the first time in
weeks. Toweling dry, I realized that I was starving, ravenous,
as if I had eaten nothing for months.

I ducked into my bedroom and found that Gran had been
true to her word. Fleece pants were laid out on the bed,
grey to match the heathered sweatshirt beside them. I
tugged the pants on and was pleased to see that the elastic
waistband was a little loose. I wouldn't market heartbreak
as the diet of choice, but a girl had to take her benefits
where she could.

Clean for the first time in days, I returned to the kitchen
to find a simple meal set out on the counter, buffet-style.
Gran loaded up a plate for me, ignoring my halfhearted
protests that she was giving me too much food. We all
decided to sit in the living room, because there weren't
enough chairs in the kitchen.

"So," Gran said, when we had settled on the hunter-
green couches.

"So," I repeated. What did they want me to say? I'd been
an idiot? I'd been a desperate fool? I filled my mouth with
turkey sandwich, trying to ignore the salty taste of renewed
tears at the back of my throat.

Clara jumped in to fill the silence. "We had quite an interesting ride back to D.C."

I wasn't interested, but I had to say something. "Really?"

Clara looked at Gran, who clicked her tongue primly before saying, "Well, your young man showed up at the farmhouse wearing nothing but his shoes. Poor Leah thought she might go into labor then and there, from the surprise."

"Leah was awake?" I asked, intrigued despite myself.

"Oh yes," Gran said. "Neko saw to that."

I turned to Neko, who was studying his manicure with pursed-lips nonchalance. He shrugged. "Well, I couldn't be sure which room you were staying in, could I? I needed to call your name from the driveway, let you know that I'd made it to the Farm after my weekend in Boston. I knew that you'd be worried."

"Your weekend in Boston," I repeated, beginning to understand the cover story that Neko had concocted.

"I got a little carried away, though," he admitted, lowering his eyes in false shame. "It must have been that Tennessee Williams retrospective I saw last month. For the record, it's much easier to bellow 'Stella' than 'Jane.'"

Melissa guffawed around a mouthful of ham sandwich, and I shook my head at his silliness. "So, Neko arrived… from Boston and woke everyone with his Stanley Kowalski imitation."

Clara nodded and said, "Just in time for us to see Jason stumble out of the woods. He had some strange story to tell—that you'd mistakenly taken his clothes when you borrowed his car to return home. He said you had an emergency back here."

Gran broke in: "Which certainly didn't please the *other* man."

"Other man?" I asked, looking at Neko, only to catch his minute nod.

Clara explained. "David, he said his name was. He came over from the Blue Cottage right after Jason."

Gran shook her head. "What a pity they didn't run into each other on the path in the woods. David could at least have given Jason his overcoat to wear."

"Pity," Neko said, with a doleful shake of his head.

Gran took up the story. "Well, at least Simon was able to loan Jason some clothes, but that poor young man was simply *swimming* in his borrowed dungarees."

"Now, Mother," Clara said. "They probably would have been okay if the twins hadn't 'pantsed' him."

I made a mental note to thank Simon's boys. Melissa asked, "So then what happened?"

"Jason insisted that Jane had left," Clara said. "David seemed rather put out. He told Neko—"

Neko interrupted. "He and I *discussed* things. In fact, we strolled back to the Blue Cottage to tidy up. And then he went on his way."

"On his way?" I asked, glancing apprehensively toward the door.

"He said that he understood that you had a lot, um, on your plate, and he'd catch up with you later in the week." Later. Great. That could be now.

Gran, oblivious to my concern, continued her story. "By the time Neko came back to the house, most people had left. We all piled into the Lincoln and drove home."

"All?" I asked.

Neko clarified. "Clara drove. And a fine driver she is—never went a mile above the speed limit. That gave us plenty of time to talk to Jason."

"Jason was with you?"

"In the backseat. With me. While your grandmother sat up front." Neko fluttered his hands in front of his eyes. "The poor man just could *not* get comfortable. I think that he was positively *chafed* by the time we got to his house."

Clara took up the tale. "Of course, we waited with him at his place, to make sure that he could get inside. He'd misplaced his house keys, somehow. Or that's what he told the woman who finally showed up."

"Ekaterina?" I asked, my voice a whisper.

"Is that her name?" Clara snorted and tossed her flame-red hair. "Sounds about right. Poor thing looked like she was going to faint away when she saw all of us. She burst into tears. No strength to her at all. No meat on her bones."

"Speaking of meat on bones," Melissa said, and she jumped up from the couch. "Neko, will you help me?"

I took the opportunity of their absence to look at my mother and grandmother, to really study these women who were so like me. I reached out to take their hands. "Thank you," I said.

Gran smiled slightly, and then Clara, and I knew that I would one day tell them everything that had happened in the Blue Cottage. Well, not *everything*…

"Gran?" I said, realizing this was the perfect time to ask them both a question. "Clara?" They looked at me expectantly. "Have you ever done…" I trailed off, realizing that I

was going to sound like an idiot. "Have you ever worked…"
That was no better. Well, there was no way to avoid this.
They'd stuck with me this long; I couldn't imagine they'd
abandon me now. "Do you believe in magic?"

Clara glanced at Gran and then quickly looked away. She
dropped my hand and raised her short, blunt fingers to her
mouth. She chewed on her fingernails distractedly until
Gran said, "Stop that!"

Clara folded her hands in her lap and finally met my eyes.
"Yes," she said. "I believe in magic."

"Clara—" Gran said.

"No!" My mother did not raise her voice, but she spoke
with great force. She looked me in the eye and said, "I
first felt it when I was a teenager. If I held my worry
beads, I could…make things happen. And when I cast
runes, they truly told the future." She swallowed. "It
frightened me. A lot. And so I drank. And got high. And
just stayed away from home, where the feelings were
strongest."

Gran looked flustered. "You know I don't believe in
those things, Clara. I never have."

"But you believe in your *traditions,* like the rhyme at the
Farm. And that old pregnancy necklace."

"Those are different," Gran countered immediately.

"And you used the crystal Jane made for you, when you
were in the hospital."

"That was a gift!"

"Mother!" Clara said, and her voice held the exact same
note of exasperation that I had perfected as a teen. Clara
turned to me. "I'm sorry, Jane. What can I say? You come

from a long line of weird women. Stubborn, wonderful, gifted, *magical* women."

There was a sudden clatter in the kitchen, and Melissa and Neko returned with a towering plate of chocolate-chip cookies, a pitcher of milk and a tray of glasses. From the studious way they avoided meeting our eyes, I figured they'd overheard all of that last bit.

Melissa slapped my familiar's hand as he attempted to drink directly from the pitcher. He settled for a tall glass of milk and a single cookie. Melissa poured for me and held the serving plate in front of my nose until I'd taken two, then three and finally four cookies. "They're best when they're hot," she said, passing the platter to Gran and Clara.

Suddenly, I realized how much I'd missed my best friend, up at the Farm. How much I'd needed her. I clutched at Melissa's free hand as she sat down. "I'm sorry," I said to her.

"What?"

"I'm so sorry. When I was, um, with Jason, I realized that I…pitied you. I thought your First Dates were ridiculous. I thought that I had everything, that I was leading some sort of dream life, and I actually felt *sorry* for you. I was an idiot."

Gran answered before Melissa could. "We're all idiots." She offered her pronouncement around a large bite of cookie, and she swallowed before she elaborated. "We women who forfeit what we believe in just to please a man. We're idiots."

I took a mournful nibble of my own. "Not you," I said to my grandmother. "You loved Grandpa, and now you love Uncle George, and you've never been an idiot."

"Except for that foolish concert opera."

"What?" I was astonished. "You *love* the opera."

"I like the *people,*" she conceded. "But the operas? I might as well listen to cats yowling at the moon." She sipped her milk. "George loves it, though. At first, I was afraid to tell him how I really felt, and now it's far too late. So I suffer half a dozen nights a year. I'm an idiot."

"Six times a year!" Clara said, helping herself to another cookie. "I was locked into a weekly meditation group for six *entire* years. That's one of the main reasons I decided to move back here."

"What happened?" I stared at her.

"I met a man at the food co-op in Sedona. He had the most sensitive hands I'd ever seen…." She sighed, and I tried to picture her scooping quinoa from a bin, standing next to her Adonis. "He told me about a meditation group he was setting up. Group chanting in the box canyon. It was utter crap."

I snorted. "Why?"

"He chose nonsense words for us to chant. Had us yip like coyotes and howl like wolves, communing with our inner carnivores. Every Wednesday night. For six long years."

"Why did you keep going back?" I asked.

"I told you. He had these hands…" Clara sighed and flexed her own fingers. Then she shook her head. "I finally stopped going when I found out that he was showing Megan McDonald those hands. Those hands, and quite a bit more. We're idiots!"

I laughed at the same time that Clara did, and it felt wonderful to share her disdain. Melissa took advantage of the moment to refill my glass. "Don't look at me," she said. "You *know* my ways with men."

I couldn't help but turn to Neko. "And you?"

"What about me?" He tilted his head at a delicate angle.

"Aren't you going to defend your gender?"

"Do I look like a fool?" He set down his empty glass of milk and stretched his arms high above his head. "I could tell all of you stories that would make your hair curl." He redirected his gaze at my tangle of drying hair. "Or straighten. Suffice to say that Roger found a way to come out to his family when he was home for his cousin's wedding. A way that involved a waiter at the reception, a microphone from the band and *way* too many glasses of champagne."

"Oh, Neko," I said, catching a glint of true hurt behind his blasé recitation. "I'm sorry. I thought that I just hadn't seen him around because I'd been busy."

"No," he said, shaking his head sharply. "You haven't seen him around because men are jerks."

I patted his hand. "Not all men," I said.

I immediately pictured Harold Weems. Poor, bespelled Harold, gaping at me like a fish out of water.

Fish. I put that image out of my mind. Now was not the time to dwell on the past. Not the time to mourn a superannuated tetra that was the last remnant of eleven wasted years. I should be grateful that I was through with Stupid Fish. That I had moved beyond him, and the rotten man he represented.

For there *were* good men. As long as we women remembered to be strong. As long as we remembered to be true to ourselves.

I took another cookie from the plate and held it high, waiting until everyone around me had one. "To ourselves," I said, saluting the air.

"To ourselves!" they echoed, and then we collapsed into a corny, girly, loving, supportive group hug.

29

Evelyn was sitting behind her desk, her tweed suit boxier than ever, her blunt-cut hair still hovering along her jawline at the absolute wrong length for her features. How did she maintain that exact cut? I ran my fingers through my own mop nervously, only to come up against the gathered band of my muslin cap. This was my first day back in colonial garb after nearly a week of heartbroken sulking, and I missed the casual comfort of my fleece pants.

"Jane, I'm very pleased that you were able to make it in to work today. I have to say, you still look a little pale. I'm glad you're back, though. So much happened while you were out."

I faked a slight cough into my hand. I'd figured that I should come in to the office and salvage at least one day of the workweek. I didn't want my boss thinking that I was a total slacker, just pretending to be sick. Somehow, I didn't think that Evelyn would give me a lot of leeway for de-stroying my love life with one of our patrons. (Although she *might* have been interested in the cataloging project that I'd taken on in my basement—in my classification skills, if not the subject matter.)

Evelyn leaned forward and settled her doughy features into her "concerned" look. "I'm afraid that you didn't have a chance to say goodbye to Harold."

"Goodbye?" What? Harold had left? Where had he gone? Icy dread painted my throat. What exactly had I screamed at him last Sunday?

Evelyn sighed deeply. "Yes, goodbye. He gave us seven long years, but it had been clear to me for quite some time that he needed to move on. I'd told him as much in his annual reviews for two years running, but he always seemed too timid to take the chance. I'd love to know exactly what you said to him."

I stammered. "I—I really don't remember. I think that I was already coming down with the flu when I saw him on Sunday. I'd been away for the weekend, and he startled me when I was opening my front door. I wasn't really thinking—"

"Well, whatever it was, it did the trick."

"The trick?" I stopped fumbling for an explanation. "What trick?"

"Helping Harold find the strength to tender his resignation," she said matter-of-factly. "He said that you always showed him the importance of being true to himself. You encouraged him to follow up on his computer skills, to hone his abilities."

I was shocked by his generous gloss on our relationship. "So what is he doing?"

"He set up his own computer firm—SuperGeek. He said that he'd been thinking about doing it for years, but your conversation on Sunday afternoon made him realize that it was finally time." She pursed her lips into a small pout. "Perhaps you were a little *too* effective with your pep talk, though. Harold insisted that he couldn't give us two weeks' notice. He was too eager to reach his first wave of customers."

"I'm sorry," I said, still stunned.

Evelyn smiled. "Don't be. It was time. Past time. I'm just sorry Harold couldn't have thanked you himself. Harold, or Professor Templeton."

"Jason?" My belly turned to ice so quickly I scarcely had time to worry about using my so-called Boyfriend's given name.

"Oh yes," Evelyn said. "We had a long conversation on Monday morning. Professor Templeton told me how hard you worked to meet his manuscript deadline. He said that he sincerely appreciated the extra hours that you put in on his behalf. He'll be donating a copy of his book to our collection when it comes out next summer, but he wanted me to know that the footnote mentioning the Peabridge does not begin to express how useful you'd been."

Useful.

Well, that was one way of looking at it. I blinked away a mental image of his hands under my sweater as we huddled beneath the stairs at La Perla. Unfortunately, it was replaced by another snapshot—our bodies tangled on the bed in the Blue Cottage. I gritted my teeth.

I supposed I should be grateful that he hadn't elaborated

on my skills. Evelyn waited for me to say something. "I was only doing my job," I finally managed.

It wasn't the truth, but it seemed to match whatever wholesome scenario Jason had carved out for us. I couldn't help but glance over my shoulder, back into the reading room, toward the table where he usually sat. How many times had I primped and preened to walk past the man? How many coats of Pick-Me-Up Pink had been wasted on him? I scratched my knee through my petticoats, wondering just how much my silly costume had turned him on, had led him to his cruel manipulation.

Cruel manipulation. Well, it sounded all grand and tragic when I thought about our relationship that way. *I* was the one who had fallen for a married man. *I* was the one who had tried to muscle in where I wasn't wanted, where I didn't belong. *I* was the one who had cast the grimoire spell.

The heartsick queasiness that I had battled during my time off swept over me with a vengeance. Still, I probed deeper into my thoughts, like a patient testing a bad tooth. Jason *had* made himself available to me. And of course he had known that he was married, that he should have been off the market. Even if he were caught in my love spell, he should have respected the truth. I couldn't really be at fault. At least not completely.

But there was something in me, something that had made me reach out for him. I had wanted him, was attracted to him, was drawn to him. Was that because of his very un-availability? Because I somehow sensed that I could never truly have him? Because I could tell that he was emotionally bound to someone else, and I would never have to commit, never have to hurt the way that I'd hurt for the past year, getting over Scott?

Yeah, right. I could ask myself questions all day, but the reality was I had fallen really hard for a jerk.

Evelyn was continuing to speak. "Professor Templeton made it clear that he won't be using our reading room in the near future. He said he's had a family emergency come up, and he'll have to spend more time at home. He specifically asked me to thank you for your...how did he phrase it? Your professional enthusiasm."

Professional, my ass.

Before I could summon up a few polite words, Evelyn leaned back in her chair. "And that brings me to the last thing I wanted to talk to you about."

I couldn't read her expression. Usually, her chair-leaning signaled something bad. It generally accompanied grave news, announcements where she wanted to read my reaction completely. In fact, the last chair-leaning conversation we'd had was the one where she'd informed me that I was not going to get a raise, that I'd be living in the cottage.

"Yes?" I said, because she seemed to need a prompt to continue. What could it be now? Maybe Harold *had* told her something about what had happened; maybe he had mentioned his so-called love for me.

Or maybe Ekaterina had called, demanding that I be disciplined for poaching her husband. Husband. I shivered.

Or maybe there was something else going on at the library, some particularly dank corner of the basement that needed organizing, some obscure collection of impossible cramped-handwriting letters that needed to be sorted through, and Evelyn had decided that I was just the woman for the job.

Finally, she spoke. "There comes a time in every library where the director has to consider the long-term viability of the institution."

Oh. My. God.

She was breaking up with me. She was giving me the "it's not you, it's me" speech, tailor-made for the reference desk. She was firing me.

I was going to be out on the street. No job. No home. No decent references, courtesies of Harold and Jason and all the insanity of my life in the past couple of months.

How was I going to feed myself? How was I going to feed Neko? And where would I put the books on witchcraft that now marched along the orderly shelves in the cottage basement?

"Evelyn, I—"

She shook her head, effectively cutting me off. "You and I face one of those times." She settled her palms on her desk blotter and finally looked me in the eye. "Jane, I spent all day yesterday in an emergency meeting with the Board."

"The Board?" I tried to keep my voice from quavering.

"The Board, and a special guest. I supposed I shouldn't be surprised that you never mentioned Mr. Potter to me. Not after our discussion about Justin Cartmoor and your grant applications."

"Mr. Potter?" I could not begin to figure out how he fit into this discussion.

"He came to see me on Monday afternoon. He brought pictures of Lucinda."

Mrs. Potter. The owner of the shih tzu. "I never met her," I said, because it sounded like I should say something.

"That's what Mr. Potter said. But he seemed certain that she would have liked you. Liked you and us. Our building. Our collection." Evelyn's face suddenly split into a broad grin. "That's why he decided to endow the Lucinda Potter Library Enhancement Fund."

"The Lucinda—" My grimoire spell had struck again. Besotted, Mr. Potter had solved the Peabridge's fiscal nightmare.

"Yes!" She couldn't contain herself any longer; she actually leaped up from her chair. "The Lucinda Potter Library Enhancement Fund. Mr. Potter—Samuel—has already spoken with his lawyers, and the paperwork is all complete. He's setting aside one pool of money for our daily operations, and another for special projects. He mentioned our diary collection in particular, said that you had told him how desperately we needed to get it in order. With his generous gift, we can hire one full-time cataloger, and at least two part-time people."

I collapsed back in my chair, thoroughly shocked. Mr. Potter had said that he and Lucinda had no children, that she would have loved to help us out with our collection needs. Nevertheless, I'd never really believed him. I'd thought that he was just engaging in cocktail-party chatter. Two full-time equivalents, plus money to run the place on a daily basis?

Somewhat dazed, I pulled off my mobcap, running my

hands through my hair to collect any stray bobby pins. Was it ethical to accept the gift of a man blinded by magic? Could my spell change the way he thought of Lucinda, of his wife and what she loved, what she believed in? I tried a shaky laugh. "Then I guess we're through with the costumes, aren't we?"

Evelyn's own guffaw was loud, horsey. "Through with the costumes! You are a kidder, aren't you! We'll need them more than ever, with all the new people who are going to come flooding through our doors! We're going to issue press releases, Jane. Host a party. We're on the Georgetown map at last!"

Well, a girl could try, couldn't she? Grudgingly, I asked, "Then I guess the coffee bar stays, as well?"

"I wouldn't think of changing a thing!" Evelyn shook her head. "Not the coffee, not the costumes and most certainly not you. Thank you, for everything you've done."

I shook my head and dropped my mobcap into my lap. "Really," I said. "It was nothing."

All's well that ends well, I tried to justify. Those were Shakespeare's words, and they should be good enough for me. But I promised myself that I would think twice, no three times—four!—before I worked another spell.

30

For the rest of the day, I was ridiculously happy. A lot of things suddenly made sense in my life. Burdens that I hadn't even realized I carried were suddenly lifted, and for the first time in ages, I found myself able to fill my lungs completely, to walk with my head high and my spirits light.

I thought about calling Melissa—it was only fair that she should hear from me on the good days, as well as the bad. Arriving home, though, I remembered that she was out on yet another First Date. The woman's persistence was remarkable, even if her choices were flawed.

Neko was waiting for me in the living room, stretched out on the couch, soaking up the last beam of afternoon sunlight. "Did you bring the candy?"

"Candy?" I looked behind me, as if some explanation for the strange request might lurk on the doorstep.

"Ghosts? Goblins? Snack-size Snickers bars? Tonight is Halloween."

Halloween. How had I forgotten that? Somehow, all of the autumn days had run together—I could have sworn that it was still September, and I had just moved into my cottage. I shrugged. "There aren't that many trick-or-treaters here in Georgetown, anyway. And I can't imagine any of them will come back here in the library gardens."

"I wanted cream caramels." Neko pouted.

"Too bad they don't make sardine taffy," I said, collapsing on the couch, then shifting to ease my whalebone stays.

"That would be heaven," Neko sighed. He stretched and got to his feet. "Should I make some mojitos?"

"For just the two of us?"

"You'd make them if Melissa were the only one here."

"That's different. She and I always have mojito therapy." I shrugged. "Besides, I don't feel like mojitos. I'm going down to the basement." All afternoon, I'd been trying to figure out some magic I could work, something that would be completely selfless, completely dedicated to the peace, harmony and well-being of another. Something to atone for my love spell and to offer up thanks for all the good news in the library.

Neko's face twitched with interest, and if he'd been an actual cat, I think his tail would have quivered in expectation. "What were you thinking of?"

"A spell. An incantation. Whatever. I have all this positive energy, and I should use it. I'm just going to change out of this stuff—" I gestured at my colonial costume "—and I'll meet you downstairs.

Neko was waiting for me when I showed up, feeling fresh

and clean in jeans and a bulky sweater. He sidled up to the shelves in the farthest corner of the basement, where I'd placed the most repugnant books in the collection. "What are you thinking of? Another love spell?"

"No!" That sounded too sharp, and I forced myself to lower my voice. "No more love spells. No more love. At least for a while."

Neko curled up on the cracked leather couch to watch me. "What, then?"

"I want to do something to thank them. Gran, Clara and Melissa. Something to let them know that I appreciate their being here last night, the stories that they told me."

Neko arched his back and settled into a more comfortable position. "You could brew an elixir of joy. Add a drop or two to a hot beverage, and the drinker feels happy for no good reason."

I turned a doubtful glance toward the spice chest, occupying place of pride beneath the reading stand. "What's in it?"

"You'd have to check the potion book for the precise amounts. It has a rainwater base, and you add a bit of bluebird wing. Some dried apple blossoms, a pinch of powdered dove's blood… You pour the whole thing over toad's skin, to filter out any lingering negativity, and then you drink it out of a silver thimble."

"Toad's skin?"

"If you don't believe me, you can read it in the potion book!"

"No, no, I believe you." And I did. For all his vanity, his narcissism, his absolute belief that the world rotated around him and only him, Neko had not led me astray about a single aspect of witchcraft.

"What then?" he asked.

"I promised Gran." I thought back to that early September day. Was it only seven weeks ago? "The day that Evelyn told me I'd be living here in the cottage. Gran called at work and made me promise not to lick any toads."

"What sort of fool would lick a toad?" Neko sounded scandalized.

"My point exactly. I promised, without considering the consequences. I think that drinking a potion poured over the skin of a toad might violate the spirit of my promise, though, if not the actual words."

"You have got to be kidding."

"Nope." I shook my head. "I'll talk to Gran. Take back my promise. But not tonight."

Neko cocked his head to one side. "Would she ever know? I mean, I don't think that the elixir of joy is what she had in mind."

"A promise is a promise." I shrugged. "We've always trusted each other. Besides, I'm pretty sure that she would know. When I was a kid, she could always tell when I was lying."

A smooth baritone spoke from the base of the stairs. "Now that sounds like a witchy power, if ever there was one."

I started at the first words, but I placed David Montrose's voice before I turned around. "I don't think that I invited you in," I said, but I wasn't truly surprised.

David inclined his head up the stairs. "Warder's rights,

remember? In any case, you shouldn't leave your front door unlocked, if you don't want visitors. Especially on Halloween. Who can say how many ghosts and goblins might take up residence here?"

Had I left the door unlocked? I looked upstairs, trying to remember whether I had automatically flipped the deadbolt when I came home. Turning back, I caught the tail end of some silent communication between David and Neko. My familiar stood and stretched. "I'll go check on it," he said.

"You don't have to," I responded quickly.

"No," he said to me, but his eyes stayed on David's. "I wanted to, um, get a drink of water." And he was gone, before I could beg him to stay.

I took a deep breath before I turned to face David directly. "So," I said.

"So," he repeated. He was dressed in clothes that I'd come to think of as "mine," comfortable khakis, a soft-as-flannel shirt. Clothes that I knew he'd chosen to make himself more attractive to me.

"Just how much trouble am I in, for Connecticut?"

He studied my face for several heartbeats. "If you'd stuck around till I arrived? You'd still be unable to use your powers. I would have locked your witchcraft down so tightly, you wouldn't be able to watch *The Wizard of Oz.*"

"But now?" I asked warily.

"Now, I've had a chance to calm down. Neko explained everything to me."

"Everything?" I felt myself blushing.

"Enough."

"I suppose you're here to gloat over the mess I made of things."

"Mess? It seems to me that everything has worked out pretty well."

I shrugged. "If you don't count lying, cheating and deception." My words were more petulant than I actually felt.

"Who did you lie to?"

"Harold?" I said the man's name louder than I'd intended. "Jason. Mr. Potter." I had a truly terrifying thought. "You! Oh my god, you, too. That was why you kissed me that night. That's why you changed your clothes, why you became something that you weren't. You were caught up in the love spell, too! Be free, dammit! Just leave me alone!"

I waited for the *ping,* the snap, the breaking of the bond that I had felt with Harold.

Nothing.

"Jane, I don't have any idea what you're talking about." He sounded amused. Tolerant. Not angry, like a man who had suddenly been released from a spell that had held him against his will. Not bemused, like a man still caught up in my magic.

I crossed to the couch and collapsed in the pool of my comfortable sweater. "That first spell I did, the grimoire spell. It worked, but it made too many men fall in love with me."

David came to stand in front of me. He crossed his arms on his chest and shook his head. "You don't get it, do you?"

"Get what?"

"The way the spells work."

"I think I've got a pretty good idea. I haven't sat around

doing nothing for the past two months. You've been a good guide to all this witchcraft stuff, and Neko helped out a lot."

"Well, neither of us taught you enough about the grimoire spell."

I heard something behind his words. Laughter, I was pretty sure, but something else. Something grave. Respect? Pity? I gritted my teeth. "No time like the present, then. What about it? Did I change the balance of the universe as we know it? Have I set the world of Faerie upside down, releasing petty spirit vengeance on all the world?"

"Nothing quite so dramatic as that." David sat down beside me. He took a deep breath and met my eyes guilelessly. "The grimoire spell only works on the first man you see after you work it."

"The first man—" I thought back to that night, to Melissa standing in the kitchen, Melissa and… "Neko!"

"No." David shook his head in brief annoyance. "Neko doesn't count. For purposes of magic, he's a part of you."

I felt my face turn crimson, but I said, "You, then."

"No. Warders are immune to their witch's workings."

"Then the first man was…Harold."

"Precisely."

"But the others? Jason, finally realizing I was alive? Mr. Zimmer, ordering coffee? Mr. Potter, talking to me at Gran's, and at the Gala, and making his donation to the Peabridge?"

"Just Harold. The spell bonds to the first man. The others weren't caught up in your magic."

I repeated his words inside my head. I couldn't believe him. Each of those men had been free to act? Free to do whatever he wanted?

"But why?" I finally asked. "Why would everything change now, all at once?"

David gestured smoothly. "Look at yourself." I stared down at my jeans, raised my fingers to my hair. "You're the one who's different, Jane."

"I'm not! I'm the same person I've always been!"

"Are you, really?" His voice was soothing, even as his next words plunged me into doubt. "You've cut your hair. You grew out your nails. You put on makeup every morning and touch it up during the day. You're wearing contact lenses."

Everything he said was true, but I found my heart beating faster to hear a man say the words. A man who had been attracted to me, spell or no spell.

Of course, he was also a man who had set me aside, like a shirt that didn't fit.

I started to get up from the couch, too embarrassed to continue the conversation. David reached out and grabbed my wrist. "We men are really dumb creatures, you know. We can be led anywhere by our…senses." I knew that he was going to identify another leader, and I was glad that he hadn't specified body parts. I was already mortified by this conversation.

"Jane," he said, and he removed his fingers from my wrist, only to cup my jaw with his palm. "You've grown. You've changed. You like yourself more, and the men in your life can see that. You have confidence. You're at ease—and that draws us like flies to honey."

And suddenly, I understood what he was saying. I saw the path that he was leading me toward, the direction he was taking me.

I liked being the woman who remembered to put on lipstick, the woman who wore a green evening gown to the Gala. I liked being the woman who organized hundreds of books, cataloging them like a true professional.

I liked myself.

I sat up straighter. "And you? If self-love and independence are symbolized by wardrobe shifts, what are you doing in those clothes?"

He glanced down and shrugged. "I've grown, too. I've changed. I'm not the same warder who was fired by my last witch. I've decided that I can let myself be comfortable. If I'm going to succeed as a warder, as *your* warder, I'm going to succeed in my ability to guide you. To protect you. No one's going to care if I wear stiff, formal clothes or magical robes inscribed with symbols." I turned my head to one side, still skeptical. "I like myself this way."

And that admission actually made me laugh out loud. "That, I understand."

He joined me in laughter, amusement that trailed off easily as he looked around the basement. "I like what you've done to the place."

"Really?"

He got up to study the nearest bookshelf, walked down to the next one, and eventually traced his way around the entire room. He nodded when he found the spice chest, took note of the tackle box full of crystals, made a mental inventory of the little cauldrons and other witchy supplies stored on their respective shelves.

"A place for everything, and everything in its place," he pronounced at last.

"It just feels…right like this. I hadn't realized how much the disorganization was bothering me."

"So now it seems like you're really ready to study. Ready to learn."

"What about the Coven? What are the chances that they'll challenge me for this? For Hannah Osgood's collection?"

David shrugged. "High. They'll say that you aren't skilled, that you aren't trained, that you don't know what to do with everything you have."

Indignation rose in my chest and I opened my mouth to protest.

"They'll *say* that. But they probably won't succeed. For one thing, they could never come up with a list of everything that's here. They'd have to, to convince the Court that the books belong to them."

I thought about the laptop computer secure beneath my bed, and the backup drive I'd left in my desk at the Peabridge that very morning. "But they'll definitely try?" I said, and my voice was suddenly very small.

"They'll definitely try," David confirmed. "But that will take a long time. And in the end, I don't think that they'll be successful. In the meantime, you can learn more about using your powers."

I caught my breath, suddenly realizing just how much I wanted to do that. "And you? You'll teach me?"

"Jane, I told you before, I'm not supposed to be a teacher. I'm a warder."

"Then, you'll…ward me? Be my guide? Keep me safe?"

He looked at me for a long time. I remembered how I'd

been drawn to him when we first met. I remembered how I'd worried about eating in front of him. But then, I recalled how I'd relaxed with him, how he'd helped me through my early spells, how he'd tucked me into bed with tender hands—hands that had no secret mission, no ulterior motive.

Men. I'd never understand them. In fact, I was ready to take a break from them. From my romantic interest in them, at least. I needed to spend some time figuring out who *I* was. I needed more nights like the one just past, gathered together with my grandmother and my mother, with my best friend. I needed to know more about Jane Madison before I tried to convert her into Jane Randall, Jane Templeton or Jane Anyone Else.

"Please," I said to David. "As warder to witch. Say you'll help me."

He nodded gravely. "As warder to witch."

I reached out to hug him and felt him tense beneath my hands. I turned my face away from his, though, and he relaxed. His ease spread to me, and I took a deep breath. A clean breath. A new breath for the new me.

"But first," I said. "Would you like a cup of tea?" He followed me upstairs to the kitchen, where Neko had already put on the kettle, set out the teapot, arranged the mugs and added a huge pitcher of cream.

My familiar looked up as we gathered around the table. He turned his head to one side, looking first at me, then at David. "Trick or treat?" he said at last.

"Treat," David and I said at the same time.

It wasn't going to be easy, I was certain. Figuring out the

new me, helping the Peabridge grow, preparing for my confrontation with the Coven…. None of it would be easy. But it was definitely going to be a treat.

Jane's got a lot of learning in store for herself!
Check back in October 2007 for the next peek into her life.
Don't miss SORCERY AND THE SINGLE GIRL

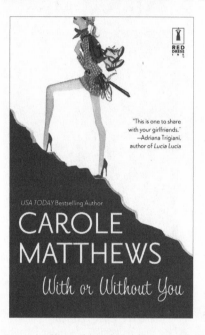

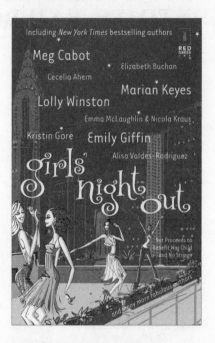

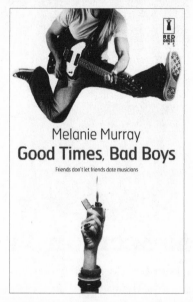

More great reads from international
bestselling author Sarah Mlynowski

As Seen on TV

Sunny Langstein has done what every modern-day
twenty-four-year-old shouldn't do. She's left her life
in Florida to move in with her boyfriend in
Manhattan. But don't judge Sunny yet, because
like any smart woman she has an ulterior motive—
to star on *Party Girls,* the latest reality-television
show. Here's the catch—*Party Girls* have to be
single. Free designer clothes and stardom versus
life with her boyfriend. What's a girl to do?

RED DRESS INK
™